© Melanie Donohue

KEITH DONOHUE is an American novelist, the author of the
national bestseller *The Stolen Child, Angels of Destruction,*
and *Centuries of June.* He has also written reviews for *The
Washington Post.* Donohue has a Ph.D. in English with a spe-
cialization in modern Irish literature and wrote the introduc-
tion to *The Complete Novels of Flann O'Brien.* He lives in
Maryland near Washington, D.C.

Also by Keith Donohue

The Stolen Child

Angels of Destruction

Centuries of June

Additional Praise for *The Boy Who Drew Monsters*

"Clearly, we are in the territory of the wholehearted, up-for-anything gothic, which even as it undertakes a melancholic exploration of the lost, forlorn, and bereft operates with the volume cranked and the plot on greased wheels. As a writer, Donohue always seems to know exactly what he is doing . . . and in *The Boy Who Drew Monsters* he twists the screw on Jack with the finesse of an expert. It is a pleasure to watch him glide along, pulling one squirming rabbit after another from his copious hat."
                                                    —Peter Straub, *The Washington Post*

"*The Boy Who Drew Monsters* dissolves notions of reality and fiction and leaves behind an eerie narrative about what haunting aberrations might lurk just outside our peripheral vision." —*Time Out* New York

"A masterfully controlled example of the literary horror genre. The setting is vividly gothic and evocative, and Donohue builds tension and fear in that strange, snowbound world at an exquisitely slow pace."
                                                    —*Richmond Times-Dispatch*

"The novel is a pressure cooker, an airtight room with limited oxygen, and an astute study of the mysterious demons that loss breeds. . . . The book's final twist—and by final I mean, like, in the very last sentence—is satisfying in a *Sixth Sense* kind of way, but the manner in which Donohue keeps us in the dark until then is the novel's real reward."
                                                    —*Popular Mechanics*

"This story is genuinely, deeply frightening. . . . *The Boy Who Drew Monsters* is dazzlingly electrifying, full of portending dread, and genuine, creepy scares. Never have I been so unnerved by a novel, at least in some time, and as a literary horror novel, this succeeds on just about every level."
                                                    —*PopMatters*

"Look out, Ichabod Crane. Let's just say [Donohue's] spirits make the headless horseman look like a friendly guy."
—*New York Post* (Required Reading)

"Donohue has created the slow, clicking, stomach-tightening anticipation of a roller coaster on the rise. He draws readers in with creative prose that outlines images that are both innocent and creepy."
—*The Portland Press Herald*

"This novel ranks with the best of modern-day supernatural thrillers."
—*Bookreporter*

"With a mind-bending final twist, *The Boy Who Drew Monsters*—much in the tradition of the classic *The Turn of the Screw*—will leave readers shaking in their boots."
—*BookPage*

"Donohue's writing is as evocative as Jack Peter's drawings, both startling and heavy with emotion. . . . A sterling example of the new breed of horror: unnerving and internal with just the right number of bumps in the night."
—*Kirkus Reviews*

"The ghostly influence of Henry James's *The Turn of the Screw* haunts this chilling novel. . . . Donohue is an adept creator of atmosphere. . . . A brisk and winningly creepy narrative."
—*Publishers Weekly*

"The novel unfolds through rich prose and a deeply imagined story. The final page—the final sentence, really—comes as a clever surprise, but one that resonates soundly. Fans of Donohue's first novel, *The Stolen Child,* will be pleased. Also recommended for readers of Joe Hill."
—*Library Journal*

"It will raise the hairs on the back of your neck. Keith Donohue manages to peer into the darkest nightmares of childhood and beckon forth the monsters from the closet. . . . Atmospheric and haunting. *The Boy Who Drew Monsters* is all the more chilling because it is grounded in real family life, with its heartbreaks and tenderness."

—Eowyn Ivey, *New York Times* bestselling
author of *The Snow Child*

"Both an eerie, engrossing tale of the supernatural, with a sting in its tale, and a superb evocation of troubled youth. *The Boy Who Drew Monsters* reminds us that there is no rage like the rage of children."

—John Connolly, *New York Times* bestselling author of
The Book of Lost Things and *The Wolf in Winter*

"An eerie, unsettling novel about the monsters outside your door . . . and the ones inside all of us. Donohue fills his pages with intimacy and dread, and whips up an ending that'll take your breath away."

—Christopher Golden, #1 *New York Times*
bestselling author of *Snowblind*

"There are no monsters. That's what Jack Peter's parents tell him, and what I kept telling myself as I got sucked deeper and deeper into this delectably chilling novel. But still, as I read, I found myself looking out the window at shadows moving in the darkness, until finally I had to get up and flip on every light switch in the house. *The Boy Who Drew Monsters* left me breathless and reeling, questioning the line between what is real and what is imagined—and realizing that the meeting of the two is where true terror dwells." —Jennifer McMahon, *New York Times* bestselling author of *The Winter People*

"Keith Donohue has crafted a brooding, Serlingesque tale of tragedy, heartbreak, and the things that go bump in the night. Creepy, nostalgic, and understated, *The Boy Who Drew Monsters* is a tale meant for the dark of night, but most will want to enjoy it with all of the lights on."

—C. Robert Cargill, author of *Dreams and Shadows*

The Boy
Who Drew
Monsters

A NOVEL

Keith Donohue

PICADOR

New York

THE BOY WHO DREW MONSTERS. Copyright © 2014 by Keith Donohue. All rights reserved. Printed in the United States of America. For information, address Picador, 175 Fifth Avenue, New York, N.Y. 10010.

www.picadorusa.com
www.twitter.com/picadorusa • www.facebook.com/picadorusa
picadorbookroom.tumblr.com

Picador® is a U.S. registered trademark and is used by St. Martin's Press under license from Pan Books Limited.

For book club information, please visit www.facebook.com/picadorbookclub or e-mail marketing@picadorusa.com.

Designed by Kathryn Parise

THE LIBRARY OF CONGRESS HAS CATALOGED THE HARDCOVER EDITION AS FOLLOWS:

Donohue, Keith.
    The boy who drew monsters : a novel / Keith Donohue.—First edition.
        pages cm
    ISBN 978-1-250-05715-0 (hardcover)
    ISBN 978-1-250-05716-7 (e-book)
    1. Boys—Maine—Fiction. 2. Monsters—Fiction. 3. Psychological fiction.
    4. Ghost stories. I. Title.
    PS3604.O5654B69 2014
    813'.6—dc23

                                                                2014018914

Picador Paperback ISBN 978-1-250-07488-1

Our books may be purchased in bulk for promotional, educational, or business use. Please contact your local bookseller or the Macmillan Corporate and Premium Sales Department at 1-800-221-7945, extension 5442, or by e-mail at MacmillanSpecialMarkets@macmillan.com.

First published by Picador

First Picador Paperback Edition: October 2015

10 9 8 7 6 5 4 3 2 1

For Robert Andrew Larson

The Boy
Who Drew
Monsters

Prologue

In the dream house, the boy listened for the monster under his bed. An awful presence in the dark had awakened him in the dead hours, and he waited for the telltale sound of breathing. Would there be breathing? Or would it arrive in silence, without warning? He would have no time to defend himself or save the treasures hidden in his old toy box. The possibility of such an attack unnerved him, but he dared not move. He did not dare lean his head over the side of his boat to check the space between the mattress and the wide blue sea of the braided sisal rug. He did not dare turn on the lamp and flood the room with light and risk spooking the monster from its hiding place. There was no breathing but his own, no sound at all but the thrum of his heart.

Dream house, that's what his mother and father used to call it, before the troubles began. "This is our dream house by the sea," they would tell the summer visitors who would come to stay for long weekends. Or his Grandpa and Grandma Keenan who would come for the chance of a genuine white Christmas in Maine. "Welcome to the dream house." The boy was not sure if it was a house in which dreams came true or if the house itself had been made out of dreams. Once upon a time, the name had made him happy, but on ice-cold nights like these, the dreams turned into nightmares, and monsters under the bed stirred in the bump of the night.

He hefted the quilt over his head until he was completely engulfed. Heavy as a wave, the weight pressed upon him, and he remembered how the rough darkness of the sea, no bottom or top, swirled all around as both boys fought for air in the green-gray chaos. Suffocating and afraid, he threw off the blankets, monsters be damned, and sat up in the bed, panting, holding off the urge to call out to his mother to come rescue him. Save me! But he did not want to wake her at this late hour. She did not believe in monsters.

Lately the monsters had been coming for him inside the dreams. They would softly lay a hand upon his shoulder. They would whisper in his ear as he slept. And he would rouse himself to find nothing, no one. In the mornings, he would wonder when and how sleep had ever arrived. He was so tired of the pictures in his head. From his bed, he could see through the top panes of the windows to the cold stars in the sky above the ocean. Moonlight cast a square upon the far wall, and he believed that if he concentrated long and hard, he could make the sun appear in that space and send the monsters away. He set his will against the night.

One

Dream boy. Holly watched her son sleep, just as she had done a thousand times before, wondering where he had gone in his dreams. Another minute will be no harm, she told herself, reluctant to disturb his peace. The birdcage of his chest rose and fell, and she found herself synchronizing her breathing to his, just as she had done a decade ago when he was a newborn. Jack clenched his hands into fists, one tucked against his cheek sure to leave a mark on his skin. Beneath his fluttering eyelids, his eyes rolled back and forth as he concentrated on a dreamscape only he could see, a film playing out in his subconscious mind. He seemed deeply under, a child like every other child, a normal son, an ordinary boy in his sleep. She held the moment in abeyance, allowing the illusion to linger.

It had been three years since she had dared to stay so close to her son for so long. A summer day on the beach, her beamish boy broke free and raced across the sand and rocks into her arms, radiant heart jangling under his ribs. Fine soft hair matted onto his scalp, he smelled of salt and sand and soap, and as he kissed her again and again, he banged the top of his crown against the ridge of her cheekbone. He was in love, love, love with her, and she loved him in return with a fierceness that

scared her often, she could eat him up. Her bright bold beautiful boy all
of seven. He had squeezed her around the neck until she winced. Now
but a memory. She watched him sleep, wishing him to come back to her.
Back before it all began.

In the middle of the night, Jack had cried out once, a screech that
woke her with its animal intensity. She was too tired and too condi-
tioned to abandon the warmth beneath the down comforter, so she
waited, tense and alert for an echo. But the quiet returned swiftly as he
stilled himself. For half an hour, she listened, fidgeting on her pillow,
watching the slow sweep of the alarm clock. Tim had turned his back to
her and was little more than a familiar contour, his body sloped like a
faraway roll of hills. In the morning, she woke first, only to find him
slumbering in the exact position, as though dead to all interruption.

"It's eight," she told her husband. "You wanted to make your rounds
this morning. Check the houses now the cold is here."

"Let me sleep."

"No rest for the wicked," Holly said, throwing off the covers so that
his back was exposed to the cooling morning, and then she went to fetch
their son.

She wanted to wake Jack gently, slowly. His long dark hair fell across
his forehead in tangled strands like a forest of kelp, which accented his
pale skin and soft features. Beautiful boy. Bending closer Holly reached
to brush back his hair, and as soon as she touched him she realized her
mistake.

Quick as a snake, his arm sprang forward by reflex. His fist struck
her just below the left eye socket, and a sharp pain radiated from the
spot where bone smacked bone. The second blow glanced off the point
of her chin and landed flush on her shoulder. She recoiled and saw his
eyes wide with fear and anger.

"Don't touch me," he screamed. "Get away, get away." He launched
himself at her again, a whirl of punches and sharp elbows, and she slid
farther away, too shocked to defend herself. A feral savagery possessed
him as he bounced on the mattress, flailing his limbs, as if he did not

know his victim. She stood and backed off, looking for a means of protection without actually laying a hand against her son.

"Stop, Jack, just stop it. What are you doing?"

As suddenly as the attack began, he froze on all fours and raised his face toward her, a wave of recognition coming over him. Penitent as a hound, he bowed his head and slumped, collapsing on his chest.

"What's gotten into you?"

Jack buried his face in the covers and began to cry. Since he was seven years old, he had not suffered easily any human touch. He would shrug off the arm around his shoulders or flinch at a hug or handshake, but he had never before come to blows with anyone. Not even when Tim would wrap him up and carry him to the car when they absolutely had to take him out of the house. Her heart pounded as she fought to calm her breathing, and she felt the contusions on her face and shoulder throb against the hot flush of her skin. Torn between the desire to comfort her son and the urge to flee, Holly could not move one way or another. She braced her feet against the braided rug, anxious for the truce to begin.

"Don't touch me," he said again, his voice now calm and muffled by the comforter.

"Don't worry," she said. "I wouldn't dream of it." With her fingertips she pressed against a spot of pain on her face.

She waited. At last the boy sat on his haunches and crossed his arms, muttering to himself, steadying his vibrating body. His eyes were fixed on a spot somewhere behind his mother, and she watched patiently for the switch in his brain to be thrown. A bubble of spit popped at the corner of his lips. The tight muscles on his neck unwound like bands.

She hoped he had given her a black eye, some mark that would prove to her husband and the doctors what she had been saying for months. He was close to becoming out of control at times, too much to handle on her own. The blankness of the boy's face refused to acknowledge her presence in the room. His porcelain skin reddened, and she stared at his eyes until he returned her gaze.

"What was that all about, young man?"

"I'm sorry," he said.

"You better be."

He frowned and his eyes welled with tears.

"You hurt me, Jack. Why did you hit me?"

The ferocity drained from his body, and all at once be became a little boy again, confused by his own actions. His shoulders drooped, and he tucked his chin into his chest and hid behind the curtain of his bangs.

"You can't do that, you can't hit Mommy."

"Sorry," he said again. "I thought you were coming to get me."

"I was coming to get you, to wake you up."

"No, I thought there was a monster under the bed."

A quick smile split her face. A boy, a boy, just a little boy lost. She clenched her teeth and scowled at him, too late; he had seen her furtive grin. She cleared her throat. "You can't go around hitting people, honey."

"I promise," he said.

So many broken promises, so many pledges to be good. Her head ached. "Get yourself dressed, then. And when you are ready, come down for breakfast, and we'll see what you can do to make it up to me."

"Sorry," he said for a third time, but she had already turned to leave.

Jack Peter dressed quickly and smoothed his quilt just like he had been taught, and then he tiptoed in his socks to the heating register nearest to the window. Lying on the floor, he put his ear close to the vent, a trick he had discovered one day by accident, as though the house itself had secret passageways for the words. If the blowers were not running, he could eavesdrop on conversations in other rooms, depending upon where he sat. In the kitchen downstairs, they were talking. He could imagine them huddled in the breakfast nook, two cups of coffee breathing their steam.

"Just out of the blue?" his father asked. "Completely unprovoked?"

"What would I do to provoke him? I barely touched him," she said.

"You're going to have a shiner."

"It isn't funny, Tim. He was like some wild animal. He's stronger than he looks."

"You'll have to be more careful."

"Careful?" Her voice rang through the heating duct like a struck gong, loud enough to be heard through the open door as well. "I have to be more careful?"

"Holly, the walls have ears."

"I don't care if he can hear me, maybe he should be listening to me. Maybe you should listen. Something has to be done."

His father dropped his voice, changed the tone, so Jack Peter had to creep closer to the register.

"It was just the one time, Hol. Just the once. I'll talk to him. We'll work on him not hitting, but I don't want to have him all doped up. Don't want to increase his meds."

"Couldn't you at least talk to the doctor?"

He stubbornly refused to answer her. They would be sitting there, silent, staring away from each other, through the window, at the newspapers, eyes following the rising coffee steam. Jack Peter had seen it before, again and again.

After some time, his father spoke calmly. "You shouldn't have startled him. Something must have set him off for him to react so . . . violently."

"He said there was a monster under his bed." She lifted her face toward the ceiling. "More like a monster in his bed."

"You shouldn't have touched him."

"My own son."

"Our son," he said. "He was just afraid and you set him off. Match to a fuse."

Jack Peter heard one of them rise from the table and cross the room, but he could no longer make out what his mother was saying, though he could hear the anger roll through her muffled voice.

"No," his father answered. "I think that would be impossible. A terrible idea. Look, I'll work harder with him."

Stealing away as quickly and quietly as possible, Jack Peter left his spot and stationed himself at the top of the staircase, careful not to give himself away. He caught the tail end of his mother's answer.

". . . if something happened to us, then we'd have to make those kind of arrangements."

"Please, Holly," his father said. "I won't send him away. He'd be miserable in one of those homes."

Send him away. Away, away, where would they send him?

"You don't know that," his mother said. "Maybe he could be happier, maybe they would find a way to better control—"

"I won't do it," his father shouted.

"—his behavior. Get him outside. Conquer his fears."

His father said, "But he's our son. I can't believe you'd even suggest such a thing."

"I can't have him hitting me, Tim. Hurting me, or hurting himself. I don't want to send him away, but I'm at my wit's end."

"I'll talk to him," his father said softly. "I'll take him to see Wilson, make the necessary adjustments."

A prolonged silence filled the void, rising like the sea from the bottom till it engulfed the whole house. Wrapping his arms behind his head, Jack Peter waited for it to end, but he dared not leave his listening post. He would not go away, he would not go outside, he would make them stop, and they would see and they would keep everything as it was. He would show them. He would make them see.

At last his father pushed away from the table. He would be walking to her for a hug. "And I'll check under the bed," he joked. "For monsters."

Freed, Jack Peter bounded down the stairs and into the kitchen, beaming for her, but she would not turn to face him. At the sink, doing dishes, she was not ready. Dressed in her jogging clothes, she looked ready to run away. His father flashed a greeting, waved his hand for the boy to join him and be still. A bowl of oatmeal with a crater lake of maple syrup in the middle had been put at his place at the table.

"Tim," she said at last. "I'll be back from my run soon, and then you can make your rounds. Make sure to fetch Nicholas on your way home. He's coming over to play with Jack this afternoon."

Jack Peter picked up his spoon and drew a line across the thick surface. The syrup ran and spread like blood. Work to be done, he told himself. Not away, not away, but here. Inside.

A pale yellow sun hung low in the salt sky. Winter had blown in overnight, and the cold gave an air of lonesomeness to the empty roads and deserted vacation homes. Tim loved the dying light of December and the absence of the people and set about his business with a kind of gleeful freedom. He had a dozen properties to take care of in the village and another dozen scattered on the eastern edge of the peninsula, and he had worked his way through three of the four homes on his list for the day with not a soul to bother him.

The Rothmans' summer place was the biggest and finest house in the village, fronting the crescent beach, ideally situated with a view of the lighthouse to the north and the unspoiled sand and rocks to the south. Tim parked the Jeep around back and stood in the driveway, admiring how seamlessly the new mansion blended in with the grand old New England Victorians that dotted the coast. But it had been built less than ten years ago. His son was older than the house. The wind cut through his jacket, so he hooked the lapels against his throat and jogged to the door and fumbled for the keys.

The house was colder inside than out, and he searched for the thermostat to turn up the heat and flipped on the lights in the pale noontime. In the kitchen, new and clean birch cabinets glowed like honey above smooth slate countertops and the spotless stove and refrigerator. A few tasteful prints lined the walls, and in the dining room, the chairs sat precisely three inches from the edge of the table, awaiting company. Alert for drafts, he wandered room to room, absentmindedly checking windows that he knew were closed. A layer of dust furred the shells and curios laid out carefully on the sideboard, and he drew a line with his fingertip along the edge of a mahogany credenza. Bound in frames, pictures of the Rothmans were everywhere: the father in his white dentist's jacket, brandishing a tool of grave menace; the mother with the same practical smile in every photograph. Two children—a boy and a girl—progressively aging from toddlers to teenagers, perfect teeth glistening in the Maine summer sun. Even the dog was perfect, a Shiba Inu regal as a coiffed fox. In a gilded mirror, Tim saw himself prowling through their possessions like a thief, and he quickly turned away.

Tim sat in Dr. Rothman's easy chair and inspected the Persian rug between his feet, wondering if he had dragged any sand or mud inside. The room was simple and elegant. A Steinway upright took up one wall. More photographs of Mrs. Rothman in her best swimsuit. Arts and Crafts mirrors and lamps. White pine beams and finishing trim. The furniture, spare pieces, summer home, finer and newer than his own. A castle built crown by crown, bridge by bridge, tooth by tooth.

Money. He dug into his front pocket and fished out a ten, the same crumpled bill he had tucked away three days ago. He knew without looking that his wallet was empty. Never enough money. The plan had been for him to go back to school, finish his degree, but when their son was born and later diagnosed, they decided after many long nights of argument that Tim would put ambition aside to care for the boy most of the time.

"I make more money," she had said, and it was true, even as a small town lawyer just starting out. "So it only makes sense, when he's still little, for me to keep my job. What's so terrible about being a stay-at-home dad? You can always find something seasonal or part-time, we'll work it out."

He had stumbled into the caretaker's position with Coast Property Management, but he often wondered if Holly had not secretly welcomed the chance to escape the responsibility of daily care for the boy, right from the beginning. When J.P. was younger, Tim took him along for odd jobs when Holly was not free or when they could not find a sitter. But after Jip developed his phobia, those excursions with his son became nearly impossible. Just as unlikely as returning to college after all these years. He was old enough to be a freshman's father.

With the sole of his boot, he scraped at a spot on the rug. The wind rattled the windowpanes behind him, and he hoisted himself from the easy chair, stiff with cold, and climbed the stairs to check for drafts in the bedrooms. In the dentist's boudoir, the king-size bed floated like a raft on a wide expanse. A single wrinkle creased the bedspread, and he smoothed it with two hands, picturing Dr. Rothman and his wife, perfect and tan, resting on a summer afternoon, worn out with relaxation. The wind whistled through a chink in the walls, and Tim followed the sound, past the daughter's room. He caught a glimpse of a giant stuffed bear, won at some seaside carnival, sitting on Goldilocks's chair.

The door at the end of the hall was closed, and when he opened it, a sharp odor leapt from the boy's bedroom, as if it had been trapped for three months. Something dead in there. On the walls were posters of all the Boston sports stars, Red Sox and Patriots, Celtics and Bruins. A pair of water skis stood in the corner, and on the shelves and dresser careful lines of shells and starfish, a dried mermaid's purse, a stick of driftwood bent like a narwhal's horn. A scrapbook lay open on the schoolboy's desk. Pages of an ordinary summer. The whaleboat out of Boothbay, a clambake on the beach, a set of printouts from the big annual fireworks in Portland. And the boy and his sister in the bright sunshine, climbing on rocks, kayaking on the calm Atlantic, holding a pair of trophy fishes no bigger than perch. The boy and his sister, darkening to bronze from July to September. He turned the last page and thought of his son.

Monster under the bed. Turning back the bedspread, Tim fell to his knees and peeked beneath the mattress. Squatting like a dried toad were a pair of swimming trunks in the shadows. He strained to reach them and recoiled when he touched the calcified folds and creases. As he dragged the stiff cloth across the floor, a trail of sand spilled out. In the pockets were four hermit crab shells reeking of the sea. He poked at the little bodies one by one but they did not flinch. Some monsters. The Rothmans must not have noticed when they packed up for the season, and that the cleaning crew must have neglected to look under the bed was no surprise to Tim, for they were quick and careless, often leaving behind surprises for him to remedy. He set the swimming trunks and the dead crabs next to the scrapbook, the shells dark against the wood.

Holly had been so angry that morning, filled with a deep disappointment that had rarely surfaced despite their hardships of the past ten years. The mark on her cheek already blossoming into a red plum. She never understood how best to deal with the boy, how to approach him sideways and give him space to come into the real world from his far-off land. Only once had Jip raised a fist against him. It was on the first day of school after the near drowning three summers ago, and Tim was sure that his son would not want to miss the chance to see his friends. He had tricked him into getting out of bed and even made it through breakfast, but as the time to go approached, the boy simply stopped moving.

"Put on your socks and shoes," Tim had barked. "We're late for school."

His son balked and bent his legs to hide his bare feet beneath his bottom.

"You know you want to go. Dammit, Jip, hurry up and do as I say." He could hear the rising anger in his voice but did nothing to stop it.

Lowering his head, the boy glowered at him, defiance steadfast in his gaze. He shifted farther away, anchoring himself in the chair, wrapping his thin arms around the rails.

"Last chance—"

"No," Jip yelled.

Tim reached and grabbed at his arm, intending to wrench him free and make him put on his socks and shoes, but in the same instant, his son twisted and swung wildly, small fists beating like a drummer against his father's hands. Realizing his mistake, Tim stepped out of range, and watched the boy flail at him and then collapse, overcome by his rage, a different creature altogether, a mad dog snarling and showing his teeth. The display alarmed Tim at first, but he thought to simply wait and betray no emotion. Just as he had guessed, his son came back into himself and settled.

Standing tall and looking down on the child, Tim said, "You must never hit."

His little boy convulsed with one short spasm, just longer than a twitch. "No," he said.

From that moment, Tim knew to take care in any sudden and unexpected touch, and that's what must have done in Holly. She forgot. She scared him. It would never happen again, Tim would find the right opportunity to talk with Jip and put the fear of God in him. Send him away, indeed.

The Rothmans would never have to send away their little boy. He would come to this room every summer until he was a young man, and probably come back with his own son in time, and that boy would be normal, too, and on it would go for them, the lucky, the untroubled, the well-to-do. And Tim would be coming here forever, checking on someone else's second home, closing up every winter and caretaking their dreams. He listened for the wind, but it had abated. No breeze whistled through the cracks. An oppressive silence gave him the uneasy sensation of being all alone in a strange place, and then the house heaved a sigh as though it had tired of him. When he realized it was just the furnace shutting off, Tim laughed at himself. Acutely aware of his own breathing and feeling like a trespasser, he turned to leave, only to be stopped by a small and uncertain sound. Something scratched, like fingernails raked across a sheet of paper, barely audible but enough to unsettle him. It clicked again, a staccato of movement emanating from inside the room. Spooked by its suddenness, he pricked up his ears. The third set of delicate clicks came from the direction of the boy's desk, and he heard and finally saw the scuttling of a pair of hermit crabs resurrecting themselves in their shells, fiddling their great claws and wriggling their legs to meander across the wooden surface.

"What the—"

All four crabs were on the march, heading off to the four corners, and he pounced, collecting them one by one in the scoop of his hands. Each quickly withdrew into its whirling cone. How they had survived for months in the boy's pockets was a mystery to Tim, but he quickly dismissed the question and carried them downstairs and put them in the sea grass behind the house. He watched for a long time to see if they would move, but they remained still as stones.

The sun had long since reached its winter day apogee and now arced toward the west as though rimed in mist. A frosty afternoon was sneaking in, and he was late. He left the crabs where they lay and hurried off. As he approached the Wellers' house, he could see their son, Nick, waiting patiently on the front porch, cold as an icicle, and he raced to the Jeep as Tim pulled into the driveway, as if he had been a prisoner a long, long time and was now released from his sentence. His cheeks were red and chapped, and the boy beamed with an eagerness nearly impossible to bear. Nick was such a good friend to have for Jip. Such a good boy.

iii.

The grays hid as best they could on the icy white field, crouching behind the random nooks and crannies folded into the landscape. By the cut of their uniforms and the odd square lip at the bottom of their helmets, they gave themselves away as Germans. In a poised fist, one man held a grenade shaped like a hammer. Two snipers stretched out on their bellies, peering through the sights to await the foe. On the white hills above the ambush site, a squad of green Americans marched to their doom. The radio man's antenna had snapped off in some ancient skirmish. The mine sweeper kept falling over on the soft surface. Five o'clock on a December Sunday, and the dusk concealed the soldiers.

A war cry, startling in its whooping ferocity, broke the stillness, and from the horizon, a band of red Indians swarmed on to the scene. Charging on red ponies, reins in their teeth, a pair of braves drew back their bows. The arrows whistled softly in long arcs and fell true. The gray captain gulped his last surprised breath as the arrowhead pierced his heart. One by one the army men turned in dumb shock at the unexpected arrival of the reinforcements, their savage intensity. From the pillows, the Americans cheered and huzzahed as they returned fire, launching grenades like winter hail. The kneeling bazooka man blasted a round, and bodies flew in all directions. In their feathered headdresses, their mohawks, and latticed breastplates, the warriors scrambled over the quilt, their hatchets raised with gleeful, murderous intent. Men fell through the ice and cried out full of panic in the frigid waters. At the height of the massacre, the bedroom door opened swiftly, throwing a rectangle of light from the hall against the far wall and illuminating the boys inside.

With a fistful of plastic Indians raised in midair, Jack Peter stared at the figure on the threshold. He froze, bewildered, as if awakened from a deep sleep. His shadow on the wall was as still as the toy soldiers strewn across the bed.

His mother kept her hand circled around the doorknob and stood halfway in the room, her gaze intent upon her son. "Boys, it's getting late. Shall we send Nicholas home, or would you care to join us for supper?" Nobody ever called him Nicholas, not even his own parents. He smiled again at her constant formality.

"I could stay, if it's okay with my mother." Nick stole a glance at Jack Peter, but he showed no reaction. A flush rose on his face, and he tightened his grip around the plastic men.

"You boys will have to clean up now, and, Jack, you never made your bed today." Mrs. Keenan took one step into the room, and her mere presence seemed to break the spell around her son. His rapid panting slowed into a gentle rhythm. He put down his toys and bowed his head like a penitent. Making parentheses of his arms, Nick scooped the soldiers and warriors to the middle of the mattress.

"Jack, Jackie." His mother snapped her fingers, trying to get his attention. "Isn't it nice Nicholas can stay for supper? But, Jack, you have to help clean up this mess. And make your bed, okay? I don't want to have to tell you again. C'mon, my boy."

In slow motion, he picked up the ponies that had fallen to the floor and added them to the pile. Mrs. Keenan turned and left the room, and in her absence, he began to move more quickly. With Nick's help, they put the plastic soldiers in a pretzel tin on top of the toy box, and then they straightened the sheets and pulled smooth the quilt. The boys went about their work quietly, as Nick knew better than to distract his friend. He was always unsteady when transitioning, and it was best to be silent and let Jack Peter find his own way. When the room was tidy and everything in order, Nick pretended to clap dust from his palms. "Finished?"

On cue, his friend became a ten-year-old boy again. "Yes!" he shouted, and they raced each other downstairs. The wind rattled the panes of the picture windows on the lower floor and flung sand against the siding. Just beyond, whitecaps frosted the Atlantic, and the surf pulsed like a heartbeat. Cold and damp pushed against the old saltbox house, the joists creaking in the wind, and the furnace pushed back with an exhalation of heat. It was good to be inside on such a night.

The living room was dark except for the glow of the tiny colored lights on the Christmas tree, and the boys nearly bounced right past Mr. Keenan, nestled in his easy chair. "What ho, lads? Mr. Nick, I see, has joined us. And what have you fine fellows been up to all afternoon?"

"War," said Jack Peter. "With the army men."

"War? Mayhem and murder, J.P.? So soon to Christmas, do you think that's wise?"

Jack Peter hovered beside his father's chair, a step away from contact. "Pretend war. Just pretend. It isn't real."

"All in the imagination, eh, Jip?"

"Up here." He tapped his skull with one finger.

"How about you, Mr. Weller? Which side were you on?"

The question embarrassed Nick, for he felt, in part, too old to be playing with toy soldiers. He had agreed at Jack Peter's insistence, just as he nearly always had. "There were no sides. They were all mixed up, the Germans and the Americans and the Indians."

"A healthy disregard for history," Mr. Keenan said. "Good for you. There are many things more important than history. Imagination, for one. And dinner, for two. Are you boys washed up and ready for some grub? Let's turn on some lights on the way. No need to be living in a graveyard."

A fish stew bubbled on the stove top. Nick watched as Mrs. Keenan sliced a loaf of bread on a wooden board. As she concentrated on her task, a bruise on her cheek deepened to purple. They sat in their usual places, the grown-ups at the ends, Jack Peter and Nick facing each other. From the saying of the blessing, Nick began to sense the difference in the atmosphere, as though something or someone was watching them eat. None of the others seemed to take heed of the situation. Mr. and Mrs. Keenan chatted idly about the weather and the food, savoring a morsel of whitefish, a hunk of bread, a sip of wine, and Jack Peter, as usual, zoned in upon his task, chewing mechanically every bite. But Nick could not shake the feeling that they were not alone.

"You boys will never guess what I found today," Mr. Keenan said. "I was up at the Rothmans' place making sure it was shipshape for the winter, and I thought I heard the wind come in, so I go checking all the windows. In one of the rooms there's a real peculiar smell. A stink, really—"

With his glass at his mouth, Jack Peter snorted into his milk.

"So I look under the bed, and what do you know, the kid had left a wet bathing suit under the bed. Been sitting since the end of summer, but that's not all. Inside the pockets, what do you think? Hermit crabs. Four of them crammed in there. But here's the weird part. I'm getting ready to leave and I hear this scribble-scrabble sound coming from where I laid them out upon the desk, and you guessed it. Those crabs come back from the dead, trying to escape the house and walk back to the ocean."

"Ghost crabs," Jack Peter said.

"That's right," Mr. Keenan said. "Figure they were hibernating or something. Nearly scared me half to death."

Mrs. Keenan rolled her eyes and pressed her hand against her painful-looking bruise. Mashing a potato with the tines of her fork, she addressed the table. "Nick, we're looking forward to having you stay over after Christmas."

He reddened, remembering how his parents had foisted him off so that they could get away on a cruise between Christmas and New Year's. Just the two of them, a second honeymoon, they said, although he wasn't sure what was wrong with the first. The trip, he sensed, was intended as remedy for what had been broken over the years, but their attempts at

rekindling left him out in the cold. They had given him the choice between a week with the Keenans or five days down in Florida with Nana
and Pap. The spare bedroom at their condo in the retirement village
was always hot no matter the temperature outside. Even Christmas
was blazing. No snow, no friends. The endless afternoons. Dinner at
five o'clock, in bed by eight. The nightly news, a game show with the
television blasting full volume. Maybe you would like to do a puzzle?
He loved his grandparents, but he'd rather be dead.

"Thanks again for having me. I'm happy to stay with you guys. And
with Jack Peter."

Across the table, his friend betrayed no emotion.

An idea jumped from Mr. Keenan's brain to his mouth. "We could
even get the old gang together during winter break. What were those
boys' names? Jip, you haven't seen some of those guys since, what, second
grade?"

Yes, second grade. Jack Peter had been an inside boy for over three
years. Hadn't been to school, rarely left the house. One by one, his few
old friends had nearly forgotten about him, and they always gave Nick
grief for continuing his strange friendship. Perhaps it would be better in
Boca Raton.

"You boys will have the run of the place," said Mr. Keenan.

A pair of eyes stared out at him from over Jack Peter's shoulders.
Mismatched askew eyes, the left larger than the right, pupils dark as
holes, glowered at him. He nearly dropped his spoon. The giant face
came into focus, a child's pencil drawing taped to the refrigerator door.
The portrait filled the entire page from side to side: a young boy with
dark tangled hair atop a high bare forehead, a rudimentary nose, a slash
of a mouth. He was primitive but intense, hatched and worked over,
shadows radiating from the wild eyes. Nick could not resist the temptation to look more closely, so he rose from his chair and walked right up
to the paper.

The drawing had a furious energy to it. There were no erasures, no
signs of uncertainty, but rather the stray lines and swirls had been in-

corporated into its overall execution. A smudge ran the length of the jaw from the left ear to the chin, as though its maker was trying to soften the line and blur the edge. Though the picture looked similar to many children's drawings, the boy on the page was animated by a different spirit, an air of unreality, that hypnotized Nick. As if the image had some power over him, life imitating art. He could not reconcile its skill with the impression he had held so long of his friend as simple, slow to talk or respond in regular ways, a boy who seemed much younger, more childish on the surface, yet there was a darkness to the drawing's depth.

"Do you like it, Nicholas?" Mrs. Keenan called from her place. "Jack drew that. Completely out of the blue."

Nick twisted his neck to look back at them over his shoulder. The boy in the picture kept watching.

Scraping his chair along the floor, Jack Peter inched around to face him, an intense expression in his eyes, flashing with a creator's ardor. "Do you ever go swim in the ocean?"

"Of course I do. Don't you remember? You and me used to go swimming all the time every summer. Not in the winter, but I still go swimming in the summer. When it gets hot."

"People drown in the ocean. Ships crash on the rocks in a storm. The people get lost and confused in the dark, and they breathe in the water, and everybody drowns. Shipwrecks. Your mommy and daddy are going on a boat."

Mr. Keenan laid his crust of bread over the top of his bowl of stew. "In the olden days, Jip, but not anymore. No more shipwrecks. The lighthouse on Mercy Point helps them steer clear. Now turn around and finish your dinner."

Dutiful son, he scooched his chair back into position with his bottom, inch by inch. Nick took it as a signal to return to his place. "Who is that picture supposed to be?"

Jack Peter did not speak but instead tapped a finger insistently against his temple. He would not stop the jabbing attack, and it alarmed everyone at the table. He poked his skull so hard that Mrs. Keenan was forced to grab her son's wrist to stop the compulsion. She strained against his strength, the veins and sinews piping along her forearm, her face colored deep red.

iv.

He had gone outside to warm up the Jeep in the driveway, leaving the motor idling in the bitter cold. In the clutter of the mudroom, Tim stomped his feet and clapped his gloved hands to get the blood flowing. The cross-country skis in the corner rattled, his breath exploded in white clouds, and the windows were laced with frost. He made a mental note to go round in the next few days to the rest of the summer houses to make sure the heat had been turned on low for the season. Nothing worse than frozen pipes bursting in the thaw. Winter was a-coming. Hell, it was already here. A single step separated the mudroom from the kitchen, and out of habit, he kicked the riser to knock the sand and dirt from the treads of his shoes before entering the house proper. The boy was already waiting for him, mittens and hat and boots, wrapped like a mummy in his overcoat and scarf.

"All bundled up and ready to go? All we need do is put a few stamps on your forehead, and we could mail you home."

Nick waddled forward a few paces and was nearly to the door when he was stopped by a tug on his sleeve. "Will you be back?" Jip asked.

"Of course. I'll come by one day after school same as always, and then we'll have the whole week after Christmas. I'll stay over."

"How many nights?"

"From the day after Christmas to New Year's Day."

"Would you stay, Nick? Would you stay if your parents ship-wrecked?"

Mrs. Keenan stepped between the boys. "That's a terrible thing to say, Jack." She turned her back on her son. "Now, don't you go worrying about that. Your parents will be fine."

"They can swim," said Jack. "But not in the cold. Don't go swimming in the cold water, Nick."

The flat order seemed to bother him, and Nick hesitated before answering. "I won't. It's too cold. Feel the window."

Laying the flat of his palm against a windowpane, Jip smiled at the sensation. Tim put his hand next to his son's. "What do you think, Jip? Below freezing?"

"Cold enough to snow. Cold enough to ice. Be careful driving, Daddy." He studied their translucent reflections in the glass and traced the shape of Nick's face with one fingertip. "Okay, you can go now."

In the old days when he went about outdoors, Jip often walked the path along Shore Road and up and over the granite rocks at Mercy Point to Nick Weller's house on the other side. They would gambol like billy goats on the rocks and while away many empty summer days. It was not more than a mile by foot, though the boys were only allowed to make the trip during daylight and in fair weather. By car, one had to dogleg inland to drive around the headlands and the cliffs, and the roundabout way turned it into a three-mile drive. Not that Tim minded the ten or fifteen minutes spent bringing Nick home. He was grateful that the boy still came over after all these years, putting up with Jip's strangeness, providing a connection to the outside world, a semblance of normalcy.

As if things were ever normal. Maybe, once upon a time, when he was a brand-new baby and would return a smile. That was the first sign, surely, that something was wrong when his reaction to every cootchy-coo was listless. He wasn't as closed off as some of the other boys Holly and Tim had met in those damned support groups. He talked where others were lost in silence or trapped in a handful of words or sounds. He could bear, with warning, to be touched, although this morning's incident gave Tim some doubts. It's a spectrum, the shrinks had said, and Jip was on the high-functioning end, but even so, it was far from normal to refuse to set foot outdoors, far from normal to live so deeply inside the mind. But Nick didn't seem to care, or perhaps his sense of loyalty trumped his aversions. Tim clamped a hand on his shoulder and led him into the cold.

The boy climbed into the Jeep and buckled his seat belt. A wave of longing flowed through Tim as he watched the boy ready for travel. Polite, obedient, a bit on the shy side, but mostly just an ordinary boy. Tim checked his emotions and shifted into reverse. "On the road again," he sang as the Jeep rolled down the driveway to Shore Road. The winter sky was filled with stars and a half-moon pulling the tides. They glided as quiet and alone as a ship on the sea.

"Sorry about that scene with the picture," Tim said. "You know Jip. Sometimes he can't find the words."

"Don't worry, Mr. Keenan."

"Do they still teach art in school? Do they still teach you kids how to draw?"

"We have art two days a week," said the boy. "And music on Fridays."

Music, he had forgotten about music for Jip. Music might do. Something to add to the home-school curriculum, and they could begin in the new year. The practice, the discipline would be good for his son. A wind instrument, perhaps the clarinet would be cool. He turned inland and began the horseshoe curve around Mercy Point. For a few hundred yards, the beam from the lighthouse crossed the road, and its brilliance never failed to surprise him. Backlit, Nick's reflection appeared in the windshield, animated as he talked. "We did drawing at the beginning of the year. And cutting shapes out of paper, a mosaic. And watercol—"

Tim mashed the brakes and stopped the Jeep, wheels crunching the gravelly shells along the edge of the road. Beyond the boy's transparent reflection in the glass, something stirred not twenty feet ahead. Uncoiling, the white mass transformed itself into a living figure rising from a crouch, its pale skin glowed sepulchral blue in the moonlight, and it turned with a hunch of the shoulders and began to shuffle away. In the beam from the lighthouse, it looked back once, illuminated for an instant. In long, urgent strides, it sped over the rocks toward the sea and then disappeared into the darkness so quickly that Tim was not sure if it had happened at all or exactly what had been spooked by the car.

"Did you see that?" he asked the boy.

Nick was rubbing his neck where the seat belt had caught him as the Jeep suddenly stopped. He did not appear to have seen a thing. "What is it?"

"Something out there. On the road." Tim shifted into park and cut the engine.

As he stepped from the Jeep, he noticed that the wind had picked up, making a cold night bitter. He took a few steps in the direction of the lighthouse where the creature had fled. Back in the car, the boy watched him, his face a puzzle under the dome light. Tim listened in the stillness but heard nothing but the far-off pulse of the surf against the rocks and the wind wrapping around the fir trees and every upright thing. No sign of it, and the thought of calling out after such an illusion blew away in the breeze. He considered the abstract landscape one last time, not much more than dark contours under a dark sky, and convinced that the creature was gone, he got back into the Jeep.

"Are you okay?" he asked the boy. "Are you sure you didn't see anything out on the road?"

Nick shrugged. "I saw you."

"I thought there was—"

"But I'm okay." He showed him his neck.

"Couldn't be," Tim muttered and shook his head to rid it of the vision. He flipped on the high beams and drove on, gripping the steering wheel as if it were going to slip out of his hands. At every bend, he imagined another shadowy presence in the darkness, and he could not force himself to relax until they had cleared the horseshoe turn and had the ocean again on their right. Tucked amid the white pines, the Weller home glowed in the December lonesomeness. A string of colored lights ran along the eaves and framed the windows and front door. No other house on this side of Mercy Point had so much as a candle for as far as the eye could see.

Fred Weller answered the door with a highball in his hand. Despite his jovial rotundity, he had the look of a man who could never get warm in the wintertime. Even indoors he bundled himself in a thick Irish sweater cinched at the waist and woollen socks beneath his slippers. He wore an expression of mild bemusement on his face, as though he wasn't expecting Nick to return that evening, and indeed, the boy slipped by without a word, shedding his hat and coat as he disappeared.

With a smile and a wave, Fred drew Tim into the living room. "What's your poison? Something to warm you up now that winter is finally here?" Fred went over to the bar and poured another Scotch.

Tim considered the invitation and was won over by the arrival of Fred's wife, Nell, who appeared by magic at the sound of new life in the room. In an old-fashioned dressing gown, she slunk across the floor, rolling her shoulder blades and hips, and kissed him on the cheek, the smell of juniper warm on her skin. "Timothy Keenan, I did not hear you come in. I hope Nick was no trouble—where is the boy?"

"No trouble at all, although . . ."

She laid a manicured hand against his chest. "Why you're as pale as an oyster, and your heart is just racing. What's the matter, dear soul? You look as if you've seen a ghost."

"That's just it. I saw something on the way over here. Out on the road down by the lighthouse."

Fred handed him a tumbler. "Seems you could use this drink after all. What was it?"

The first sip was as warm as a match.

"I can't say for sure. We were just making the way around Mercy Point when I saw this thing, white as paper, I thought at first, a naked man—"

A laugh burst through Nell's lips. "Maybe I should have a drink, too. Naked as a jaybird?"

"Right, couldn't be," said Tim. "A person without any clothes would freeze to death on such a night. Hypothermia in ten minutes flat. So it simply couldn't be a man."

From the bar, Fred grunted his agreement as he ladled ice into a glass.

"And there's the way that it moved. No sooner did I see it, but it just skittered up the rocks like a kite that's snapped its string, and then the wind grabs ahold and pushes it so hard that it vanishes in an instant."

Fred handed Nell a small cocktail. "Happened to me once. Nicky and I go fishing out at the Long Pier, and just as we climb onto the boards, a breeze snatches my Red Sox cap clean off my head, and it cartwheels the whole length till it ends up cattywampus in the ocean. My hat, not my head. My favorite one."

"Honestly, Fred. You're comparing some ratty baseball cap to a naked man in the middle of the road on the coldest night of the year—"

"He just said it couldn't have been a man. Not to be blown about like that. I was making a simple comparison."

"And I'm just pointing out the flaws in your analogy."

"Not an analogy. Just an observation. A comment on the power of the wind."

"You're being a bit windy yourself," said Nell. "Let the poor soul finish his story."

Tim downed another slug of Scotch and set the empty glass on the table. "That's the long and short of it, I'm afraid. I got out of the car to take a look, but the thing was gone. And Nick didn't see it at all. You may want to check up on him. He caught his collarbone on the seat belt when I hit the brakes. For the life of me, I can't imagine what else it might have been."

"A dog," said Fred. "A big hairy white dog. Or a coyote."

Nell sneered at the proposition.

"What, I saw a coyote round here just last summer coming down a cul-de-sac. Could have been a wild animal. A deer."

"Don't be absurd," Nell said. "You really don't listen, do you? He said it was white as a sheet."

"An old beach towel. A blanket. One of those beach umbrellas caught in the wind."

Nell smiled to herself. "I still think it was a naked man."

"You're always imagining naked men," Fred said.

Nobody could think of a proper retort, so they all waited for a change of subject. Ice cubes rattled in empty glasses.

"How is Holly?" Nell offered at last. "And your boy?"

"Ah, Jip . . . Nick and I were talking on the way over, and perhaps we can invite some of his school friends to the house while we have the two of them over Christmas break."

Some signal passed between the Wellers, a sideways glance that the couple had imbued with shared meaning over the years. They offered no reaction to his suggestion, and he began to regret having raised the possibility.

"I think we might have discovered a hidden talent. He's taken up drawing."

The notion sparked her interest. "You ought to get him one of those artist's kits for Christmas."

"Does he take commissions? Perhaps my wife would model for you."

"Honestly, Fred." She swiveled to put her back to him. "You know, Tim, one of those sets of colored pencils and some fancy paper and maybe some simple paint. Watercolors. Courage the boy." She laughed at her tipsy slip of the tongue.

Yes, he thought as he rose to make his good-byes. Young artist. Self-expression and all that. What boy, even his own, could not use a proper bit of encouragement?

He was not used to drinking, never more than one beer unless he was out with the neighbors or the vacation home owners, and then only to be sociable. The Scotch grumbled in his stomach, and his head felt heavy as Fred and Nell wished him good night. In the driver's seat, he took a few deep breaths to stave off the light dizziness. She never changed, desirable as ever. His lips buzzed numbly, so he kissed the air a few times, pretending it was Nell, before driving away.

Ordinarily he loved the deserted shore on a winter's night, enveloped in solitude for a few moments out of his crowded life. But tonight he could not rid his mind of the image by the roadside. Rounding Mercy Point, he slowed, filled with dread and hope of another sighting. When it did not appear, he pulled off at the spot of his earlier encounter with that strange hallucination. He shut the engine but left the headlights on and slid out of the Jeep. Starry, starry night, and the bitter air filled his lungs. No sign of the thing, not so much as a footprint in the sand. Tim climbed the rocks toward the lighthouse, blinded momentarily by its intense glare, and stopped only when he was high enough to see the whitecaps on the black tide, phosphorescent in the distance, line upon line rolling in.

He should be getting back. They would be wondering what took him so long.

What was out there? Nick hadn't seen a thing. What had the creature been, after all, but an illusion, a spot of indigestion from Holly's bouillabaisse? A dog, a deer, a white coyote? Or a figment of an overtired imagination, a phantom conjured by the wildness running through his son. A boy who hits his mother when she wakes him from his dreams. His boy, always just beyond reach, always swirling away from him like a windblown kite. More encouragement, she had said. More courage. He inhaled one last taste of the salt-sweet tang of the sea and then made his way home.

v.

Holly held her breath and sank beneath the water's surface until she was resting completely on the bottom of the bathtub. Her hair floated like seaweed above her face, her hands bobbed weightlessly, and once she held still, she could hear nothing but the intense rhythm of her own pulse. She closed her eyes so that the only sensation came from the warm water against her skin and the pressure from the air trapped in her lungs. After a moment, a few bubbles escaped through her nose. This is what it must feel like to drown, she thought, and how strangely peaceful in the end. Fifteen seconds more passed before the initial impulse of panic and survival. She arched her back and lifted her shoulders until she could breathe again, and she opened her eyes and saw the white porcelain of the tub, the turquoise tiles on the bathroom wall, and the ceiling bright as a cloud. The skin above her cheekbone throbbed in the humidity. She rolled a towel and laid it beneath her neck and leaned back to rest. Wisps of steam rose from the freckled skin of her knees, a pair of islands peeking out from the water.

The steam reminded her of the priest that morning and his frosty breath as he stood outside Star of the Sea Church, greeting the eight o'clock parishioners after Mass. Cold enough on the steps to see the puffs of air escape with his words. She wanted to sneak past him, just as she had sneaked inside, but he reached for her, extended his hand, and it would have been impolite to refuse the gesture. "Good morning," he said, as earnest as a politician, and when he grasped her hand in both of his and held her in his palms, she could feel the blood warm her cheeks. He was as old as her father, long gone from this world. The people all got in their cars and drove away, and there was nobody left in the church. Last one out.

"Going for a run?" the priest asked.

She wrapped her coat more tightly over her sweatshirt and leggings and shuffled her feet beneath her as if she could hide her sneakers. The decision to come to Mass after all these years had been spontaneous, and she was not dressed properly at all. That morning she had put some concealer on her black eye and donned her jogging gear and bolted from the house, intending to drive down to the high school for a few laps around the oval track. When she saw the handful of cars dotting the church's parking lot, she pulled into Star of the Sea instead. An apology worked its way to her lips, which the priest anticipated and dismissed with the wave of a hand and a wan smile. "We're happy to have you in any disguise. Father Bolden. Joseph." He introduced himself with a curt bow and a smart click of the heels like a Prussian officer washed up on New England's shores.

"Holly Keenan," she said. "I was raised a Catholic."

"But you haven't been back in some time?"

"No. Not since I was married, and before that." A century ago, before Jack, before Tim, when her greatest care was herself. Had she even had such a life?

"Well, welcome back."

For a moment she considered his remark by chewing on her bottom lip. She thought of her mother, no doubt on the way to Mass at this very hour. "I'm not sure I've come back."

"Let's just say 'welcome.' As in, anytime at all. Whatever you're looking for, Mrs. Keenan—"

He must have noticed my wedding ring, she thought. There was a balm in his voice, an unexpected patience.

"If you ever need someone to talk to, someplace to go."

"Thank you, Father." She felt strange calling him Father, after all these years away from priests. An old station wagon turned into the parking lot, the first to arrive for the next scheduled Mass.

"You're always welcome, Holly Keenan. Have a good run."

The bath had cooled, so she lifted her right foot and turned the hot water faucet with her toes till the warmth enveloped her. The morning seemed so long ago. Someone to talk to, he had said, and why else had she come? Someone to talk to about Jack. Someone other than Tim, who was nearly past any conversation about the boy, locked inside his misconceptions of how their son would outgrow his maladies and transform into a normal, fully functional child. She often wondered if Tim's fantasies outstripped Jack's delusions. No, she had not been able to talk about Jack with him in a long time. Many mornings she had jogged past the church without a thought.

Of course, early on she had been tempted to go in, find help or solace or reconciliation, but Tim put more faith in doctors and neurologists, therapists and psychologists, brain specialists and herbalists to locate some remedy even as Holly knew none was to be had. In the beginning, when they first realized something was wrong with their son, she had longed for the comfort of the religion of her youth, its rites and ceremonies, but the plain fact was that Jack's inability to connect with her, with anyone, had seemed such a cruel joke and prayer an empty promise. And that was when he was a little boy, but now, now, just tonight, he nearly had been too strong for her. Her face hurt. Her biceps still ached from the strain of trying to stop Jack from poking at his skull.

She had left him downstairs, parrying with *The Simpsons*, knowing that he would not disturb her bath as long as the cartoon played. Besides, any minute Tim would be back from taking Nicholas home. She shut her eyes and imagined the priest, drifting, trying to relax for just a moment more.

A loud noise, like a single knock at the door, interrupted her reverie, the sharp percussion of a large object striking a hard surface with considerable force. Holly sat upright in the tub, the water rolling off her shoulders and chest, and listened for a following sound, a reply to the first. Her son, perhaps, calling out in surprise or pain, but she could not hear a thing. "Jack!" she shouted. A few beats of silence passed as she waited for his answer, caught between her wish for just a few extra minutes alone versus her instinct to investigate. She could not pinpoint the source. Had something fallen downstairs, was he okay, or had the noise originated elsewhere, maybe Tim's car door slamming? The old house creaked and shuddered in the wintertime, and every stray thud was made louder and more ominous in the emptiness of the season. Perhaps the wind had blown over the trash cans. It's nothing, she told herself, and just as she slid back into the comfort of the water, another knock disquieted her. She pulled the plug from the drain and stood, dripping onto the bath rug, wrapped a thick towel around her torso, and swung open the bathroom door. Her feet left wet prints on the hallway floor.

"Jack," she called from the landing. The familiar swing-time tune from the cartoon's ending credits filtered upstairs. He did not answer, so she went to the top of the stairs and called a third time. "Is everything all right down there?"

"I'm okay, Mom." An annoyed tone in his voice, but no fear or panic.

Another thump sent vibrations through the house, though Holly could not tell if it came from within or without. She hurried into her bedroom, discarded the damp towel on the bed, and put on a nightgown, robe, and slippers. The banging grew frequent and insistent. What is that boy up to? she thought, and hurried down the stairs.

Perched on the couch where she had left him, an afghan wrapped around his legs, Jack now watched a nature program on public television. "Where is your father?" she demanded, but he had slipped into a TV coma and would not be distracted from the show. A brown bear lumbered across the screen. She stood in the middle of the room, alert to the possibilities.

The next blow made her jump. It seemed to have come from the northeast corner of the house, but as she turned, the hammering began, a rapid-fire staccato that traveled the length of the waterfront wall. She raced to a window but could see nothing in the darkness. The southern wall came under attack, a rain of cannonballs against the siding.

"What the hell is going on?"

Curled beneath his blankets, Jack stared at the screen and smiled, as though he had not heard anything.

Her overcoat hung on a hook by the front door, and Holly struggled to fit her robed arms into the sleeves. "Stay inside," she said to Jack, catching the irony of her admonition as she stepped over the threshold.

The air on her bare legs and wet hair chilled her quickly and crept up through her slippers and gripped the soles of her feet. Almost immediately she regretted her decision to leave the house. Tim should be out here in the cold, protecting them, looking for burglars or whatever strange thing was attacking their home. Where is that man? Where was that Father Bolden to protect her with his faith? She murmured a prayer from her childhood as she skirted the perimeter, creeping in darkness, listening for the whistle of cannon fire, watching for the madman with a maul, and shaking with anticipation. The thought of confrontation alarmed her. She had no weapon, not even a baseball bat, and she must have been a fearsome sight in her overcoat and slippers. Perhaps her attacker would perish with laughter. Windblown clouds passed between the moon and the landscape, creating patches of light and shadow on the beach and against the house. In the intermittent exposure, Holly inspected the siding for damage, but the blows had not so much as scratched a shingle. Where she had expected gaping holes with splintered edges, there was nothing. In the quiet of the night, the ocean, to which she had been long accustomed, fell and rose like a child's respiration.

Baby's breath. When Jack was a baby, Holly used to hold him against her chest and sit out on the deck summer afternoons until she and the child breathed in rhythm to the tide. That first magical year when she could not get enough of him, before they fully suspected there was something wrong, before all the doctors, before all the talk of personality disorders. He was simply a baby. Asleep, he would leave a warm slick of perspiration against her skin, wet as a seal, face muzzled against her breast, his tiny fists working toward his mouth. Her baby. She missed him, wanted him to be outside with her, an infant in her arms or the toddler who held one of her fingers in the vise of his fist. Just as she looked for him in the windows, light pouring into the night, a shadow crossed the rectangle of glass and then a second shadow in pursuit.

Jack was waving his hands above his head as though trying to scare away someone inside with him. Someone, she thought, that had been banging against the side of the house trying to get in. A man, a murderer, a monster.

Rays of panic pierced her, and she scrambled through the pillowy sand, desperate to reach him. A hand reached out and grabbed her as she turned the corner, the monstrous thing that had been pounding to enter the house, but turning in the half-light, Holly realized it was only the sleeve of her coat snagged on the cyclone fence that ran along the border between the house and the beach. She tugged and stumbled free, falling into the sand and beach grass.

When the thing did not pounce upon her, when it did not swoop from the sky trailing a long tattered black shroud, when nothing overtook her but her own sense of the absurd, Holly laughed, sprawled on the ground. She had found nothing banging at the siding, no wolf at the door, huffing and puffing to get in. She convinced herself that Tim had come home, and that explained the second figure in her living room. All a misunderstanding, jangle of nerves. Picking herself up, she brushed the sand from her palms, certain that there was no one else inside with Jack, no maniac in a hockey mask, that indeed the only madness came from her own strung-out imagination. A relieved laugh, a laugh to stop from crying, a laugh she was afraid would never end.

Through the fir trees, a pair of headlights appeared small and distant as Tim's Jeep snaked along Shore Road, returning home at last. If that was Tim on the road, she thought, who was the second shadow? Abandoning her search altogether, she hustled inside the house, pulled off her coat, and hooked it by the door. "Were you walking around while I was outside? I thought I saw someone here with you."

Serene as a Buddha, Jack sat on the couch just where she had left him, still tuned in to the nature program, a gang of grizzlies catching salmon as they laddered their way up a stream. His expression had not changed. He seemed not to have moved. She ran her fingers through the frost clotting her hair and kicked off her slippers under the Christmas tree.

"You saw no one? You heard nothing?" she asked, and he nodded without looking at her, though she could not tell whether he had been unaware or was consenting to a conspiracy. Dashing from room to room, she confirmed the house was just as she left it. At the foot of the stairs, she listened for a stranger hiding above, and she called once and was embarrassed by the echo of her voice. Every time she passed him on the couch she noticed Jack's stare, as though he was daring her to ask again. He looked as though he had snatched the truth in his mouth and it was still squirming behind his teeth.

By the time the Jeep pulled into the driveway, the scene was set. Holly had positioned herself next to their son and crossed her arms, affecting nonchalance.

Blooms of red dotted Tim's cheeks as he came in from the cold, smacking the meat of his arms and stomping his feet. "Brrr . . ." He shivered and chattered his teeth with great exaggeration like windup choppers. Jack squealed with delight.

"Where have you been?" Holly asked.

He unwound the scarf from his neck as he crossed the room to greet her with a kiss, the taste of liquor on his lips. "Sorry that took so long."

"Have you been drinking?"

"Mr. Jip, isn't it getting time for bed?" He checked his watch and mussed the boy's hair. Squirming out of reach, Jack burrowed deeper beneath the afghan and snuggled closer to his mother. "Just one," Tim said to her. "You know Fred and Nell. They are so grateful that we've agreed to take Nick off their hands. Second honeymoon, what do you think of that? What have the two of you been up to?"

She considered letting the moment pass, but could not resist. "There was a noise. Outside."

"What sort of noise?" He seemed nonplussed by her demeanor. "Jip, seriously, time to hit the sack."

Irritation floated in her voice. "At first it was just a random knock, I thought something falling over, but then it went on, bang-bang-bang. Striking the siding like gunshot. And you weren't here to go check, so I had to hop out of the bathtub sopping wet to see what was the matter. And then I thought there was someone in the house when Jack was all alone. I swear there was something else inside." With a sneer, she added, "While you were out, sipping Scotch with Fred and Nell Weller."

With a bow of his head, he showed his contrition.

"Honestly, Tim, I was out creeping around in the dark like some teenager in a slasher movie. Lord knows what's waiting behind the corner—"

"So what did you find?"

"Nothing," she said. "I have no idea what was making those noises."

Jack's head popped out from beneath the blanket. "Trying to get in."

Tim snatched away the blanket. "Seriously, bud, let's go. Say good night to your mother."

The boy stood, snapped to attention. "G'night." He saluted and marched upstairs. Even after all these years, she was still disappointed that he did not kiss her before going to bed. She could not remember the last time he had kissed her good night.

After Tim apologized once again, they did not discuss it any further. Without evidence was there a crime? She had Christmas cards to write, and he did penance by folding a load of laundry. In the background, Jack made his slow retreat to bed, stalling in the bathroom before the mirror, brushing his teeth with meticulous care, undressing in slow motion, and then quickly donning pajamas against the cold. His light went out at half-past nine, but his parents knew to give him another thirty minutes to fall asleep.

The house grew still and quiet. Holly sneezed in the kitchen, and Tim said gesundheit from the bedroom upstairs. When she came to bed, she found him already beneath the covers, staring at the curtains drawn across the window on his side. She turned off the light and slipped in beside him. "Something on your mind?"

He rolled over to face her and laid his hand upon her hip. "I'm truly sorry. You know, Jip could be right, could have been something trying to get in. Fred Weller was telling me that people have been spotting coyotes in the area. First thing tomorrow, I'll do a thorough check around the premises—"

"You're forgiven," she said. Silly man. They both knew he would forget by morning. In the pitch dark, she reached out to find his face, laid her palm against his cheek, and waited to feel his smile. He kissed her and fingered his way to the hem of her nightgown and slid the thin fabric to bare her skin. She raised no objections to his touch, but moments later, when he climbed upon her, she breathed out the softest of sighs.

vi.

From the darkness of his room, Nick listened to the dying of the evening, waiting for them to go to sleep. The plain white sheets and his thick comforter covered him, and he did not move while his parents were still up and about. Their muffled conversation slow and regular as the tides, the sound of a glass against a bottle, weary tread upon the stairs. Not too long, usually, when they were besotted, and then they would pass out, exhausted, and purr like kittens in their dreams. Drunken kittens. The telltale signs began: his father singing in falsetto as he stripped off his shoes, his mother stumbling and cursing the rug. After these weekend binges had become routine, Nick could time almost to the quarter hour when they would end. In the beginning, his parents used to show up plastered and sloppy and throw open his door to watch him sleep, but he stopped all that one evening when he screamed in their faces as they hovered over him. That night he had scared them away once and for all.

When it was safe and quiet, he clicked on the lamp and tiptoed to his dresser, opened the bottom drawer, and reached beneath the sweaters stuffed inside. Curled into a tube, the paper seemed a pirate map entrusted to him for safekeeping, though he knew already that it revealed no treasure. At the Keenans' house, as they were saying good-bye, Jack Peter had pressed the scroll upon him in the mudroom. "Don't open it till you are in secret where no one can see," he had said, but Nick could not resist. He had sneaked a look at it in the Jeep while waiting for Mr. Keenan to drive him home. Sitting on the edge of his bed, Nick unfurled it again and smoothed the edges.

Sketched in pencil was that man from the road, the figure that he and Mr. Keenan had encountered earlier that evening. No mistaking the scarecrow features, the pale skin stretched taut over bones, and the deranged hair twisted like a mop. Jack Peter had captured him in the act of rising from the ground, one hand lifted and begging, the other flat on the ground, supporting his weight. The drawing showed the same incomplete face and the figure's blank stare, as if Jack Peter, too, had witnessed him on that same deserted road. He knew it was impossible, but Nick could not ignore the similarities. Above the man, penciled in his friend's familiar block letters, were the instructions: DRAW MORE MONSTERS.

They had been playing this game for years, passing secret messages to each other, hiding notes in coat pockets and underneath pillows where they surely would be discovered later after the friends had parted. For the past month, Jack Peter had been obsessed with war. Through a series of orders and communiqués, their mutual forces had been marshaled. Old soldiers, long forgotten, emerged from their hiding places in shoe boxes on closet floors and dusty cookie tins rescued from underneath the bed. Epic battles featured cowboys versus Nazis, Indians versus the French foreign legion, the blue minutemen versus the red Russians. One battle begat the next in a war without end. Maps to imaginary lands were plotted and then destroyed to prevent the intelligence from falling into enemy hands. Week after week, the carnage continued in the bedroom, behind the Christmas tree, and in one daylong siege in the workshop in the basement among all the dangerous tools. Many men were lost, abandoned beneath sofa cushions or dropped into the abyss below the heating registers.

Before the wars, it had been board games. Hours and hours of Monopoly and Risk. Two weeks to master checkers, and a month of chess. Before the games began, they had gone through a phase of comic books, beginning with *Batman* and *Superman* and ending with *Tintin*, reading side by side with hardly a word between them. They never bothered with the Internet or video games on the computer. The closeness of the big monitor and the brightness of the screen and the quickness of the action gave Jack hammering headaches. Summertime was given over to baseball on the radio, the Red Sox mostly, but on long August nights, they could pick up on AM radio faraway Pittsburgh and Chicago and, for one magic evening, the golden glow of a Dodgers game all the way from southern California. Last spring they had devoted to model ships, whalers and clippers, and over a long Easter break, a scale model of the U.S.S. *Constitution*, complete with cloth sails and string lines and the intoxicating smell of glue and black paint. What mania came before that, Nick could no longer remember, but anything was acceptable, as long as it was safely indoors.

And now, as with every obsession, this war had its natural limits, a moment when the luster faded suddenly and without reason, and the bored boy would cast around for novelty. His latest passion would be drawing monsters. Not bad, he thought, I could get into monsters. And yet.

Yet he had seen that thing on the road. He pretended to Mr. Keenan that he had witnessed nothing—in part because he could not believe his eyes and in part because he was not completely sure the figure was not simply of his own imagining, an illusion based on Jack Peter's sketches and the power of suggestion. Whatever it really was. By the time Mr. Keenan had exited the car in pursuit, it was too late for Nick to confess. Anyhow, he had shut his eyes when it looked his way, and then the creature simply vanished into the night, no more presence than if he had never appeared in the first place. Even now, with the drawing spread across his lap, Nick could no more be sure what he had seen or what he may have conjured.

He blamed Jack Peter. That boy had always had a way of pulling him into his inner world, with a strange hold stemmed from their shared affinities and lifelong history. They had been linked from the cradle. Born just two weeks apart, they were raised together. Their mothers seemed like best friends to Nick, and he could not remember a single birthday or Halloween or Christmas that they had not spent together. Separated only by Mercy Point, they were always playing at either the Keenans' or the Wellers' house, especially in those long winter months when life at the shore can be so lonesome.

Of course, Nick had other friends, boys from school mostly, but he rarely saw them outside the classroom. They were scattered widely across the peninsula; but most of them, he knew, avoided him on account of his parents. Couple of drunks. By default, his family had remained loyal with their oldest friends, the Keenans, and he to Jack Peter. Once upon a time, they had been equals, or so it seemed to him now, looking back to those years when Jack Peter was unafraid of the outdoors. They would play hide-and-seek in the fir trees that bordered the Keenans' house, or fly kites in May and June. They were just friends, but all that changed after the accident. Jack Peter emerged out of the ocean an entirely different child, more demanding and in control, and without thinking, Nick began to bend to his wishes. From that time on, he had followed Jack Peter's lead, always. He, too, had been changed by that day on the beach, though not in the same way.

Daring one more glance at the monster, he rolled up the scroll and tucked it back into the hiding place. The hard wooden floor felt cold beneath his bare feet, and his bed beckoned, soft and warm. He hopped across the room and just as he snapped off the light and settled under the comforter, a crash came from beyond his closed door. A thump of something heavy landing on the floor.

The first thought to flash through his mind was the image of the bogeyman from the drawing come to get him. Hadn't that thing crossed the headlands moving northerly? Right in this direction. Nick pictured the creature as just beyond, pacing the hallway, readying itself to smash the door and wrest him from the covers. Counting to ten, he steadied himself and waited. A game of hide-and-seek, but when no bony fist turned the knob and no curdling groan was uttered, he realized that his imagination had raced ahead of all reason. He eased his way from under the covers to investigate.

At the far end of the dark hall, his parents' bedroom door stood ajar, but no light shone from within, so he tiptoed to the entrance and peeked inside. After his eyes adjusted to the dimness, Nick could make out the general contours of the furniture, the pair of mirrored bureaus, and the king bed with one body curled beneath the blankets. His mother snored quietly in her usual spot. On the far side, the white sheets were twisted and wound like wind-wrecked sails. Nick crept over and saw his father passed out in a heap of limbs on the floor. From the angle of repose, his father looked as if he had no head, and for a moment in the stillness, Nick wondered where it might have gone.

"Dad?" he whispered in a soft voice, and when the body did not respond, he laid one hand on his father's shoulder and shook him gently. "Dad, are you all right?"

His father grumbled something in his sleep but did not respond to his son's entreaties, so Nick pushed harder with both hands.

"Whozat? Ah, Nicky. I seemed to have missed the bed." Whiskey breath, but his clothes smelled like sour milk. Still dressed in his bulky sweater and trousers, he had at least remembered to take off his shoes and socks, for his bare feet shone white in the darkened room. As he tried to stand, he struck a pose that mirrored the man in Jack Peter's picture, a kind of fishlike crawl from out of the primordial ooze. Nick bent to offer support, and his father used him as a crutch to stand, wobbling and uncertain. "You're a good boy."

Nick helped him back into bed, untangling the sheets as best he could and tucking him in. His mother sighed in her sleep but did not stir. For a long while, he watched them to make sure that in their unconscious states they would not be tossed about by their boozy dreams. On other nights like this, they could be trusted to lie as still as a pair of corpses, but he wanted to be sure his father would not fall out of bed again. He swore to himself, as he had a dozen or more times these past few years, that he would never touch a drop of liquor. They had been better able to handle it when he was younger, but over the past few years their drinking had grown worse. Sometimes they seemed to willingly remove themselves so far from reality as to lose their place in it.

Gently shutting the door behind him, Nick returned to his own room and eased into bed. Outside the cold wind blew, and the sheets and pillowcases were ice against his bare skin. With a wriggle he wrapped the comforter around his feet to warm them. He knew that he would be awake as long as he was frozen, that he would not be able to get to sleep anytime soon, and a mild panic set in over the lateness of the hour and the prospect of school in the morning.

"Sleep," he told himself. "Just go to sleep."

But he could not sleep. The man on the road filled his thoughts. Mr. Keenan had stopped short and the car jerked them forward against the restraints of their seat belts. Nick had pretended not to see, but he had seen all. Uncurling like a fern, the man had risen from the ground and stood half hunched in anticipation. In the pale moonlight, his bare skin shone white, and he moved with a wild animal's hesitancy and sudden alarm. A deer caught by surprise, here and then gone, disappearing into the night. He wondered where the man had run off, for to the east lay bare rock tumbling down to the endless sea. Summer days Nick and Jack Peter had hopped about over that same rough slate, dodging crevasses and tidal pools, but he could not imagine how a barefoot man could make his escape or where he might hide or how he might avoid the dark and freezing waters.

The room had grown stifling and close with the constant blast of forced air. He flipped over his pillow and laid his head against the cool fabric, reaching back with his free hand to throw off all the covers except for the thin sheet. Blood rushed to his cheeks, and he felt a slick of perspiration pool along the ridge of his spine. Hot as August. The faint aroma of salt water, sunshine on the beach wafted into the room. He could smell fish and the broken bits of crab and lobster shells too long in the heat. The odor of rot made his eyes water, and he sat up in the dark room, wondering where the smell originated. The rank and humid foulness hit him full blast in the face. The bed seemed to totter momentarily, a boat rocking on a wave, before it settled again, and then the wave reached the wall and slid into the closed closet. Something heavy inside bumped against the surface of the door, hard the first time and then softly again. The hangers rattled like metal chains.

He did not want to get out of bed. The thought of opening the closet frightened him, but the clatter would not stop and the odor intensified with his every breath. Sweat beaded along his brow, and his pajamas clung to his skin like wet napkins. In their bedroom, his parents were out cold. He could call till hoarse, but they would not waken till morning. He knew he would have to face the thing itself. The closet would not let him go.

Curious and afraid, he put one foot on the floor as though to test whether it was safe. Tender as a wing, a flutter beat in rhythm on the inside of the closed door. The stench was now awful, fetid and briny. He wished he had just left the door open, so he could see inside without taking a further step, even if that meant, as it sometimes did, that he would have to deal with the amorphous shapes of his clothes tricking him with their ghostly transformations. The scraping from inside the door continued, insistent as a whisper. The heat pressed upon him, palpable as fog. Nick gingerly put his other foot down and crept across the floor, anxious that he might awaken the man inside, or that thing from the road that he was now sure lingered there, ready to pounce as soon as he turned the doorknob. Muttering a prayer, he steadied his nerves and, deciding at the last moment to get it over with quickly, he flung open the door.

Even in dim light, the blur of white blazed before his eyes. Hung from the closet rod, the two naked bodies, twined together as if bound, swung in the draft he had created. Despite their disfigurement, they were recognizable at once as the corpses of his parents joined together in one final dance. The rotting smell rolled off the corpses, burning his sinuses and lingering in his mouth. Their skin was the color of bone yet waxy, the consistency of soft cheese peeling off in curled ribbons, and when they swirled into view, their crimson faces were bloated, lips blue, noses scarred as though nibbled by fishes, their wet hair flat and plastered along the contours of their skulls. Their mouths hung open and their tongues lolled hideous as eels. Worst of all, their open eyes stared straight at him, sunken in the folds of skin thick as wet dough. A dead look of accusation. They seemed to have been dragged from the bottom of the sea like a pair of large fish hung on a string to dry.

Nick did not cry out at first, for he could not reconcile the difference between what he was seeing and what his mind knew to be true. Two simultaneous versions of reality from which to choose: the swinging bodies in the closet and the surety that his parents slept not twenty feet away in their own bed, dead drunk to the world, just out of reach. It was the incompatibility of these truths that made him crack, and he screamed, running down the dark hallway to the safety of their room. He kept on screaming until he saw his mother shift beneath the blankets and turn on the small lamp on her crowded night table. In the soft glow, her eyes blinked, bloodshot, and she struggled to sit up against the pillows, fighting the stupor in her mind, and disoriented by the sudden presence of her terrified son.

"What it is, pet? Did you have a nightmare?" She held out her arms to him.

He slipped in beside her on the empty space between her and the edge of the mattress. Roping her arms around his shoulders, his mother pulled him toward her.

"There were bodies in the closet," Nick said, realizing at once that it could not be so. She was right here. And in there, swinging on a rope next to Dad.

"Are you sure? Skeletons in the closet." She laughed to herself despite her best efforts at restraint.

"You and Dad were drowned."

"Drowned? We're right here." Her breath smelled of sour wine. She blinked her eyes, fighting sleep, as she tightened her grip around his wrist. He would have stayed there forever had she not nodded off and then suddenly snapped awake, as if she finally remembered who he was. "Still scared? Let's go see about those bodies in the closet. I'll bet you anything it's a couple of coats that just seemed to be something else in the dark."

Nick started to object, but his mother had already let go and was forcing him off the edge of the bed with her hip. She reeled in the darkness and flipped on the light in the hallway and then again as they entered his room, mother bold and protective with her son hiding behind her nightgown. He was as intimidated by her speed and confidence as he was frightened of what was behind the closed closet door. Had he closed it when he fled? She did not hesitate to reach for the knob and fling it open. Just as she had promised, nothing inside but his old familiar clothes. They stood together for a while considering its emptiness.

"See," she said in a calm and comforting voice, guiding him to his place. "Nothing to fear. We'll leave it open if you like, but it was just your imagination."

Nick climbed back into his bed with a dozen pictures in his head, and as she kissed him good night, he wanted to beg her to stay, at least until he could fall asleep, but he let her go, stumbling back to her room. He turned on the lamp on his nightstand for he knew he could not sleep in the dark.

vii.

His bedroom faced the ocean, and in the morning, the rising sun would blaze fire over water and shine through his window. If he had not drawn the curtains the night before, Jack Peter would watch the reflection of the dawn in the bureau mirror on the opposite side of the room. With a rapt devotion, he would study the way the light chased away the dark. Find the pattern, watch how it repeats itself. He would not move until it was over. He tried not to blink until he saw the whole sun. The glass would slowly come to life, changing by degrees nearly imperceptible, but with patience he could distinguish each shade and hue when the pale lavender sky was shot through by the circle of the sun. Soon he could see the long trail of glowing orange run from the horizon to the shore along the smooth surface of the sea and the gentle breaking of the waves along the bottom of the mirror. Then the burning disk would continue its slow ascent, the sky would yellow then blue, and a new day had begun.

He got out of bed and scurried to his desk. Although the winter sunshine now filled his room, he switched on the lamp to throw a spotlight on his work. Last night's drawings lay hidden under sheets of virgin white. The stub of a pencil weighed down the papers, and he stared at the blank surface, waiting for an image to appear, some transfer from his mind, and then with the pencil in hand, he carefully drew the first curved line, satisfied that he had at least, at last, started. Within those first few moments, he was free from all exterior distraction and possessed by the flow of lines against the page. A face appeared slowly out of nothing, not a real face, but facelike enough to stand for the thing itself, so that the image on the page became a substitute for the image that had been in his mind.

He had nearly completed his new picture when the others began to awaken. The alarm clock in his parents' room disturbed him from his work, and his mother rose from her bed, the box springs creaking, and out slipped a mild curse as she stubbed a toe. She would be in soon to awaken him, after she had made a pit stop in the bathroom, so he had just enough time to put away his drawing, turn off the light, climb back into bed, and pretend to be asleep.

"Jack," she called from above, and when he refused to answer, she spoke his name again, careful not to touch him. "Rise and shine. I can't afford to be late today."

With a long and deep moan, he rolled away from her entreaties, so she circled around to the other side and sat on the edge of the bed. He opened his eyes and offered himself to her, remembering yesterday morning he had struck her by accident and wanting to make peace. He pulled her hand to his face, and she caressed his cheek and then brushed his mussed hair with her fingers. "C'mon, Jack, you've got to help me out here. Wake up, wake up, buttercup. Time to get out of bed, sleepy-head. We need to get dressed and have some breakfast." After a few moments of cajoling, she succeeded at last in raising him to a seated position. He pretended to rub the sleep from his eyes.

Mornings had become a game between the two of them. He would dawdle as long as possible whether actually tired or not, and she would coax as long as patience held out. "Lift your arms," his mother said, and when he had surrendered, she tugged his pajama top over his head. The cold gave him the shivers and he yearned for his sweater.

From the direction of his desk came a rattle, and as they turned toward it, they saw the top drawer shake slightly in its slides as though something inside wanted to get out. Her fingers flew to her mouth to trap in her apprehension. They waited, still and quiet, until the scrabbling began again.

"You've got a little visitor, Jack."

He hugged himself, his thin, bare arms as pale as his undershirt. "What is it?"

The drawer jerked lightly on its rails.

"Sounds like a big mouse." She smiled and joked, "Or a small rat."

Gathering the fabric into a circle, she guided the sweater over his head, and he smiled, as always, once he'd pushed his way through the opening. As he worked his way into the sleeves, Jack Peter asked, "Aren't you going to see what's in there?"

"Are you kidding? I have no intention of opening that drawer. Would scare me half to death, whatever's in there. I'll have your father take a look. That's why I keep him around—to kill spiders and get rid of mice."

"But don't you want to know?"

"I do not. Now, do you think you can put on your pants by yourself and some socks and shoes and march down to breakfast?"

He nodded, so she kissed him on the forehead. She lingered a moment at the foot of the bed, regarding him with tenderness and a short smile, and then she was gone. Jack Peter gathered the blankets around his legs and listened to the next part of the morning routine.

Through his open doorway floated the familiar rhythm of his parents' fleeting conversation. His mother roused his father from his slumber and readied herself for work. Reminders of the day's schedule were exchanged, and this morning, words about a mouse in a drawer. She hurried downstairs, poured herself a mug of coffee for the trip to the office, and left, closing the front door with an emphatic click. Some days, after his mother had gone, a brief interval of silence returned to the house, a sure sign that his father had gone back to bed. No such luck today. Down the hall, the pipes rattled and the shower gushed. He had seven minutes before his father would arrive.

As he quickly dressed and straightened his sheets and blankets, he stole glances at the desk drawer to make sure it did not suddenly pop open and release its contents. He sat on the smoothed quilt and counted off the remaining minutes, tapping his left foot on the floor to keep time. At the seven-minute mark, he got up and went to the doorway, anxious for the schedule to be maintained. Even though he knew it was coming, when the door swung open, he was caught by surprise. Clad in a yellow robe bright as a canary, his father stepped out of the bathroom in a cloud of steam that trailed him to the bedroom door. "Up and ready to get cracking? We have Dr. Wilson this morning."

"I don't want to go. I don't like Dr. Wilson."

"Look, I had to call and get them to squeeze you in this morning. I know you don't want to go, but it's mandatory, I'm afraid. No Dr. Wilson, no magic pills."

"I don't want to take the magic pills."

His father scowled at him. "Jip, I've told you a hundred times, that's not an option. Now hurry and get ready. We've barely enough time for breakfast." Just as he was about to leave, the scrabbling and bumping in the drawer began again.

"Wait!" The boy held out his arms like a toddler. "Didn't Mommy tell you about the noise in the drawer?"

"The mouse?"

Jack Peter took two steps back into the room, hoping to entice him to follow. "Aren't you curious? Aren't you going to check?"

His father followed him in. "Curiosity killed the cat, my boy. Or, in this case, the mouse." He quickly opened the drawer and peered inside, pretending to shuffle the contents. "Nothing here to meet the eye. But not to worry, if there's a mouse in here, it won't eat much. We'll take care of it later. First, Dr. Wilson. There's no time for games."

The eggs had gone cold and the little triangles of toast had become hard and dry by the time he came downstairs. He pushed the food with his fork and sipped at a mug of lukewarm cocoa, stealing glances at his father, who was spying on him from behind the newspaper. With a bit of effort, he thought he could dawdle all day, but his father folded the sports section with a crisp crease and laid it down beside his empty coffee cup. "Time to go."

Condemned, he pushed away from the table and followed his father to the mudroom. First came the dark sunglasses, which made the day into night, and then his coat and hat, his scarf and mittens. He tried to screw his feet into the floor, but he hadn't the strength to resist his father's tug at his hand. On with the red boots. They marched to the doorway, and Tim left him standing at the threshold while he went to start up the Jeep. The sun fell brightly upon his face and the cold air wormed its way through the layers of clothing and fingered his skin. He tucked his chin against his chest and shivered. The engine roared to life and his father came trudging from the driveway with an old stadium blanket they kept in the back for just such occasions.

"I can't," Jack Peter said.

"Of course you can," his father answered, and he threw the blanket over Jack Peter's head and shoulders and wrapped him up so tightly that only his face could be seen. With a firm hand against his son's back, Tim guided him onto the driveway. On the first step outside, the boy let out a low moan that rose to a steady wail as he was herded the few feet to the car. His father pushed him into the passenger's seat and slammed the door behind him. Jack Peter banged the seat with his back over and over until he was strapped into place. His cries subsided to a quiet singsong whimper that Tim drowned out by turning on the radio.

"Honestly, Jip, can you cool it just this once?"

Behind his dark glasses and buried in his swaddling, the boy whined softly all the way to the psychiatrist's office. Once a month to Dr. Wilson. Once every other month to the state-provided therapist. Twice a year to the dentist's. The odd trip to the pediatrician for other maladies. Every time a little hell.

Even so, it was better now than in the beginning. They had not understood at first what triggered the seizures, and it was only through months of tribulation that they realized that it was being outside that made him panic. When their son first started having the attacks, Tim had to carry him, seven years old, bawling like a rabbit in a trap, pleading not to be taken from inside.

The ordeal with Dr. Wilson took the rest of the morning. First, they had to move from the car to the medical building and then unwrap the blankets once inside. Then Jip had to adjust to the new environment of the pediatric waiting room filled with people. He liked to sit on an end seat with his father next to him, but no two seats together were available, so they stood by the water cooler affecting a casual air. As usual, they went in together for the interrogation.

Wilson rose from his chair, a giant of a man, and reached down to shake Tim's hand in his huge paw. Emerging from his bushy beard, his smile of greeting was alarming, for he usually wore a severe expression on his face. His joker's grin was his attempt at appearing nonjudgmental, which often had the opposite effect. While he settled into his throne across from them, Wilson invited them to sit on the couch. He gave Tim one last cursory glance and then turned to the boy.

"So how are we doing these days, Jack? Ready for Christmas?"

Jip said nothing and tucked his chin to his chest. The doctor bent forward, made himself smaller, and put his face closer. "Come now, it's me. What's new and exciting? Are you working on anything?"

"He's doing much better," Tim volunteered. "Been drawing, haven't you?"

Like a hummingbird, Jip's hand darted forward and he used one finger to trace a pattern in the air.

"What do you like to draw?" Dr. Wilson asked.

Jip dropped his hand back into his lap and stared straight ahead.

"What is it that you see?"

He rolled his eyes quickly in the direction of his father. Like a wooden contraption, Wilson unfolded himself, straightening his body, and then leaned back in the chair. He put the tips of his index fingers against his lips, considering his next steps, before addressing Tim. "Perhaps you could leave us alone for a while. Perhaps there's something Jack would like to talk about in private?" He arched his eyebrows, eliciting a small smile from the boy.

"I'll call you back in when we are done," Wilson said. "And we can talk about his routine, whether his meds are working for the anxiety. We won't be long, eh, Jack?"

In the reception room, Tim waited with the other parents and their children arranged on the furniture, each caught up with a private malady. A yawning boy with circles dark as a raccoon's mask. A teenaged girl twisting a tissue in her nervous hands. Another child, face upturned and as blank as a stone, counting the tiny squares in the ceiling tiles, a kindred soul perhaps. Twenty minutes passed like eternity. When at last they stepped out into the room, Jip and Dr. Wilson looked as chummy as conspirators.

"You have yourself a good Christmas, Jack," the psychiatrist said. He towered over Tim and put a hand upon his shoulder. "Mr. Keenan, I think we're okay for now with the dosage, but I want you back here next month, and we really should talk about group again, or somewhere he can talk, let some of his anxieties out in a constructive way."

"It's just so hard to get him out of the house, doctor."

"I'm not sure how much his agoraphobia is actually making his overall anxieties worse, but he's worried that whatever he's afraid of outside is trying to come inside the house. It's probably best we tackle this latest beastie while we can. Let's give it a try, maybe in the new year? Meanwhile, I think it's healthy to encourage the drawing, eh? Jack, why don't you grab your coat and get your father's."

When the boy was out of earshot, Wilson took Tim aside and spoke softly. "Keep an eye on what he's drawing, would you? Bring some in next time. There's usually a story there."

Lunchtime had come and gone by the time they made it back home and repeated the whole process in reverse, shuttling him from the Jeep and those fifteen feet into the mudroom. Tim unwound the swaddling from the boy, and he was whole again. They talked about his homeschool lessons over tomato soup and grilled cheese sandwiches. At two o'clock, as usual during the school year, his father left to attend to the few chores and errands of the day, checking on the properties he looked after, making sure the winter was not invading the summer homes of his wealthy clients. For a glorious hour or so, Jack Peter had the whole house to himself.

He was supposed to be reading. That was the deal they had made that past September when Tim and Holly finally agreed they could leave him alone for a small part of the day. Prior to that, one parent stayed at home while the other was at work, and during the summertime, when Tim's duties kept him busy, there had been a nurse two afternoons a week and a string of babysitters, college girls mostly, whose company he both enjoyed and resented.

"I'm almost eleven," he had argued. "Too old to be babysat."

"You're just ten," his mother had said. "How do we know we can trust you?"

"He'll be fine with a book," his father had countered, and that settled the matter.

Today, however, he merely cracked the text at hand and left it spread upon the table. He wandered through the old house as aimless as a ghost. In the living room, he peeked in the coat closet and stared at the hidden presents wrapped in bright Christmas paper. He turned on the lights on the Christmas tree and then turned them off again. In the kitchen, he opened the refrigerator and straightened out the bottles and leftovers on the shelves. Each time he passed a window, he checked the locks, and double-checked the front door and the side entrance. He wrote his name in the dust on the coffee table and erased it with his sleeve. At three o'clock, he went into the mudroom to stare through the picture windows at the road that wound through the fir trees. He counted off the minutes between the first flash of yellow in the distance to the moment when the school bus turned the corner and came into full view. At the next driveway, the Quigley twins skipped down the steps in their matching plaid skirts and green jackets. Alert to the possibility of any oncoming traffic, he watched them cross the road and followed with his gaze until they were safely through the front door. Their obsessive border collie nearly knocked them over when they stepped inside. "Hello," he mouthed silently. "Good-bye." The red lights of the school bus stopped blinking, and with a belch of smoke it rumbled away. Framed in the windows, the children's heads bobbed like dolls.

Right after the twins got home, his father was due. Sometimes it was just a few minutes after, sometimes up to half an hour. There was no way to count on him. Better to go back to the kitchen table and pretend to be reading when he arrived. Pretend, because he had already read the book three times. First on Friday, when his father had handed it to him. They always overestimated how long it would take, and the books in the fifth-grade home curriculum were much too easy. For those first few books, when the hour finally arrived for his father to quiz him, Jack Peter often had forgotten some of the details, so now he spent the week going over the text again and again. His parents thought him a slow reader because he never seemed to get any further along in a book, but he was faster and smarter than they could ever guess.

His thoughts strayed from the page. Nick would be home by now, and he could picture his friend sitting down to an afternoon snack, Mrs. Weller flitting around in the background, asking about school, and good old Nick letting her know that everything was just fine, nothing new, and maybe he had drawn some monsters in his notebook.

At four o'clock, the front door opened suddenly and in came his father, tired and disheveled. A black slick of grease crossed his pants at midthigh, and his hands were covered with the same goo. He saluted his son and went to the kitchen sink to lather and scrub. "Sorry it got so late, Jip. I went over to check on the Hollisters' place, up by the crescent, and something had gotten in through a hole in the crawl space. Dug a big, big hole and squeezed right in underneath and made itself at home. I could fit my whole self in it. Nothing worse than trying to keep out something that wants to come in."

"Did you see who it was?"

"What?" He laughed and rubbed his hands furiously under the hot running water. "Not a who. A what. And, no, I didn't ever find out if it was a cat or a raccoon or a whatever. Maybe a skunk by the smell of things, but I had a devil of a time fixing up the hole so it won't get in again."

Jack Peter sidled up to his father and leaned against the counter next to him. "Maybe it was a big mouse."

"Right, like the one your mother said was hiding in your room. This old place is crawling with mice," he said. "Just last week, I found a whole bunch of them had made a nursery school down in my workshop. Let's go take a look. Get to the bottom of the secret of the hidden mouse."

They went upstairs together, and though he had not heard the rattle from the desk since the morning, Jack Peter knew what to expect. His father removed his left shoe and held it in his hand. "They're wicked quick," he said. "You've got to be ready before you see 'em or you haven't got a chance."

"What are you going to do with that shoe?"

"If there's a mouse in there, Jip, your mother said we've got to get rid of it. Don't want it running loose in the house."

"You're not going to kill it."

He put a hand on his son's shoulder to steady himself. "Well . . . no, not if I can help it, I guess. We'll just stun the critter and then I'll take it outside and let it go, if you want. Now, slowly open the drawer while I get ready. One, two—"

"I don't want to. You'll kill it."

"Never." He pulled on the handle and yanked open the drawer with a start. There was no startling flash of brown, no tail zipping like a pulled string. No evidence that there had ever been a mouse at all, no seedy droppings, no chewed paper. Tim rooted around in the clutter and found nothing, and only as he was about to close it and admit defeat did he spy the scroll of paper. As he unrolled it, the drawing took shape, a picture of a boy alone on the shore, emerging from the sea, behind him the lines of waves breaking in the distance. Half unfurled, the picture amazed him, and had he bothered to open it all the way, Tim would have seen the legs of the other figure running off the page.

"When did you do this?"

But Jack Peter would not answer. His eyelids fluttered, and his eyes rolled back into his head, the whites showing as blank as clouds. He fainted onto the bed, and he remembered nothing more till the sound of his father's voice gently calling his name brought him back fully into the world.

viii.

Did you get rid of it?" Holly leaned across him and spat in the sink. Bits of foam stuck to the corners of her mouth. In the mirror, Tim was startled by his own reflection and his frown of disgust. He uncurled his lip and considered his appearance, the deepening lines across his forehead and the crow's-feet radiating from his eyes. The outside man in the mirror looked back at the inside man, both thinking the same thoughts, just a second apart. He tried to remember his wife's question.

She rinsed the toothpaste from her mouth and checked her teeth, running her tongue over the enamel. "Well, did you get rid of it?"

The mouse, right. He had nearly forgotten the mouse given their son's peculiar reaction to the hidden drawing. "I put down some traps."

Moving on in her preparations for bed, Holly took up the brush and ran it through her hair, counting the strokes, the numbers passing stealthily through her lips. "Not where Jack can hurt himself?"

"Of course not. One in the back of the closet and one between his desk and his old toy box."

Like a marionette on a string, she tilted her head so that her long hair spilled to one side, and she brushed the flow of it. "Make sure you check on those traps. I can't imagine anything worse than a dead mouse in the room for a couple of days."

He had stopped looking at himself and now squeezed behind her on his way out of the bathroom. "Not that there was any sign of it. No droppings, no shredded tissues on the floor."

"I didn't see it," Holly said, "but I sure heard it in the desk drawer. Jack's not going to step on a trap in the middle of the night?" She turned and followed him into the bedroom. The small table lamp was the last one on in the house, and Tim imagined how it might appear to those out on the sea, a tiny pinprick of illumination against the blackness of the night, one small star upon the shore. If there were a man out there in the cold, he would be drawn, surely, to any sign of life.

"No way he can step on the one in the closet, and I'm sure he doesn't go near that toy box anymore. Why do we keep it, anyhow? It's probably full of nothing but baby things and stuff he's outgrown."

Holly folded back a triangle of the covers and bedsheet, but rather than climb in, she sat on the edge of the mattress as though trying to remember some unfinished task before going to sleep. "How was he at the psychiatrist's?"

"Same as ever. Lots of questions, few good answers."

They slipped into bed and lay flat on their backs side by side, and Tim turned out the light.

"Honestly," he said, "I don't know why we keep going to that guy. Jip is never different afterwards, just gets a different pill."

"To keep Jack under control."

"That's just it. Maybe keeping him under control is what's keeping the problem alive. Maybe if we trusted him, Jip could make it on his own. Without the pills. Everybody is on something these days. It's a racket. Overprescribing, masking the problem."

"I can't have this argument again," she said. "I'm tired."

"I'm just saying that maybe there's less than meets the eye. Take the Weller boy. He's shy, introverted, but you don't see Nell rushing off for a pill."

"Please"—her voice cut the darkness—"don't hold up Nell Weller as your example."

Without another word, Tim rolled away from her and into the privacy of his thoughts. She said nothing either, but he could hear her breathing, steadily and in sync with the ticking of the alarm clock. Longtime combatants on this matter, each could not find sleep easily, and an hour passed in wary détente.

Just past midnight, he heard her calling his name softly from a far-away spot on the opposite shore of his consciousness. She laid her hand upon his shoulder. "Tim, are you awake? Did you hear that?"

Halfway between sleep and dreaming, he opened his eyes in the darkness of the room and struggled to orient himself. Familiar objects, shades of gray, began to take shape, and he became aware of his wife's entreaties. "Listen," she commanded in a hoarse whisper, and he strained to discover what she had heard, but he could find no stray sound.

"There's someone in the house."

He heard nothing.

"Something's walking around."

"Are you sure it's not Jip, going to the bathroom?"

She cricked her neck toward the bedroom door and looked at the gap where it met the floor. "The hall light's not on. He's afraid of the dark and always turns on the light."

Fumbling for the table lamp, he nearly knocked it off the nightstand and had to grab the base to stop it from rocking. In the burst of light, he blinked and then hoisted himself against the pillow. She was already up, the quilt pooled across her lap, her feet twitching under the covers.

"It was on the roof," she said. "Footsteps crossing from one edge to the other, and then they stopped."

"Could be a bird," he said.

"Like a man's."

"But they stopped?"

Her face was flushed, and she frowned at him. "I didn't wake you up at first. Thought it might be my imagination. But now it seems like it's in the house. Listen."

They held their breath and did not budge. Beyond the door, a board creaked, the sound of a foot upon the stair. He swung his legs over the edge and stood.

"Shouldn't you have a baseball bat or something?" she asked.

"Where would I get a baseball bat?"

"Some protection," she said. "In case you have to defend yourself."

"There's a hammer in the workshop, and a shovel out in the mud-room. But I'd have to get by *it* to get them."

"Be careful," she admonished from the bed. Tim looked back once to see her trembling, her hands clasped at the bunched cloth at her neck-line. The bruise on her face pulsed like a siren.

The idea that he could move without a sound proved false from his very first steps. His weight made the pine boards squeak, but he could not shake the desire to sneak up on whatever was making noises in the bowels of the house. He tiptoed in his bare feet, an impractical cat bur-glar, and made his way around the bed to the door. The hall was dark and quiet. No light shone from Jip's room, and nothing scurried out of the way as he walked along the runner that covered the corridor floor. Tim crept down the stairs, alert for any signs, but he met no one as he checked the rooms one by one. The house seemed undisturbed. Only the Christmas tree in the living room suprised him, and he laughed at his foolish reaction to its bulk looming out of the darkness. He checked the knobs and latches, even to the workroom down below, but the doors and windows were locked for the night. He found himself slightly dis-appointed by the lack of anything out of the ordinary. In the kitchen, he snapped on the lights and drank a glass of water to assert his authority over intruders real or imagined. His only cause for unease was the sen-sation that his wife was upstairs waiting for him and would continue to insist that she had heard something. But what could he do? He couldn't conjure a visitor by sheer imagination.

Tim considered waking Jip to see if he had been the cause of the strange noises, but there would be hell to pay if he disturbed the boy and overturned the night any further than it had already been. He yawned, long and hard, fatigued by the lateness of the hour. Holly would not be placated easily, but he rehearsed his explanation. Birds on the roof, the house settling in the changing weather.

At the top of the stairs, his left foot landed in dampness, cold as ice. So cold that he yelped and withdrew his bare sole from the rug. "Son of a bitch," he muttered to himself and bent to feel the dampness with his hand, but it was not wet, just cold, and it seemed to be no larger than the span of his fingers. He blindly ran his palms along the borders of the spot and made it out as a footprint. On his hands and knees, he crawled along the floor and came upon another frozen patch embedded in the runner. A third appeared and a fourth, but he could not tell from the shape of the prints which direction they followed. He crabwalked along the trail to his bedroom door, and then he worked his way back down the hall to his son's bedroom. A set of icy prints stopped in front of Jip's room, and Tim squatted there, his eyes even with the doorknob. He grasped the frosted metal, icy as a school yard flagpole, and against his pressure, it turned in his hand, forcing his wrist to twist sharply, and all at once the boy was in the open doorway, backlit, looking down quizzically at his father.

"Feel this," Tim said, and he pulled his son's arm until the boy was on his knees, and he pushed the boy's hand against the rug. Tim expected him to recoil against the strange temperature, but Jip knelt there implacable.

"What am I supposed to feel?"

Pressing his own palms against the corded fabric, Tim could no longer sense the icy prints. He waddled down the hall, testing the runner with his hands and bare feet, but it was warm and dry.

"It was stone cold just a minute ago," he told his son. "Someone had been walking on it with frigid feet. Did you hear anything just now? Something on the roof?" He laughed at the absurdity in his own question.

"No, nothing, nothing at all."

"And you've been in your room the whole time?"

The boy nodded and rubbed the sleep from his eyes.

"And you didn't feel the cold? Didn't see a thing?"

"Probably in your head. I see things all the time."

For a long time, his father stared at him, opening his mouth a few times as though to reply before reconsidering. Like a pale ghost, Holly emerged from the bedroom, anxious to find them both standing there. In her thin nightgown, she shivered as she stood, waiting for some explanation.

He thought to tell her about the icy footprints in the hall, but he was not sure that she would believe him without any proof, and he was not sure if it was not all some trick of the mind like that thing on Shore Road. Instead he put an arm around her waist and tried to reassure her with a hug. She trembled in his arms.

"It was nothing," Tim said. "All in your imagination."

"Are you sure? I heard sounds, I felt something moving around."

"A bad dream," her husband whispered, and her breathing slowed. Over her shoulder, he could see his son, small and slight in his little boy's pajamas. Up and alert when he should have been long asleep in his bed. Jip stood there staring right through them, with his inscrutable eyes, as if they were the intruders in his house, the unexpected visitors in the middle of the night.

Two

Holly lied to her husband and son so she could sneak off to see the priest. Early on the Saturday before Christmas, she announced that she had some last-minute shopping to do and that she might return late because of the crowds. Midway through their oatmeal, the boys offered no rebuttal, just a wave of their spoons as she fled the house, winding a scarf around her neck, wrapped in layers of wool.

A wet wind blew against the car, so she cranked up the heater for the short ride. Fat gray clouds scudded across the sky, heading over the ocean. She turned on the radio in time to catch the last few lines of "The Little Drummer Boy." *Blech*, she mimed shoving her finger down her throat. That insipid lyric, that numbing tune. She poked the button on the dashboard to silence the song.

She had been on edge for two weeks now, ever since that morning when Jack surprised her with a punch to the face. The bruise had faded, but she could still feel the sting. And then there was the weirdness with her husband, how he was seeing things out in the snow, how he refused to believe her when she heard those strange noises in the night. Her sleep, never truly peaceful, had grown erratic, and she was a mess at the office, chewing out the poor receptionist over one missed call. Ten days of that tension rolled by before she picked up the phone and called Father Bolden, and that first conversation felt like going to confession when she was a little girl. Bless me, Father, these are my sins, and the sheer relief when stepping out of the dark box and saying a few prayers to erase the slate.

By the time Holly pulled into the church parking lot, she had nearly banished the maddening carol from her mind, but the damn thing had thrown off all that she had rehearsed in the days leading up to her appointment with Father Bolden. They had gotten through the preliminaries over the phone, yet ever since that hesitant exchange, she had been practicing what she wanted to say, feeling a bit guilty that she had omitted to tell the worst of her worries. Now the "rump-a-pum-pum" had drummed it from her mind. For a long time, she sat in the cooling car, wondering where to begin. With the strange events of the past two weeks, the weird noises in her head. Or back to that summer when Jack first refused to come out of the house? Or further still, to when he was a toddler, unresponsive in his high chair? A rap on the window made her jump, and in the glass, a fist pale and spangled with age spots, and beyond that, the smiling face of the priest. He stepped back to let her out and shoved his fingers into the deep pockets of his gray cardigan.

"I saw you from the house and didn't know if you'd had a change of heart."

"Just collecting my thoughts. It's good of you to see me on such short notice."

"Have you managed to find them all?"

"My thoughts? No, I suppose if I had, I wouldn't need to come in."

"Well, now, if there are any stray thoughts wandering about, they better come in out of the cold. Shall we?" He laid a hand against the small of her back to guide her to the rectory.

Inside, the house was less austere than she had imagined. No monks, no Spartan cells, but a plain New England home, the walls a Bristol green, the wainscoting two shades darker. Here and there, evidence of an old man's miscellany: a rocker and a plaid stadium blanket, bookshelves cluttered with classics, a framed nautical chart of the coastline, a pair of snowshoes hanging by the door. The house smelled faintly of witch hazel and incense.

He led her to a sparse but elegant dining room. Beside a pot of coffee, a ring cake had been laid out in the middle of a lace doily on an old plate with a braided rim, perfectly centered on a mahogany table. Probably the work of a housekeeper, there were always these devout ladies in the rectory in her day, who served as maid and cook and chaste hausfrau for the priest. The woman herself was absent, although Holly sensed another presence in the house, an organizing spirit. Perhaps she was dusting the priest's plain room or hovering behind a doorway to eavesdrop. The dining room walls were unadorned, save for the crucifix atop the lintel and one painting that drew the eye by virtue of its solitude. She circled the table to take a closer look.

As with so many paintings she had encountered in this part of the country, the subject was the roiling sea with a ship barreling toward the viewer, the sky a chaos of yellows and grays. Sails swollen with wind, the cloth tattered at the edges, the ship listed slightly forward with the bow pointed toward the deep. The painter had been clever enough to show a coil of rope uncurling and an unmoored barrel smashing against the rails. A silver plate fixed to the bottom of the frame showed the title in tarnished letters: *Wreck of the Porthleven, 1849.*

"I see you've discovered the *Porthleven*," Father Bolden said. "A tragic tale."

"So, you know the story behind this painting?"

Holding a hand against his belly, Father Bolden chuckled and walked around the table to join Holly as she faced the painting. "I pride myself, if it is not too great a sin, on the history of these parts."

"Was there really a shipwreck around here?"

"Legend has it that the spirits of those who died on board still haunt these waters," Father Bolden said. "Fact is, she left Cornwall in a calm November, a small crew and passengers bound for America to find a better life. The *Porthleven* ran into rough seas just as they came within sight of Maine. One December evening, a nor'easter blew in, and the ship floundered in a blizzard. A scrim of white so thick the poor captain could not have known how close they were to land. This whole area was snowed in, not fit for man nor beast, and of course, that lighthouse had not been built. The crew laid anchor but it did not hold. She hit a ledge of rocks and broke apart in twenty feet of water. Six crew and thirteen Englishmen, women, and children, including a vicar from Cornwall, and not a soul survived the freezing sea. People in the village discovered the first bodies next morning, stiff and coated with ice, and story goes that not all the passengers were found, that some still lie at the bottom of the sea, and you can hear them keening on stormy nights, anxious in their watery graves."

She shivered and wrapped her arms against her chest.

"You'll have some of Miss Tiramaku's crumb cake." He pointed at the table, as she turned. "She's a sensitive soul and will be heartbroken if we don't finish at least half of it."

Taking a chair, Holly allowed the old priest to pour her a cup while she sliced two helpings of cake. The cup rattled in its saucer as he set it before her. The dollop of cream she added left an oily slick on the surface, the color of foam on the back of a wave. She stirred and at once the hue brightened, and in the whirlpool created by her spoon, she imagined the foundering ship and the passengers pell-mell on the decks. The image so disconcerted her that she had to look away from the cup. Through the picture window, scattered flurries danced in the cold air.

"I've been thinking about your situation ever since we spoke on the phone."

Holly looked up, flabbergasted by the sudden appearance of the priest already seated in his chair across the table. A sip of hot coffee helped shake off the visions of those people drowning in the sea.

"Where should we begin?" He bit into a forkful of cake, allowing her time to consider the question.

"Would it be a sin, Father, to say that I hate him sometimes?"

Crumbs caught at the back of his throat set him into paroxysms of choking and sputtering. Red-faced, he gulped at his coffee and composed his demeanor. "Surely, Mrs. Keenan, you don't mean *hate*."

She studied her fingernails and reconsidered her opening gambit. "Perhaps 'hate' is a strong word."

"A four-letter word. My late mother, God rest her soul, never allowed such a word to be uttered in our house. She would have given you a clap on the ear. Perhaps you meant something else?"

"Of course, I don't hate him. He's my boy. But I do hate the way our lives have changed. The Asperger's is one thing, but this fear of the outdoors just adds to the struggle. Everything revolves around his needs, his care. Do you know what an ordeal it is just to get him to the doctor's or the dentist? I have to trick him, offer a bribe, wrap him in blankets so he's not exposed to the outside."

"Why, what happens when he goes outside?"

"Panic. Terror. First he gasps for breath, can't get enough air in his lungs. His eyes bulge out like he is afraid of what's out there. Visible to Jack but invisible to the rest of us. Then come the spasms and convulsions. You would swear some physical presence is sitting on his chest, crushing his ribs. His arms flail out, but he can't move, can't get rid of the thing kneeling atop him. Becomes helpless as a newborn, crying and shouting for rescue, but there's nothing to be done. And I can't bear to watch it, can't stand the gulping and retching sounds coming from my own son; and it doesn't stop, only intensifies to the point where all we can do is bring him out of the sun and air and back inside. And suddenly Jack calms himself, but it takes a lot out of him. He acts as if he's been in a fight or just been chased, panting, slipping into fatigue, and then he falls asleep like a baby after a crying jag. But he's no baby. He's growing up, getting bigger, too strong for me to handle, and I'm worried that there'll come a day . . ." She stopped herself with a shudder.

"And these . . . incidents happen only when you try to take him outside?"

"Lately he's been worse. Two weeks ago, he hit me when I woke him up. To be fair, I had startled him, but he's never done that before. And that same day, he started jabbing his finger against his skull, like he was trying to drill a hole into his brain, completely unprovoked. He seemed possessed."

Father Bolden curled his lip over the brim of his cup and took a considered sip of coffee. One eyebrow arched like a snake as he swallowed. Far off in the rectory, a telephone rang.

"Do you have to get that?" Holly asked.

"Miss Tiramaku is here," the priest said. "She'll answer the call. Why do you say 'possessed'?"

She laughed and began smashing the crumbs on her plate with the tines of her fork. "Not possessed in the way you mean. I'm not looking for an exorcist, God forbid."

"God forbid, I never thought anything of the kind. Just an interesting choice of words."

The fork dropped from her hands, and her voice rose an octave. "I don't know what to do anymore, Father. I'm afraid of my own son, afraid of what he might do to me, to himself. The punching, the fits, the way he looks at us sometimes, like he's scheming. Out to get us. He sees things, monsters under his bed, but he's trapped as well by his thoughts and dreams and his inability to just say what he feels—"

A loud knock at the front door made her jump. Not two seconds later, the doorbell chimed, then chimed again. Father Bolden pushed back from the table and stood, bowing slightly to his guest. "You'll forgive me, but I believe my housekeeper may still be on the phone, and whoever's at the door insists on an immediate answer."

The doorbell rang again.

"Unfortunately, talented though she may be, Miss Tiramaku has not yet mastered the trick of being in two places at the same time. You will excuse me, Mrs. Keenan, for a brief moment."

The priest shuffled off, leaving Holly quite alone in the room. She imagined voices in the distance, the woman chatting on the telephone and a conversation in a lower register at the front door, but in truth, silence had insinuated itself upon the room, and all she heard were her own questions. Why had she come here this morning? What made her think the priest might offer some answers or consolation? Years ago when Jack was first diagnosed, she could hardly bear to name his condition; an ocean of prayer poured out of her, only subsiding in time as he grew worse, not better.

Outside, the flurries and bleak sky had given way to weak sunshine, and as the warmth reached the windowpanes, the glass ticked as it expanded. A sense of folly crept into her thoughts. She resolved to simply go, make some excuse to the priest in the foyer, and escape this austere place. She licked the wet crumbs from her fork and sipped her coffee, but it had grown cold. Behind the aroma of cake and coffee came the musky smell of the old man's house covered over by furniture polish, the sharpness of unaired rooms. Across from her, the painting on the wall took on a new aspect in the changing light that made her feel woozy. She could feel the sea roll, and the doomed ship pitched ever so slightly on the swells. Those poor people soon to drown. Land in sight, but no way to reach it past the icy waters. The wooden deck groaned in the storm. Another presence had entered the room, the floorboards creaked beneath the shifting weight. The noise reminded her of that night in the house when something had landed on the roof, disturbing the stillness. Holly thought it must be Father Bolden returned from the interruption, and in that moment, she resolved to mumble her apologies and be on her way. As she rose and pivoted to leave, she cried out softly at the sight at the door, an older Japanese woman with one dark eye and the other clouded by a milky scale. Her gray hair was pulled back severely, accentuating the left side of her face, which drooped a bit, as though she had once suffered a stroke. Her lips hung open at one corner, exposing pink gums and small, white teeth. Like one of Jack's off-kilter drawings.

"Jesus," Holly whispered. "You shocked me."

The woman's good eye searched the room, and when it landed on Holly, her expression turned to mild disdain.

"Are you Miss Tiramaku? If you're looking for Father Bolden, there was someone at the door."

The woman nodded, as if to thank her and acknowledge that indeed she was the housekeeper and in search of the pastor, but she did not depart and, in fact, appeared to be considering some remark in the back of her mind. Impassive as a statue, she wore a black dress that hung like sackcloth and plain sensible shoes out of fashion a generation ago.

"Good cake," Holly said at last. "You were kind to make it."

"You shouldn't say that."

"About the cake?"

"No, you shouldn't say 'Jesus' unless you mean it."

She had forgotten she was in a priest's house. "Sorry, but it was only because you startled me—my mind was elsewhere." She hid her mouth behind her hand.

"You were frightened by the painting, the *Wreck of the Porthleven*? I don't know why he insists on keeping it there. Did he tell you about the *yurei*, too?"

"The what?"

Stepping closer, Miss Tiramaku cast a glance toward the entrance to the room, making sure the priest was not close enough to overhear. "The *yurei* are spirits of the dead condemned to haunt the living until the wrong that has been done to them has been set right. Did he tell you about the people who drowned? Legend has it that the captain took a foolish risk in a storm. The *yurei* want to be freed from their misery."

"I'm sorry," Holly said, "but I don't believe in ghosts. Or *yurei*."

"Don't be so sure of things you cannot see. The mind conjures the mystery, but the spirit provides the key." With a nod, she gestured to the painting. "Poor souls beneath the sea."

Coming here was a mistake, Holly thought. She searched for some polite way to excuse herself.

Like a spider scrutinizing a fly, Miss Tiramaku stepped closer, a look of sudden recognition on her face. "You are Mrs. Keenan. The mother of that boy."

Her words sounded like an accusation. What had the priest been telling her about Jack? Or was it common knowledge around town that her son would not willingly leave the house? Was there some cabal of housekeepers gossiping about the strange child and his hapless family? That Keenan boy. Stricken by a dizzying nausea, Holly wanted to run away, but the one-eyed witch in the doorway blocked the passage.

Whistling from the hallway saved her. The tune of "O Tannenbaum" pitched loud and clear on his lips, Father Bolden trundled toward them, his face red with exertion and pine needles clinging to his cardigan and the front of his black trousers. "The Christmas tree is here. That was the man come with our big balsam, and I had to instruct him how best to set it up in the parlor. Free delivery can't wait. It's a beauty, Miss Tiramaku, seven feet if I'm any judge. I see you two have made introductions in my absence."

The housekeeper had stepped aside when he had entered the room, and in his presence, she seemed far less frightening. "Yes, Father. Mrs. Keenan was just telling me how much she enjoyed my coffee cake."

He looked anxiously at the remaining pieces on the dessert plate. "You'll stay, Holly, and help us with the decorations. My mother left me the most exquisite glass ornaments from the old country. Been in the family over one hundred years."

"I couldn't—"

"But I insist," said the priest. "We can continue our little talk while we trim the tree."

"No, I really must be going. Last-minute shopping, I'm afraid."

Fiddling with the thick buttons of his sweater, the priest looked as crestfallen as a schoolboy. "Perhaps the tree can wait."

"Not on account of me. Thank you for your hospitality, but I've got to run."

The priest and the housekeeper took a step toward her, but it was not till she had breezed between them that she realized they had only wanted to shake her hand. The antiseptic aroma of a pine forest drenched the front hall, and she burst out of the house, wiggling into her coat, glad to breathe in the fresh cold air. Safely in her car, she looked back at the rectory, and on the front steps stood the priest and his housekeeper, refugees from a gothic fairy tale, waving good-bye. She ripped the gearshift into reverse and gunned her way out of there.

Rather than heading straight into town for shopping, she drove along the shoreline and stopped at an overlook and parked the car. The engine ticked like a bomb when she pulled the key from the ignition. Christ, one more thing, she thought, and then it purred to silence. The gray Atlantic pushed its waves against the rocks below the cliffs, and the clouds dumped snow far out at sea. *Yurei*, ghosts of the drowned. She shook her head in disbelief. Her hands trembled as she stepped out into the cold, and she longed for a brandy. The wind pressed against her body. Mother of that boy. *That boy.* She longed for some way to force a good cry, but it was too cold for that now. There were gifts to buy, an alibi for her deceit, and so much to do before the holidays.

ii.

Tim skinned an orange for the boy and poured himself another cup of coffee. No reason not to take it easy for a while. Holly would be gone for hours, granting them a reprieve. The oatmeal bowls soaked in the sink. The list of chores on the fridge was an artifact from a distant age. A lazy Saturday morning stretched out before them, promising idleness. Padding in his slippers to his easy chair, Tim wrapped his robe tightly against the cold and settled in with the crossword from the newspaper. He scanned the clues, filling in those boxes with words readily known or deduced. On the carpet by the Christmas tree, Jip curled like a cat in his old favorite threadbare pajamas, frayed at the cuffs and outgrown by two sizes. Intent at his drawing, he hummed softly to himself, and only when Tim listened closely could he make out the tune his son was singing. "Little Drummer Boy." Stray flurries wandered across the picture window. He thought for a moment of turning on the Christmas lights against the dismal morning, but he had settled in too deeply to move his bones. Stuck at his puzzle, Tim leaned back in the chair, nestled his head against the cushion, and closed his eyes.

In what seemed mere seconds, his son appeared at his side and was softly smacking him on the cheek. He opened his eyes to the sight of the boy hovering above him, bouncing on the balls of his feet, mouthing a silent admonition to wake up, wake up. The newspaper had fallen from his lap, though he still held the pen in his clenched fist.

"What is it, Jip?"

"Someone at the door."

"I'm awake, I was never asleep. Why didn't you just answer?" he asked, realizing at once his mistake. Jip would never risk bringing the outside in. Rousing himself from the chair, Tim gathered his robe together as he marched to the front door. Standing on the stoop were Nell Weller and her son, flakes of wet snow melting in their hair.

"Nick, you little ray of sunshine. Were we expecting you this morning?"

Cupping her hand around the back of his head, Nell guided the boy inside with a gentle nudge. As he was taking off his coat, Nick sneezed, covering his mouth with the lining. Nell followed her reluctant son, taking in the scene of the Keenan men in their robes, the room in quiet disarray.

"Don't worry," she said. "Not a cold, I don't think. Allergies. We had to put up a fake tree this year, took Fred all day to figure out the branches. You don't seem to be prepared for visitors at all. Is Holly home?"

Tim rubbed the stubble on his chin and smoothed his bed head hair. "Out Christmas shopping. You just missed her."

"Shopping? I wish she had told me. I would have gone with." She unbuttoned her winter coat and slipped out of it with a shimmy. Beneath it she wore a tight red sweater that showed off her figure and a black pleated skirt that rippled as she moved about the room, tidying as she went. "Husbands," she said, but the tone was amused, not exasperated. "Maybe you forgot? She agreed to have Nick over for the day. Is that okay by you, or do you two have plans?"

Tim looked for his son, but the boys had disappeared, already at play in another room. "Free as a bird. Do you have time for a cup of coffee?"

She nodded and followed him into the kitchen, taking a seat at the table for two tucked in the breakfast nook. Through the bay window that overlooked the ocean, she watched the few stray flakes spin wildly, launched upon the wind. With the insouciance of a waiter at a café, he set down the ceramic bowl filled with sugar cubes, the dairy creamer in the shape of a cow, and her coffee in a cup and saucer.

"Something out there caught your fancy?" He took the seat opposite.

"The sky, the sea. Funny, same as my underwear. Black on top and blue on the bottom."

He was not sure if she was flirting with him, but he decided to try his luck. "You are looking especially gorgeous. All dressed up this morning."

"Christmas party," she said. "Fred's work. He's already at the office in his Santa suit for the little frights. Bad as their mommies and daddies. I'm skipping all the early folderol and am timing my arrival to coincide with the annual spiking of the eggnog. I can barely stand the people he works with. We would have taken Nick along, but he's such a pill these days. Too old, he says, for Santa Claus. You're sure it's no inconvenience to have him here?"

"No trouble at all. Jip lives for the company."

Red lipstick marked the edge of her cup. She leaned across the table and took his hand in hers.

"You are an angel. You both are, and I can't thank you enough for taking Nick for the holidays. Fred and I need to get away. Some time to ourselves, patch things up a bit. You know how it can be, sometimes you just want to start all over. And, failing that, a few days on the cruise will make the winter that much shorter."

He squeezed her fingers and then withdrew. For the length of a cup, they talked about the Caribbean trip, the ports of call, the likelihood of shuffleboard and endless buffets. Her excitement bubbled along, and he found himself watching how she spoke instead of what she actually said. He'd give a nod now and again, a smile to keep her there. He remembered that same contented look from years ago, animated by their secret. At last she looked at her watch, let out a sharp gasp, and said a hasty good-bye. From the open door, he watched her go, standing at the threshold long after she had driven away, an ache small and persistent in the pit of his soul. He waited till he caught himself shivering when the chill crept up his pajamas.

The boys did not answer when Tim called them, and he had no idea where they might be. In Jip's room, most likely, but perhaps they were prowling around below in Tim's workshop. He went to tidy the kitchen, pausing to look at the beach through the bay window, his thoughts drifting back to that summer's day, the last time all of them had been outside together. Holly lost in a paperback on a distant rock, Fred asleep on a bright yellow towel. The boys, seven that year, were down in the water, as usual. A gull or two, white as paper, roamed the blue skies. Nell was stretched out facing him, a gesture intimate but guileless. Her maroon bathing suit clung to her curves, and they were talking of summer's end, idly chatting in that circuitous way they spoke to each other, saying nothing that was not coded in a language of longing. No one saw what happened. No one could say for sure when precisely Jip and Nick had gone missing.

He turned from the view of the water, and there the boys had suddenly appeared at the kitchen table, intent on a notebook. In unison, they looked up at him and flashed two grins. The tip of Nick's nose was red from sniffling, but they otherwise seemed quite normal. How had they managed to sneak in without his notice? He shook the befuddlement from his brain.

"You're like a couple of ghosts. Time for me to hit the shower, boys. You two be all right without me?"

With a wide grin and a slow nod, his son dismissed him.

Curlicues of steam rose from the sink as he lathered his cheeks with shaving cream. He dipped the razor into the stream of hot water and began to shave in confident strokes. Just as he scraped the last bit of foam, the dull blade nicked his skin and a bright red berry of blood appeared on his throat. A short agitated cough escaped his lips, for he could not remember the last time he had cut himself shaving. He pressed his thumb to the spot on his neck below his left ear, and in a moment, the bleeding stopped. The hot water had fogged the mirror, and behind him, a cold breeze fluttered the curtain. Someone had left the window open, so he forced it shut. The snow had given way to pale sunshine. He shrugged out of his robe and stripped to the skin.

The room was freezing, so he let the water run till great clouds of smoke rose, and then he slipped into the shower and closed the glass door behind him. The heat and humidity unkinked his muscles and relaxed

his joints as readily as a sauna. Working shampoo into his hair, he massaged his scalp. Images of Nell on the beach crossed his mind, how she
leaned toward him close enough to touch. A line of perspiration runs
between her breasts, and the fine hairs at her nape glisten in the sunlight. He cupped his scrotum in his free hand. *Where are the boys?* She
was the first to notice, springing to her feet, casting a shadow over him
as he turned on his belly. Shampoo began to drip in his eyes. The temperature dropped suddenly as though someone had opened the door, and
when he strained to focus his stinging eyes, he thought he saw her enter
the room. Just as abruptly, the sensation vanished, and he saw on the
glass shower door, now visible in the condensation, a crude drawing of
a naked woman, stylized and slightly misshapen, long curly hair, contours
of breasts, the thumbprints of two nipples. He rubbed at the drawing,
only to discover that it had been traced on the outside surface. "Jip," he
bellowed, but of course, the boy was too far away to hear, and besides,
why would he have drawn such a thing? Surely, he is too young to be
thinking of naked women. For all Tim knew, his son never thought of
sex at all, or at least he had never said a word about it. The fog from the
shower rose and bumped into the ceiling, billowing across the room and
settling into every corner. He rinsed his hair and stepped from the shower,
wrapping a towel around his waist.

Slowly swiping his hand, Tim erased the image on the glass, leaving
behind a beaded trail. He felt like a criminal destroying evidence and
could not shake the sensation that there was a conspirator in the room,
just behind him. As he turned, a face in the mirror leapt into view. Finger-
drawn on the surface was another face, a woman's surely, but more
haggard and distorted than the other. The hair was just a suggestion on
a high and prominent forehead, and one eye drooped, its iris clouded
and vacant as the blind gaze of a Roman statue. As he smeared the
drawing, Tim wondered momentarily how he had not noticed it earlier
when he shaved. "That kid," he muttered to himself. "He's drawing everywhere." Just beyond his reflection, he thought he saw the one-eyed
woman again, and in the glass of the shower door, the memory of the

naked woman seemed to rearrange itself from the constellation of water drops. He quickly combed his hair and dressed in a pullover and sweatpants, anxious to be out of there. The mist followed him into the hallway, and he raced down the stairs.

The kitchen was cold as a morgue, but the boys were just where he had left them, busy at the table with a pile of papers. Around their heads they had fitted the hoods of their sweatshirts, so they resembled a pair of medieval scribes illuminating a manuscript. In a frigid cell without a fire. He shivered and found the problem at once: an open window funneled winter into the room. Hurrying to close it, he barked at his son. "What's wrong with you, Jip? Why are you leaving all these windows open in the dead of winter? The bathroom was as cold as a witch's tit, and now this. And the heat has been on all day."

Jack Peter stopped his drawing in the middle of a line. The point of his pencil hung an inch above the surface, and he sat still and expressionless, as his father stormed around the room looking for other open windows. Nick followed with his gaze, waiting for the chance to answer the charge.

"We didn't do it." A line of clear mucus escaped from his nose, and he sniffed and wiped it with his sleeve.

With grave concentration, Jack Peter tapped his pencil on the tabletop, slowly at first, but then with greater speed and force.

"Don't," his father said. "You'll ruin it, J.P." But the boy kept tapping.

"Stop, Jip. I said stop."

He was more frantic and forceful. The point left small marks in the soft wood.

"It wasn't us," Nick said.

The pencil sounded like a woodpecker hammering on an oak. Tim grabbed his son's wrist, the boy's pulse racing in rhythm to the tapping. By tightening his grip, Tim forced him to stillness. "Dammit. Just quit, Jack. Who did it then? Who let the cold in?"

"Him," he growled. "The monster."

"The what?" He looked carelessly at the drawings on the table, fabrications of the ten-year-old mind. "Don't be silly."

His son refused to look him in the eye.

"What is he talking about, Nick?"

"Maybe Mrs. Keenan left it open before she went out. Or maybe you forgot. It wasn't us, I swear."

With a sigh, Tim loosened his grip around his son's thin arm, and Jip wriggled free like a bird from a snare and skittered from the table to a chair in the breakfast nook. He turned his back on his father. There was no reasoning with him when he was so angry, Holly would say. Leave him be.

A bolus of air, cold as the December sea, tumbled across the room and wrapped itself around his legs and lower body. He whispered a curse and searched for the source of the sudden gust, but the windows and doors were shut fast. The boys seemed unaware of the lump of winter sitting in the room. At the dining table, Nick contemplating the space between his two hands against the wood. Jip remained at the window, chanting barely audible nonsense like some mad monk at prayer. Seeking forgiveness and the restoration of equilibrium, Tim carefully approached his son, and bent down so their faces were on the same plane.

"Why is it so cold in here?" he asked.

Jip stopped muttering and leaned forward to tap his finger against the glass. "Him. He's trying to come inside."

"Who him?"

"The man, the monster." He spoke quietly, glaring at his father. "Don't you know anything?"

He reached out to his son, but stopped his open palm inches from the boy's hair, afraid that Jip would flinch and withdraw from the touch. A wave of helplessness nearly overcame him. "There are no monsters."

The boy faced him, a baleful expression in his eyes. "Just look, Daddy. He's out there now."

The green ocean filled the window frame in a band across its width, and above it only sky, thick with gray clouds stretching to the far horizon. To see the shoreline, Tim had to come closer and nearly press his nose against the pane, his breath leaving a fog on the glass. To the right, the rocks wandered in the sand, and directly below the window he could make out the bow of a small wooden boat stored beneath the house. To the left, the headlands rose gradually to the lighthouse, and he worked his gaze back from that landmark to the irregular granite. He would have surely missed the figure crouched in the ledges had he not been expecting to find something. Straining to get a better look in the dim light, he bumped his forehead against the glass. He pushed ever so slightly, as if that slight pressure might burst the seam between the inner and outer worlds. The figure on the rocks moved, shifting in its crouch, and it cocked its head toward the house. Tim could not be sure, but it appeared to be a man, a figure that reminded him of the strange thing he had seen that night on the road. White as winter, the hair a clot of whirls, a mangy beard. A wild and lonesome thing.

"What the hell is that?" He peeled himself from the window and went straight to find his boots and coat.

"We didn't do it," Nick said from the table.

"You boys stay here. I just want to see what that is."

On the mudroom floor, a trail of sandy clumps led from the kitchen to the outer door. Tim left his boots untied and coat unbuttoned and hurried round to the back of the house, scrambling to the shore. Where the man had been, there was nothing.

He stepped into the empty landscape, hoping to catch sight of the figure, but it had vanished. A sudden patch of sunlight brightened the rocks and sand, throwing momentary shadows until the clouds passed by and erased the fine detail. Glancing over his shoulder, Tim saw the boys standing side by side in the frame of the bay window. Jip's head was turned to the northeast, as though he was watching something, trying to direct his father's attention. Tim followed his son's gaze, spying at last a flash of white movement, quick as a breath. He raced toward it, coat flapping in the wind, bootlaces lashing his shins, sinking in the sand, and scrambling across the rough rock.

It was impossible, he told himself, for the naked man to have outrun him, even with such a head start, but after that one glimpse, he saw him no more. Only the illusion of movement, the desire of the chase. On a promontory, he stopped to catch his breath and surveyed the sighing sea, the desolate rock, and realized how the world had swallowed them both. He was panting, his chest pounding, and feeling a bit dizzy. Exhausted, he bent over, resting his hands upon his knees, allowing his head to hang down. Between his feet, fresh wet drops had darkened the ground, and at first, he wondered if the thing he was chasing had passed this same way, wounded and bleeding. A bright red coin splashed on the rock, and then another. He raised a cold hand to his warm throat and felt the slick where he had cut himself earlier, shaving, and when he drew back his hand, he was surprised to find it covered in blood. At the sight of it, he fell to the ground in a dead faint.

iii.

The first thing Nick saw that morning was a swath of red velour stretched tightly across the drum of his father's belly. From his bed, his faced muffled by a pillow, Nick blinked to focus, and the red balloon in his field of vision swelled and receded. He rolled over to get a better look.

"Ho, ho, ho. Something wicked this way comes."

Nick rubbed the sleep from his eyes. His father wore his annual Santa Claus outfit, sans beard and cap.

"Sure you don't want to come with? It's going to be a real fun party."

"Dad—"

"Had to make sure the suit still fits. One of these years I'll be too fat."

"—do I have to?"

"Too old, are we? Where are the sons of yesteryear? How our childhood swiftly passes. Once around the block in a little red wagon and then you're all grown up. Now look at you. Can't get out of bed in the morning. Even when it's snowing."

His father pulled up the blinds. A few flurries danced across the sky. In the light from the window, motes of dust caught in the draft drifted and fell. Nick wanted nothing more than to sink into the warmth of his bed.

"Your mother will take you over to the Keenans. But you better hop to. She's already in the bathroom, working her magic. Mirror, mirror, on the wall."

Nick sat on the edge of the bed and stared at his bare feet. "Do I have to go over there? Can't I stay home by myself?"

"Not unless you want to see me sent to prison. The law is very clear on this point: you're too young to be left alone all day by yourself." His father sat next to him, the mattress sagging under his girth, the bedsprings complaining of the burden. "Imagine what those outlaws would do if old Santa Claus showed up in the holding cell. Destroy their faith in mankind, it would."

The sleeves of his Santa suit rode up, exposing two inches of pale skin thatched with wiry black hairs. Nick wished he would put on some gloves.

"I thought you liked hanging out with your old pal Jack. Something gone wrong between you two?"

"He's just weird sometimes."

"Weird? A bit of an odd duck, but aren't we all? I've come to the firm conclusion that everybody's got something wrong up there." He tapped his skull with his middle finger. "Odd ducks, all. But he's your best friend, Nick, and you've got to stick by your friends."

The door swung open slowly, pushed by a hip, and Nick's mother came in, a hairbrush in one hand, a coffee in the other. She was wearing nothing but blue underwear and a black bra. "Have either of you seen my red sweater?"

"The one with the tiny Christmas trees on it?" Fred asked.

She rolled her eyes. "Not that one. The nice one."

"I like the one with the tiny Christmas trees on it. Very festive. Seasonal. Besides, I gave you the one with the tiny Christmas trees on it last Christmas, and you never wear it. You're naughty, not nice. And you'll get coal in your stocking this year."

"Aren't you going to be late?" she asked.

When Fred looked at his watch, he noticed how the sleeves on his suit rode up on his arms, and he hitched the fabric in vain. "Is it just me, or is everything getting smaller? I must load up the sleigh and hitch the reindeer to it." As he exited, he recited their names, "On, Comet and Cupid and Vixen and Dixie. . . ."

"Good grief," Nell said, pretending to give him a kick in his broad backside. She chased him down the hall, threatening him with the hairbrush, laughing all the way.

After she had gone and he was safely alone, Nick slid his hand beneath the mattress and pulled out the notebook. He had been dreaming about it all night, imagining the pages white as snow, the ink turning to blood red. Hold it close, he decided, bury it under his overcoat, beneath his hoodie sweatshirt, keep it next to the skin.

Nick smuggled in the monsters. While his mother was engaged at the door with Mr. Keenan, he managed to sneak past them both and scurry off with Jack Peter. At the top of the stairs, Jack Peter whispered, "Wait here" and ran into the bathroom. Nick loitered in the hallway, spying through the open door to Mr. and Mrs. Keenan's room. The unmade bed looked like a crime scene, a red quilt flowing to the floor and tangled sheets the dreadful evidence of their recent presence. He was not sure why, but the disorder unnerved him. He listened for a flush from the toilet, but heard only laughter coming from the kitchen. Jack Peter burst from the bathroom and they crept into his room. Behind the closed door, Nick slipped the notebook from beneath his sweatshirt and handed it to his conspirator.

For the whole week, he had been busy dutifully following the instructions to keep his creations bound in a secret notebook, and on lined paper stood one monster per page. With a mix of nerves and pride, he watched Jack Peter peruse them one by one. The first few creatures imitated their pop culture counterparts: the old movie Frankenstein complete with flat top and neck bolts, and his Bride with the electric beehive hairdo, a cloaked vampire with brilliantined hair and bared fangs, a mummy in peeling wrappers, a skeleton with dancing bones. He had copied the Creature from the Black Lagoon, a winged monstrosity labeled Mothman, a witch and her flying monkeys. There were a stylized werewolf and floating Dementors straight out of *Harry Potter*, an orc from the *Lord of the Rings*, and a fire-breathing dragon patched together from a dozen movie dragons. Jack Peter raced through the images like a critic, vaguely dissatisfied with the work, searching for something that was not there. When he reached the last page, he flipped back to the beginning to scrutinize each drawing, tracing with a fingertip the path of certain lines, muttering beneath his breath. He did not speak directly to Nick but rather seemed lost in the process of seeing.

When at last Nick understood what was taking place, he could no longer bear to sit and watch. He took a turn about the bedroom, inspecting for the hundredth time its attractions. On the other side of the closet door, he imagined, one of their monsters, snarling quietly to itself, peered through the keyhole, waiting. On the bookcase carefully arranged treasures gathered dust. Toy cowboys and Indians and colorful plastic soldiers from many wars tangled in a knot inside a clear jar labeled Sebago Pretzel Co. Next to that contained jumble stood a stack of puzzles and board games—chess and checkers, backgammon and Parcheesi, marathon Monopoly and Risk that could occupy entire afternoons. He touched the box of a German game called *Waldschattenspiel* that they had played all the time last winter, a game requiring candlelight in darkness, where trolls in pointy felt hats hid behind wooden trees, moving away from a relentless seeker, winning by keeping to the shadows.

On the floor between Jack Peter's old toy box and the desk, a mousetrap had been baited with a chunk of hard cheese, its killing bar poised to snap. Nick squatted on his haunches to inspect, resisting the urge to spring the mechanism with a quick finger. "What's this for?"

From the bed, Jack Peter did not look up from the picture. "My mother thinks we have a mouse."

"Have you ever seen it?" Nick sat on the toy box, remembering when it held their childish treasures.

Jack Peter bent closer to the drawing. "I've never seen it because it isn't a mouse."

As usual, the desk was clean and ordered, schoolbooks piled on the back right corner, paper stacked neatly on the left. The single drawer in the middle sealed in a mystery he dared not release. Atop the bureau, the mirror reflected the falling snow and the ocean through the window on the opposite wall. Nick idled away a few moments, transfixed by the waves caught in the silvered glass. The melody of his mother's voice rose from below, joined by the nervous reply from Mr. Keenan in the breakfast nook. Theirs was a different rhythm from the muffled sounds his parents made, and he was distracted by its music.

He sneezed and rubbed the tip of his nose with his fingers. His own face in the mirror stared back at him, its knitted brow and puckered frown, and he exaggerated the effect, trying to look angry and disappointed, practicing the scowl until it felt convincing. The sudden appearance of a pale white arm surprised him, but it was only Jack Peter in a state of undress, shucking off his pajamas to reveal a reedy chest and two nipples like staring eyes. Bone-white skin glowed in the thin light, for he was an inside boy who rarely left the house, rarely stood directly in the sun or the rain or the wind. The sunlight might pass right through him, and the very air bruise his skin. Jack Peter pulled on a dark hooded sweatshirt and a pair of jeans and then sat on the floor to wrestle his feet into his socks.

At the window, Jack Peter wrote on the glass with his fingertip. "Do you know this trick?" He breathed hard upon the window, and in the condensation appeared the word "wicked."

"Epic," Nick said, hiding an edge of sarcasm.

"Let's go scare my daddy." Raising his hood like a cowl around his head, Jack Peter gathered the notebook from the bed and a fistful of pencils from his desk. With a crook of a finger, he bid Nick follow, and they sneaked down and stationed themselves at the kitchen table without a sound.

Nick's mother had gone off to her party, leaving Mr. Keenan all alone. He was just staring through the bay window, unaware and lost in his thoughts. When he finally noticed them at the table, he seemed mildly distressed at how they had managed to materialize unnoticed.

"You're like a couple of ghosts. Time for me to hit the shower, boys," he said at last. "You two be all right without me?"

Soon the plumbing moaned as water gushed in the shower overhead. Taking the notebook in hand, Jack Peter leafed through the pages again, stopping momentarily at pictures that caught his eye. "These are good," he said. "Some scary. Did you make some of them up?"

Small guilt pulled at Nick's stomach, as though he had somehow failed him. A string of mucus ran from his nose, and he wiped it away with the back of his sleeve. "No, I copied them from books or movies. Some I remembered in my head."

Jack Peter grunted and closed the book. "Did you ever see someone who was dead?"

"Besides that time you drowned and everyone thought you were dead for a few minutes?"

A rare laugh escaped Jack Peter's mouth. "I mean someone who was dead a long time?"

Once when he was cutting through the pine forest on his way home from school, Nick had come across a dead cat, half buried in dry needles. Weatherworn, it was a desiccated bag of matted fur and bones, but when he flipped over the corpse with a stick, a squirm of maggots writhed in its guts, and he retched and ran away. But he had never seen a dead person, much less a body dead a long time. Nick thought of his parents, drowned and hanging in his closet, but he figured they did not count because he could not prove they were real. He shook his head.

Taking a clean sheet of paper, Jack Peter began to draw, concentrating intently on moving the pencil. Nick watched in silence, curious and patient, wondering what strange thoughts danced in his friend's mind.

"Do you mean dead like zombies?"

The boy across the table paused and lifted his eyes. "Not zombies."

"They're called the living dead."

"Not zombies." He continued his line, the tip of his tongue peeking from the corner of his mouth. "Zombies eat brains. And they are slow. Not zombies."

"But dead, anyhow."

"Definitely," Jack Peter said. "Or at least I think so."

Above them the shower stopped, and Nick thought he heard Mr. Keenan call out, but Jack Peter made no move to answer. He finished and rotated the paper so Nick could take a look. The creature faced him from a head-on perspective, a man of sorts, his arms longer than his legs and bent at the elbows, the legs bent at the knees, so that he appeared crablike, scrabbling toward the viewer. His hands and feet were splayed outward, and his face, full front, was wild and ruined. Bug-eyed, he stared beneath a tangle of hair thick as seaweed. He wore no clothes, which only emphasized his preternatural physique, as though made of skin stretched over wire. Nick recognized him at once. The creature he had encountered on the road that night with Mr. Keenan.

"That's him. I've seen his face before." He stared at the page and laughed to himself. "You missed one thing though. He's got no pecker."

"What's a pecker?"

"You know, your thing between your legs. If this dude is naked, you'd see his pecker."

Jack Peter giggled and tilted his head at the image. "You mean his penis."

"Whatever you want to call it. His is missing."

Across the room, a window flew open, snapping as though spring-loaded, and the curtains unfurled like two flags. A gust of cold wind blew and scattered the loose pages onto the floor.

"What the heck was that?" Nick rose to close the window.

Jack Peter stopped him. "Wait, get those papers first. I'm not finished yet." He was already busy drawing again.

Mr. Keenan strode into the room, his face red with anger. Hollering at the boys, he raced to shut the window, and he turned on Jack Peter, demanding to know why he was opening all the windows in the house and didn't he realize the heat was on. But Jack Peter simply withdrew, tapping the pencil against the table. Nick had seen that gesture many times and knew that his friend was retreating deep into himself and would not be reached. Mr. Keenan kept hollering at them to tell the truth. When Jack Peter finally confessed that there was someone on the beach, his father did not believe him at first. He had to go to the window to see for himself, to press his hands and face against the glass, searching the shoreline for what had spooked his son. "What the hell is that?"

In a blur, he dressed in boots and an old winter coat and was out the door searching for what they thought they had seen. The boys watched as he stumbled across the sand and rocks, looking back once as if to ask them for directions or whether to go on, but it was too late, he was too far gone, and he disappeared into the midday nothing, and they were all alone in the empty house.

iv.

Trying to stem the pain, Holly pressed the heel of her hand against her forehead. Behind her a line of customers shifted impatiently in place, and the teenaged clerk at the counter waited for a credit card with indifference. Perhaps it was the fluorescent light or the incessant piped-in music or the hustle and bustle of the determined shoppers, each on their merry mission, unaware of the other people in the world, thank you, at least one of whom had a thwacking headache. She hated the mall, and at the moment she was not too fond of Christmas either.

The Rose Art Gift Set, with its sixty-four-piece assortment of premium-quality drawing components, included twenty-four colored pencils, eight watercolor pencils, oils, pastels, duo-tip markers, sharpener, eraser, and illustrated instructions, along with the sixty-sheet Deluxe Sketchbook, may have been overkill, for her son's interests were often fleeting. There were scads of toys abandoned in his room, gathering dust on the shelves, archived in his old toy box. He'll like it, she reassured herself, although she never knew with Jack from day to day what he liked, much less what he loved. If he loved.

Shopping bag in hand, she exited the store and threaded her way through the groups of gawkers wandering the faux boulevards. Knots of bored teenagers aimlessly passing another afternoon. Boys in football jackets, girls with wires twisting from their ears, everyone tapping messages to one another on their smart phones. Young husbands, helpless and clueless, searching for that perfect gift for their wives. Young mothers pushing strollers, their babies ordinary as could be. Children queuing for photographs with an ersatz Santa Claus. Holly lingered awhile before a shop window displaying ridiculously expensive women's boots and wished she were twenty years old again. What different decisions she would make. Better shoes, not the least of them.

In the plate glass window, the reflection of her son appeared. Dressed in a winter coat and a watch cap, Jack was walking directly behind her, hand in hand with a tall blond woman in a long black coat and black boots with silver clasps. By the time Holly realized who she had seen and turned to find them, they had vanished. Sure that she had seen Jack, if only fleetingly, she looked up and down the long broad corridors. They had simply disappeared, though she was certain that the blonde would stand out in the crowd. Convinced that they must have gone into the bookshop directly opposite, she walked briskly to the entrance, whispering his name to herself.

The front of the bookstore was stuffed with tchotchkes, T-shirts printed with portraits of Shakespeare and Austen and Dickens, bookmarks and book lights, playing cards and lap desks, kitschy souvenirs of Maine. She hurried past the fiction and poetry, searching for the pair of them, her son and his kidnapper, and at last Holly spotted the blond woman in the black coat. Transfixed in the cookbook section, she held in her hand a fat book about cupcakes. Jack was missing from her side.

Holly hesitated, caught by the realization of just how illogical her request would seem. She cleared her throat, and the woman in black faced her with an inquisitive stare. Young, too young, to have a ten-year-old boy. Too innocent to have abducted him.

"So sorry to bother you," Holly said, "but I saw you passing by in the window across the hall, and I thought . . ."

The blonde smiled at her, signaling to continue.

"I'm looking for my son," Holly said. "He's ten years old. A blue coat and watch cap?"

"Sorry, I haven't seen any little boys. Is he lost?"

"Yes, no." She clutched her bag and shouted at her, "Didn't I just see you walk in here with a little boy?"

The blonde took two steps away and pretended to study the pages, casting a backward glance over the crazy woman behind her. Holly brushed past her and searched the rest of the store, scouring the children's section, asking a bewildered clerk if he had seen a ten-year-old boy in the past few minutes. Wandering the maze of aisles, Holly saw not a single child, and when she passed the blonde with the cupcake book in line at the cashiers, she convinced herself that she had been mistaken. She had conjured a mirage. How could it be Jack? He never leaves the house.

The instant she walked out of the bookstore, Holly began hearing a tapping sound, thinking at first it was just the clack of her shoes on the linoleum, but it was a far steadier sound hidden in a melody piped over the sound system. The noise seemed natural at first, part of the song, but even when the tune changed, the rhythm persisted, so softly that she thought it must be a mistake, but then the drumming intensified into the following song. She looked around at the other shoppers to see if they could hear it, too, but they were anesthetized by the general bustle. In front of the soft-pretzel stand, she saw an older man in a trim white beard who reminded her of the actor who played Kris Kringle in that old black-and-white movie *Miracle on 34th Street*. "I believe, I believe, it's silly but I believe," she whispered to herself, "and if you can't trust St. Nick, you can't trust a soul." She grabbed his arm and asked, "Do you hear that?"

"Hear what?"

She pointed to the ceiling in the direction of the speakers. "That knocking sound. It doesn't go with the music."

He tilted his head and cocked an ear to the ceiling and listened for a couple of measures. Laying a finger against his pursed lips, he contemplated his response with detached bemusement. "I'm sorry, but I don't hear it."

"No, no, listen. There, just beneath the piano, like someone's rapping on a table." She beat out the time on the glass counter of the pretzel stand. "A code. Don't you hear it?"

"I'm sorry, I don't hear any secret code."

"You're kidding me. Like a séance. Listen: tap-tap, tap-tap-tap. . . ."

The man shot out his free hand and grabbed her wrist until she let go of his arm. "Look, lady, there is no tapping, just the regular old Christmas songs. Do you want me to get you something? Water? Would you like to go somewhere and sit down?"

Holly backed away. The knocking followed her as she looked for the correct exit, the one nearest to where she had parked the car. Along the way, nobody else had noticed that the sound system had run amok, that a mad drummer boy played a steady and diabolical tattoo. She fought her way outside where the music stopped, and the drumbeat faded into the wind blowing across the parking lot. While she could no longer hear it, Holly felt the throbbing pulse in her forehead. A green bench beckoned, and she sat on the cold metal and held her head in her hands, wanting nothing more than to get home and lie down in a darkened room till the pain went away. She closed her eyes and willed the ache to end.

She sensed the presence of another, a shadow hovering over her. "There you are," a disembodied voice said. "I was hoping to catch you."

Holly shielded her eyes with one hand and squinted at the man with the short white beard. She was alarmed to see him and thought at first that he had followed her to confess that he, too, had heard the strange tapping over the sound system, but he was holding up a bag that read Sharon's Arts & Crafts. "You left this at the pretzel counter. I'm glad I was able to find you before you got away." He set the bag beside her on the bench. "Are you okay?"

"Gifts for my son. He loves to draw. I don't know how I could have forgotten him."

He eased onto the empty spot on the bench and jumped a bit when his rump came in contact with the cold surface.

"He's just so hard to shop for. My son. He's ten, and you would think that a boy of ten might be the easiest child in the world, but he's special needs, for one thing." Her voice faltered and she choked back the urge to cry.

"And he never leaves the house."

"I'm so sorry—"

She pressed her hand against his arm, trapping him. "Not unless we force him, of course, and there are times when we have to take him to the doctor's or whatnot, but it's like moving a prisoner." She rocked back and forth on the bench, subconsciously imitating her son.

He flexed his bicep, hoping she would take the hint, but she tightened her grip. The man shifted in his seat, as though he could not decide how to gracefully flee.

"No, he was fine until a few years ago, as fine as a boy with his condition can be. On top of it he has this phobia, and it's getting worse. Do you understand?"

Head on a spring, the man nodded.

"My big fear is that he's never going to be normal . . . enough to mainstream. I mean, you know, what would happen to him when we aren't around anymore?"

"It must be difficult."

"Difficult? He's missing this, the snow, the mad rush of the holidays, the whole wide world." A tear escaped the corner of her eye, and her nose was about to run, when suddenly a sensation came over her, one she had not experienced since she was a child, and all at once a gush of blood sputtered from her nose. She raised her hand to cover and catch it, but the blood ran over her fingers. The man was reaching for his handkerchief, and she coughed, and another clot burst and ran down her chin. Before she realized it, her blood had spread across the white cloth in her hand, and the man with the beard had reached over and tilted her head back and was holding her still, his hand cupped along the base of her skull, and telling her that it will be all right, it will be all right.

"I'm so embarrassed." Her voice was muffled by the fabric. "I used to get these all the time growing up, but it's been ages."

They sat together, quiet and still, and waited for the bleeding to stop. There were fine flecks of her blood in his beard.

"Funny, but here I am confessing all my sins, and I was just talking to a priest this morning."

"People say I have a trusting face, but I think it's just the beard." He stood and leaned close to get a better look. "Maybe it's stopping. Do you want to try to sit up?"

As she nodded, she felt the reassuring cradle of his hand lift her. He kept his fingers on the base of her neck while she steadied herself and daubed the wet mess beneath her nose and mouth. A red spray had speckled the sleeve of his jacket, and the handkerchief looked like a crimson flag. She touched her face with her fingertips to determine how far the stain had spread.

"Let's get you to the ladies' washroom where you can clean up proper."

In the bathroom mirror, she was shocked by the red map on her face. One of Jack's pictures gone awry, her eyes half-crazed with horror and the blood running nearly ear to ear and curling beneath her chin to the throat. She washed her face gingerly till all traces had disappeared, and as she was inspecting her reflection, she saw the word over her shoulder, scratched into the paint of one of the stalls. It was backwards and foreign and she could not make out what it spelled. Turning round, she read it clearly: "wicked." Wicked, indeed, the wicked witch of the mall.

The first thing she saw when she left the bathroom was the gallant man holding up the shopping bag as a sign of his fidelity. A bright smile emerged from the forest of his beard. "Feeling better?"

"I'm so embarrassed, and you've been so kind."

"No more nosebleed? No more spirits tapping under the table?"

"All better," she said and held out her hand in gratitude. He hooked the handle of the bag over her wrist.

"Merry Christmas," he said. "I hope your son enjoys his gifts."

Low clouds bruised the late afternoon, and the sun kept disappearing, then reappearing as a faint halo on the misty sky. On the drive home, she delighted in the houses strung with bright lights, little beacons of cheer in the gloom. Along Mercy Point, she glimpsed a cargo ship far out at sea, its blinking lights sending off some melancholy signal, and she wondered if the captain and crew would make it home for the holidays, or if their turkey dinner would be a lonesome affair on the vast and wasteful ocean. Her thoughts drifted to the *Porthleven* and its doomed passengers. What terror it must have been for those poor souls taking on frigid water within sight of land.

The front rooms of the house were dark when Holly pulled into the driveway. Strange for Tim not to have lit the way for her, and by this late hour, he surely would have supper on the stove, but the place looked empty. She grabbed the bags from the passenger seat and hoped to sneak them past any prying eyes. Beneath the map light, she checked in the rearview mirror for any trace of blood on her face, and satisfied that she had removed all evidence, she stepped into the gloaming.

The front door swung open when she turned the knob, and she called out for her family and flipped on the lights. Nobody appeared. Tim should have heard her arrive, seen the car in the driveway, and Jack usually greeted her after she had been away all day. The room was cold and quiet. She left her coat and hat on the edge of the sofa and turned up the thermostat, the furnace blowers thumping, as though the house itself had been holding its breath for her. On the kitchen table were the remnants of a male bacchanal, dirty plates with pizza crusts, an open bin of pretzels, the peel of an orange curling upon itself. But no boy, no father. Where the hell were they?

Something pattered across the floor overhead, and she stuck her head into the stairwell to call for her son. Nick Weller appeared on the landing, followed by Jack, a wild grin on his face. Bounding down the steps in their hooded sweatshirts, they looked like trolls descending from the hills, and Jack nearly bowled her over. She circled her arms around his head and shoulders to return the embrace, but he pulled away at her touch. Beyond him, Nick stood on the stairs, watching.

"Nick, what a surprise."

When he bowed his head, his hood concealed his eyes. "My mother dropped me off so they could go to my dad's Christmas party. I guess they forgot me."

Holly suddenly remembered the last-minute phone call the night before from Nell with an urgent request that they watch Nick. Not the
first time they had left him late, but the boy before her was so penitent,
abject really, that she sensed trouble far greater than his parents' absent-
mindedness. "But where's Mr. Keenan?"

"Gone," Nick said.

"What do you mean gone? How long has he been gone?"

"I went out to look for him, but I couldn't find him anywhere."

Clamoring for attention, Jack stuck his face next to hers. "He chased
it. He went outside and chased it."

"Chased who? What are you talking about?"

"He's out there." He pulled at her arm. "Daddy tried to catch it."

"Jack, please—"

"The monster."

She wriggled free from his grasp. "Nick, tell me what really happened.
Where's Mr. Keenan?"

"It's true, Mrs. Keenan. He saw something out there on the rocks, by
the ocean. And he wanted to get a closer look."

"Mom, do you want to see my drawing of it?"

"Jack, honey, I have to listen to Nick, now—can you please be quiet,
please?"

He did not like it when anyone raised their voice or reproached him,
so Jack turned his back to her and faced the wall, but at this particular
moment, she did not have any desire to consider his feelings. Nick was
acting queer as well, shrinking into that ridiculous hood like a turtle
retreating into its carapace. But she had no room for his feelings either,
and she pressed the question by stepping closer so that she was nearly
touching Nick. The boy's face shone with perspiration and a dark red
stripe of skin above his upper lip had been rubbed raw.

"When Mr. Keenan didn't come back, I got worried. Not at first. We
watched him go over the rocks, but then he vanished, and I didn't know
what to do." He wiped his nose with the sleeve of his jacket.

"And what was he after?"

Nick moved to put himself between Jack and his mother. "I can't tell what it was. Me and Jack watched him and then he never came back and then it just was later and later and Jack said he was hungry. I didn't know if I was supposed to stay inside with him or if I should try helping Mr. Keenan, so I made him some lunch, but we got hungry and ate it. After, when he still didn't come home, I thought maybe something bad happened out there, and I told Jack to stay here, and I went out—as far as the ocean and up to the highest rocks I could—but I never saw him, I'm sorry."

"How long ago was this?"

"Maybe three or four hours."

"Jesus," she said and then covered her mouth with her fingers. A kind of paralysis came over her, and she could not decide whether it was wiser to search for her husband, flashlight in hand, or wait for him at home with the boys. Or perhaps she should call the police or the fire department, and what would she say, my husband ran out of the house and hasn't come back for four hours? Darkness swallowed the last of the twilight, and she stared through the bay window as the land and sea lost shape. "Tim, Tim, Tim," she whispered under her breath until his name became mere rhythm, the drum on her heart, and still he did not come. The sudden closing of a car door in the cold air gave her a moment of hope—he's home—but it was only Fred and Nell come to fetch their son. They rolled into the house, slightly drunk and worn from the party. One look at her snapped them into sobriety.

Big Fred Weller swayed in the middle of the living room and then steadied himself next to the Christmas tree. "You look both tragic and worried," he said. "Have you just seen Hamlet's ghost?"

"It's Tim," Holly said. "He's disappeared."

v.

Nothing. First, he was there, plain to see, but then he became part of nothing. Through the window, the boys watched Mr. Keenan climb over the rocks chasing shadows that were not there. His coat blowing in the wind like a loose sail, he stopped to scan the landscape, study the ocean, the rocks, and then launch himself, tacking to the northeast and falling off the edge of the visible world. The glass shielded them from the outside, but Nick could see in the noonday light the waves rolling in, crashing silently against the rocks, the clouds banked in the sky, and the bareness of December. He shivered where he stood, but his friend was placid as a statue. In a few moments, Jack Peter stopped staring and walked across the kitchen to his papers scattered on the table. The chill in the room gave way to enveloping warmth as the furnace kicked in, and when the air blew through the vents, the smell of the balsam Christmas greens perfumed the whole house. Shortly after Mr. Keenan had disappeared from view, Nick asked if they should go look for him.

"He'll be back, don't worry."

"But we're all alone," Nick said.

Jack Peter looked up from his work. "I said don't worry. I know what's going on. He's just out on a hunt, but he'll never catch it. He's not smart enough."

They passed an innocent hour talking about monsters. For each of his drawings, Nick had a story—the first time he had seen *Frankenstein* on the late late show, the mummy from a comic book, Harry Potter facing down the Dementors.

"Those were scary," said Jack Peter. "But I know how to make a real monster."

Nick laughed at his assertion. "Okay, big shot, how do you make a monster?"

"I can't show you," he said with a laugh. "You can't do it."

The big clock on the kitchen wall scraped away the time, and Nick grew more concerned by Mr. Keenan's absence each time he stared at its face. He had not realized just how much he depended on having an adult in the house when he was alone with Jack Peter. That boy was unpredictable and possibly dangerous. Wary as a hare, Nick twitched and watched for signs.

Early in the afternoon, Jack Peter moved without a word to the refrigerator and took out the milk and cocoa syrup. With mechanical precision, he poured the milk into a pot and set it atop the gas burner on the stove, which flamed to life with a few clicks. He watched and waited, his face as expressionless as a stone, and Nick joined him, the lads hovering above the hot pot like a pair of witches at a steaming cauldron. The scalded milk hissed when he poured it into the mugs, and the aroma of chocolate bloomed and made them hungry. They raided the refrigerator and the pantry for their lunch. Jack Peter popped frozen mini pizzas in the toaster oven and Nick cracked open a fresh bucket of pretzels. While they were waiting for the pizzas to cook, they layered saltines with peanut butter into towers as tall as their mouths would stretch, laughing as they ate them, spraying crumbs across the room. For their second lunch, Nick peeled himself an orange and Jack Peter munched on a leg of leftover roast chicken.

After their meal, the stuffed boys waddled into the living room and nested like a couple of pashas. Jack Peter flung his legs across the arm of his father's easy chair and stared at the blank ceiling, moving his finger from time to time as though drawing. Perched next to the Christmas tree, Nick watched the glass ornaments catch the slant light and sparkle on their hooks. Silence settled inside the house, broken only by the occasional bark from the border collie across the way in the Quigleys' backyard. They had fallen into inertia, the heaviness in their small stomachs weighing them to their spots. Nick patted his stomach and burped, and they giggled at how it interrupted the silence. Jack Peter tried to copy his friend but his belch was loud as a grown man's. He fell into a fit of laughter that was too loud and went on too long.

"Are you sure your father is coming back?"

"He'll return."

"And your mother's just out shopping? When will she come home?"

"She'll be back. You worry too much."

"What are we going to do? We ought to do something."

"Nothing to be done." Jack Peter pulled a magazine from the rack by the chair and flipped through it, pausing only when a photograph caught his eye.

"Shouldn't we go look for your father?"

He did not glance at Nick but kept thumbing the pages. "I'm not going out there with you."

Nick knew why his friend would not leave, but he could not shake the nagging unease about what had happened to Mr. Keenan. Ignoring Jack Peter's insistent stare, he went to the coatrack and dressed to go outdoors. At the entrance to the mudroom, he looked back at Jack Peter, who had not stirred and now slouched in the chair, watching Nick's every movement. Without another word, Nick left the house and stepped out into the cold.

No one else was out on such a gray day, and the only sign of life was the curl of smoke from the Quigleys' chimney. He made his way from the mudroom to the tilt of sand that separated the yard from the sea. The insistent waves pulsed along the shore, and he walked out slowly, climbing the rocks as if stepping stones, watchful for any telltale movement, but the entire vista was blank and desolate. In the summertime, there might have been gulls overhead or a person or two sunning themselves or casting a fishing line into the dark waters, but here in the dead winter, such memories flitted briefly in his imagination. He marched on, looking back once at the bay window, half hoping that Jack Peter would be watching at least, but there was no one there. Perhaps he didn't care, perhaps he wasn't involved. Fingers of damp iciness reached into the gaps of his jacket, and he zipped himself in up to the throat. When he reached the place where Mr. Keenan had last been seen, Nick crouched to inspect the ground. There was no trace of him, not so much as a footprint in the patches of sand between the clumps of rock. To the south, a few sentinel-like houses clung to the edge of the dunes, and to the north rose Mercy Point and the lighthouse, its rooftop globe clear and unseeing as a glass eye. He called once for Mr. Keenan, though there was no answer, and his own voice sounded small and weak.

If the thing he had been chasing was frightened, it might be running still, like a rabbit escaping a fox, trotting away and hiding and trembling, and then when flushed, dashing off farther, and Mr. Keenan might just have been drawn recklessly into pursuit, and might be miles off now. Or perhaps the creature was some preying beast and had waited in ambush to snatch and carry him to its lair and was only now gnawing on his flesh, and years later, the human bones would turn up when some hiker stumbled upon a cave. Or maybe Mr. Keenan had suffered some accident on the rocks or stumbled into the sea. The body could be any number of places, hidden from view. In the gathering twilight, Nick walked toward the ocean, half expecting to see a corpse bobbing on the water.

Spindrift blew off the waves and foam gathered in clots that rolled along the shore, full of bubbles like scalded milk. Stretched to the far boundaries, the gray-green sea appeared lifeless, though Nick knew below the waves lived fishes and crabs and lobsters scuttling across the sandy bottom. He remembered the day when he and Jack Peter had last been together on this same spot three years ago, and how they had looked out upon this same ocean, and how he wished he had never met such a strange boy. His parents made him play with him, he didn't want to, he wanted to be normal. Jack Peter had angered him that day with one careless sentence.

If I could run away, he thought, I would. If I could swim across the ocean, I would not stop till I reached the other shore. And I would live there in a cottage on the shore of Ireland or England or France. And I would learn to be someone else and speak the way they do and eat their food and give myself a new name. And though my parents would miss me and my friends would know that I am gone, they would forget about me in time, and I could find somebody new. And I would cut that string. *I would be rid of him for good.*

There was no body swirling in the waves. Squatting on his haunches, he took off his gloves and put his bare hands on the cold sand, where the ocean would come and cover them in ice water. The sound and motion of the waves matched the rhythm of his breathing until the winter wind and water seeped past his fears. He kept his hands in place until they stung and reddened, but he could not go farther. Shoving them into his pockets, he shivered and stared out at the Atlantic. How long he stood there he did not know. Sometimes when he was alone, Nick felt as if he was the last boy on earth. He moved through the landscape without volition, compelled by an unseen force to be here, a living thing in an artificial world, made to breathe and act and move beyond his own control. The sun at his back slipped down below the tops of the fir trees and cast one brief and final play of light and shadow on the surface of the sea. The shift in temperature awakened him as if from a trance, and he turned and walked back through the lengthening shadows to the darkening house.

Inside, no lamps had been turned on against the dying of the light, and Jack Peter had not moved. He was where Nick had left him, splayed across the easy chair, studying the ceiling as though some picture had been sketched upon the surface. He greeted Nick with a grunt. "What did you find outside?"

"Nothing."

The news didn't seem to faze him one way or another. He swung his legs around and sat up straight. "I'm bored. What should we do?"

"Aren't you worried about what happened to your father? Where's your mother?"

"We just have to wait. We should do something to make the waiting go faster. Do you want to draw more monsters?"

"I'm tired of drawing."

As if a switch had been thrown, Jack Peter stood suddenly and clapped his hands together. "Let's have another war. You always like a good war. You can be the greens." Without waiting for an answer, he took off for his bedroom and the bucket of plastic army men. Nick looked once at the door, willing it to open, for an adult to push through, but it remained closed fast against the outside world. He gathered his resolve and took the stairs two by two to join the battle.

The bodies were piling up when he heard a voice calling from below. They dropped their toys, and Nick ran to greet Mrs. Keenan at the top of the stairs. She was full of questions about her husband, questions for which he had no good answer. So instead, she sat quietly on the sofa murmuring Tim's name when the Wellers arrived, full of drink and curiosity.

The five of them kept vigil in the living room. Nick's mother put on a pot of coffee, and his father turned on the Christmas tree lights and built a fire in the fireplace. In a corner, Jack Peter examined the monster notebook again, scrutinizing each page. Mrs. Keenan waited by the telephone, and his parents took up the sofa, collecting their wits and sobriety. A current of anxiety flowed from person to person, and now and again, the notion of a search party was proposed and rejected. Night had fallen completely, and it would be dangerous out on those wet rocks with just a flashlight.

Minutes after six o'clock, Nick heard a scratching outside the mudroom, like a mouse gnawing at the wood, and just as he rose to investigate, the door creaked open. They raced to find Mr. Keenan standing there in the threshold, his face and hands beet red and raw, wildness in his eyes. A slash of dried blood arced across his throat and more blood was spattered on the front of his overcoat in a dark constellation.

The blood, Jack Peter was mostly interested in the blood. The pattern that it made on his face and clothes, the way the color changed from bright fresh crimson to deep magenta, nearly black. He positioned himself in the middle of the room, and as usual, they were oblivious to his presence, as he studied their every movement and noted every word. The grown-ups wanted the whole story from his father, and they fussed over him when he came in. His mother peeled off his stiff coat and tugged the wet gummy boots from his feet. Mrs. Weller went to the kitchen sink and doused a dish towel in hot water to dab at the crusted blood at his throat. Mr. Weller poured a mug of hot black coffee and stripped the throw from the back of the sofa to wrap around Daddy's shoulders. Nick sat on a chair at the edge of the room, frightened by the blood and chaos, biting his fingernails. But Jack Peter watched with greedy curiosity as the man slowly emerged from the wind-chapped and dirty skin.

The ragged gashes on his throat resembled the nail marks of an animal, and the wounds would not stop bleeding. When one towel turned red, it was discarded for a fresh one. Running back between the chair and the sink and the cupboards, Jack Peter replaced four towels before the color faded to pink and subsided. His father took a sip of the coffee and winced when it hit the roof of his mouth. His mother's hands were shaking, and she clasped her fingers together as though in prayer to still the tremors. Mrs. Weller asked for a first-aid kit, and Mommy left the room to hunt for it.

The Wellers threw their questions at Tim, but he could not find the words to answer. His face reddened in the warmth of the house, and the frost in his matted hair melted. From behind the scrim of adults, Jack

Peter caught his father's eye, and he looked as if he was conjuring a plausible explanation. "You had us worried absolutely sick," Mrs. Weller said.

"There was someone out there. The same thing I saw on the road that night I brought Nick back to you."

"Coyote," Mr. Weller said. "You're not the only one who's seen it. The Hill brothers found one had been at their trash cans just last week, and it nearly ate the Rivards' little dog. Some of the fellas were playing poker in the basement there, and they heard all this yapping, and out in the yard, a mangy old coyote snapping its teeth, ready to carry the poor pooch away."

"It wasn't a coyote but taller than a man. The boys saw it, too. Tell them."

Jack Peter waved the bloodied towel in his hand. "It was a monster. Trying to get in our house."

All of the adults stared at him as if he were crazy. He hid his face behind the wing of his crooked arm and retreated from their scrutiny.

Mr. Weller laid his hand on Nick's shoulder. "How 'bout it, son. Man, or something else? Maybe a werewolf out in the middle of the day. Did you get a good look at the beast?"

The boy's lips quivered and his eyes blinked rapidly as he fought the urge to cry. "I don't know. It was far and we turned away and when we looked back, it was gone."

Tim rose from his chair, as if emerging from a cocoon of ice, crackling and stiff in his joints. Anger contorted his features, and he stepped between Nick and his father to confront the boy. "But you saw him, clear as I did. You saw him today and you saw him that night."

Nick chewed his lip and stared at the floor.

"Tell the truth, boy. A man, wild and naked."

Everyone now watched Nick for some affirmation or denial, but the boy was in a panic that threatened to drown him.

From his crouch, Jack Peter listened as they questioned his friend, saw how scared he looked, and jumped up to save him. "He didn't have a pecker."

In unison, their heads swiveled to face him. Mrs. Weller laughed at the comment.

"That's what Nick said."

His father croaked a warning. "Jip—"

"I never said that."

"You did," Jack Peter said. "You saw the drawing and you said he had no penis."

The adults, even his father, laughed again. Jack Peter hated it when people laughed at him, and he wrung the bloody towel in his hands and waved it to make them quit. When he saw the shock on their faces, he stopped and clasped his hands behind his head to keep still, to show them they should not be afraid.

His mother entered the room, bearing the first-aid kit, and she came at once to his side. "I'm just going to help you," she said and laid her hand upon his knotted fingers, prying gently to get him to relax his grip, but he didn't want to, not yet, he wasn't finished telling them about the monster, but she kept tugging at his hands and speaking slowly, words full of music, till he finally gave in to her and let go of the towel. She held his left hand in her right, rubbing his thumb with her thumb, and he was okay.

"What's going on? What happened here?"

Nobody wanted to tell her. Each person avoided her gaze.

"Who set off Jack?"

"It was nothing," his father said. "Just a misunderstanding about what's appropriate in mixed company."

"Heavens, Tim," Mrs. Weller said. "I've heard 'pecker' plenty of times."

"Mixed, children," he said.

Rising for the defense, Mr. Weller tottered to the middle of the room. "Jack here was trying to tell us what he saw—or didn't see—in regards to that creature your husband chased all the way to Canada."

His mother took out some gauze and a bandage and went back to patch up his father. She pressed the nail marks with her fingertips. "So much blood. Do you think you might need stitches?"

He dismissed her anxiety with a wave of his hand. "I saw something out on the rocks, white as a ghost, and I chased it. I must have passed out, and when I came to, it was early dark and I was so cold. My neck was bleeding. I could feel something had been at my throat. All the way home, I kept hearing noises out in the blackness, following me, footsteps behind me, all around, that would stop when I stopped and start up again whenever I moved."

"White as a ghost," his mother said. Mrs. Weller kept pulling at the hem of her sleeve, and Mr. Weller was quite nearly smiling, skeptical and bemused.

"A couple times I yelled out, but whatever it was would run away— you could hear it scamper over the rocks—but then it came around again the way a dog will circle back on you. Or maybe there was more than one of them. Maybe you're right, Fred, maybe there's coyotes or a pack of wild dogs out there. Maybe that's what got my throat."

Mr. Weller's smile broadened, and then he blushed.

"Were you just frightened to death?" Mrs. Weller asked. She had inched closer.

"Let me tell you, I was scared, and didn't know where I was half the time. Only by keeping the sea on my left could I figure out the way home."

He pictured his father out in the dark, using his mind to turn the landscape so that the sea would be on his left-hand side, rotating the darkened sky like tilting a picture. Maybe the monsters would just slide off the page. He wanted his father to open the doors and shake out the Wellers. Erase Nick from the page. He was tired of them. Without hesitation, he yawned wide and roared a protracted sigh.

"Seems we've overstayed our welcome," Mr. Weller said, nodding to the sleepy boy. "We really ought to be getting home. Thanks for having Nick."

Mrs. Weller stared at her husband as though he had said a bad word. "Not until Tim finishes his story."

"Of course not, dear," Mr. Weller said, folding his arms across his chest. "Tim, we're pins and needles."

"There's not much more to it. I picked up a rock and threw it, and whatever it is stopped following me. The boys must have forgotten to turn on the outside lights, which would have been a beacon, so I stumbled around in the dark, looking for the house, till I spotted Jip's bedroom window. Go to the light at the end of the tunnel. Isn't that what they say you do when you die. Look, I'm all right. A bit frosty around the edges, and the blood—"

"I think you should see a doctor," Holly said. "If not tonight, at least in the morning."

"But you must have been out cold for hours," Mrs. Weller said. "You could have a concussion."

"Did you hit your head?" Jack Peter asked.

From the corner of the room, Nick coughed, reminding them of his presence.

"I don't remember." He touched his forehead. "Maybe that's one symptom of amnesia. You can't remember if you have it."

Mr. Weller fetched their coats and hats. "No more monsters for tonight."

"No more monsters," his father said.

"Peckerless or otherwise, no more monsters. Doctor's orders." Mrs. Weller stood to join her husband. "You get him to bed, Holly, and we'll give you a call in the morning, eh?"

"You've been too kind," his mother said. "I'll take care of Tim, now."

Jack Peter studied the Wellers as they readied themselves to go, wrapping themselves until they nearly lost all shape. At the door, Mrs. Weller leaned over and kissed his father on the cheek. Mr. Weller grabbed him in a bear hug and squeezed so hard it made his father gasp, and then they stepped into the night. Through the window Jack Peter watched them pass through the beam from the porch light. Nick looked left and right and all around as if worried about what lurked in the shadows, ready to pounce. They made it safely to the car, which trailed away, two red taillights that narrowed to pinpoints and vanished.

Beside the easy chair, his mother crouched next to his father so that their faces were on the same plane. She had led him back to comfort and warmth, wrapped a blanket around his legs, and now they conspired in secret looks and low voices. They often spoke this way, in a language of gestures foreign and inscrutable. She laid her hand upon his forearm. He bowed his head toward hers.

"How about I run you a nice hot bath? And while you're soaking, I'll make us something to eat—you must be starving."

Careworn, she slowly stood and made her way upstairs. Rushing water overhead broke the silence. His father reclined in the easy chair, head back, resting his eyes. Jack Peter read the angles of his face, normal color returning to his skin, and listened to the soft purring of his steady breathing. From afar, he traced the three long lines swiped across his throat and a nick beneath his left ear. Just when he seemed to have fallen fully asleep, his father arched an eyebrow and popped open one eye. They considered each other from a short distance before Jack Peter had to turn away.

His father closed his eyes again and spoke in a calm and measured tone. "Who do you think was out there, Jip?"

He cleared his throat and whispered. "A monster."

"But there are no such things as monsters, son."

"Then I don't know."

The roar of water upstairs ended abruptly, and he knew his mother was now testing the temperature with her elbow. He had seen her do so a hundred times before, rolling back her sleeve and hunching over the tub to make sure the bath was not too hot or too cold. She specialized in making things just right. In a moment, she would call his father when it was all set, but Daddy was already moving, untangling the blanket from his legs and lifting his sore and tired body from the chair.

His mother stayed with him and did not return immediately to make their dinner, leaving Jack Peter alone downstairs. He gazed at the strings of colored lights on the Christmas tree, touching the different ones to feel if blue was hotter than red or if green was as cool as grass, but the bulbs were all the same, the heat as tiny as the heart of a bird. When he tired of that experiment, he wandered to the kitchen and found the bloodied dishcloths soaking in the sink next to the dirty dishes from his feast with Nick. Battle wounds from the wars of the toy soldiers. On the refrigerator door, the boy in the picture seemed to be following him with his eyes, so Jack Peter turned his back on him and saw at once in the opposite window a white flash of movement. A face watching him had turned away. The man was in the yard. Jack Peter ran to the glass, but all he could see was the pitch of night and his own reflection smattered with light from the kitchen. His warm hands on the cold surface left ghost impressions when he withdrew, a sign on the windowpane, hello, goodbye. He decided that he would not tell them about the visitor, that he would not let on that he was losing control. *Better to keep some secrets to yourself.*

An hour after she had said she would be right back, his mother came down to the kitchen in a bathrobe, her wet hair turbaned in a high towel, her face flushed against her white smile. His father followed shortly thereafter, he too in a robe and slippers, moving with rejuvenated assurance, as if nothing had happened. Only the bandage at his neck hinted otherwise. Each parent nodded upon first seeing their son but was otherwise indifferent to his presence. They worked together at the stove and counter, throwing together a boiling pot of pasta and a jar of tomato sauce, a casual salad, and frozen rolls heated and brushed with olive oil and garlic. Believing himself invisible, Jack Peter was surprised when they remembered to invite him to the table. He saw how they had changed. They were a team again, and he would have to see what he should do about that. The blush of red wine filled the room when his father uncorked the bottle. Piping hot, the spaghetti was no sooner set on the table than they were at it like a pair of wild beasts. They chomped at the bread, slurped at the sauce, and drained their glasses to the lees. They ate as though they had been starving, abandoning themselves to desire, as if the raw act of eating was somehow wicked when true wickedness was just outside the door.

Three

The man next to Holly took the light from his son, a boy of Jack's age, and passed it to her, tipping the small candle to her wick, a drop of wax falling to the circle of cardboard protecting her hand against just such accidents, and then she turned to the stranger on the other side to send the dot of flame on down the pew. Soon the darkened church was illuminated by hundreds of such candles, and at the altar the priest, resplendent in his white and gold vestments, was saying something about the child who brought light into the world, but Holly could not understand his prayer, for she was caught in the yellow and blue flickering before her eyes, remembering similar ceremonies with her parents and sisters at the midnight Masses of her youth. She had nearly forgotten how it felt to be so carefree and filled with expectation. The congregation listened to the first measure from the organ and then all voices rose in song, and the music carried the altar boys and the deacon and Father Bolden on their recessional along the center aisle. She had just found her place in the hymnal when it all ended, the carol complete, the parishioners blew out their candles and wished friends and fellows alike a Merry Christmas.

In mere moments, the flock had flown, leaving behind a few kneeling penitents, heads bowed, whispering their prayers. In front of her an elderly woman in a lace mantilla reminded Holly of her grandmother. Across the aisle, a family with six children as well dressed and well behaved as the von Trapps were putting on their overcoats atop their suits and dresses, the youngest crying softly as he was roused to be bundled up. A toddler in a tiny vest and red bow tie could not keep from staring at Holly, and when she smiled back and waved, he buried his head on his father's shoulder. The crowd at the rear of the church thinned to a manageable few, so she slipped into her coat and headed toward the vestibule. She hovered at the edge so she could be among the last people there, greeting the priest.

Father Bolden brightened when she came into view and grabbed her extended hand with both of his and pulled her to him, close enough so that she could smell the wine on his breath and the incense lingering in the folds of his vestments. She was aware of a few souls around her, but at the same time, his gesture created an intimate space, perfect for what she had come to say.

"A very Merry Christmas to you, Mrs. Keenan. I'm so delighted to see you here." He squeezed her hand in his. "After you left so suddenly, I was afraid I had scared you off and would never see you again." Noticing someone over her shoulder, he let go with his right hand but held on to her arm with his left. "Just who I was looking for."

Bundled in her winter coat, Miss Tiramaku shuffled to his side. She gave Father Bolden a kiss on his cheek and offered her hand to Holly. In the soft light of the church, Miss Tiramaku was no more substantial than a will-o'-the-wisp, but Holly felt a strange warmth in her touch.

"Mrs. Keenan," she said. "Merry Christmas. I was hoping to see you tonight. I think I may have left you with a bad impression."

"No," Holly said. "I was just a little thrown by our talk. And that painting of the shipwreck. And your ghosts."

Miss Tiramaku was massaging her hand. "I'd like to talk with you about your son. He and I share the same condition, that is to say, we're on the same spectrum, though they never called it autism when I was a child."

"Asperger's," Holly said. "But you are fine now? Functioning?"

Suppressing a laugh, she nodded. "If you call this functioning. I'd like to meet your son sometime, see if I can be of any help."

For a moment, Holly felt a surge of hope, a fleeting possibility that Jack might not be forever trapped inside.

The priest turned around to the two women. "Cinnamon buns in the morning, Miss T.?"

"It wouldn't be Christmas without them." She smiled. "May we meet again soon, Mrs. Keenan."

"Holly," she said. "And a very merry Christmas to you."

Miss Tiramaku went on her way, pushing open the doors and disappearing into the night, leaving the church nearly empty.

"When I was a little girl, we used to come to midnight Mass every Christmas eve," Holly said.

"Welcome home. And how is that boy of yours?"

"I need to talk with you, Father. It's not just Jack but my husband, too. He's been acting strangely. Wandering around at night, seeing things."

"Seeing things?"

She leaned forward and spoke in a hoarse whisper. "He left the boys alone and went out by the ocean because he saw something. All day long, came back with these wicked deep scratches in his throat. He was a bloody mess. Claims it was ghosts."

The von Trapps marched up to them in single file, a song waiting to be born if she ever saw one. In order to give them a proper greeting, Father Bolden released her, and shook each hand one by one and gave the littlest among them a pat on his sleepy head. The moment was ideal for her escape, but Holly found herself bound to the priest by invisible wires. She had said too much, and having heard "ghosts" emerge from her mouth, she felt slightly embarrassed by the ridiculousness of the word. She did not believe in ghosts, and thought all those who believed in them to be slightly mad. Even the Japanese housekeeper with her *yurei*. Perhaps Tim had gone mad as well, out wandering the shoreline, pursued by monsters. She wanted to retract her confession, rewind the conversation to its beginnings and beyond, to the moment she had ever decided to come to this place. Her husband and child were asleep in their beds. She should be home, dreaming of sugarplums.

Just as she was about to leave, Holly felt a tug at her sleeve and saw that the old priest had latched on to her again and would not let go. The last of the von Trapps bid him auf Wiedersehen, adieu, and they trooped off. Father Bolden drew her closer. He reminded her of a Cub Scout at a campfire, ready for the thrill of the story. "What do you mean by ghosts?"

"That was wrong. I'm not sure if he really meant ghosts or something else. What I meant to say was that he's been acting strangely lately. My husband. My son, too. I just needed an hour's peace. Jack will be up at the crack of dawn, waiting by the Christmas tree, and it's just been madness. Chaos, the holidays, you know?"

"Better than most. A case of the Christmas spirits."

She shrugged at his joke and offered him half a smile.

"The offer stands," he said. "You come see me anytime you want or need to. There's always a lull after Christmas." He relinquished his grip and sent her on her way.

The clouds had fallen during the service, and a soft fog settled upon the landscape. In the mist, the lights in the parking lot sprouted halos. A minivan purred to life, its headlights picking the way through the gloom. The von Trapps, she imagined, heading home to bed, and in the morning there would be confetti of wrapping paper and ribbons and bows, and whiskers on kittens, and a few of her favorite things. Why isn't my life more like a musical? As she reached her car, Holly stuck her hand inside her purse to search for her keys but was surprised instead by the candle and its cardboard circle concealed like a gun. She debated whether she should return it to the church, but decided a small white sin was preferable to further embarrassing conversation with the priest.

Gripping the steering wheel, she leaned close to the windshield to try to see where she was going. The thick mist parted as the car pushed forward, and she toyed with the wipers to little improvement. She drove cautiously, grateful that no one else was around, and to ease her anxiety, she replayed the Christmas hymns on the soundtrack in her mind. At the turn onto Shore Road, a shadow crossed the pavement in front of her, and she braked, uncertain of what she had seen. Ahead on the driver's side, the object seemed to move again, the mist rippling in its wake, and she rolled down her window and stuck out her head into the dark night. "Hello," she said, but only the purr of the engine returned her call. Bitter air rushed into the car, and the blast rejuvenated her in that sleepy hour. The clock radio read half-past one.

An answer rose up from the silence. Initially she thought there must be a problem with the car, the scrape of the wipers on a dry window or whining from the parking brake. She pulled onto the shoulder and shut off the engine. The ever-present ocean bashed against the rocky coast somewhere below, but on top of that familiar rhythm a human sound filtered through the dense cloud, like a party nearby, the last of the revelers blurting out a song, and then she took it for an argument heading to violence, a husband and wife hollering at each other. Or Fred Weller's pack of coyotes howling at the moon, but those were no animal sounds. The voices had a different tenor, a tone of desperation. She opened the door and stepped out into the night.

Where were they coming from? Holly crossed the road and looked down the embankment toward the water, but it was hopeless. The mist around her swallowed everything, made all invisible. She could be forty yards or four hundred yards from the edge, and even if she could manage to find the shore, what then? Far off and out at sea came the sounds. Voices, she imagined, in the cold and darkness, the passengers from the *Porthleven*, begging for rescue and an end to their terror. Couldn't be, but still, something out in the water could not be seen, could not be saved. Her heart raced and panic tugged at her limbs. She felt the urge to plunge forward and launch herself into the rocks, but an equal force kept her locked to the spot, dread rising in her gut. The fog tasted of salt. She bent over at the waist and rested her hands on her knees to prevent hyperventilating, and when she looked up, there was no wooden ship sinking in the ocean. As abruptly as the screaming began, it suddenly stopped, like a recording cut off in midmeasure.

The calmness frightened her more than the sound. She listened in vain, waiting for the screams to resume, but the voices had been interrupted and abandoned. Fear crystallizes time, makes it slow and still. Only once before had she experienced this feeling, the day her son had vanished from the beach. To make the world spin again, she would have to will it to motion, so she inhaled a deep breath and let it spool from her lungs. The car across the road seemed miles away, the murkiness as thick as blood. Her husband and son were asleep in their beds, the Christmas house was waiting for her to return. For a few moments, she sat in the car, running the heater. It's late, she told herself, I should just crawl into bed. The ocean was just an idea, a sound and nothing more. No *Porthleven* rock-riven and filling with cold water. No mysterious lupine figure wandering in the night air. No pair of boys playing in the surf and tumbling beneath the waves. No inside boy, no strange and penetrating stares from the babe at her breast. No strangers accusing her. No husband. How long ago had she known? How soon had her instinct told her the truth about Jack? The world of ifs, the land of so.

Tim had left the twinkling lights on, glowing softly like a chain of stars, guiding her into the driveway. Her Christmas boy was not ever going to be well. Pretty soon he would be stronger than she was, and bigger, some real violence in his fist. The day was coming when the ordinary demons of adolescence would wrestle with his private devils, and it could be a hell. And she knew that her love for Jack would not be enough to protect him forever, that one day she would have to give him up or send him away or have someone else, a nurse, a ward, a home to mother him.

A lamp was on in one of the windows, and as soon as she faced it, the light went out so quickly that she could not determine from which room it had shone. Upstairs, yes, but Jack's room or her own? Or perhaps it was one of them using the bathroom in the middle of the night.

Seat down, fellas. Still, the sudden flicker unnerved her, as if the house itself had been spying, waiting for her to make the next move. The house was cold inside and the air damp against her skin as though the hazy vapors had crept in through the cracks. She turned up the thermostat a few clicks until the heat came on and pumped warm air into the room. During her absence, Tim had arranged the presents below the Christmas tree in a small mountain of many colors and ribbons and bows. She stood before the pile of gifts, admiring the artful care he had shown in placing each one. Just so. In the morning, he would play the elf, dispensing the packages one by one in an order of his own devising.

She tiptoed up the stairs and changed into the nightgown hanging from the back of the bathroom door. As she readied for bed, the lateness of the hour weighed heavily. Other Christmas eves had been spent in last-minute preparations for the morning to come. Once Tim had stayed up till three, assembling a recalcitrant bicycle, now long neglected. The year Jack Peter was born, they spent the night listening through the baby monitor, hoping he might awaken, and nestling together for his midnight feed, all three of them asleep, the baby against her breast, her husband at her side. Or that terrible fight that one Christmas when she could not fully forgive Tim's transgressions and amends. Ancient history, she thought, and slid into bed, careful not to wake her sleeping husband.

Belowdecks the sea poured in through the hole created when the ship struck the rocks. In their quarters, preparing for arrival in the new land, she and Tim were tossed to the floor by the scraping collision. The ship listed to the breach and knocked the feet from under them again as they tried to rise. Their trunk of clothes and goods slid across the room and burst open, and the small loose articles—a brush and hand mirror, a sheaf of paper and pens, a secret flask of rum—fell and scattered pell-mell. Seeping through the oaken decks and streaming beneath the door, the sea stained the wood, slowly at first like spilled milk, and then all at once, a torrent that gushed by inches as they regained their feet. She screamed at Tim to do something, but he simply sucked on the long stem of his clay pipe and considered the situation with a detached, almost amused air. The coldness of the water shocked and then numbed them. Tim sloshed to the cabin door, but he could not open it against the pressure of the incoming sea and he hulloed and called for the captain, but it was instantly apparent that no one could hear them. Holly struggled to his side in a panic as the water girdled her hips and waist, and she beat her fists against the door, hollering for help. *Come save us.* She drummed and cried out, but the ship rocked and pitched by thirty degrees, and the cold water rose to their shoulders. Tim banged against the ceiling, the sea sweeping them off their feet, so that they were treading water now, and the wooden walls burst ecstatically. They were under, breathing in the sea in one last desperate gesture, the air bubbling from their mouths, a bewildered look frozen on their faces. Suspended in the green sea, the bodies floated toward the cabin walls and then sank, white as fish bellies, dead as dead could be, bobbing in slow motion, and knocking dully against the confines of the little room in the coffin of the *Porthleven*.

As if she had stopped breathing, Holly choked and gasped for breath. She opened her eyes from the nightmare, and almost reflexively, she sat up in the bed to check on her husband. Tim snored gently into his pillow. She threw off the covers and went to see about her son, gently opening Jack's door. In the dim light, she made out his figure curled on the bed. He twitched in his sleep and his shoulders jerked as if she had caught him in some erotic throes, but his movements were sporadic, as if he dreamt of wrestling or of running or swimming away from her. The memory of those drowned bodies gave her a chill. She wanted to lay her hands on her son, but she knew that he might jump from her touch or scream or strike her. From the edge of his bed she spoke his name softly, and he rolled over and went still, sighing once. Just as quietly, she inched off the mattress and stood, watching him a moment longer.

Tim was still sleeping when she crawled into bed, but he woke as soon as her cold feet grazed the warmth of his calves. He rolled over to her, and she could feel his gaze upon her.

"You're back," he whispered. "How was church?"

Midnight Mass seemed a lifetime ago. "Just fine," she said. "Beautiful, really, but it's been a strange night. On the way home, I could have sworn there was a group of people out there. A ship at sea, drowning. It's so foggy, I couldn't see a thing."

The hinge of his jaw made a snapping sound when he yawned. "Try to get some sleep. Who knows when our little boy will be up in the morning? Could be the crack of dawn. Just like when he was a baby."

Neither one of them spoke again, and soon her husband was asleep and snoring. She stared at the ceiling for a while and then at the gap between the window and the shade, that small space where in a few short hours the rising sun would slice through the darkness to announce another morning.

ii.

On Christmas morning, Nick remembered Baby. He had not even thrown off the covers, and Baby was on his mind, which was odd, because he hardly ever thought of Baby anymore, and he could not understand why it had to happen on such a festive day. This time Baby showed up fully made, swaddled in pastel blankets, bald and cheerful, a toothless searching mouth. Nick imagined it crying in the other room, in the crib that had never been assembled but still sat in a box in the attic, and he could almost smell the talcum powder and the baby shampoo, could almost see his mother cross the floor and bring Baby to him, and it would curl its fingers around his pinkie, and he could almost feel its phantom weight in his arms. But there was no baby, he knew, and there never was, but that did not alter the strength of the sensation that Baby was here, had come at last.

His parents told him one day after school. In the beginning, the news meant no more to him than that night's menu or their planned summer vacation up north to look for moose. They were happy, so he felt he should be happy, too, and he was. We're going to have a baby, they said, a little brother or sister of your own. A due date around the Fourth of July. Which was miles away. Eons. He could barely remember last year's fireworks, so the announcement that his mother was expecting was as mythical as every other expectation. What will come, will come. But once they told him about Baby, they could talk of little else. We have to get the spare room ready for Baby. You know when Baby comes, Nana and Pap will come from Florida and stay for a while to help. You'll have to play quietly. Whenever guests visited the house, they wanted to talk of nothing but the plans for Baby. His father touched his mother on her tummy every night in case Baby wanted to kick, and one time, she asked

Nick if he would put his hand on her to feel for Baby, but he did not. It was enough to see how her skin moved.

His mother had disappeared one morning, gone early to the hospital, but not to worry, his father would take care of him. On a hot day in June, Nick had come home from playing with Jack Peter on the rocks behind his house. He burst into the kitchen with a plastic pail laden with bits of shell and small fishes they had trapped in the tidal pools, and he was excited to show his mother the treasures. The house was cool and dark, and the screen door slammed behind him.

"Dad!" Nick yelled. "You'll never guess what we found out there—"

There in the middle of the afternoon sat his father at the kitchen table, an ice-filled glass at his elbow, and the day's crossword puzzle. He put a finger to his lips and said, "Hush." Scraping the chair legs on the linoleum floor, he pushed away from the table and motioned for Nick to come sit in his lap. But that's what he did when he was little, so instead he went to his father's side and stood there, close enough to have a big arm around his shoulder. His father's face looked puffy and red.

"I've got a bit of sad news for you, Nick." His father used his serious voice. "Your mother lost the baby, son."

"Lost Baby?"

"Yes, you see, sometimes the baby won't be able to make it out in the world, and then the mother has what they call stillborn—"

"So the baby isn't going to come?"

His father bent his neck and looked down. "No, Baby died and isn't coming. Not anymore, not ever."

"But Mom is going to be okay?"

The rest of his memory exists in a fog. He could not remember if his mother was at home that afternoon or had gone to the hospital for another day or two. Mrs. Keenan came and fetched him, and he stayed with Jack Peter overnight or longer. When he came back home, he found his mother lying on the couch in a robe and pajamas, bundled in June as though for December. His mother was never sick, and he never before saw her resting on the couch in the middle of the day. His father, yes, asleep in front of the TV tuned in to some dumb golf match, but never his mother. She was a life force, whirl of motion, always making and doing, and now washed out and wasted. Without the baby in her middle, she looked smaller and weaker than ever before. He could not tell, really, with her robe and pajamas as she stretched out, but it looked as if Baby was gone for good. "Come here, pet." She held out her arms and he rushed into her embrace, and she engulfed him so tightly that he could feel the pulse in her neck beat against the side of his cheek. "Daddy tell you?"

He nodded in the swim of her, warm and soft and clean.

"I'm so so sorry, Nicky." He did not understand why she was apologizing to him. Losing Baby was not her fault, and besides, he was not sure if he wanted Baby to come at all. She was crying softly in his ear. "It was a brother. A beautiful boy."

For that whole summer she cried, or so it seemed at the time, but now he realized that only a few days passed when she could not bother to dress or leave the couch. When he was seven, he thought her sorrow would never end, and as she suffered, so did he. He moped about the living room, staring at cartoons on the television, not letting her far from his sight. He watched his father come from work and fill a glass with booze and drink until he remembered to order Nick to bed. He tiptoed around their misery. Sent out to play, he would sit on a rock and stare at the ocean. More often, he was shipped off to spend some time with Jack Peter, who never seemed to care about Nick's feelings, unaware of anyone's emotions but his own.

She got better like she said she would. The weight fell away in her sadness, and sometimes the whole pregnancy seemed nothing but a dream from beginning to end. His mother slowly came back into herself, and by late August, she was well enough to accept an invitation to the clambake the Keenans had planned to mark the end of another summer. Nick had looked forward to it for ages, a chance to return to normalcy, the Wellers and the Keenans on their own private stretch of paradise, just in sight of their dream house by the sea. The days were hot enough to go into the water, and the two boys were jumping over waves as they ran to the shoreline. They had been getting along just fine that day. He looked back over his shoulder. His mother was chatting with Jack's father, his hand on her bare shoulder. Mrs. Keenan sat alone, reading a book, but he could not find his father anywhere. Nick pulled Jack into deeper water so that the swells nearly knocked them over. And then, in the middle of the ocean, Jack Peter had to ask about how they lost the baby. Why couldn't he have been quiet and pretended all of it had never happened? Why did he have to make him angry? A word from Jack Peter about Baby, and he could have killed him on the spot.

Like a siren, the stereo downstairs blared with the soundtrack of Christmas and broke his memories. The same songs every year. His mom and dad were up and puttering about in their robes, probably wondering where he was and what was taking him so long and what kind of kid doesn't come running on Christmas morning to see what Santa left and why is he the way he is. His mother would be putting cinnamon buns into the oven, the first whiff of hot sweetness just moments away. His father would be running the old electric train from his youth, the elaborate village set up beneath the tree with its endlessly fascinating circulation on the tracks. One or the other parent would be calling him soon, and he resolved to beat them to it by springing downstairs with a smile pasted on his face.

They hugged him and they kissed him, and they all wished one another a Merry Christmas. The cinnamon rolls popped out of the oven in gooey glory, and the train went round and round with a giraffe bobbing its head up and down, and they opened the gifts they had for one another with oohs and ahs and thank-yous. He watched his mother more intently than usual, following her actions so closely that several times she gave him a slightly reproachful look, and he would stop and pretend to be entranced by hockey skates or some new book rather than the changing patterns of her face. In some respects, his mother was the same as she had been that awful summer, and in her robe and jammies, she echoed the woman who had been stretched out on the sofa, mourning

Baby. But in other aspects, she appeared much older, worn somehow, a crease in her brow every time she frowned. Faint lines at the corners of her eyes. A thin streak of gray spiraling from the hairline. The veins in the backs of her hands thick as vines. It wasn't just the physical traits, really, but her manner that had aged her. She rarely laughed without restraint any more, not when she was sober, that giddy head-thrown-back cackle. Nick watched her watching her husband, regarding him coolly as if he had done something wrong that could never be forgiven.

Baby would have changed everything. A little kid around the house who still believed in Santa Claus and the tooth fairy and the bogeyman. Nick would be a big brother, not the only child, not the only one to take care of them. And maybe they would not drink so much, and maybe Nick could play with Baby instead of having to go to the Keenans all the time. The last gift exchanged and unwrapped, they all settled into their places, the easy chair, the sofa, the floor. Over the next hour, they drifted away, each heading nowhere, and by midday the morning's happiness was but a memory.

"Don't forget to pack your things," his mother said later that afternoon. Sunlight struggled through the dirty windows, and he felt the day was ending all too soon. Alone in his room, he was working on the final pieces of a plastic hybrid man-machine, a postmodern warrior that snapped together in forty-nine easy moves. Lost in the task at hand, Nick did not comprehend at first what she was talking about.

"We have to leave early to make our flight in order to catch the boat on time to make the cruise. We drop you off at half-past eight in the morning, so be ready."

He tossed the toy on the bed and tried not to look crestfallen. If Baby were here, they would never leave.

"You could have gone to Florida, Nick. Seen your grandparents for a few days. It was your decision." His mother picked up his discarded soldier. "What's the matter, pet?"

"Couldn't I just stay here alone? I can take care of myself."

"We've been over this a million times. It's just a few days, and he's your oldest friend in the world. It won't kill you to be nice to him for a little while. He has no one else, really." She marched the toy soldier across the blankets and pretended it was attacking her son. He swatted her away playfully.

"Do you want me to help you pack?"

"I can do it myself."

She rose to leave. "You're such a big boy," she teased at the door. "You were always like that, so independent. All grown up before I knew what was happening to my baby."

He opened the closet, wary of the bodies that had been there, and worried about his parents on that ship far out to sea. He pulled down his suitcase from the shelf and began counting out socks and underwear for each day, and crammed in some pajamas, two jeans, and a couple of shirts and sweaters. On top of the packing, he laid his monster journal and pencils. Sick to his stomach, he did not want to go. Jack Peter was weirder than ever. Mrs. Keenan was hearing voices, and Mr. Keenan was seeing things. The man lurking out there. He put on his pajamas and waited for his parents to tell him it was bedtime.

They were seven years old and playing in the surf that August afternoon, letting the waves crash into their thin bodies while they stood their ground. Up on the shore, his mother was alone with Jack's father, who seemed to be consoling her, his hand upon her shoulder. A pair of gulls circled overheard in the bright blue sky. The boys were laughing, having fun, daring the sea to defeat them. They went in deeper.

Jack Peter wiped spray from his mouth. "Won't this be funner when we can bring your baby brother?"

A swell buoyed against Nick's chest, so he jumped and landed on his toes in the soft sand. "Baby's dead," he yelled. "My mother lost the baby." He had not said so aloud to anyone, and only in so saying did it become real. He wanted to get out, leave right now, and be away from Jack Peter and everyone, so he would not cry.

"What kind of a stupid loses a baby that's not even born?" The question angered Nick, and his mother was not stupid, Jack Peter was. Stupid, stupid. When the next wave curled over and threatened to swamp them, Nick took a deep breath and pulled him under, dragging him to the bottom. The dark water rolled over them and churned the sand and shells against their skin, and the ocean tossed them like rag dolls, but Nick dug in his feet in the grit and pressed his hand against the boy's chest with all the strength he could muster. In the green murk, he opened his eyes and saw Jack Peter staring back at him, playing some private game, blank and untroubled, ready to stay down. Nick wanted to hurt him for saying that about his mother. He wanted to make him go away and bring back his mother's lost child, and so Nick held him there until they both began to thrash for breath and the adults came rushing into the waves to search for their missing sons.

iii.

He had trouble figuring out how to fit the bones together.

Skeletons were hard enough to draw, but in his mind, all the bones were jumbled in a pile of pickup sticks. Long legs, shorter arms, the connect-the-dots of the vertebrae. The fingers and toes were puzzle pieces that could be made to fit together only just so. Even the skull had come apart, the lower jaw separated from the face, and some of the tiny teeth gone missing. He took a long time to lay out the skeleton, but Jack Peter wasn't bothered, he had all day to move the bones from his mind to the picture he had to draw. The pencil fit precisely in his hand, and the sketch paper was clean and white as a bedsheet. He ran his palm against the smooth blank surface, pleased at how it felt against his skin.

When the package was presented to him off the Christmas mound and he tore the wrapping paper, he was both surprised and dismayed. Surprised by the sheer variety of the Young Artist's Gift Set, the watercolors and the assorted colored pencils and the sharpener and eraser and the formal elegance of the sketch pad, but dismayed by what to do with it, for he had been drawing forever with pencil stubs on scraps and bits of found paper, and his pictures had always done what he desired.

"But I can already draw," he told his parents.

"Of course you *can*," said his mother. "This isn't going to teach you to draw any better, but having the right tools is essential to any artist. Just imagine what you can do."

All through the morning, he waited to try out the new pencils and paper, waited while his parents opened their presents to each other, waited to whittle away the remains from his mountain of gifts. They took their time, since it was just the three of them, and fussed over each new package. He waited through their coffee and the big brunch of bacon and Daddy's special flapjacks, "stacked as high as an elephant's eye." He waited through the obligatory phone call to his grandparents, the long-distance thank-you for the sweater and hope you have a Merry good Christmas. By noon, there were no more festivities planned.

In his easy chair, Daddy would soon fall asleep. The bandages had come off, but the three slashes across his neck were still pink and vicious. His mother sat across from him, playing with her new tablet, the glow from the screen shining on her face.

"There's plenty online," she said, "but it's a mile wide and an inch deep. Here's a whole database with shipwrecks off the coast from as far back as 1710."

Her husband opened his eyes briefly and nodded.

"But where's the *Porthleven?*" she asked, and the question lingered in the air. From time to time, she mentioned another discovery, lost for a while in the Cornish village for which the ship had been named, but the news drew no response.

"It's here," his mother said to no one in particular. "Records of the *Porthleven* at the Maine Maritime Museum over in Bath." She dug deeper into the digital archives, while stealing glances at the Christmas tree and the fire dancing in the fireplace. His father lounged around in his robe and slippers, spending a great deal of energy doing nothing.

By one o'clock, Jack Peter abandoned the concept of family time. Alone at the kitchen table, he wore his new sweater, the red and blue of the Union Jack, his favorite flag, and he had on a pair of those thick woolen socks that had been balled up in the toe of his Christmas stocking. From the corner of his mouth, a peppermint candy cane hung like a cigarette. He had already tried out the high-powered binoculars he had begged for, and had been searching the rocks and the ocean, though he did not tell his parents what he saw through the lenses, because they wouldn't believe him. They never believed him.

The bones had been dancing around in his imagination since the night before Christmas. Where such persistent images came from, he did not know. Sometimes the image appeared quite suddenly, and he was compelled to put it to paper as quickly as he could. Other times he drew things simply because he wanted to make them, and those were the pictures he controlled. But lately, they had come unbidden. The skeleton was one such mystery, and he was dying to get it down. He spent the next hour at the kitchen table carefully drawing all of the bones from memory. Nobody bothered him the whole time.

Jack Peter drew the bones, starting with the ones closest to the surface. He could render in detail the forearm sticking up from the hole in the sand, but the buried ones were much more difficult to see and harder to render. The candy cane in the corner of his mouth thinned to a sliver. He finished by drawing a few waves in the distance, with one grinning head poked above the foam, a little joke that only he would ever get.

The paper curled slightly along the edges, the drawing smeared where he had laid an oily fist to steady it, but when he looked down upon his work, he was well pleased. Rolling it into a scroll, he carried the page to his room and spread it out upon the bed so that he could compare what he had created with the scene outside his window. A conspiracy of ravens gathered on the storm fence that ran along the path to the sea. A stray gull, far north for this time of year, had spotted the bones and was laughing on the dune. High tide rolling in had swept clean any footprints on the beach, but the big hole in the sand remained.

Back and forth he went between his drawing and the landscape, comparing the differences in detail. Lost in the process, he did not hear his mother come in. From the doorway, she watched her son, first his reflection in the mirror, framed by the sea, and then the real boy at the window. Distracted by the optical illusion of two boys, she failed to notice both his drawing and the scene on the shore below. He was surprised to see her and wondered how long she had been there.

"What have you been up to, Jack? We miss you downstairs. Hardly seems Christmas with you locked away."

"I was drawing," he said. "With my new paper and pencils."

"All day? You must really like them, I'm glad."

"All day."

She stepped into the room and struck a casual pose by leaning against the edge of his desk. Careful not to look at him directly, she stared instead at the toys on the bookcase. He tracked her movements warily, wondering why she had come. These days she seemed frightened to enter his room or wake him in the mornings, and she only came in when he wasn't there, to tidy up or put away his clean clothes in the dresser.

"Can I ask you a question, Jack? I don't want to scare you, but do you know anything about the strange things that have been happening around here?"

"You don't scare me."

"I'm glad about that." She laughed. "But, seriously, have you seen anything unusual?"

Twisting his arms over his head, he tried to escape her question.

She took a few steps closer to him and bent down to see his face. "Or voices in the night. Do you ever hear voices out there, in the ocean, like someone calling for help?"

He looked at her as if she had gone crazy.

"What about the other day when your father left you and Nick alone in the house?"

"We were good. We didn't mean to make a mess."

His mother sat on the window seat, her face halved in the afternoon light. She had approached him cautiously, and he felt bad again for having hit her, but it was an accident. One minute she was across the room, and the next, she could have held him in her lap. "Have you ever seen that thing your father was chasing?"

"The monster." He held up his fingers curled into giant claws.

She laughed again. "Mr. Weller thinks it might be a coyote or a dog run wild."

"A dog with a bone."

"There's something out there," she said. "I just don't know what."

Out there. Jack looked through the glass. The sun shone in a cloudless sky, and he could see the dry grass and bare beach rosebushes move in the breeze. His father had followed the thing across the rocks and then disappeared. You could be so easily lost, over the horizon, into the sea. One minute here, one minute gone. Nothing certain.

"Sometimes I see things," he told his mother. "And then they go away. But I have never seen anything in here. Not even a mouse."

" 'Not a creature was stirring,' " she said. " 'Not even a mouse.' "

He remembered how she used to read "The Night Before Christmas" to him each year. Sitting in her lap, he had learned to memorize it and then read it himself. His mother taught him to read, taught him how to write. She wrapped her hand around his, around the pencil, and together they made the lines, the circle O and the combed E and the wavy W. Spelling was hard to remember, and even now he was not the best of writers, but he could draw.

He smiled at her. "Safer in here."

She did not answer him but went far away in her thoughts. Her silence unnerved him, and he drummed his fingers on the windowsill until the noise reached her. Waking from her reverie, she smiled at him and laid her hand over his beating fingers. "So, what have you been drawing? Show me your latest masterpiece."

With a grand flourish, he gave her the binoculars and told her to look toward the rocks on the left. She soon found the hole on the beach and a strange white sticklike object raised in the sand next to it.

"What's that?" she asked.

He unrolled his drawing and spread the paper along the width of the windowsill. Her hand flew up to cover her mouth. Her eyes darted from the bones on the paper to the rocks and sea.

"Like an arm," she whispered, and then she was at the door, calling loudly for Tim to please come upstairs right away.

iv.

The red and blue lights from the police car beat against the windows and the side of the house, the reflection pulsating into the sky. Tim wondered whether the young policeman behind the wheel had left on the lights for show, some excitement in a sleepy tourist town on a peaceful Christmas Day. The few neighbors would no doubt speculate about the presence of the cruiser in the driveway, but he did not know the protocol for the flashing lights. Perhaps he could just ask him to shut them off, but he wasn't even sure that calling the police was the right move in such a situation. Holly had insisted that he do something about the bone in the hole on the beach. She had freaked out when she saw it from Jip's bedroom window, waking him from a nap in the easy chair to come upstairs and see.

Just a pup, the county trooper appeared barely older than their son. He stepped from the car stiffly and put on his hat as though this was some traffic citation. Tim and Holly had been awaiting his arrival, and they nearly leapt from the house to greet him.

"You the folks with the bones?" He had the singsong rhythm of a native.

"The Keenans," Tim said. "It's just one bone."

"What happened to you?" He lifted his chin. "That's quite a gash there on your neck. Cut yourself shaving?"

Tim laughed and gently touched the raw skin on his throat. "As a matter of fact, I did, but this happened later. I was out the other day on the rocks and must have slipped and hit my head. Some kind of animal must have gotten at me while I was unconscious."

The policeman leaned in and inspected Tim's neck. He held up three fingers and made a slashing motion. "Looks like they were made by fingernails. Human. And mad."

"The crime scene is around back," Tim said.

"Let's have a look-see." He stepped aside so that Tim and Holly could lead the way on the path between the dunes. The ravens perched on the snow fence took off, cawing madly over the disturbance.

As she looked back to the policeman, Holly noticed his name tag pinned to the breast of his jacket. "Is that your name? Officer Pollock? Bet you get joshed about that all the time, around here. What with all the fish."

"No, ma'am. First time."

At the crest of the hill, they could see the hole in the sand above the high-tide mark, and they hurried down to take a closer look. Five feet long and four feet deep at its lowest point, it was empty save for a shallow pool of water resting at the very bottom. A slab of rock on the northern side cast a shadow into the crater. On the seaward side, most of the sand had been piled, and signs of disturbance ringed its perimeter. Although there were no footprints, indentations in several spots showed that whatever had been digging had shifted positions to get a better angle and go deeper. The wind had blown some of the piled sand toward the ocean, exposing a single bone, weatherworn as driftwood. Midway along its length, the bone twisted slightly and ended in a notch designed to fit the head of another bone. Tim had seen this type of bone before on an X-ray. In high school, he had broken his right arm playing football, a compound fracture of the radius. They all bent down and looked at the surface as bleached as a cloud.

"It's an arm," Tim said. "A human arm."

"Could be," Pollock said. He pulled it from the pile and the sand spilled into the space where the bone had been. "Smallish, but human most likely. A child, perhaps a small adult."

"Where did it come from?" Holly asked. "How did it get here?"

"Can't say. Could've washed up ashore. You would never believe what the ocean coughs up. Found a foot once, still inside a boot. Could've been here a long time. Looks old. And got dug up by whatever was here last night."

Holly shuddered and wrapped her coat more tightly around her shoulders. "What was here last night?"

With a grunt, the policeman stood and tapped the arm bone against his thigh like a riding crop. "Probably smelt it or could tell there was a buried bone. There's been a big white dog running loose around these parts. Dogs can smell bones a mile away. Even ancient ones. Seen any other holes? Any other bones lying around?"

Tim frowned at him. "Shouldn't you be treating this more like a crime scene? Isn't that kind of evidence of foul play?"

They could read the reflection in his sunglasses as Pollock held up the bone to the sunlight and inspected it closely. "This arm has been detached from a living thing for a long, long time."

"How long?" Holly asked. "Can you tell how old a bone is?"

Brightening to her question, he turned to her and away from Tim. "Look at these striations here, the way the knob is worn as an old croquet ball. Course I can't tell simply by eyeballing it, but I'd say that bone has been here for years, decades even. What I can do is send it off to the crime lab in Augusta—they might be able to say for certainty."

"That's it?" Tim asked. "You don't want to investigate? Call in the CSI?"

Pollock jammed the bone back into the sand pile. "I could, if you insist. We could run some tape around this hole and call the state police, but they might want to bring in a backhoe, chew up this whole waterfront. This being Christmas Day, I'd be loath to disturb those boys. Ruin the rest of your holiday, all for an old bone. But if you insist, Mr. Keenan, I could radio in. Or I could write up my report, send this upstate, and, turns out I'm wrong, we can always come back. Bring a big crew. If there's more bones, likely they're not moving out on their own."

Slipping her hand under Tim's arm, Holly pulled herself closer. "It is Christmas."

"Could you at least see if there are any other bones in the hole?"

His leather holster rubbed and squeaked as Pollock hopped down into the hole. He looked like a gravedigger halfway done with the job, chest deep in the earth. When he bent to investigate the bottom, he was swallowed whole. "The sand's packed solid here. You can see the marks from whatever made this. Sure no shovel."

"Any signs of other bones?" Tim shouted from the edge as though speaking to a man in a deep well.

Pollock popped up and brushed the sand from his jacket. Laying the bone on the edge, he waited for Tim to offer a hand and then climbed back to the top. "There's no one else down there."

"What'll we do about the hole?" Tim asked.

"Get yourself a couple of shovels, and you could fill it in no time. You wouldn't want someone to stumble into it and hurt himself. Maybe you and the boy could do the job." With his thumb, he pointed to the second-story window. Jip had been watching their every move.

"Not going to happen," Holly said. "He doesn't ever leave the house."

"Never?"

Tim answered quickly. "Agoraphobia. He's afraid of the outside."

"It's not a phobia," Holly said. "It's not like he's just afraid of the dark or scared of heights. It's all part of his illness, a condition of the mind. He's much worse than that."

Her words hung in the air like an executioner's verdict. Pollock reached for the bone at his feet, and in the distance one of the ravens on the beach screeched at a thief. Wrapping his coat more tightly, Tim shivered and pondered their life together. He wished she would not be so free with her opinions in public and be so adamant in her analysis. Jip was getting better day by day. Once upon a time, he would have no more stayed in the light of the window than venture onto the beach. But he was up there now, watching them from on high.

"Would you like to meet him?" Holly asked. "Our son, Jack. He doesn't get many visitors, as you might imagine, and I'm not sure he's ever met a real live policeman. He would be thrilled."

Tim put his hand on the trooper's shoulder. "Come inside and warm up a little before you go on your way. There's a pot of coffee on, and nobody can resist my wife's Christmas cookies."

"I'll make you a hot chocolate," Holly said. "You seem more of a cocoa kind of guy. Oh, it will be all right. You're worried about missing a crime. Nothing ever happens on Christmas, especially around here, and you won't be missed. We'll never tell." She hooked her arm in the crook of his and had him lead her to the house.

Inside, they made another fire in the fireplace and warmed the milk on the stove, fussing over the policeman like a prodigal son. Their own Jack Peter lingered in the stairwell, listening to their conversation from the shadows while the adults gathered round the kitchen table. Tim held his chin in one hand and stared at the bone, now wrapped in an old kitchen towel. Steam from the mugs curled and vanished.

"I've got another mystery for you," she said. "Last night after Mass, I was driving home, and the fog was so thick I thought I'd never make it. In fact, I had to stop, and this was about one, one thirty a.m., and it was the most curious thing. First some kind of creature crossed the road ahead of me, not near enough for me to make out what it was but near enough to be something. And Tim has been seeing things in the shadows, and we were wondering if the police have come across an unusual amount of weirdness lately."

Pollock brushed cookie crumbs from the corners of his lips. "Can't say that there's been anything unusual. Same amount of weirdness."

"Thing is," Holly went on, "I heard voices, too. People in trouble. Or fighting, screaming out in the dark. And I was wondering if the police took any calls last night, if you can tell me, for a domestic disturbance."

"Last night? No. Quietest Christmas in ages."

Tim sat up straight and addressed him pointedly. "Could it be something else? The noises. Some creature in the fog."

"Round here, nothing would surprise me. We have a pair of foxes behind the house. I don't hear them so much, but my parents do. Sound like hell, my dad says, when they're out there mating."

"Could it be coyotes?" Tim asked. "Friend of mine says coyotes have been seen around town. Right on the beach."

Pollock shifted his gaze around the room as if to ensure that no one was eavesdropping. "My guess is that you've been troubled by that big white dog running wild around here. Probably the same fella that dug up your beach. I'd be careful around dark."

Quiet as a ghost, Jip materialized in the kitchen. He must have slid across the wooden floors in his thick woolen socks to have arrived without a sound, without a twitch. His features were set still on his face, as though he had been listening for a while, and when Pollock met his glance, Jip gave no sign of distress or displeasure, not even a blink of the eyes. His mother rose to usher him over to the policeman. "How long have you been there, quiet as the morning?"

"Officer Pollock," Tim said, "this is Jack Peter. J.P. I call him Jip. Jip, this is the policeman they sent."

Pollock extended his hand, but Jip stood a safe distance from the stranger. They considered each other like two gunslingers, and the stand-off ended when Jip noticed the holstered gun at his hip.

"Are you a real policeman?"

"Sure am. Past two years, least."

"Is that a real gun?"

Pollock rested his hand on the butt of his pistol. "Sure is."

"Do you ever shoot anyone?"

"Only if I had to, as a last resort."

"What about a German soldier or pirates or monsters? What if they were trying to kill you, could you shoot them so they would stop?"

Tapping her nails on the table, Holly drew their attention. "That's enough about that, Jack. Did you see his police car parked in the driveway?"

He nodded but did not take his eyes off the pistol.

"Did you see the lights, Jack?"

"There's a pattern," he said. "My sweater is red and blue."

"Red and blue so people notice when you're driving up behind them. Same idea with the siren."

"You ever see a dead body?" Jip asked.

The policeman stood and paced the floor by the back window, facing the ocean. "I have to confess, I never have."

"I saw my friend Nick when he was dead."

Tim interrupted. "He wasn't really dead, Jip. Just unconscious." He turned to the policeman. "When they were seven, Jip and his friend Nick nearly drowned one day. We had to pull them out of the ocean, give them mouth-to-mouth."

"I drew Nick."

Holly gestured toward the picture hanging on the fridge. "That's Nick right there. On the door."

His father stood, prepared to reach out to his son. "Yes, Jip, you drew him. Right, we see. But there's no need to make a big deal out of it."

"But the bones," Jip said.

The policeman took the package from the table and peeled back the towel. "It's an old bone. Washed up on the shore."

"I drew bones." The boy raised his voice.

Holly rose from her chair and insinuated herself between the child and the policeman. "He drew a picture of bones. We bought him an art set for Christmas. From Sharon's. Superdeluxe. Pencils and markers and a giant sketch pad. He's been drawing things. You saw his picture of Nick on the refrigerator. Jack, why don't you get the drawing you were working on today? You can show Officer Pollock."

His stocking feet spun on the wooden floor like a cartoon character's until he found traction and raced upstairs.

Once her son was out of earshot, Holly said, "Look, he gets stuck in his head sometimes, and he needs a way out, so that's why we're urging the drawing. For when he is nonverbal."

After a sip of cocoa, the policeman had a light milky mustache above his lip. His face reddened against his navy shirt.

The boy returned, laid the scroll upon the table, and backed away three steps. With a soft scraping sound, the paper uncurled to reveal the pile of human bones, a whole skeleton mixed in a hole.

"That's quite remarkable," said Pollock. "Did you copy that picture from a book?"

"I did it," Jip shouted. "The bones, the hole."

"Easy there, sport," Tim said.

Frustration bubbled in the boy. He rocked and swayed where he stood, hands clenched, and under his breath, he muttered, "Murder." Nobody else had noticed that Officer Pollock was now squeezing into his jacket and reaching for his hat.

"I've stayed too long, and you seem to have a situation on your hands. Best I leave."

"Oh, no," Holly said. "You haven't finished your cocoa."

"Thanks all the same, but I'm really on duty. Sorry to have upset anyone. You going to be okay there, Jip?"

The boy had turned toward the living room and the bright light from the fireplace, and he did not answer.

Tim and Holly walked the trooper to the door. "Thank you for coming," said Tim. "And sorry for the situation. He gets upset sometimes when he can't make himself understood."

"Or when he thinks you don't believe him," Holly said.

The policeman looked back at the boy framed now by the fireplace. He waved the bone at him playfully. "I'll get this up to Augusta and we should hear soon. But dollars to doughnuts, it's old as can be. Remember to fill in that hole, Mr. Keenan, before someone falls in and gets hurt. I'll turn on the cherry top when I leave. For the boy."

At the door, they wished him a merry Christmas. Arm in arm, they went to the window to watch him get into his car and turn on the red and blue strobe, beating like the waves. As the black-and-white cruiser left the driveway, Holly turned toward her son to make sure that he was not missing the display. Jack was at the fireplace, carefully feeding strips of paper into the fire, his beautiful picture, bone by bone, turning to ashes, bits of blackness escaping from the hearth, rising up and out into the bare sky, the very opposite of snow.

v.

She could not sleep. In the dead of night, Holly prowled like a ghost through the dream house. Earlier that afternoon, while the turkey was in the oven and the potatoes boiling away, she had spent hours on the Internet, chasing link after link, the search engines churning up all kinds of doings in their algorithms. Bodies in water decompose quickly, depending upon the temperature and the depth, but bones are a bit more resistant to decay. In the right circumstances, bones can last for centuries. She saw pictures of a skull from a shipwreck off the coast of Texas in 1686, and the Neolithic skeletons of a mother and child found in the Mediterranean Sea near Israel. In due course, she considered herself an expert on what happens to those who drown, but at some point in the process, the idea occurred that surfing hours online was an inappropriate way to spend a family holiday. Bleary-eyed, she found the boys on the sofa, catching the end of yet another football game.

There had been a scene after the policeman left, a protracted negotiation from discord to blowup to harmony. Tim saw Jack throwing the papers in the fire and lost his temper, shouting at their son to stop. Despite his father's warnings, Jack kept ripping strips of paper and tossing them into the flames, until the last of the evidence vanished.

"What's gotten into you?" Tim asked. "Get away from that fire. You could burn yourself."

The tears started flowing.

"Jip, that's enough. You know better than playing with fire. And why would you burn up your drawing?"

Holly rose to intervene, but it was too late.

"What is wrong with you?" Tim shouted. "You've been misbehaving for weeks. First, your mother. And then you leave the windows open, and how could you be so rude when we had company? He turned his police lights on for you and everything."

Holly could see her son's face reflected in the glass door of the fireplace, a pale replica of the boy that appeared to be consumed by fire. He quaked on the spot, threatening tears again. "Go easy," she said.

"I will not go easy." Tim turned from her to their son. The red scabs on his neck had opened and thin lines of watery blood oozed from the cracks. "I would like some answers, young man. You have to talk to people when they talk to you. Otherwise they will not want to turn on their siren for you or talk to you about being a policeman or even want to come into the house. Do you understand? Is that what you want?"

"No," he said. Simply and slowly, revealing none of the emotions she knew swirled within him. Holly was shocked that her son replied at all, that he had summoned the courage rather than retreat into the safety of his mind.

"If that's the case, Jip. If that's the case, then you need to make more of an effort. If you want people to be nice to you, you have to be nice to them. Or at least pretend. You can't just say nothing."

He had nothing to say, but simply bent away from his father's approach.

"And why would you rip up your drawing and burn it in the fire? You worked so hard all day long."

The boy blinked and said nothing.

"I used to think I could at least rely on you to talk to me."

Tim grabbed Jack's arm and shook him once, not hard, but startling in its suddenness. She watched her son's eyes, saw how he vanished into his impenetrable depths. His left arm jerked out of his father's grasp and then straight up as if pulled on a string, and then he reached around with his right hand to grab it by the elbow to keep the arm from flying away. His face reddened and his head swayed from side to side under the branches of his arms. Chirps escaped from his lips, birdsong with no melody. Holly stood by, paralyzed by indecision. No matter how many times she had seen him this way, she felt powerless. A bad mother. Tim, however, tried to reach through the barrier their son had constructed. "Jip, Jip, stay with me, boy. It's Daddy, and everything's okay. We don't have to talk about the pictures."

But the moment for rescue had passed. Nothing to be done but observe, to make sure he did no harm to himself or to anyone else. Three years ago, when the fits first began and they had no way to predict what might happen, he got loose from them on the way through the front door and bashed into the ceramic umbrella stand, sending it to the floor and breaking it into a dozen pieces. Jack had stepped on a shard in his bare feet and cut his heel deeply, the gash bright as a red smile pumping blood. Holly did not know which was worse, the accident itself or trying to get their hysterical child out of the house and to the emergency room. And it was just as bad on the way home, the stitches and bandages, the howling assault against the world passing just beyond the thin glass window. By hard experience, they knew now to leave him be until the episode played out. He would tire eventually.

Tim sat on the bottom step of the staircase, and Holly posted herself on a kitchen stool. They pretended not to notice him, for often he responded more quickly if he thought he was being ignored. She stole glances with her husband, trying to convey with the stoniness of her features her dissatisfaction with his direct and clumsy approach. The chirping stopped abruptly, and Jack unlocked the pretzel of his arms. Expression returned slowly to his eyes like tinder catching flame, and as suddenly as he had departed behind the veil, Jack returned. He blinked and then smiled at his mother. When he asked if he could run upstairs and work on his drawings, she let him go with a sigh.

The rest of their Christmas was quiet and uneventful. A turkey dinner with the trimmings. A video chat over the Web with her faraway sister. A long complicated board game for three before Jack was sent to bed for the night. He was asleep within ten minutes, as guiltless as a newborn, snug in his blankets. Tim turned in an hour later and was lightly snoring beside his lit reading lamp. Holly slipped in beside him as the clock struck eleven, but she could not let go of the day so easily.

When she could no longer bear the insomnia, she left Tim in the bed and wandered down the hall. The door to her son's room was closed as she had left it, but she could not resist turning the knob carefully and opening the door, with a whisper from the hinges. His room was chilly, and through the window even the moon and stars looked cold. In the pale light, she saw the scattered papers and pencils on his desk, a sign that he had been busy working on some new project. She resisted the temptation to steal a look and resolved instead to ask about his drawings in the morning.

She floated downstairs, moving from room to room with no real purpose other than to defeat her restlessness. The Internet beckoned. She had a theory about the bones and the wreck of the *Porthleven*, but the thought of investigating more leads online just depressed her. She touched the glass tablet, which was smooth as ice.

Bones, she thought, who collects the bones? A ghoulish task. Who came to retrieve the drowned, how did they recover those shipwrecked corpses washed ashore? Near her head, the window rattled long and hard as though something was trying to force its way inside the house, and in the rooms above, someone had awoken and was moving the furniture.

He could not sleep. In the dead of night, Tim opened his eyes and realized he was alone in the bed. His wife was gone, sleepless too, no doubt. Lately Holly had been uneasy and agitated, seeing and hearing things, strange things that were not there, but then who was he to judge? Not with that pale wild man running naked over hill and dale, or was it just a chimera, a conflation of a white dog and his own frazzled nerves? Turning over in the bed, he flipped his pillow to the cool side, trying to go back to sleep. Useless.

Huffing, he threw off the covers and swung his legs over the edge to sit up in the bed. The room was gloomier without her in it. As a boy he could not bear to stay alone in a darkened space. Where had she gone, what was she chasing now? He walked across the creaky floorboards and threw on his robe. Just past midnight, the alarm clock said. Another Christmas come and gone. That Weller boy would be over in the morning, just hours away, their houseguest for the next week. He envied Fred and Nell, ditching the kid and heading for warmer climes, a week at sea away from the wintery murk of Maine. He imagined them promenading on the deck, Fred in a tuxedo and Nell in an evening dress, and then at once he laughed at the absurdity of his vision, the notion that people today traveled like they were Astaire and Rogers in some black-and-white 1930s film, when in reality it was probably polo shirts and khaki shorts, or maybe a charming little sundress, her peach one that gives the impression that she is wearing nothing at all. He banished her from his thoughts.

As soon as he stepped into the hall, Tim could tell where Holly had been. The door to their son's room was ajar, so he traced her steps and pushed it open with his toes just enough so that he, too, could spy on Jip asleep. A crack of light zigzagged across the boy's face, giving it a gentle and peaceful aspect, a marked contrast to the sullen child hours ago who could not be contained. Why did he push his son so hard? Why did Jip have to go so far away sometimes? Love from a distance was so much more difficult when it is your own child. And Tim loved Jip with a depth that amazed him in such quiet moments. Still, he cursed the doctors and the therapists, wishing for a thousandth time to have a different boy.

Perhaps Holly was right, perhaps their son wasn't ever going to be normal. Surely they had more difficulty recently in forcing him to comply with their wishes. Jip had deliberately torn apart that drawing long after he had been told to stop, and he persisted despite their warnings. They would have to work harder with Jip, Tim thought, at listening and obeying. Go easy, Holly had said, but that was just the problem. They had been too easy on the boy, coddling him, when he's smart enough to understand the moral consequences of his actions, right from wrong. He'd talk with Dr. Wilson next time. He'd find a way to get Jip to obey more readily once it becomes clear that he has no choice. They would work harder on achieving some equilibrium.

How much easier it had been in the beginning, before they knew the facts about Jip. He came into the dream house as an answer to their long-held prayers for a child. After years of trial and failure, the miracle pregnancy, and nine months later the baby was born, pure and simple, a baby who did baby things. Who would know, without any experience in raising a child, what to expect at each stage of development? They took his affect as normal, his long naps were a blessing. *Aren't you lucky*, Fred Weller had said, *to have one that sleeps through the night?* The baby's sudden disinterest in play or food was chalked up to boredom. Only when periods of withdrawal grew more frequent and alarming did they begin to suspect. They made countless trips to the doctor, but they resisted nearly every diagnosis. *On the spectrum*, one had said. *Asperger's*, said the next one. But he refused to believe it for the longest time, and even now, he pressed against the cold hard language every chance he could. Words, words, but no real explanation, no cure. An *abnormality*—one quack had actually used that word. As if that was a reasonable way to talk about a human being or to discuss the future of a child with his parents. Tim looked at his son, sleeping like a baby, and wished he could buy back those days and hold him in his arms again, unaware of the darkness ahead. Bring me back my baby, my little boy.

When he closed the door, the knob clicked softly. He listened to whether he had awakened his son by accident, but heard instead his wife moving through the rooms downstairs, furtive as a mouse. Sneaking around lately, holding secrets, off to church for the first time in years, a signal of her deeper unrest.

"I just miss it," she said, when the prospect of midnight Mass had been broached. "Not so much for the religion but for the ceremony, the ritual, the order, and certainty of it."

"Go then," he had said. "I'll stay here with Jip. But I hope this doesn't mean you've gone soft in the head and are interested in all that superstition—"

She kissed him, now that he thought about it, to shut him up.

And then after the service itself, she had come home more upset than ever, with stories about voices filtering out of the sea in the middle of the night. She'd gone off her nut with the stress.

A gust of wind hit the house and rattled the windows. The whole wall seemed to shake. From Jip's room came a scraping sound as if the bed had been pushed across the floor. Downstairs Holly whooped at the noise, an involuntary yell of apprehension. He raced to her quickly and had reached the first floor when the rattling happened again, this time much more violently at the kitchen windows, the wind zeroing in on the spot. Then two thumps, one right after the other, striking against the glass. Holly found him in the dim light, and she latched onto the sleeves of his robe.

"Did you hear that?" she asked. "There's someone trying to get in."

"No, it's the wind."

As if on cue, the glass rattled till it hummed.

"No, Tim, that's someone outside the house trying all the windows. Listen."

The rattling moved, in fact, to the mudroom, the windows shaking one by one, as if the thing outside was testing each as it moved from the back of the house toward the front. The outer door shook briefly, and the doorknob trembled. Tim loosed himself from her grip and went to the front closet and pulled out the brand-new baseball bat he'd bought himself for Christmas for just such emergencies.

"Don't, Tim."

"Be quiet. I just want to be protected if there is someone out there, but I tell you it's the wind."

They crouched together in the dark. A minute passed in silence, and another, and then they breathed more easily. Another five minutes crawled by, and nothing.

"We could turn on a light," Tim said.

"Are you kidding? And have whatever's out there see us in here?"

"There's nothing out there. Gales. A front moving through."

"How could it be the wind? Does the wind turn doorknobs? Does the wind knock on the kitchen windows? Something's trying to get inside, Tim. Inside the house, inside our lives. I hear it all the time."

"Those back windows are twelve feet off the ground. Just listen, you can still hear the wind in the distance. It's just moving off. A squall."

"It's not the first time," she said. "It has been going on for weeks. Weird noises around the house, things that go bump in the night."

He held out his arms and she nestled into him, feeling a light clunk from the baseball bat as he embraced her. "You're overwrought. It's about Jip, isn't it? I know he's been a handful lately, but I've got a plan. A New Year's resolution to work harder with him."

She sighed and buried herself deeper in his arms. They stood together in the middle of the room anticipating another sound, but the only noises were the wind whistling and blowing in the distance and the creaks and ticks of the old house.

"You're tired," he said. "Been doing too much for the rest of us."

"I am tired, but my mind won't shut off."

He laid the baseball bat on the sofa. "We'll get you a sleeping pill."

"Perchance to dream."

He put his arm around her hips and led her to the bottom of the stairs. Shrouded in darkness at the top of the stairwell, Jip stood looking down upon them.

"Jesus," she said. "You gave me a fright. How long have you been up there?"

"J.P., what are you doing out of bed?" Tim turned on the light, and the three of them blinked and shielded their eyes from the sudden illumination.

"I had a dream," he said, rubbing his eye. "There was a monster under my bed."

They walked up to him, pausing a few steps below, so that they could see him face-to-face.

"Too much turkey and apple pie," his father said. "Gives you bad dreams. It was just the wind you heard. Shook things up. No monsters, remember?"

"It was a nightmare," his mother said. "Everything will look better in the morning light." He stepped toward her and opened his arms. She touched him lightly on the arm and then brushed the hair from his eyes, and he was her little boy again.

vi.

His old-fashioned suitcase looked like a small coffin, or so Nick thought in the midst of his overwhelming anxiety that morning after Christmas. His parents were rushing around the house, preparing to go on their grand holiday cruise without him, leaving him instead with the Keenans for the rest of the week. He dreaded the whole idea the way he dreaded the last day of summer and the prospect of school, or the semi-annual torture in the dentist's chair, the wet kiss from Nana when she came to visit. He dreaded it the way he hated tuna noodle casserole and rope climbing in gym class and cleaning out his room. Dread sat like a troll on his stomach the whole time he had to wait for his parents. They had planned the trip months ago, but even now were wondering where was the hair dryer—no, the travel-size one—and did you remember to pack sandals? He sat on the sofa in his coat and hat, his suitcase at his feet, but he was not surprised to hear his father and his mother ask, independently, if he was all set and ready to go. I'll never be ready, he thought, but I'll go.

Strapped in the backseat of the car, Nick the prisoner was being driven to his place of execution. The early hour and overcast skies combined to extend the gloom of the night, and in the windows of the car, he could make out his reflection superimposed over a scattershot of frost. His glum face peppered white. In the front seat, his parents were discussing still what they might have left behind, and he secretly wished they had forgotten about him, like that *Home Alone* kid, to live by his wits. He could picture himself fighting the bad guys, outsmarting anyone who tried to break in.

The drive to the Keenans was much too short, and when they pulled up to the house, Nick realized that he just could not bear the idea of a week with Jack Peter, that he had changed his mind and would visit his grandparents in Florida after all, or if that was out of the question, would they consider smuggling him aboard the ship? He had always wanted to see the Caribbean and play the pirate, *savvy?*, but it was all too late. His father had killed the engine. His mother had already left the car and was jabbing the doorbell.

Mrs. Keenan answered the door in her robe, and Nick had the uneasy feeling that they had awakened the whole house with their early arrival. Tangled against one side of her head, her hair was unbrushed, and she still had a line from the pillowcase creasing one cheek. When she bent over to pick up the morning newspaper on the stoop, her robe and nightgown gaped open, exposing her naked breasts, heavy and full, with brown nipples at the curve, and he felt both a surge of strange excitement and awful embarrassment in a single instant. She did not seem to notice either the momentary exposure or his dumb amazement, and she waved them all in and clutched at her collar against the chill. Nick was not sure if his father, trailing behind him, had caught the same peep show, but if he had he kept the matter to himself.

Mr. Keenan was nowhere to be seen, and Nick wondered if he had forgotten and was still asleep. Jack Peter, of course, was up and dressed, a ball of excitement and anticipation. Without being asked, he took Nick's suitcase and propped it against the banister, and he bounced around aimlessly, waiting for the adults to finish their business so that the fun might begin.

"I hope we didn't wake you," Nick's mother said. "It wouldn't be so early, but it's all so complicated. We've got to be in the airport an hour ahead, just to make it through security, though I don't expect we'll see too many people the day after Christmas. And then we have a connecting flight in Atlanta, of all places. You can't get theah from heah. And we have to make that, or we miss our boarding time. I'll be glad when it'll be over."

"We've been up for hours," Mrs. Keenan said. "Coffee?"

His father winked at her. "Only if it's already on. We can't stay too long. Time waits for no man, and neither does our airplane."

"Won't be a sec." She headed off to the kitchen, and Nick was inclined to follow her, but he stayed put. Mr. Keenan came lurching down the stairs, alert to the guests in his house, his hair mussed from bed and a shadow of whiskers on his cheeks. He waved to the Wellers but saved his real greetings for Nick.

"Nicholas, moving in with us, I see." He bowed formally like a butler in a comedy of manners. Not knowing what was expected, Nick returned with a bow of his own, and not to be left out, Jack Peter bowed as well, as stiff and angular as a T square.

Mr. Keenan asked, "You have come about the bones, *Herr Veller?*" They played these games all the time with Nick. Mr. Keenan acting like a clown, nearly desperate to make him feel welcome.

"*Ja.*" Nick answered, taking up his part. "I have come to see about *ze skeleton.*"

Nick's father wanted in on the fun. "What's all this about skeletons and bones?"

Mrs. Weller ignored her husband and said, "Tim, you're looking better. Your throat." She raised her fingers to her neck, and Mr. Keenan copied her gesture.

Nick turned to Jack Peter to see if her remark had registered, but the kid had his usual blank expression and he seemed to be caught in a game involving his interlocking fingers.

With her rump, Mrs. Keenan pushed through the door from the kitchen. She carried a tray with a package of store-bought muffins, the coffeepot, cream, sugar, and mugs, and Mr. Keenan sprang to help her. "Oh, you're up. Give me a hand with these things. Nell and Fred only have time for a quick nip."

"A nip and a nibble," Mr. Weller said. "Now what's all this talk about bones? Got a skeleton in the closet?"

"You're right, Fred," said Mr. Keenan. "But not the closet. In a hole on the beach."

"I don't know which is worse. A scandal hiding safely away, or a skeleton out in the open for all to see."

"Didn't you see the police at our place yesterday afternoon?" Mr. Keenan asked. "Quite a show, and the neighbors must think a crime was committed. Dead body in the attic, or a cat burglar swiped the family jewels, but nothing of the sort."

Looking up to the ceiling, Nick imagined a corpse moldering in the rafters. Old man dread roiled again in his curdling stomach, warning him of the pending dangers the moment his parents left him alone with these people.

"Well," Mr. Keenan continued, "we called them out to the house ourselves. There wasn't any murder that we know of. But something dug a big hole on our property, and in it we found a bone."

"A real human bone," Mrs. Keenan said. "Washed up from the sea."

Mr. Keenan seemed anxious to tell the story. "Actually, the arm bone from a child about Nick's age or maybe a little younger, although the police seem to think that the bone itself is fairly old, judging from the erosion. But it is the damndest thing. Something must have dug it up during the night before Christmas, 'cause we saw it in the afternoon. Didn't know what to do."

Jack Peter bounced on the sofa. "I drew a hole—"

"So we called the police, that's why you might have noticed the squad car parked—"

"—full of bones."

"That's enough, Jack," Mrs. Keenan said.

With a sharp bang, Mrs. Weller cracked her empty cup on the coffee table, setting it down too hard, causing everyone to jump in their seats. A rill of nervous laughter flowed from person to person. Embarrassed, she lifted it again and set it down softly on the surface. "So, all that trouble about an old bone?"

"And a hole, big as a grave," Mr. Keenan said. "The police think it might have been dug up by a wild dog running loose. That's your coyote, Fred, a big white dog. We're supposed to fill in the hole so nobody will stumble across it and get hurt. That's what the trooper told us. You should have seen him, Nell. They're making them younger and younger. A baby."

Jack Peter piped up from the sofa. "What happened to baby?"

His mother put her finger to her lips just like a kiss. Jack Peter rocked in place, stifling an impulse, rocked so hard he nearly made Nick ill.

"The hole is still out there," Mr. Keenan said. "C'mon, take a look from the kitchen."

"Just one quick peek," said Mrs. Weller. "And then we have to get going or we'll miss our plane."

Single file they followed Mr. Keenan into the kitchen and marched straight to the window that faced the sea. With the flair of a game show model, he waved his arm to present the scene below.

His audience leaned forward and strained to see what had been promised. Squinting and searching, the Wellers walked up to the glass, and Mrs. Keenan followed, laying her hands on Nick's shoulders from behind. The beach was empty, rocks and sand leading to the sea, a stick of driftwood washed ashore, but nothing else. No hole, no grave, not so much as a small dent in the sand. Mr. Keenan had been watching their faces, and when he saw how puzzled they were, he turned to look out.

"I guess someone must have buried your body," said Mr. Weller.

"Where did it go?" Mrs. Keenan asked. She looked as if she was running through the possibilities in her mind and rejecting every one.

"No," said Mr. Keenan. "I'm telling you it was right there, six feet deep. Holly, you saw it. Jip, you drew a picture of it. And the policeman saw it, wrote a report. Officer Haddock."

"Pollock," said Mrs. Keenan.

But her husband was already halfway out the door. Moments later, he reappeared far below on the shore, a tiny mad toy soldier, coat wrapped over his robe, the cuffs of his pajamas jammed into untied boots. Darting from rock to rock, he searched the beach for the missing hole.

Jack Peter pressed his palms against the windowpanes. "There he goes again."

"He'll catch his death," said Mrs. Keenan, and she peeled off from the group, heading for the mudroom for her coat and boots. Everyone but Jack followed, flying out into the morning wind, shocked by how

cold and empty the world was. They blew around in crazy circles, looking for the nonexistent bones and the missing hole, until the whole bunch
caught up with Mr. Keenan on top of a wet rock at the tideline. The hem
on his robe fluttered like a flag. A fine cold spray coated his hair and
clothing, and his eyes were frantic in their sockets.

"It was here just yesterday," he said. "How could we lose a hole?
You must think I'm crazy, but there's no way it could have just disappeared—"

The others tried to talk Mr. Keenan down from the rock, urging him
to come in from the cold, for the Wellers really have a plane to catch,
and inventing for him a handful of plausible explanations. Nick had
stopped listening to their fairy tales and turned his back on them and
raised his gaze to focus on the boy inside the panoramic window, distant
and indifferent as a god on high.

Four

Imaginary friends often leave without warning. Lying across from him on the other pillow was the head of Nicholas Weller, and Jack Peter wanted to reach out and poke his friend's cheek with his finger, but if that was really Nick, he might just get angry. Then again, even imaginary friends can lose their tempers. Take Red, for instance. He could be as mad as a jar of wasps. Good thing he was dead.

His mother first showed Jack Peter when he was five years old how to make a little boy out of red clay. First you get some dough and roll it into a cigar and then you pinch the bottom and separate it in two for the legs and two again for the arms and leave a bit at the top for the head. Each morning he would take Red out of the cardboard can and unfold his limbs. He put the clay boy on the shelf like a voodoo doll. As long as it was out of the can, the imaginary boy was alive, not Red at all, but a boy same as him, who was just his size and just his age. He would be there all day, someone to talk to, someone to play with, someone to tell his secrets, and Red would tell him things as well. Stories about what he did when Jack Peter was not around. Stories about his parents, about Nick and the other boys and girls, stories about the world beyond the front door. Jack Peter could make the boy, but once made, Red was beyond his control. Red lived his own life apart from their time together, going places Jack Peter could not go, seeing things Jack Peter never saw, thinking things unimaginable to his creator. Most of the time, Jack Peter was simply glad for the company and the chance to learn the secrets Red would tell. But sometimes Red would get mad at him, call him dummy, and threaten to share Jack Peter's thoughts with Mommy and Daddy. And then Jack Peter wished he had never made the boy of clay and was so tired of him that he hoped Red would go away and never come back or maybe a giant could come and flatten him like a pancake.

And then one night, he forgot to put away the clay boy, and the next morning, it was all dried out and the boy crumbled to bits, and Red was dead and never came back anymore. Jack Peter thought he might make another boy, someone to be his friend, but he did not. Instead he went to school in the fall, to morning kindergarten, and the other children were there and if you be nice, they will be nice to you, and then Nick would come over to play sometimes after school or especially in the summertime, and then came first grade and a new class with a lot more children, and then summer again, and nearly dead beneath the waves. Better to stay away from the ocean. Best to stay inside.

Long time ago. Now Nick was here, the real Nick, for a whole week. A few more days and it would all be over. He wanted Nick to stay, but the monsters were already here. It had taken all day for his parents to stop talking about the bones in the hole. He could have told them where the rest of the skeleton went. He would have said *dig deeper*, but now it didn't matter. The paper with the skeleton bones was in the fire.

They had stayed up late, the four of them, with hot cocoa and popcorn and a movie on TV, and over the hours, his parents' worries melted away. His father laughed at some silliness on the show. His mother stopped fretting and was nodding by the fire before she declared universal bedtime and off they all went. The mood, if not festive, had certainly improved from the anxiety of the afternoon. The boys brushed their teeth and put on their pajamas and went to his big warm double bed.

Mommy and Daddy's old bed, first bed, and now his own. They were still awake when the adults finished getting ready and the lights went out all over the house.

In the dark, they whispered to each other.

"Do you miss them?"

Nick drew out a sigh. "My parents? No, I guess I don't. Maybe later, but not now. Parents always think you are going to miss them, but they don't know that sometimes you wish they would just leave you alone."

"I wish my parents would go away," Jack Peter said. "Instead of me."

"You would miss them if they went away for good."

"Like you miss the baby."

Nick did not answer but rolled over to stare at him. How did Jack Peter know he had been thinking about Baby?

Kicking off the comforter, Jack Peter slid out of bed and walked to his desk and turned on the table lamp. The light seemed to scream against the darkness, but he sat quietly and began to draw. He worked quickly and with great purpose.

"What are you doing?" Nick called from the bed. "We'll get in trouble if your parents see the light under the door."

"I need to make something before I forget," Jack Peter said. He dashed off the drawing in minutes and scampered back to bed. In the closeness of the room, they soon fell asleep as if drugged.

At three in the morning, the baby began to cry. The sound came from far below and outside, persistent as a cat yowling on a fence, but Nick heard it clearly enough over the constant ocean. Unholy as a siren, the baby's cries rode the wind and wound their way into the room. Beside him, Jack Peter did not move, even as the clamor drew nearer, and Nick was tempted to wake him or bang on the door to the room where Mr. and Mrs. Keenan slept so they might hear what he heard and come to his rescue. But he did no such thing. He lay in bed beneath the comforter, stiff as a bug on a pin.

The baby did not bawl continuously but would stop and start again, each time louder than before, so that it seemed to be getting closer and closer. Nick pulled up the covers and waited helplessly in the darkness. With his foot, he nudged Jack Peter on his bum, but it was like trying to wake the dead. The body shifted slightly and then rolled back into the soft trough in the mattress. Not that his friend would have been of any use. Despite Jack Peter's presence next to him, Nick felt desperately alone.

A gentle drumming noise made him uneasy, and he squeezed his eyelids tight so he could listen without distraction. He thought it might be the sound of hail or sleet against the side of the house. He could be hallucinating, as his mother had said about the bodies in the closet, conjuring a figment in his imagination, mistaking something quite innocent for something more sinister. Stepping from the bed, he felt the warmth of the braid rug give way to the chill of the wooden floor. The crying had stopped, and he felt it safe to go to the window to investigate, holding his breath as he approached. The shape of a tiny hand swiped across the bottom of the glass. He waited for it again, convinced that his eyes were playing tricks. Impossible. He pressed his nose against a pane, resting his forehead on the sash. No snow was falling that night, and the bright moon shone over the Atlantic, casting faint light across the waves, illuminating the rock faces upon the shore. He could see there was nothing out there, nothing to fear, and for a moment, he wondered if the noises had all been in his head. Just as he was about to turn away from the window, a fleeting motion above his head, no more than a passing change of light, convinced Nick to look out again.

The glass clinked when he forced open the sticky window, and something scratched against the clapboard overhead. Nick stuck his head through the opening and into the dark night. The frosty air smacked him in the face. He had forgotten how high up the second story was from the ground. His vertigo made him feel as if he was going to pitch forward out of the window and plummet into the sand below, but the dizziness gave way to shock at what he saw clinging to the side of the wooden clapboards. Babies, darting away on all fours in jerky bursts and hesitations, a swarm of babies, scuttling on the surface like silverfish across a page. Defying gravity, defying reason. They were familiar but strange, almost alien with their bald round heads, and they paid little heed to him, other than moving away and considering him with odd backward glances from a safe distance. Their bodies were soft and naked, their faces cold and inhuman, their eyes black as holes. One opened its toothless mouth and out came a harsh mechanical cry, and when it screamed, Nick screamed back at it. The thing crawled right for him, and Nick pulled himself in and banged the sash against the windowsill. The sickly pale creature streaked across the glass. Jack Peter was sitting up in the bed, wide-eyed and rapt at what he was witnessing, but he gave no sign of help or comfort. Nick screamed again and ran from the room.

When she heard the window slam and the boy cry out in the middle of the night, Holly was already awake, as though her unconscious mind had anticipated trouble. Her sleep had been fitful for weeks now, and as she opened her eyes, Holly was sure that she had not slept at all that night. And so she was not dreaming of those sounds outside, babies crying far away, or that Nicholas, too, had heard them and was now in a panic. As usual, Tim was comatose, sleeping deeply as ever. He did not revive when she hoisted herself out of bed, and he did not wake when she stepped into the hallway and threw on the light. The poor child was shivering, hunched in a corner.

"Nicholas, what's the matter? Did you have a bad dream?"

Like a rescued cat, he sprang to his feet and leapt into her embrace, putting his arms around her waist and pulling himself so tightly against her body that she could feel his bones pressing her bones. Sense memories rushed into her, the feeling of her own child in her arms before he had grown too distant and reserved, and the force of Nicholas's faith and reliance nearly made her weep. His spindly body was crushing her, leaving her breathless. She resisted this surge of need and then gave in, mothering the child next to her breast, fiercely holding on to him.

"My goodness," she said. "Whatever's gotten into you?"

Sobbing, he burrowed deeper into the safety of her arms.

"Did you have a nightmare? Did Jack Peter do something to you? Did he hurt you?"

At the mention of his friend's name, Nick let go of her and covered his eyes with a free hand. She hung onto him, searching his face for clues.

"There's something out there."

"What, Nicholas, what? You can tell me."

"They were crawling like lizards on the walls. Babies."

An involuntary laugh filled her with instant regret. She pulled him closer as though to apologize.

"They were just outside, all over the house, and I got scared. Didn't you hear them crying?" Tears welled in his eyes.

Holly licked her dry lips before answering. "You say you heard noises out there, from the ocean?"

"Crying. Loud like a baby. And then I went to the window to see what it was. I'm sorry I opened it and let the cold in, but I had to see what was making that noise. That's when I saw the baby monsters. They turned their heads and looked at me like bugs. And then they scooted away for a minute. Stopping and thinking what to do. When they came back toward me again, I got out of there."

"What was Jack Peter doing this whole time?"

Nick paused, considering whether he should tell on him. "Just watching me."

"We have to go see if he's all right," she said, and together they opened the door to his bedroom.

Light from the hallway threw a rectangular shaft across the foot of the bed. Sprawled beneath the covers, Jack Peter slept soundly. The windows were shut and the curtains drawn. Going past the bed, Holly speculated what she might do if Nicholas was right, if there was something out there clinging to the walls. The boy followed, several steps behind, shielded by her nightgown.

Facing the sea, the old wooden window frames were swollen and difficult to open. She maneuvered her shoulders so that she could give one good hard push and was thrown off balance when the window opened as smoothly as the door. A blast of icy air gave her goose bumps, and in came the smell of the salt water and the everlasting sound of the surf. Out there in the sand between the rocks was a grave full of sailor bones. In the bed, Jack Peter muttered and curled beneath the blankets, and Nicholas crept one step closer to her. For a moment, Holly considered asking him to hold onto her waist, but realized that it might be more likely that they would fall together if she slipped. Grabbing onto the sash, she ducked her head and passed it through the opening into the night.

There were no babies, no monsters, no giant lizards crawling on the outside of the house, not that she suspected there might be, but still, a faint disappointment clouded her thoughts. Holly knew she had to make a show for the boy, however, and so searched carefully in every direction, shifting her position to better see. Her hair blew across her face, and she was as cold as a stone. Nothing to be seen, so she pulled herself back inside and closed the window with defiance.

"I heard something out there, too, but I'm glad to say, Nicholas, whatever you might have seen is gone. Perhaps you just had a nightmare?"

"No, they were there, crawling like lobsters."

The boy in the bed grunted and rolled over.

Holly gathered Nick in her arms and led him into the patch of light by the door. "You're upset, I know, and a little scared and I don't blame you. Lots of strange goings-on around here lately. How 'bout you come sleep in my bedroom, I'll make a bed on the floor out of some blankets and a pillow, and you'd be safe as a kitten. I'm sure Mr. Keenan wouldn't mind, and maybe then we could all get some sleep. And then it will all seem different in the light of morning."

"What about Jack Peter?"

When was the last time their son had come to their room to be comforted in the middle of the night? Surely not since he had become an inside boy. But perhaps just earlier, she could not remember when exactly, there was a time when his fear or lonesomeness overwhelmed his reluctance for human contact. Five years old. Four? She sat on the bed next to her son and said his name, softly so as to not alarm him. He fussed, and then she was uncertain as to whether he really had been sleeping or if he had been pretending. Holding his hand over his eyes to shield against the hall light, he sat up in the bed. The hair on the left side of his head stuck up like a wild mane, and he yawned like a lion, a magnificent stretch spiked with teeth.

Speaking in a whisper, she asked, "Did you not hear Nicholas shouting and then leave the room? Didn't you hear the noise outside? What were you doing in all this commotion?"

"I was sleeping. Why did you wake me up?"

She resisted the urge to smooth his mussed hair. "Nicholas had a fright, and he's going to come sleep in my room, and I wanted to let you know in case you woke up in the night and wondered what had happened to him."

"No," Nick said. "It's okay now. I'll stay here."

He stared at the floor when she tried to look in his eyes, and she could hear the embarrassment in his voice. "Nicholas—"

"It's fine, it's all right, I just need to go back to sleep. Could you just leave the door open a bit and the hall light on?" He climbed into bed next to Jack Peter and rolled away from her. For a few minutes, she stood like a statue in the middle of the room, watching and listening as they settled themselves. Miniature men, desperate to be brave.

"What was it?" Jack Peter asked.

"Nothing. Just a dream like she said."

She hoped that they would ask her to stay, but they had no more use for her, so she left the room and went back to her own bed. No more babies crying in the darkness, no more little boys curling in her arms.

Holly read the names of the dead. Names that had not been spoken in ages, whispering each spirit to herself. The archivist at the Maritime Museum had brought her a gray box filled with old letters and ledgers, reports of several shipwrecks off the coast of Maine, and she eventually found the list on a water-stained sheet of lined paper, the account written in the beautiful cursive hand of some anonymous nineteenth-century scribe:

Drowned on the *Porthleven*, 29 Dec. 1849

Very Rev. Thomas Vingoe 51 yrs and wife Mary
David, Thomas & Mary, children of T & M Vingoe
Bodies taken by Friends
James Chenoweth, 28 yrs, taken by Friends
Edward Conklin, 18 yrs old
Unknown Female child about 9 yrs old
Mathew Jones, wife & two infants (wife & 1 child not found)
Mr. Purcell (Captain)

Bodies not found

John Nance and his son, about 7 yrs old
Sir Charles Arundell
James Mayhew
T. Clark
Sailor (stranger) originating from Helston, about 30 yrs

Bodies not found. They could be out there still, she thought, just beyond our house, and that bone could be from one of those poor children. The tick of the big clock in the room filled her ears. Nobody else haunted the library that morning. She was tempted to slip the beautiful old page from the folder and into her purse as evidence to bear out her suspicions, but instead carefully wrote out each name on a small pad. *Bodies taken by Friends.*

The library was cold, as if they were conserving heat with so few patrons, and Holly blew on her fingers to bring some life back to her hands. She had been led to these files, she thought, from the moment she first saw the painting in the priest's dining room, and the voices, the bones, even Tim's phantoms in the night all pointed to the *Porthleven.* And maybe those ghosts had infected her son with this obsession with monsters. She thought of Jack's strange detached look when she had gone in to check on the screams coming from his room. And Nicholas, that poor trembling child she had abandoned the night before. She should have insisted he sleep with them, Tim be damned, rather than let him spend the long dark hours with Jack and who knows what they might have conjured in their late-night whispers, all their constant monsters. They had been careful to hide their notebooks filled with creatures, but she had found them out. Pages of horrors from the movies and television, and Jack's burnt skeleton. She would speak to them that afternoon, recommend a change of subject for their artistic endeavors. Still life or landscapes. Or cars, didn't ten-year-old boys love to draw cars and tanks and airplanes? The kids had taken a wrong path that week, and she was determined to correct matters, if only so the Weller boy would agree to come back someday and not be so frightened that he would stay away forever, like a mind-blown visitor who flees screaming from a haunted house never to return. That would be a disaster for her son.

But who could blame Nicholas, really? The Wellers had been good friends and neighbors, virtually insisting that the two boys remain friends no matter what. They never spoke of it as a chore or obligation, but

Holly suspected that they were proving to themselves how decent and generous they could be with their son's time. For just one week, Nick was her responsibility, and here she was about to deliver him back as damaged goods. When she held him against her breast last night, she could feel his heart beating like a jackrabbit's. Now in the library, she heard that ticking rhythm, constant and familiar as the patterns of her own breathing. Like someone knocking on her brain. What did the spirits want from her? Why were they trying to reach her family?

Heading down Highway 1 for home, Holly had the urge to study the *Wreck of the Porthleven* again. Now that she had the names of the dead, the shipwreck had become more vivid in her imagination. The Reverend Vingoe and his three small children, the Nance lad, the unnamed sailor, and the unknown girl. Perhaps they simply wished to be named and remembered. The painting would give her an even stronger sense of the events surrounding that terrible night and why the ghosts were haunting her. Father Bolden had looked perplexed when she had brought the matter up on Christmas eve, and now she rehearsed an explanation of her interest in the painting, playing up the local history angle, and isn't it interesting what can be found in the archives? By the time she reached the Star of the Sea, she nearly had her story straight.

The housekeeper answered the door, bowing slightly in greeting, and Holly reached out to shake her hand.

"Mrs. Keenan, how nice to see you." With a firm grip, she pulled Holly into the foyer. "I'm sorry to say that Father Bolden is out, but please come in. I was hoping to see you, and here you are."

"I've done some research," Holly said. "Found some details about the *Porthleven* that he might be interested in."

Miss Tiramaku took Holly's coat and then led her into the dining room, moving quickly as if she owned the place. "I was going to bring a little something to your house when Father came back. Something for your troubles. Just wait right here . . ."

Dominating the space, the *Porthleven* seemed to rock gently in its frame. In those last few moments before the ship broke apart, the men and women on board must have realized their fate. Purcell and the sailor did their bravest to keep her afloat, and the Rev. Vingoe led the others in prayer, but they all knew, they knew, they had no hope. *The water rushes over us and we are drowned.* There were no people visible in the painting, just the storm-tossed boat, the black clouds, and the frothing sea. They would have gone into freezing shock, breathed in, and it was all over, she hoped, with no more struggle. Or they would hear their own muffled heartbeats as they held their breath underwater, fighting to survive.

Miss Tiramaku glided into the room and handed her a small package in red gift wrap. "Merry Christmas."

"Thank you," Holly said and sat, dumbfounded, at the table. With a child's curiosity, she ripped at the pretty paper and found a pressed block of dried leaves in a cellophane wrapper. Inscrutable kanji decorated one side. Putting the brick under her nose, she inhaled deeply, detecting a hint of anise, a suggestion of tea.

"You're not going to get me into trouble with the police, are you? No controlled substances involved?"

Hiding her smile with her hand, Miss Tiramaku giggled. "A special tea. A little licorice and gingko and other secret ingredients. For anxiety. Completely harmless," she said. "But you never know, it might work. Or perhaps you would like to try acupuncture. I know a man in Portland."

"It was very kind of you to think of me."

Miss Tiramaku dismissed the gesture. "For when you are stressed. You can even drink it at night. No caffeine."

"That's a good thing. I can't seem to sleep as it is." Holly toyed with the ribbon from the package. "I should apologize for the other day when we first met. I was upset before you had even shown up. I'm sorry if I came across as frightened of you. How rude that was of me."

"Even the oyster hides a pearl."

"Ancient saying?"

"No, it's from a commercial," Miss Tiramaku smiled. "I was planning to come see you. About your boy."

"What do you know about my son?"

"Not much, in particular, just what I hear. I've been working at Star of the Sea for nearly twenty years. Father and I are like an old married couple. No secrets. Don't get me wrong, he didn't break a confidence. I figured it out in hints and pieces. Besides, this is a small, small town. Everybody knows at least the outlines of everybody's business, particularly when you work in a rectory. It's like the village green, only inside, where it's warm."

"What do you know? What do people say about him?"

"That he is a special child. A boy trapped inside his own mind."

Holly slid her hand from her lap and drummed her nails on the tabletop. Inside boy.

"You mustn't worry about what the others say. He is your boy."

A tear crept to her eye. Holly wiped it with one finger, determined not to cry. They sat for a while, finding their way back to equanimity.

"I have a confession to make," Miss Tiramaku said. "My parents died when I was quite young, and I went to live in an orphanage run by the nuns. Too old for adoption, everyone wants a baby. But I was also considered a bit too odd. Lost in the clouds of my own mind. They didn't say Asperger's syndrome in those days. This was almost sixty years ago, you understand. The diagnosis was much more pointed, and the treatment severe, but it made no difference for me. No psychiatrists ever came to the orphanage. I was just a special case, a little girl apart from all the other little girls. I kept to myself, stuck in my mind. Truth be told, I was a difficult child, but, praise the Lord, the nuns did what they could for me."

Holly cradled the gift in her lap.

"Don't be sorry, my dear. That was a long time ago, and look at me now. I've found a place in the world. Here with Father."

"Nobody understands Jack," Holly said. "He's what they call high functioning, but that's misleading, isn't it? It was hard enough before he developed his fear of the outdoors. And lately, he's been even harder to reach. Just the other morning, I went to wake him, barely laid a hand on his shoulder, and he woke up in a terror and hit me."

"You may have knocked on a door that he thought he had shut."

"Nobody knows what it is like."

"I do," Miss Tiramaku said. "Maybe that's what drew you here. I'd like to meet him. Your son. That's partly why the gift of the tea. A little ruse. Father Bolden was going to drive me over this evening."

The brick of tea atop the wrapping paper looked like an altar. Holly smiled at the deception. "I'll take you now if you like, and you can meet Jack. And then I can run you back, it's not far."

Miss Tiramaku stood at once. "Let's go."

On the drive, they chatted about her life in the rectory, the pastor's quirks and quiddities, and how they had both arrived in Maine from faraway places. How he took her in, gave her a job and a place to stay, and how they grew closer over the years. When the ocean came into view along Shore Road, Miss Tiramaku asked if they might stop for a while. Holly pulled over into the verge and left the engine idling. From their vantage point they could see a wide swath of the Atlantic, the breakers rolling white cotton across the gray sea.

"I never tire of this view," Miss Tiramaku said. "Sometimes I think that people born on islands are never completely content without the smell and sound of the ocean."

"I love it," Holly said. "We settled here—in our dream house—just before Jack was born. Though I still feel as if I'm an outsider to a degree, never completely accepted by the locals."

"We are not from heah. We're *from away*."

Holly laughed at the localism. "Outsiders. We could live here for a hundred years and still be from away. It's like a secret society all its own."

On the silvery water, the wooden ship bobbed along, sails full, the sailors on deck in their antique costumes manning the lines and skipping up the rigging, Captain Purcell hollering orders from behind the wheel. A woman made her way from aft to stern, holding the rail to keep her balance, a small boy in tow. Doomed, they went about their tasks unaware of their fate. Holly would save them if she could, even knowing that the ship, the crew, the woman and her son, and all the other passengers were but a moment's hallucination. She was drawn to them, pulled by the vacuum of their sinking. In the seat next to her, Miss Tiramaku stared vacantly at the same distant spot.

Holly reached into her bag and pulled out her notes. "When I first came to Father Bolden, he told me the story of that painting in your dining room. *The Wreck of the Porthleven.* Ever since, I can't shake the image of those poor drowning people. They were outsiders, too, looking for a new start, only to come to a bad end. So this morning, I went to the Maritime Museum to research the story, and I found a list of the dead."

Flipping through the pages, she handed over her notes of the ship's manifest. "People on the shore came to take those who washed up from the sea. But some bodies were never found." Holly pointed in the direction of where she imagined the phantom ship. "I think I may have heard them out there. Voices on Christmas eve. And I've been hearing other things banging and knocking, and cries on the water, late at night."

"You poor thing." Miss Tiramaku turned to face her. "You may have heard the *funa-yurei*."

"Tell me more about these ghosts," Holly said. "These *yurei*."

"Father would not want me to say."

"Father would not have to know."

In a near whisper, Miss Tiramaku told her tale. "I saw the first ones when I was a little girl in the orphanage. We slept in a ward, perhaps twelve of us, and the nuns told us we must stay in our beds after lights-out, but in the small hours of the morning, I had to go to the toilet. To wet the bed was a great shame, so I crept out in the dark, careful not to wake my sister orphans, and made my way by feel along the wall. I noticed a strange light at the far end of the hallway, and curiosity pulled me. Floating in the air in the corner were two girls, twin sisters maybe five or six years old, with bright red faces and bobbed black hair like my own. 'What are you doing out of bed, little princess?' one of them said, and I knew at once who they were."

A gust of wind rocked the car, making them laugh nervously.

"They were the murdered children of the woman who owned the house before the church bought it to make the orphanage. The mother had strangled them in their sleep and then drowned herself in a small stream that runs along the property. All the orphans knew the legend, but as far as I know I was the only one to see the ghost children."

"What did you do?" Holly asked.

"I ran away and hid beneath the covers, for I was frightened. But I would see them all the time, and they would talk to me in my sleep, and sometimes I saw their footprints in the ashes from the fireplace. It gave me the idea to have a funeral. I made two dolls that look just like them and burned the effigies in the fire with six coins to send them on their journey. And the *yurei* departed."

"Six coins?" Holly asked.

"For the River of Three Crossings, from this world to the next. But there are many kinds of *yurei*, Holly." She had the faraway look Jack sometimes had, blank and distant. "The *funa-yurei* are ghosts of those who died at sea, and they are horrible creatures who want to bring the living under the water with them. Sometimes they appear as flames; and sometimes they are men with horrid faces, floating through the air above the waves saying 'bring me a *hishaku*,' and when they are given a ladle, they fill the victim's boat with seawater."

"Good God," Holly said, and Miss Tiramaku chided her with a wagging finger.

"You mustn't tell Father about the spirits," she said. "He doesn't believe."

Holly put the car into gear, grabbed hold of the steering wheel, and eased onto the road. "We should get going. Maybe I could use a cup of your tea, and you can meet that boy of mine. And his little friend."

"He has a friend?"

"Nicholas Weller. The neighbor boy we're watching. His parents went off on a cruise for a week. Second honeymoon, a chance to start over. Nicholas is really Jack's only friend, and we're lucky to have him. They've known each other since they were babies."

"A friend," Miss Tiramaku said, the astonishment in her voice resounding the rest of the way.

iii.

The morning after he had seen the babies on the wall, Nick made sure to wake up earlier than Jack Peter. Moaning quietly to himself, he tiptoed over to the desk to see the drawings from the night before. Even in the blue light of early morning, all of the pages on the desk were blank as new snow. Nothing upon nothing, but Nick clearly remembered Jack Peter hunched over the page, furious pencil in hand. The drawings had to be there still. Hidden somewhere. Quietly he opened the desk drawer, but there were only a few clean sheets of paper.

A small trash basket sat on the floor next to the toy box, and in it, curled like a nest of snakes, were strips of torn paper. He gathered the pieces into a loose ball and looked for a place to stash the evidence till he had time and light enough to inspect what Jack Peter had drawn and destroyed. From the bed, his friend grumbled in his sleep. Nick shoved the scraps into the pocket of his robe hanging by the door, and then sneaked back beneath the covers to wait for a more natural waking hour.

At nine o'clock Mr. Keenan came in and threw open the drapes. In came the brilliant sun, its light bouncing off the mirror, doubling the brightness inside. Disoriented, the boys woke slowly. "Rise and shine," he encouraged them. "Don't let the whole day slip away." Just as soon as they had vacated the bed, he stripped the sheets and pillowcases for the wash. He was about to toss Nick's bathrobe in the basket of clothes when the boy cried that he needed the robe because it was so cold.

"You're getting soft in your old age, Nick."

"That's because I've been stuck inside." He wrapped himself in the terry cloth and knotted the belt. "Would it be okay if I went out for a bit today, took a walk after breakfast?"

Mr. Keenan went to the window to check on the weather. The morning was clear and bright, and nothing lurked on the beach. He pressed his hand against the cold glass. "Bundle up, if you go, and don't be gone too long. But first have some breakfast. Pumpkin waffles on the griddle."

A short time later, a fully stuffed Nick Weller excused himself from the table, leaving Jack Peter in the middle of a short stack of waffles, and hurried upstairs to change clothes in the privacy of the bedroom. He fished the scraps of paper from his robe and crammed the lot into a front pocket of his jeans. Careful not to rustle as he walked, he returned downstairs in search of his coat and gloves and watch cap. Mr. Keenan was at the kitchen sink, washing the sticky dishes, and Jack Peter sawed through his last waffle, all the time watching Nick prepare to leave. With his little finger, he chased and cornered a bead of maple syrup and stuck it in his mouth, and his words came out garbled. "Whey youf going?"

"Just out," Nick said. "A little fresh air. Maybe I'll walk to Mercy Point and back."

"Mebbe I'll go wif you."

"Ha-ha, very funny," he said. "I won't be long. Maybe when I get back, we can do something different today."

"We can always draw."

"I'm tired of monsters."

Jack Peter picked up a strip of bacon and munched it like a bone.

From the mudroom, Nick heard the Quigleys' dog barking, so he made his way quickly around the house and climbed the hillock to the safety of the ocean and the beach. Colder air blew off the water, and he considered for a moment just hunkering down on the spot and looking at the clues, but he feared Mr. Keenan might wander about and accidentally catch him. As he walked away from the house, Nick kept glancing over his shoulder at the back facade, now drenched in sunshine. The windows of Jack Peter's room shone like great eyeglasses, and he could picture himself with his head through the opening of one of the lenses and seeing those terrible infants swarm all over the walls. The memory gave him the willies, and he resolved to put some distance between himself and the house.

Not another soul on the beach as far as he could see, and he inhaled and savored the lonesome feeling. Since he had arrived at the Keenans', he had not been alone except for stolen interludes in the bathroom, and wherever else he went there was always someone not far away. At home he might go hours without seeing his mom or dad. No, Mr. and Mrs. Keenan seemed to be hovering, ready with the next meal or popcorn in front of the television set. And Jack Peter was incessantly following him like a puppy that couldn't be shaken. Not that he was particularly demanding, but all the more bothersome for his dumb attentiveness. His friend seemed unable to abide being alone, as though he had saved up years of solitude and was now cashing in on Nick's company. Even when they were doing nothing or sleeping or drawing those stupid pictures, Jack Peter was suffocating him. It felt good to be away from that particular burden.

Bound by his thoughts, Nick did not realize how far he had traveled till he looked back and saw the sloping roof of the Keenans' house. He rightly figured that if he could not see them, they could not see him either. Looking for a windbreak, he walked further and found a trio of pines rooted in a fissure. Beneath the boughs, he crouched and dug out the scraps from his pocket. The spot was calm, but he made sure to weigh down each strip with a little stick or pinecone or piece of shell. He spent a good twenty minutes figuring out the jigsaw puzzle, and he would have been done sooner had not the images bothered him so.

Jack Peter had drawn the babies.

They were as horrible as he remembered, the distorted faces and limbs, the pale misshapen bodies, the lizardlike way they clung to the walls. The torn paper halved some of the images, while others escaped from the page entirely. He had drawn them before they showed up, and then he had ripped the drawing to shreds after they fled. Why? When could he have possibly seen them? Why would he not wake up when they threatened to climb into the room?

Nick gathered the ribbons of paper and shoved them in his pocket. I won't go back, he said to himself. I can't. If he just kept walking, he eventually could reach his own house, break a window, and hide out until his parents came back. But that would be the first place the Keenans would check. He could hide elsewhere, not outdoors, he'd never survive the cold, but in one of the vacation homes boarded up for the winter, it wouldn't be too hard for a few days. The Mackintosh place was nearby, and he could make it there before anyone came looking for him. If someone stumbled upon him, Nick would say he was running away from a haunted house. But he knew that the Keenans would only come searching or call the cops. He could picture Mrs. Keenan worrying, frantic in the kitchen, and could feel how safe he had been in her embrace. She would know what to do, he decided. She would know what the picture meant. Hitching up his pants, he headed back to the house.

As he climbed the last rocks before reaching the Keenans' waterfront, Nick noticed a soft spot in the sand, a mound just big enough to hide a body or two. He guessed the bone had been found there, and he could picture the whole skeleton at the bottom of the grave. The grinning skull, the birdcage ribs, the long leg bones, and the arm missing its radius. Nick ran the final forty yards to a safer place beneath the deck. Overturned and resting in the sand, a little wooden boat tempted him with a means of escape, but the hull would not budge. He screwed up his courage and went inside. For the rest of the morning, they circled each other, wary as two bears, Jack Peter suspicious and resentful that his friend had left him and Nick paranoid about the games his friend was playing. Mr. Keenan flitted around the edge, cleaning house and looking in on them, vaguely aware of the tension between the boys.

No one greeted them when they entered the house. She hung their coats by the door and called out that she was home, but no one answered. They went through the living room and into the kitchen, where Holly put the kettle on. Miss Tiramaku took a turn around the room, stopping at the refrigerator to admire Jack's drawing affixed to the door with four magnets.

"Your son?" she asked.

"No," Holly laughed. "That's Nicholas in the picture, but Jack drew it. That's his latest thing, one of many portraits, who knows how long it'll last. He's taken it up recently and has become something of a fiend for it. I bought him art supplies for Christmas, and he's nearly gone through the whole sketch pad already. And poor Nicholas. I'm not sure he's as interested, but that's all they do. Draw, draw, draw."

"He has a certain eye."

"You think so? A mother can't be objective."

"You have a lovely home," she said.

"Thank you. It's a work in progress, even after all these years. I'll give you the grand tour once our tea is ready. Can't imagine where my husband's gone off to."

Overhead a loud clump on the floor let them know they were not alone after all. Holly hullooed again, and the boys came tumbling downstairs, Nick arriving first and Jack on his heels. They stopped in the threshold at the sight of Miss Tiramaku, wary of her strange presence. From his work-room below came Tim, his arms laden with the day's laundry, ready for folding, in a green plastic basket.

"Where have you been hiding?" Holly asked. "This is a friend of mine. Miss Tiramaku, this is my husband, Tim, and the boy with no socks is our son, Jack, and the sensible one is Nicholas Weller."

The males waved hello in their dopey shyness. Finding his manners, Tim came over to shake hands properly, but she bowed slightly instead, confusing him, and then they resorted to an awkward exchange of greetings.

"Where did you two meet?" Tim asked.

"Out and about," Holly said.

"I work for Father Bolden," Miss Tiramaku spoke over her. "At the Star of the Sea, and I met your wife there. How come I didn't see you at Mass on Christmas eve?"

The scowl on his face came and went in an instant, but everyone noticed. "I don't go to church. I don't believe in such things. I only believe in what my senses tell me, what is real."

"*Spiritus est qui vivificat*, Mr. Keenan. 'It is the Spirit which gives us life.'"

Holly could see that he was growing annoyed, so she changed the subject. "Boys, Miss Tiramaku came all the way from Japan, clear on the other side of the world."

"How did you end up all the way in Maine?" Tim asked. "At a Catholic church, no less."

"I was an orphan raised by nuns," she said. "Years later I came here as a young woman, intended for the religious life, but God had other plans for me. I keep house for the priest."

The teakettle whistled, and Holly asked if anyone cared to join her in a cup. Tim crossed his arms and slouched against the back of his chair.

"It's called tiger tea," Miss Tiramaku said as she joined the boys at the table. "The secret ingredient is the stripes of a tiger."

Jack giggled at her remark, but Nick rolled his eyes. They added teaspoons of sugar and a schlook of milk to their cups. Everyone sat up straight in their chairs, good posture, and Holly smiled to herself when she saw Jack mimic Miss Tiramaku's grip on the handle, one dainty pinkie sticking out. Tim sulked at the end of the table, nursing his drink.

"You boys have a good Christmas?" Miss Tiramaku asked. "Santa Claus was generous this year?"

They nodded. Nick's face flushed with embarrassment.

"You are so lucky," she said. "At Christmastime, there wasn't too much for all the children in the orphanage. We all got some special treat, a slice of fruitcake and some roast turkey, but only one present, you see—there wasn't too much money. And all the other girls, they wanted a doll, perhaps, or maybe a teddy bear or something they could hold and carry around like little mothers. But not me. Do you know what I wished for?"

The boys looked down into their teacups and had no answers.

"I saw a picture in a magazine about a windup fish. It was a koi, with a tiny key and golden scales and jade eyes. The most magnificent thing ever. So I prayed for it, and told the nuns about it, and would you guess, bless them, there was the windup goldfish for my Christmas gift, and it was as lovely as I had imagined. The special thing was that if you wound the key and put it into the water, the fish would really swim. All through that winter, I would play with the windup fish in a basin, or when they would give us a bath it would circle round the tub, and I never tired of it. Often I dreamt of it at night, swimming in my dreams. When spring came, I took it outdoors. There was a stream behind the orphanage, and one day, I wound it up and put the koi in the water, and it could swim just like a real fish. The most astonishing thing. But then the fish kept going down the stream and I ran beside it, chasing from the banks, but I was not fast enough. It swam out into the river and from the river into the sea and across the sea to America, and though my heart was broken, that is how I knew I would one day end up here in this country."

When she had finished her story, Miss Tiramaku folded her hands in front of her atop the table. The boys fidgeted in their seats, freed from the spell.

"I like to draw," Jack said.

"So I hear," said Miss Tiramaku. "What do you like to draw?"

"What is in my head." His right hand began to twitch, as though he could not control the impulse to draw even at this moment.

Tim tapped a spoon against his teacup. "I think that's enough, Jip."

Miss Tiramaku unfolded her hands and placed one on each side of Jack's teacup, and in a near whisper, she asked, "What do you imagine in that mind of yours?"

"Monsters," said Nick. "He draws monsters."

She reached out to still Jack's hands, and he did not even flinch.

"Would you mind if I talked alone with your son?" Miss Tiramaku asked. "Somewhere the two of us could have a private chat. Give us the chance to speak frankly. I'll come get you when we are through. It won't be long, but I feel certain that Jack wants to say some things, if he could take me into his confidence." She raised one eyebrow, and Holly took the cue, and pushed Tim and Nick into the living room, shutting the door behind them with a firm click.

"Why is *she* here?" He was simmering anger just below the surface. "What are you doing in church, Holly? You mean more than just at Christmas?"

Holly frowned at him. "I needed to talk with someone. About Jack."

"So you went to see a priest without saying anything, and he sent his . . . minion over here to plant ideas in our son. She kicked me out of the kitchen, my own kitchen."

"Would you keep your voice down? They're right in the next room."

He raised his voice. "I will not. What sort of monkey business are you trying to pull, Holly? I don't approve—"

"Please don't shout."

"I'm not shouting," he shouted.

From the corner of her eye, she could see Nick pretending to inspect the ornaments on the Christmas tree, as if he were oblivious to their conversation, but those boys heard everything, noticed every little detail. Turning her back on her husband, Holly went straight to the stereo cabinet and chose an album from their collection, and then put the record on the old-fashioned turntable and switched it on. The stereo had belonged to her parents, and it was one last link to her childhood and family. The arm swung in motion and dropped the needle precisely in the groove for the first track. "Jingle Bells" by Frank Sinatra. The music was loud enough to drown out their conversation.

"I don't like this," said Tim. His tone had changed, his manner much calmer. "Did you ever see such a creature? That eye. There's no call to bring in strangers to talk to our son. Especially without my permission."

"I don't need your permission, Tim."

"He's my boy, too."

"I'm going out of my mind, and if you won't do something, I will."

Tim perched on the arm of the sofa. "How long has this been going on?"

"For years," Holly said. "He's going to be out of control one day. And despite what you think, he's getting worse. Not worse, but more difficult."

"I don't mean Jip. I mean, how long have you been seeing this priest and this voodoo woman? She gives me the creeps."

"Just a little while, and you shouldn't judge people by how they look. Even an oyster hides a pearl." She uncrossed her arms and leaned on the opposite wing of the sofa. "It's getting to me, Tim. It all started when I surprised Jack in his sleep. My head is hammering all the time. Noises, tap-tapping, and then you come in a bloody mess, and poor Nicholas comes crying in the middle of the night."

Nick looked away, as if embarrassed to be remembered.

"We're all on edge, and you have to admit there's trouble with Jack—"

"It's a phase," he said.

"Not a phase, Tim. Not another damned chapter, but the whole rest of the story."

He looked away from her, and she turned her head in the opposite direction. Cemented in place, just as Nick had seen his own parents so many times, and he began to wonder if this was not part of what it meant to be a grown-up, to reach an impasse in the argument too deep for words. Even for adults. Sinatra kept crooning, and when the songs were over, she flipped the record and they listened to the other side, trapped in the living room by the circumstances of the day.

When the door opened, the woman, bowed with fatigue, ushered in the boy with a hand on his shoulder. Her face was wilted but she seemed clearly pleased by the conversation. Jack Peter looked the same as ever, a bit tamer perhaps, or calm enough at last to bear the weight of human contact. Mr. and Mrs. Keenan rose from their places, expecting some news from beyond, and they both seemed surprised by the simple presence of their son.

"We had a good talk," Miss Tiramaku said. "Didn't we, Jack?"

Jack Peter smiled and nodded his head.

"We'll have to talk again, if that's okay with you."

"Do you think you can help?" Mrs. Keenan asked.

There was a moment's hesitation that stretched and swallowed hope. "Yes," Miss Tiramaku finally said. "I'll help."

By her side, with the deft motions of his fingers, Jack Peter drew figures in the air.

iv.

Tim could no longer remember with any clarity the moment he realized the truth about his son. As first-time parents living on their own far away from any family, how could they be expected to read the signs? Their pediatrician had told them not to worry—each child develops at its own pace, there's no strict timetable for rolling over or sitting up or vocalizing, no matter what the books might say. The only other baby in their sphere was Nell's son, Nick, and he wasn't exactly a prodigy but more or less the same, so what could Tim be expected to know? They eat, they cry, they sleep. They need their diapers to be changed. One day they seem to recognize you, respond to the sound of your voice. They coo, they drool, they smile. They work as designed. The way they are meant to work. Until they don't.

And then the experts tell you the truth. The doctors, all supremely diffident even when they mean to convey empathy and good bedside manners, they tell you something is not right with your son, and your wife goes to pieces, and you tell yourself that he can be fixed. Everything broken can be made whole again. Bit by bit, day by day, measured in minor victories, Jip could be restored. Faith and hard work will make it so, and then suddenly she says, no, he's getting worse, if such a thing is possible. She doesn't know, she doesn't know what a father can do. No need for priests and one-eyed witches and their hocus-pocus.

Ever the good host, Tim saw Miss Tiramaku to the door, said the obligatory "so nice to meet you," and then watched with relief as Holly drove her back to the rectory. The boys, too, seemed glad to see her go and to have a measure of the old order restored. From the front window, they watched the car drive away, but Tim could detect no signs upon their faces, no hints that they had been spellbound.

Holly must have passed the police car on the road heading in the opposite direction, for no more than five minutes elapsed between her de-
parture and the arrival of the big cruiser in the Keenans' driveway. Across
the street, the Quigleys' dog barked madly at the man in uniform. The
boys drew up at the sight of the policeman, exiting the car, zipping his
jacket against the cold, and by habit checking in all directions for some
danger. In the gray wash of the winter's day, his sunglasses seemed fairly
ridiculous, a stab at authority and menace but out of place on such a
youthful face. With a few brisk steps, he was at the front door. The boys
swung around as smartly as soldiers and stood at attention. Officer Pollock saluted them when he came in and flashed his baby-toothed smile
when they returned the salute. He shook hands with Tim and then removed his hat, holding it in his hand.

"You just missed my wife, she'll be sorry. But if you've come about the
bones, you're too late," Tim said. "We've lost the hole, too, I'm afraid."

"Ah, right. The bone." The young policeman looked baffled. "What
do you mean, lost the hole?"

"That's just it. The hole was gone the next morning. Completely vanished."

"That's a head-scratcher. Maybe the wind filled it in, or the tide came
up farther than we thought. But I didn't come about the bone. Haven't
had the chance yet to send it to the lab. I came about your monster. I've
got the DB in the back of my rig."

"DB?" Tim asked.

"Dead body."

The boys rushed to the window to spy on whatever might be in the
squad car.

"You've got a monster in there?" Jack Peter asked.

Pollock shifted his weight and slid a thumb into the waistband of his
trousers. "Remember how we thought there might be a wild thing roaming around these parts? Well, Mr. Keenan, you weren't too far off. We've
found it. It's in the trunk. If the boys want to come out and see it with
you, they can."

"My son never leaves the house."

"Ah, right. I'd forget my head sometimes. Then you and the other boy come out and have a look-see."

Bundled in their coats, Tim and Nick followed Officer Pollock into the yard, stranding Jip like a jailbird in a glass cage. Thick clouds gathered in the west, full of long-promised snow, and Tim's joints and spine ached with the moist threat of it. In the driveway, the car sat like a cold metal sarcophagus, and as they made their way back to the trunk, Tim couldn't help but tingle with fear. Suppose the policeman had found the white man and now had bound the creature and stowed it in the back for safekeeping? An image flashed in his mind, the thing that had attacked him on the beach. He could picture the constrained wildness, snarling and straining against the rope at its wrists and ankles, the awful nakedness of the creature, its dead fish smell, its tangled hair and beard, the rotting teeth and filthy nails. Its fearsome prospect thrilled him as well, for he could at last prove that he had not hallucinated and willed the thing into being. He was doubly glad to have Nick along with him as a witness.

"It was frozen when I found it," Officer Pollock said. "Probably been dead overnight." He fumbled for the keys to the trunk, and then motioned for them both to stand back, as though he did not believe his own words. They retreated a step and craned their necks to see what might be inside.

The first glimpse of white nearly stopped Tim's heart, but when the fullness of the color and its nature became apparent, he had to stifle a laugh, despite himself. It was a dead dog, a big white German shepherd curled into a sleeping position, the black nails on its paws ragged and broken, its great pink tongue lolling between two rows of sharp teeth. Lying on a piece of old tarp, the dead body took up virtually the entire space. Were it not for the open eyes, the corpse might be mistaken for merely resting. Nick leaned in close and reached out with tentative fingers, caught between the desire to prove the dogness and revulsion over its deadness.

"Here's your monster, Mr. Keenan. Found it on the road near the tree line on Mercy." He took the muzzle in hand and turned the head so a large red contusion could be seen. "Blunt object, if you ask me. Bumper of a car, poor thing, and then it must've wandered off to die. But take a good look, Mr. Keenan, that there is bigger than any coyote, big as a wolf. A great white wolf—that explains a lot, I expect."

"Are you sure it's dead?" Nick asked.

"Sure as sure can be," he said. "I had to kinda fold it to get it into the trunk, so you better believe it would have bit me if it had breath. No tags, no collar, who knows how long it was out there, terrifying the public. I guess that's what you seen, Mr. Keenan. What dug your hole and found that bone. I guess that's what's been running round these parts."

Nick brushed his hands through the dead dog's fur. The hairs bristled at odd angles, and the body was as cold as a tombstone.

"That's not it," said Mr. Keenan. He turned his back on the car and caressed the wounds on his neck. "That's not what I saw, sorry to say. Or at least, I don't think so. What I saw was big as a man. That's quite a large dog, but still—"

"You sure you don't want another look? If the evidence points in one direction, it's hard not to trust what's right in front of your eyes. You said there was something wild roaming about, and I find you a wild thing. Pretty much locks down the case."

They stood for a while considering the dead animal, like uncertain mourners at a funeral. Nick poked at the corpse as though attempting to get it to move or bark or growl.

"A man," Mr. Keenan began, but then he cut himself short and just smiled at the trooper. "Could be," he finally said. "You could be right. Maybe it was just a big white wolf-dog all along. Thanks so much for taking the trouble to bring it by."

"Knew you and your wife had been concerned."

"She'll be sorry she missed you."

Pollock reached for the lip of the trunk lid and was surprised to find Nick leaning inside the well. "You'll have to get out of there. I've got places to go and criminals to catch."

Slipping out of harm's way, Nick straightened and shielded his eyes to look at the policeman. "You are a superhero."

"Officer Pollock," he said. "To the rescue." With a grin, he slammed the trunk, got into the car, and drove away.

"Hi-yo, Silver," Tim said, and then he put his arm around the boy's shoulders and they walked back inside.

Waiting like a fledgling in the nest, Jip began pestering them at once. "What was in the car? I couldn't see, I couldn't see."

"A monster," Nick said. "Hairy white beast straight out of your nightmares."

Tossing his jacket over the back of a chair, Tim grimaced at the boy. "Don't pay any attention to him. It was just a dog. A poor misfortunate German shepherd dog, white as winter. Must have been a beautiful thing before it met something bigger and more dangerous. Now it's just a broken body in the back of a police car."

"That's right." Nick sniffed. "Just a dog."

Holly could not remember a time over the past few weeks when she had such an unbroken stretch of peace without the constant drumming in her head. The talk with Miss Tiramaku had done her good she was certain, and on the ride back to the rectory, they had discussed more of Jack's case history from the very beginning. Holly told her about the first time she had noticed her son's strange affect. He was cradled in her lap, laid lengthwise against her propped-up legs, and she bent down to kiss him again and again, soft zerberts on his tummy and cheeks, but he didn't respond as she'd hoped, didn't respond as other babies with a yelp of glee or belly giggles or even just a sharp inhalation. No, he seemed to resent her affections. Her suspicions played out in the months to come, Tim fighting her all the way when she sought out specialists. The pediatricians were missing it. She knew. A mother knows her child.

"Sometimes a father is too close to tell," Miss Tiramaku said. "Or maybe your husband doesn't want to admit his child is different. I can connect with Jack, and I'd like to talk with him again. Maybe next time Nicholas, too. Do you think he is angry with Nick?"

"Angry?"

"Or resents him, perhaps. Resents the difference he feels?"

"No, Nick's a good boy. He's like a brother."

"A brother," Miss Tiramaku repeated and stared through the window, chewing on the word.

They had arrived at the rectory and sat in the car, plotting the next steps. To be sure that Miss Tiramaku hadn't been locked out, Holly watched her go to the door, changing from spry to tottering as though she were a windup doll herself in need of another turn of the key. Father Bolden met her on the porch, held the storm door for her in a gesture of familiar welcome. Holly did not bother to wave good-bye, but turned the car around and drove home.

In the last navy blue moments of the day, she pulled into the driveway. The Christmas lights were on, and when she walked in, the rich aroma of a beef stew made her dizzy with hunger. The boys were busy setting the table, and Tim stirred the pot with a big wooden spoon. A glass of red wine sat breathing at her place at the table, and she felt a surge of tranquility shoot through her veins with the first sip.

After a quick hello kiss, Tim shared the news. "You'll never guess who came by the house, not ten minutes after you left."

"Santa Claus," she said. "Come to deliver that Caribbean cruise he forgot?"

"Very funny." Tim reached for the wine bottle to top off her glass. "It was Haddock. That policeman who was here Christmas Day."

"Pollock," she said. "To check up on the case of the mystery bone? I have a theory where it came from."

"That's what I thought too, at first, but no. Not that at all. You'll never guess what he had in the back of his car."

Jack Peter shouted, "A monster."

"Now, Jip, let your mother guess."

"A monster?" Holly asked.

"Sort of," said Tim. "Remember that thing I saw on the rocks, that thing that got at my throat? Well it wasn't a coyote, it was a big white dog, the size of a wolf. Found it dead at the Point. Pollock had to stuff it in the back of his rig. Been roaming round here for weeks. Isn't that great?"

"That's terrible," she said. "Poor thing."

"It was already dead, of course, but don't you see? It proves there's been something out there, just like I thought, and it explains everything— the noises, the dog across the street going crazy, the feeling like you're being watched all the time out there."

She drained her glass of wine. "If you say so, dear."

"What do you mean, if I say so? Don't you understand, this fixes everything."

"A big white dog?"

"Precisely."

"Precisely." She helped herself to the bottle and refilled her glass and lifted it in a toast to her husband. "Case closed."

The boys were already seated at the table, quietly waiting for the start of dinner. The oven timer buzzed, and Tim retrieved a pan of biscuits and set in motion the whole process of clattering bowls and spoons and fetching the milk from the fridge and getting dinner on the table. They all tucked in, and in those first moments, appetite trumped conversation, and they ate as though this meal was their first in ages.

Tim speared a chunk of potato on the end of his fork and blew to cool it down. "It looked like it was asleep, all curled up like they do, in the bottom of the trunk."

"If you cut them open to let the steam out, you wouldn't have to blow on your food," Holly said. "Potatoes stay hot a long time."

"That's what I like about living in a small town. Mighty nice of that young policeman to keep us informed." He fanned his open mouth with his free hand.

Jack Peter blew on his potato.

"Same goes for you," she said. "Let the steam out, so you can eat them sooner."

"At first I didn't believe him," said Tim. "About a big dog, but the more I got to thinking, the more it makes sense."

She buttered a biscuit and ignored him. "Jack, Miss Tiramaku said you and she had a good talk, is that right?"

When he heard his name, Jack stopped chasing a pearl onion around the bottom of his bowl and stared at his mother.

"Says she wants to talk with you some more. Would that be all right, son?" Holly sank her teeth into the biscuit, and Jack nodded and resumed his game.

Tim waggled an empty fork at her. "I'm not sure it's all right with me."

"It doesn't have to be with your approval, Tim. He needs somebody. I don't think there's any harm in her talking with the boy."

"Bunch of superstition."

Her spoon clattered when she dropped it into the bowl. For the next few moments, they ate in deep silence.

"Didn't seem real at first," Nick said. "A make-believe dog. Like something Jack Peter would dream up."

They all made their peace after supper, managing a few hands of cards before bed. On the calendar in the boys' bedroom, Nick drew a big black X through another number and calculated how long it would be until his parents returned. Just a few more days. While Jack Peter was in the bathroom brushing his teeth, Nick changed his clothes. He stripped off his shirt, and as he undid his belt buckle, he felt the lump in his jeans pocket. He pulled out a wad of papers, the torn strips from the drawing adhering together like a ball of yarn, ragged and matted. The drawing. The babies. It seemed so long ago in retrospect, and with all of the strange visitors, Nick had forgotten to ask Mrs. Keenan about it, and he had not dared mention the drawing to Jack Peter. From down the hall came the sound of the bathroom door opening with a burst. He would be back soon, so Nick shoved the pulpy mass under his side of the mattress.

He was tired, oh so tired.

When the lights went out, he had hoped to go straight to sleep, but instead, Jack Peter rolled to his side and faced him in the darkness, wanting to talk. Nick could smell the mint toothpaste on his breath and the scent of soap on his skin. Go away, he wanted to shout, but he said nothing and tried to will his friend to sleep.

"What do you want, Jack Peter?"

Up on one elbow, he was eager to talk. "I wasn't scared of the lady with one eye."

"She had two eyes. A cataract on one. My nana in Florida has 'em all the time. She had a surgery to cut one out."

"They cut her eyeball?"

"With a knife. A scalpel."

"I would not want a knife in my eye."

"Me neither. I'm glad you weren't scared of her."

"She was nice." There was an air around Jack Peter's sentence, a kind of wistfulness that Nick associated with school when one of the boys or girls had a crush on a teacher. A teacher's pet.

"You should talk to her," Nick said. "Tell her everything, all your secrets."

No reply. All was still for a while, quiet enough for Nick to hope their conversation was over and he could sleep. He had nearly dropped off when another question disturbed him.

"What about that dog?"

"It was a big white dog, big as a wolf. Kinda scary to look at since it was dead."

"I wonder what it is like being dead."

Nick did not answer. The question hung over the bed palpable as a thick and heavy cloud. There was no answer to it, and in time, the boys fell asleep.

Hours later, when the house was quiet for the night, a scratching at the door awakened Nick. He had heard that sound before. At his grandparents' house, their little Yorkie would paw at the door whenever it wanted to be let out or let back into the house. Nails scraped the wood, more desperately now, as if something was trying to dig its way into the room, and a canine whine came through the space between the floor and the door. Nick could hear it snuffle and breathe and then the low-pitched growl rumble from its chest. In the trunk of the police car, the dead dog's mouth was pulled back exposing two rows of sharp teeth. He could see them clearly now, the long fangs snapping at him. He could feel the canines ripping at his pajamas, hear the vicious mad barking. With a whimper, he turned away and shook Jack Peter by the shoulder. Nick knew he had been drawing again. "Make it go away," he whispered, repeating and repeating until the boy rose from his dreams and whatever was beyond the closed door padded down the hall and went back to that special hell where nightmares are born.

v.

The dream house now sat at the bottom of the sea. Waves broke six feet above the roof, and bubbles escaped from the chimney and streamed one by one to the surface. In between the fronds of the kelp forest swam the windup fish, shining brightly as it passed through columns of sunlight. An octopus hid in the mailbox, two arms slithering through the slot. Starfish clung to the balustrade along the front porch. One fish, two fish, red fish, blue fish. With great care he drew dorsal fins, walleyes, scales, and the little beard beneath the mouth open for one underwater breath. The cod took a long time to draw, but Jack Peter didn't mind, he had all morning, he lost track entirely. The pencil weighed just right in his hand, the lines certain and crisp, and the sketch paper was smooth and willing.

One fish, two fish, red fish, blue fish. He remembered the sound of the Dr. Seuss book, its music in the background of his mind as he drew, and he could picture the illustrations and how the book was about counting things and observing details. Say, what a lot of fish there are. Windup fish swimming in the sea all the way from Japan, and the lady with the cloudy eye knows how he works. Inside his head. All these fishes need deep water, and if the ocean came and rose above the roof, Daddy would be dead, and Mommy, too, and Nick, bodies floating in the deep. Their friends could come and gather the dead and drowned and hang them up to dry. The end. No more pictures to draw, no more secrets. His hand cramped, and then the pencil grew as heavy as a spade.

He studied the house, vaguely dissatisfied with how he had drawn it, the difference between the perfect construct in his brain and the finished images on the page. He felt a bit sick to his stomach and slid the paper to the bottom of the stack on his desk. He turned off the light and sat in the gathering dawn. The others slept, slumbering in dreamland. Nick sprawled across the mattress, twisted sheets wrapped around his body like a fishing net. Late in the night, he had been crying again. Always crying. Always wanting something else. Nick could be such a chore; there was a limit to Jack Peter's patience. Down the hall, his parents drifted, two on a raft. They would be up soon enough, his mother off to work, his father wandering restlessly from room to room. If they were drowned and dead, who would take care of him? "Be careful," he whispered, and then all at once, the whole house sprang to life.

"Wake up," he said to Nick, and the boy obeyed at once, sitting up in the bed, wiping the sleep from his eyes. A glimmer of leftover resentment lingered, but Nick said nothing, just dutifully rose and hurried off to the bathroom. Jack Peter heard the others make way, the quiet *good mornings* exchanged in the ebb and bustle of another daybreak. His father stuck his head into the room, and from the chair at the desk, Jack Peter nodded at him.

"You're up. Just us boys today," Tim said. "Your mother's back to work. Come have some breakfast with us and say good-bye."

Good-bye, he thought after his father departed. Good-bye, mother; good-bye, father. Good-bye, Mr. and Mrs. Weller. Good-bye, Nick at the bottom of the sea.

At the breakfast table, Jack Peter watched his parents get ready for the day. They moved like bees from flower to flower. Coffee on, muffins in the toaster. Cereal bowls and spoons, a bottle of milk, cornflakes, a ripe banana cut into coins. The newspaper rescued from the front stoop, shedding its plastic skin. She was trying to tell his father a story, but had trouble keeping his attention. A manila folder on the counter contained her evidence, and she kept returning to it and brandishing different sheets of paper.

"There's a painting in the rectory at Star of the Sea," she said. "That's where I first heard of it. All these years and I never knew, a shipwreck right in our backyard."

Shuffling across the floor in his bare feet, Nick entered the kitchen.

His hair stood on end like a cartoon character just frightened out of his wits. I suppose he had been, Jack Peter thought. I mustn't forget about the dog.

His father tousled Nick's hair. "Orange juice?"

Nick and Jack Peter nodded, and he fetched two glasses from the cupboard.

"So I went to the Maritime Museum yesterday," she said. "Did you know they have an archives there with a record of every ship that hit the rocks from here to Machias?"

His father poured the juice. "Say when."

She buttered a muffin and chomped a half-moon from the edge. "And here's a list of all the passengers. No survivors, can you imagine? And some of the drowned came ashore. Listen: 'bodies taken by friends.' And the others were never found. Do you understand what I mean? Tim, are you listening?"

"Bodies taken," he said.

"Not that. Some bodies were never found. And I looked on the Internet to find out what happens to bodies left at sea."

Gingerly, he stroked the red marks on his neck. "Honestly, Holly. In front of the boys."

She chewed another bite. "You boys can take it, can't you? It's not as if it happened just yesterday. Bodies disappear quickly, but in the right conditions, the bones can last for years, for centuries. The bone, Tim, the arm bone."

In the next chair, Nick shoved a spoonful of cornflakes into his mouth and crunched.

"I'll bet you anything," she said, "when the tests come back, they'll say just how old it is, just how long it has been in the water: 1849."

His father pulled out the sports page from the newspaper. "And the dog just found it on the beach?"

"Don't you get it? The bone, the shipwreck, the weird voices in the night. Miss Tiramaku says there might be ghosts. *Funa-yurei*, she says."

Clearing his throat, Tim leaned back against the counter, regarding her with wonder. "Tiramaku," he said at last, making the name sound like an insult.

His parents stared at each other from their respective corners, a truce passing between them before any shots could be fired. His mother was the first to break, glancing at her watch. "I'm late. You boys be good."

They mumbled their promises through their cornflakes.

The boys vanished after breakfast, off to their secret games. Tim let them go with a smile. They were close as brothers sometimes. On the counter lay the jumble of Holly's papers, and he stacked them neatly in their folder, sighing at his wife's latest obsession. Old bones, ghost ships. That ridiculous Japanese woman with her crazy ideas. He washed the dishes and gathered the plastic garbage bag to take outside to the trash cans. He shivered as he looked out to the snow clouds collecting off to the west. He had just lifted the lid from the metal can when a blur of white in the yard frightened him.

Flushed from his hiding place, the white man bristled alert and then darted between the fir trees and crossed the road. All angled arms and legs, he galloped along the edge of the Quigleys' house and disappeared from view. It all happened so quickly that Tim could not believe what he was seeing. He shoved the trash bag into the can and considered following, but knew from hard experience that it would be as futile as chasing a rabbit. The cold handle cut into his palm, so he screwed the lid back in place.

White as a ghost, white as paper. Tim had thought it was dead, if such a thing could ever be called alive. Or shown to be a great white dog. Or a figment of his mind, but there was the white man again, running not twenty feet from the house. Where the man had brushed against the evergreen branches, needles still swept the air. For the longest time, Tim stared at the path the thing had taken like a deer caught in the open and gone to cover. He thought if he waited long enough he might make him reappear.

Across the street, in the parlor window of the Quigleys' house, the curtains parted and suddenly closed. How strange to have someone home in the middle of the day, but of course, the children were on Christmas break. Perhaps they had witnessed the white man, too. Tim turned his collar against the wind and walked over to the neighbors'. Behind the front door, their dog barked madly. He listened for the approach of someone coming to calm him. Staring him in the face was a brass door knocker in the shape of a humpback's fluke, covered in a pale green patina and pitted with salt. Three knocks until one of the twins answered through a crack no wider than her face. She kept the dog at bay with one firm leg against its chest.

"Howdy," he said to the child.

"Nobody's home," she said. "My mother went out."

"That's okay." He could not remember which one of the identicals she was. They were two halves of the same peach. Without expression, she simply waited for him to continue. "Did you see anything strange go by just now? Something as big as a man?"

She shook her head and started to close the door. Slick as a salesman, he stuck his foot in the opening. "Wait, let me at least have my guess this time. I'd say Edie, is that right?"

"No," the girl said. "It's Janie."

"Ah, you're right. I should have known by your obvious charm and intelligence. Tell me, Janie, were you just peeking through the curtains?"

A guilty smile spread from ear to ear. "No."

"In that case, you better fetch me Miss Edie."

The head disappeared, and the collie stepped into the void, sniffing him in the crotch. Tim pushed away the sharp muzzle, and then both twins appeared side by side on the threshold. "Hello, Edie. I've just come over to ask you girls a question."

They stared at him, through him, waiting.

"Have either of you seen a man running around the neighborhood? A tall man, with white bare skin, with long hair and a tangled beard? I thought maybe one of you was spying from behind the curtains."

The girls stiffened slightly and inched closer to each other.

"I didn't mean to scare you. I could be all wrong, just my imagination."

The twins shook their heads in matching rhythm.

"Nothing strange at all?"

Edie wiped her nose with the back of her hand. "We saw the police come to your house on Christmas."

"That? It was about something we found on our beach, is all."

Janie wiped her nose as well. "Did they arrest him and take him away?"

Tim bent down so his face was on their level. "Arrest who?"

"Jack Peter," they said, and the certainty in their voices took him aback.

"Whatever gave you the idea that the police would come for my son?"

Each girl chewed on the inside of her cheek, one left one right, mirroring her twin. They stared past him to the house, where the two boys were playing.

"Our mother isn't home," Edie said. "And we aren't supposed to open the door for anybody no matter what." Janie closed it in his face.

One hard kick and the lock would break. Or at the very least, he could hammer with his fists until they opened up and answered his questions. Instead, he retreated without complaint, wondering the whole time what they must think about Jip. "Weird kids," he muttered, exhaling each word in a cloud of condensation. In the few minutes he had been outside, the temperature had dropped by several degrees. Cold air from Canada rushed in, and if the weather folk were right, conditions were ripe for a nor'easter. Batten down the hatches, and, Lord, it was freezing. He walked out into the yard, wondering if he should try to track the white man. The wound at his throat throbbed, and he remembered the last time he had given chase. Besides, the thing was long gone, no doubt racing over the headlands or in some rocky hiding place. What kind of creature had come crouching from his dreams? Bone cruncher, throat slasher, nightmare vision.

Back inside his own house, Tim called upstairs to the boys, and Jip answered as if nothing had happened. Safe, in any case. He flipped through the pages in Holly's ghost files. *Bodies not found. Sailor (stranger).* Perhaps she was right after all. Had some phantoms risen from the bones of a ship? Impossible.

The central heat cycled off and the blowers stopped, and within minutes, it was chilly enough inside for him to need an afghan to wrap round his shoulders. With a cup of coffee in hand, he nested in an armchair, staring through the window for signs of the white man prowling around outside. He brooded over the Quigley twins and their dark suspicions. Children had always found Jip strange, and they could be such emotional thugs. Even when Jip was just a little boy, the others chastised or shunned him, and Tim still remembered picking him up from his first day of nursery school to find him scowling and alone in a corner. As he grew older, kids called him retarded or stupid or crazy. No wonder he withdrew, no wonder he angered so easily.

Adults were no better, and in certain aspects, they were much worse than children. At least children had an excuse for the most blatant stares and finger-pointing, but catch an adult gawking at your child, and they would pretend to have not looked in the first place. But he knew. Questions were just on their lips: *What is wrong with him? Why does he act that way?* Strangers were bad, and friends could be unintentionally hurtful. Summers Jip used to join Tim on his rounds of the rental properties, back in the days when his son could still bear to be outdoors. Most of the annual vacationers or the owners of the grand houses would be too busy having their fun to pay much attention to such a quiet little boy. But some remembered him even when he no longer tagged along. The Schroeders, who had always offered lemonade, would make a point of saying "Tell your son hello." Jeff Hook at the barbershop would often ask, "What happened to that boy of yours?"

What happened, what happened?

He drew the thick blanket round his shoulders and leaned his head on the wing of his chair. Against the chill in the room, he felt warm and drowsy. For just a minute, he closed his eyes. Just a catnap. His coffee went cold.

Young again, the four of them, before the boys, before the nightmare years. The last September before the girls were expecting, right before the nine-month watch began. The summer people had gone away, the rows of cars parked bumper-to-bumper along the seaward lane, the French Canadians with their canvas rolling carts and beach umbrellas took their sandals and sun hats back to Montreal and Quebec. The millionaires returned to work in New York and Boston, making money once again. Gone the college kids on their endless breaks, the hordes of temporary workers at the beach bodegas and lobster shacks. All cleared out. An Indian summer Saturday upon them, bright and clear September, and it was just the four of them at the Wellers' home, Tim and Holly, Fred and Nell. Still new and fresh to one another, late twenties and free of care.

The red shells and splintered claws were strewn on dirty dishes like bones in a boneyard. Remains of a salad wilted in a wooden bowl. Empty wineglasses stood tall in ranks of red and white, here and there puddled with the dregs, one comrade toppled on its side, the merlot stain spread like blood on the tablecloth. A pinched roach had been extinguished in a saucer of drawn butter. They had started early that afternoon, firing up another couple of joints on the sun-drenched deck, the glorious feast at dusk, and after the food and wine, a cold dip in the ocean under a full moon. And then back for more wine, another smoke, and Fred fell asleep outside on a chaise longue wrapped in a beach towel against the chill. Around midnight, Holly curled up on a settee in the Wellers' living room till she, too, was lost in deep slumber. The windows were open to the sound of the lapping waves. Another bottle of wine uncorked, another pair of wineglasses in the low light of the dining room. From his chair, Tim watched Nell glide across the floor, her sheer wrap parting along the seam at one tan thigh.

"Happy?" she asked. Her smile anticipated his reply.

"Delirious," he said. "Stupendous, wonderful."

"What makes you so wonderful, Mr. Keenan?"

With a grand sweep of his arm, he took in the whole room and the outside world beyond. "Good food, good drink, good company. A splendid end to summer."

She stood before him, the wine in her tipped glass rolling like a wave. "I thought it might be me, Mr. Keenan, that made you happy tonight."

Looking up from his chair, he studied her face, realizing at last that she was playing, flirting with him. "Yes, you, too. I'm always happy when you're around."

Her wrap came undone, exposing the red and blue of her swimsuit. She laughed. "You've been staring at my tits all evening, Mr. Keenan."

"They are magnificent," he said and drained his glass. "You are magnificent."

In an instant her expression changed from smiling to sober, her eyes catching the light from the overhead lamp as she drew near. Close enough to smell the ocean on her skin, she stood above him and leaned forward, trapping him with her hands wrapped around the arms of the chair. He made no escape but sat quite still, his breathing matching hers.

"There was a wicked man," she said, "who had a wicked thought." She laid her hand against his bare chest and drew one fingernail down his breastbone. When she kissed him, her mouth tasted of smoke and butter, and he reached his hands beneath the fabric of her cover-up. She turned her wrist and slid her hand under the waistband of his trunks, and with the pad of her thumb she rubbed the tip of his erect penis. His hands wandered to the bottom of her bikini, sliding it quickly to the floor, and she stepped out of it, kissing him deeply. With a practiced shift, she rolled his swimsuit from his lap and straddled him in the chair. It all happened so quickly, punctuated by her faint moans, and he drank her in, the softness of the skin at her nape, the way her hair fell and covered his face.

"But Fred. And Holly—"

With one finger against his lips, she hushed him. "Our little secret," she said, each word accompanied by the roll of her hips. When they were finished, she kissed him on the forehead, and he closed his eyes. When he opened them again, she was dressed, and glancing back once at the spent man in the chair, Nell sauntered away on bare feet and went through the patio doors to check on her husband asleep under the stars. Inside, Tim watched them from behind the transparent doors, bodies by the ocean, trapped in his own dark reflection.

vi.

As she left the house early that morning, Holly felt a surge of relief, as if going to the office would prove a distraction to the weirdness of the past few days. The timebomb in her head, the jangled nerves. Priests and ghosts and haunted ships, the voices in the night. She was glad of the mundane pleasures of the job during Christmas week. It was quiet there, and she was alone except for Becker at the front desk, but even boredom has its limits. At three o'clock, she decided to go home, dawdled on the Internet, searching for ghost ships. The afternoon was nearly over when she packed her briefcase and stepped out into the deserted street.

Wind pushed around her car, and she had to lean forward and keep both hands on the steering wheel to maintain control. The sky was gray and thick with low clouds, and the sea had turned a dull pewter. In the wooden belly of the *Porthleven*, Fred and Nell saw the water breach the seams between the boards. At first, the leak spread slowly, a dribble through the cracks, and then one by one jets sprang free and sprayed the room. Then like a burst dam, a huge hole opened and in gushed the ocean, soaking the floor, and they began to panic, wading through the cold dark water, rising quickly to their ankles, over their knees. Serves her right, for seducing Tim and nearly ruining her marriage. And poor, poor Fred. But Nell and Fred were not out there. They were on the decks of some mammoth cruise ship, basking in sunshine, sipping brightly colored cocktails with tiny paper umbrellas. Away from it all—what Holly wouldn't give to be away from it all.

The infernal dream house loomed as she turned the corner. She parked in the driveway and waited, resting her head against the top of the steering wheel and closing her eyes for just a minute. Her pulse beat as steady as a clock. If the wind had not been buffeting the car, she might have catnapped, but as it was, a chill slipped in, and she was soon too frozen for one more stolen moment.

Stepping inside, she thought at first that nobody was home, and the place was an icebox, as though the boys had left open a window again. Hidden beside the Christmas tree, Tim slept sitting up in his easy chair. She leaned over and touched his knee. Tim's eyes popped open in terror, and he cowered under the blanket.

"Sorry," she said. "Didn't mean to startle you."

Her husband was still blinking and searching for his bearings as the boys came charging down the stairs. They were soaking. Jack Peter's hair was plastered against his scalp and Nick was as wet as a drowned kitten. Their shirtsleeves were damp to the elbows and their trousers were sodden from their socks to their knees. "Tim, what happened to the boys?"

"What happened, what happened?"

"The house is freezing, and the boys probably have pneumonia." Holly went to the coat closet and fetched a pair of blankets. "C'mere, honey," she said to Nick. "How did you get so wet?"

He trembled. "The walls."

"What walls?" Tim asked.

"It's like they were bleeding water. The walls in Jack Peter's room."

For a man half-awake, Tim raced quickly up the stairs, trailing a string of curses.

"Let's get you out of these clothes," Holly said, and then turned her back to give them the blush of privacy.

The boys struggled free of their shirts and pants, the wet fabric sticking to their skin. Both were pale and thin, shoulder blades sharp as fins. They wrapped blankets across their shoulders, marching up the steps ahead of her. Grousing about the cold, they entered Jack Peter's bedroom and found Tim standing in front of the wall, dumbfounded by what he had discovered.

There was no flood on the second floor, no puddles of standing water, and no broken pipes from the bathroom down the hall that had

leaked into the bedrooms. At first, Holly could not discern any difference at all in the room, except for its irrefutable coldness. The boys
hopped to the relative warmth of the bed and rolled themselves under
the quilt. Holly blew out clouds of her breath, which vanished in thin
wisps. Ice had formed on the inside of the windows, fractal patterns
etched on the glass. With her thumbnail, she scratched the surface to
gauge the thickness of the frost, as deep as glazing on a cake. Scanning
the room, she could not find any opening for the cold, and the iced window reminded her of her childhood home and the winters there in the
unheated upstairs bedrooms. Overnight anything damp would freeze
over until Daddy got the woodstove going in the kitchen. But in all the
years they had lived in the dream house, she had never seen ice form on
the inside of the windows.

Tim studied the walls, running his fingers across the plane as if tracing the lines in a drawing, and only when she stood beside him and aped
the tilt of his head could Holly see what he had divined. In the paint ran a
raised design, a water stain, but dry to the touch. With the palms of their
hands, they rubbed against the marks on the wall, which left a powdery
residue on their skin.

"Feels like sand," Tim said.

"Salt." She licked her fingertips. "Salt water."

He smoothed out a fragment of the stain and then inspected the dust
on his hand. The watermark spread in all directions from the ceiling to
the floor. On the edge of the trim and the bit of wooden floor beneath
the desk and dresser, the bookcase and the toy box, traces of salt remained. He toed the rug and dried flakes rose and dissipated. "How in
the world did salt water get up into this room?"

"Boys, put on some dry clothes and tell us what happened."

When the shock of the cold hit them, they hollered and danced across
the floor, their bare skin mottled red and blue, and just as quickly, they
dashed into fresh clothes, luxuriating in the warmth of thick socks and
corduroys and the bulk of wool sweaters. Tim measured the breadth of
the damage, feeling his way along the wall. He clucked his tongue

against the roof of his mouth as he calculated the meager possibilities of cause and remedy. After she had helped her son dress, Holly sat on the bed and took each boy by an arm and pulled them to her. "Tell me."

"It still seems like a dream," said Nick. "Jack Peter was over there by the window, and I was on the floor. All of a sudden, I am sitting in wet. My legs are cold like when you sit down in the grass and don't know the ground is wet and it creeps up on you and goes through your pants, and you don't realize what's happening till it's too late."

"Don't worry," Jack Peter said. "I tore up the picture."

"Please don't interrupt. Would you please let Nicholas tell his story?"

"When I stood up that's when I noticed Jack Peter staring at the walls. Water was coming in, not gushing, but . . ."

"Seeping," Jack Peter said.

"Slow, same as when you get a cut and it's coming out and won't stop, but not so fast that there's blood all over the place. We tried to hold it back, but the water just seeped onto us till we were all wet."

Inching closer to his mother, Jack Peter said, "Inside a wave. If the ocean came in and tried to drown the whole house."

Holly and Tim looked up at the ceiling. The salt left a swirling line as pronounced as the mark that waves leave upon the sand.

"I was afraid," Nick said.

"That he would drown," said Jack Peter.

"But just like that the water stopped. Just like ebb tide, when everything gets dry again. But cold and dark in the room. The ice came on the windows fast as paint, and that's when we thought to yell for Mr. Keenan, but he never answered."

Upon hearing his name, Tim stopped examining the filigree of salt upon the ceiling and faced the others with a blank expression. Holly raised her eyebrows at him. "And what were you doing this whole time? Where were you?"

"I never heard a thing—"

Nick joined the defense. "We couldn't wake him. We tried, but at first, he didn't ever move, like he was dead, and then when I shook him by the shoulder, he moaned in an awful way, and I thought he might be sick."

"I don't remember any of this," Tim said. "I had just closed my eyes for a minute, and the next thing I know, you're waking us all up. From a dream."

"To a nightmare," she said. Far below in the basement, the furnace roared and the blowers breathed to life. Slowly, the heat returned. For the rest of the day, Tim went to check on the thaw. They spent the night camped out in the living room by a roaring fire, huddled in blankets with the television on all night, afraid of their own house.

Five

At dawn, Tim woke before the others but found he could not move from beneath the blanket on the couch. An incapacitating fatigue. Daylight arced across the ceiling, and he watched the whitening surface, thinking, thinking of the man he had seen, the wild white man, first on that night when driving Nick, the amazing shape of the creature crouching by the road. And on the beach, again the hunched-over thing spied from a window. Giving chase, he had stumbled and fallen and came to with blood on his throat. He rubbed the sores and winced. Just when he had found a logical explanation—the dead white dog in the trunk of the policeman's car—Tim had seen it again. The white man running, but what if it was a hallucination? He never had hallucinations. He lived in the real world. Work to be done, problems to solve.

Through the windows he saw the clouds amassing in the west, and the sky filled with promise. He carried the idea of snow in his mind as he set about his chores. Upstairs, the boys' bedroom had dried out completely and was warm and snug. The salty residue on the walls had vanished. No ice frosted the windows. He checked for leaks where the winter might come in and furred each window with weather stripping, glancing now and again at the beach below for any signs of the bogeyman.

Beside the rocks he found a dark patch of sand that he thought might be the bone spot, but he could have been mistaken. He worked deliberately and quietly, the weight of the past few days lifted by the mundane task. When finished, Tim crept back downstairs and found the bodies at rest where he had left them. Holly and the boys looked like New Year's revelers on the morning after, crashed in the easy chair and on the floor, sleeping it off. He was grateful for the respite from his anxieties.

As soon as Holly spoke, he knew that she had been awake for some moments staring at him in the crepuscular light. He went to her side and bent to face her when she opened her lips. "What are you thinking about?"

"These strange days. Ghosts and the boys."

"You think so, too?"

With an arched eyebrow, he conveyed his skepticism. "Jip's bedroom is just as it always was. Not a trace of the ice or salt. Weird."

She sat up slowly and stretched her arms straight out and rolled her shoulders as fluidly as a cat. "Like it never happened."

The boys were sleeping side by side on the floor between the fireplace and the Christmas tree. Chests falling and rising, their breathing synchronized. Twins. In the dimness, they looked alike, their flyaway hair, the way they had wrapped themselves in blankets. Two versions of one boy.

"It's good that he has Nick," said Tim.

"He won't always be here," Holly whispered. "We need help with Jack."

"I suppose you are right." He laid his hands on her shoulders.

"So you're okay with this? With finding someone to talk with Jack?" He leaned over and kissed her on the forehead.

Holly held him off. "I'm serious, Tim. I worry about him all the time, about how strong he's becoming, and how scared I already am of him. And what happens when we're no longer around to take care of him?"

"Whoa, one step at a time," he said.

"It doesn't have to be Miss Tiramaku, but they seem to have already developed a rapport," she said. "They're on the same wavelength, the one that never reaches us."

With the white of his smile, he surrendered. "Okay, okay. What harm can it be to have him talk with her?"

She slid from beneath his hands and wriggled out of the chair. Free, she kissed him and headed off to the bathroom. She sang in the shower, moved with élan through her morning ablutions. At breakfast, he caught himself staring at her, marveling at her newfound energy, and in her moments of grace and beauty, she restored his energy.

"Put down that pencil," Nick said. Jack Peter did not obey, perhaps was not even listening, but instead leaned further into his work, hunching over his paper, the pencil moving in a series of cross-hatchings to indicate the shadowed eyes, a delicate fury in his speed and gestures. In the flow of his innermost thoughts, he worked without hesitation, the lines appearing by destiny, with no consciousness behind them, the picture having existed there on the blank page from the beginning and needing only the instrument in Jack Peter's hand in order to appear.

"Stop," Nick insisted. "I will wait here until you stop. You have to quit sometime."

Jack Peter ignored his friend's request and began drawing the man's beard, hair by hair, the full face coming into being, mesmerizing and filled with menace.

The choice became clear: Nick could either remain there looking over Jack Peter's shoulder until he finished or he could deliberately interrupt the act. Taking the patchwork paper from beneath the mattress, he smoothed the wrinkles and laid it on the desk, just in front of Jack Peter, evidence of the crime. More tape than paper, the image had taken forever to reconstruct from its torn bits. The jigsaw page was all that remained from the ruined picture of the babies. The artist laid down his pencil.

"I want to know," Nick said. "Whether you draw these things before or after you see them."

Bristling with anger, Jack Peter tapped the end of the pencil like a jackhammer against the surface of the desk.

"Where do these creatures come from?" Nick demanded.

Jack Peter struck his temple with the soft eraser on the pencil's other end. He seemed to be beating out some telegraphic code only he could comprehend. A pile of his drawings lay stacked to his left, and Nick picked up the sheets and rifled through them, searching for a particular image.

"You need to tell me. Where's the one of the ocean coming into the house? I know you made that happen."

Nothing could deter Jack Peter from creating the monster at hand.

"Where's the dog? The one I heard two nights ago." Nick tossed the papers back on the desk. "In the trash? Shredded to pieces?"

Jack Peter refused to answer and could not be further distracted from the drawing in front of him. He bore down, concentrating on the unfinished man, moving his gaze from line to line, imagining how to complete it. No expression, just an intensity to his eyes, a furrow bisecting his forehead. The pencil snapped in his hand. They could play this game all day, Nick decided, and Jack Peter would not budge an inch. He was stronger that way. Stubborn.

"Did you put the bodies in the closet?"

"Were you scared?" Jack Peter asked, picking up a fresh pencil. "Did you want to run away? Why don't you go away, and I can stay here."

No course remained except surrender. With a sigh that began deep in his core, Nick withdrew and plopped down on the bed. He stared at the reflection of the gray sea and gray sky in the dresser mirror, slowly realizing that the spots in the glass were not flaws in the silvering, but the movement of falling snow. The weathermen on TV had been calling for a nor'easter all week, and it was finally here. The thought of snowmen and sledding gave Nick a thrill, a chance to be outside, and he roused himself from the bed and went to the window to stare at the real thing.

"Snowing," he said in a gleeful tone, but Jack Peter did not so much as turn his head.

For the rest of the morning, Tim puttered downstairs in the little work-room beneath the kitchen, sorting through a jumble of lobster pots that he had long planned on fixing and selling that coming summer to the tourists. Repair on the traps proved a mindless distraction, reworking tangled mesh, cutting slats on the table saw and tacking them to replace the broken pieces. He figured he would haul them all outside and by June they would be weathered gray. Tucked beneath the house in the small space behind the dune, the workshop was his sanctuary. No windows let in the light, so he toiled shut off from the world. In his workshop he often thought of those city folk who lived year-round in windowless cubicles, yearning for their two weeks, three if they were lucky, on the summer beaches. They would arrive, blinking moles, washed out from their arti-ficial days, just to have a taste of sun and salt and wind on their faces. He, on the other hand, was outdoors every day of the year, and in the peak tourist season, often from dawn to past dusk. An outside man with an inside boy.

He pounded a nail into the wood, resolving again to fix his son. Once these strange days had passed, he would figure out some new tactics for getting Jip over his phobia. Reintroduce him to the fresh air, give him something to do with his hands. She was wrong about Jip, dead wrong. He could be reached, he could be mended. The son Tim had always wanted. The son that should be his.

When his work on the pots was finished, he climbed the stairs to the kitchen and saw, as he opened the door, how the light had changed, and at once he knew that snow was falling, and felt just like a kid again, waking on a school day to the spectacular white of a blizzard. He called upstairs to the boys with the news. "It's snowing!"

"We know!" Nick shouted from the top of the stairs.

Tim thought at once that Nick would want to go outside, and later, perhaps after Holly came home and could stay with Jip, he could have a real winter's day again and take Nick on a sled or build a snowman.

Along with that delight came a pang of regret that Jip would not agree to join them. Nick hopped down the stairs and slid across the wooden floor in his stocking feet. Together they hurried to the picture window to watch the first real storm of the season. A thin palimpsest of white covered the ground, and the snow was now falling in waves, flakes hissing into the sea, painting the cold rocks, and still melting against the patches of sand.

"Maybe we'll go out later," Tim said. "Just the two of us, when Mrs. Keenan comes home."

The boy beside him nodded with joy.

"Nothing better," Tim said, "than a snowy day."

The first wet fat flakes began to tumble from the clouds just as Holly sneaked away from her office to drive to the Star of the Sea rectory. On her way, she had picked up a cherry strudel at Schroeder's Bakery, for she wanted to stay in Father Bolden's good graces since he would have to agree to spare his housekeeper the time to be with her child. Holly was certain she could arrange her help, now that Tim was no longer the main impediment.

The boys, too, had seemed changed. At the breakfast table, they had been nattering on in their own private language about their plans for the day. She studied Nicholas closely to see if he had gotten enough sleep after his nightmares. Honestly, babies on the walls, a flood that came and went like the tides. He seemed to have recovered somewhat, although when the Wellers returned, his mother would no doubt notice the dark circles under his eyes and his pale complexion from being inside since Christmas. Nick would have tales to tell her, dogs and bones and weeping rooms. They might never let him come back again.

The snow flew in a frenzy against the windshield and made the storm seem more threatening, enough so that she considered heading straight for home. But when she pulled the old car into the parking lot, sliding slightly to the left, the motion slowed, and stepping into the snow shower, she was surprised by how gentle and harmless and beautiful it was. On such days when Jack was a toddler, she had dressed him in a blue snowsuit, thick overalls with suspenders and a matching down coat, so that he could barely move. Stiff legged and waddling in his rubber boots, he would come outside into the wonder, and within minutes his cheeks would brighten to red and his nose was a cherry button. She'd fling him onto a sled and pull him to the top of a small hill, and there he would consent to sit in her lap for a ride to the bottom. The weight of him was just as real after all these years, his back pressed against her chest as they whooshed along, snow spray in their faces, and his laughter erupting from deep within, so hard that she could feel it in her bones. She would give anything to hear that laugh again.

Father Bolden answered the door in a worn black shirt and collar, his oversized gray cardigan around his shoulders like an old friend. The sly fox pretended he was surprised to see her and a little put out by her unannounced visit, but his ruse fell apart the moment he spied the white bakery box hanging by the twine curled around her fingers. She held it up to his eye level. "Strudel," she said. "I hear your favorite is cherry."

"How did you know?"

With her chin, Holly gestured past him toward the kitchen.

He frowned and nodded over his shoulder. "A man might keep a secret from a wife, but never from the housekeeper. Don't let the snow in. Come along, come along. I'll put on a fresh pot of coffee."

Brushing the snow from her shoulders, Holly entered the rectory and made her way to the dining room. Excusing himself to find Miss Tiramaku, Father Bolden left her alone. She stared at the painting of the drowning ship, trying to convince herself that there were no such things as ghosts.

Father Bolden touched her shoulder and she leapt from her skin. He had slipped into the room with the pastry, plates, and a wicked-looking knife, while out in the kitchen, Miss Tiramaku was taking cups and saucers from the cupboards. Holly had heard none of this. She pressed her fingertips over her heart to slow its beating.

"I didn't mean to frighten you," Father Bolden said. "You were in a bit of a trance."

"Just this painting," Holly said. "I'm not sure why, but it seems so vivid to me, so real. I've found out more about it."

"Miss Tiramaku said you were off to the archives to research."

"Damn," she said. "I left all the papers at the house."

Carrying a tray with three cups and a pot of coffee, Miss Tiramaku appeared to be struggling, and when Holly offered, she allowed her to remove the weight of the carafe in order to set down the service on the table. When her hands were free, Miss Tiramaku greeted her in a quick embrace, stiff as a hug from Jack. She looked much older again, as if being in the rectory or the company of the priest had given her more gravitas, but even so, she was a welcome sight.

The priest began to pour. "Mrs. Keenan here was—"

"Holly," she said. "Please call me Holly."

He smiled and moved to the next cup. "Holly found herself lost in the *Wreck*, and I may have given her a bit of a fright."

"No, it's just that after the last time I saw it, I started having dreams about the shipwreck and hearing things, imagining things. Knocking on the walls of the house. Tapping inside my head." She turned her face away, eyes downward. "Tell me, Father, where does the church stand on the matter of ghosts?"

"Ghosts?" He looked at her over the top of the frames of his eyeglasses. "You seem to be preoccupied with ghosts. That's the second time you've brought them up."

"On Christmas eve, after midnight, I was driving home in the fog and I stopped when it was getting too thick. There were voices coming out from the sea. I thought it was a party or a husband and wife having an argument, but now I could swear they were the crew and passengers on that ship. I had to find out. I went to the museum and dug up records from the *Porthleven*. A handwritten list of the passengers. Did you know that people around here came and claimed the bodies found in the wreck? And some bodies were never found, just left there at the bottom of the sea? And then this bone turned up, a human bone, the arm bone of a child, right on our property. Don't you see, it all adds up. Ghosts."

Setting a cup and saucer before her, he picked up the knife to attack the strudel. "In general, no to ghosts or wandering spirits. Tell me, Holly, have you been talking with my housekeeper here? About the *yurei*? Have you no shame, Miss Tiramaku?"

Miss Tiramaku poured a shot of cream in her cup, and it swirled round like a cloud.

The snow reminded him of that woman who had come to the house yesterday. In one eye, snow had swirled like a shaken globe. Jack Peter knew he should not stare, but he could not resist the strangeness of the white flakes in the black of her eyes. She was speaking to him, telling a story, but he was not listening, for he was watching the snow fall in her eye. His parents and Nick were in the other room, listening to Frank Sinatra. She had been talking for some time, and he had no idea what she was saying, and he looked for some way out so he would not be lost.

"Your mother tells me you like to draw."

"I got an artist's kit for Christmas. And paper."

She pretended to look away, the way adults sometimes do, to show they are not that interested in the conversation and try to throw off suspicion. "What do you draw? Things you see or things you imagine?"

He turned his head in the opposite direction and drummed his fingertips on the table.

"Maybe sometime I can see your drawings?" she asked. "Even your secret ones."

He nodded. That would be okay.

"I know you like monsters. Do you draw monsters, too?"

"Yes," he said. "And Nick."

She looked puzzled. "You like to draw pictures of Nick, or do you like to draw with Nick?"

He did not understand her question and did not reply.

"Nick seems to be a nice boy," she said. "Is he a good friend?"

He nodded. "He comes over here to play. He stays inside with me."

She leaned in closer, so close they nearly touched, and she asked, "Does that make you happy?"

"Sometimes," he said. "And sometimes I am mad. They said they might send me away."

"Your mother and father?"

Jack Peter nodded. "And Nick," he said. "He held me underwater. He wanted to get rid of me."

She gasped. "Did that make you angry?"

"They should send him away. Not me."

"You are a special boy," Miss Tiramaku said. "I understand, because I was a special girl, too, just like you, and other people, they don't know, do they? They think we are not listening, but we hear everything. They think we are not watching, but we see everything. They think our heads are filled with made-up things, but we know the difference between what is real and what is not."

"I am tired of having to draw all of the time, every day, to take care of everything. Nobody listens, nobody knows."

"I know your secret," she said, and in her eye raged a storm.

"Snowing," Nick said at the window, jarring Jack back from his memory of the conversation with the woman who could see the pictures inside his mind. She vanished from his mind as suddenly as she had arrived.

From downstairs, his father called to tell them, too, that it was snowing. Jack Peter laid down his pencil. He wanted out.

ii.

At first the storm mesmerized the three of them, and they watched for a long time as if drugged by the shifting patterns of white. One by one, they peeled away, off to do other things while the snow fell in the background, slowly accumulating without their awareness, an inch sneaking up on another inch. Tim loved the feeling of the first heavy storm of the season, how it covered the ground and blanketed the house. He had switched on a lamp in the living room, but the rest of the house had softened to a muted gray. The snow deadened outside sounds to a whisper, while the old house creaked and groaned like a timbered hull rolling in the waves. The sensation made him sleepy, and he would have settled on the easy chair for a nap if not for the vague anxiety brought on by Holly's absence. She had taken the car that morning, not his Jeep, and if the conditions worsened, she might have trouble on the roads.

At one o'clock, he climbed the darkened stairs to find the boys. Pausing outside the door, he heard them bicker.

"Where did you see him?" Nick asked. "You couldn't have seen him, because he's only been outside."

"I've seen him through the window."

"Yes, but only from faraway. You've never seen him up close."

"I've seen him, I've heard him."

"How could you hear him?"

"He's been to the house," Jip said. "Many times."

"That's not what he looks like anyway. His arms aren't as long as that."

"What do you know? You don't know what I make—"

With one knuckle, Tim tapped on the door, and the boys halted their conversation immediately. Like a ghoul in a horror movie, he opened the door as slowly as possible so that its hinges squealed, and he stepped into the room in a stiff-legged gait. They had moved furtively to the bed, papers rustling beneath the blankets. Guilty little buggers. "What's all this, then?"

"Nothing," Jip said. To silence his conspirator, all he had to do was gaze in Nick's direction.

"A secret," Nick said.

"It's not nice to keep secrets from your father." Tim folded his arms across his chest, but when no confession was forthcoming, he relaxed and smiled at them. "Boys will be boys, and every one of them a scoundrel."

The quilt twitched up and down like a mouse hopping in the bed, and Jip quickly removed a bare foot from under the covers.

"You boys trying to scare me? How about some beans and toast for lunch and a couple of fried eggs?"

Excited by the prospect of their favorite meal, the boys sprang from the bed. In their wake, they left a trail of paper in the folds of the blankets, and Tim was tempted to call them back to clean their mess. Drawings on the floor, pencils on the pillows. Or, he thought, he could straighten the scattered pages for them, but then he let the moment pass.

They were just toddlers when he had first made them toast and beans, but he was already a dab hand at the Maine way, with a healthy dollop of maple syrup whisked into the pot, sweet as candy. At the meal's end, their faces had been slick with brown sauce and their fingers were glued together. He wet the corner of a napkin with warm water from the sink and scrubbed them clean. Nick was pliant, giggling, his mouth pressed against the cloth in stern resistance. Washing Jip, by contrast, was like dealing with a stiff doll. Clenched against his father's touch, he offered no fight, no assistance, no squeals of joy in the simple act. The difference between the two toddlers had saddened him, and he could not smell the sweetness of baked beans in maple syrup without a faint echo in memory.

Older now, and slightly more hygienic, the boys did not need his help in cleaning up after the meal. Like two lobstermen come in off the North Atlantic, they gulped down their food and wiped their plates with triangles of toast. He sat with them, modeling fastidiousness to no avail, and they ate in silence, content for the company and satisfied without conversation. Every speck gone, they waited for him to finish before asking to be excused, and between bites, he watched them watching him. He noticed for the thousandth time just how much Nick favored his mother's looks, but the point of view made it seem a fresh observation, like seeing one of Jip's distorted drawings, the long-familiar suddenly made new.

The face of the mother in the face of the child. She was on some Caribbean beach, port of call, looking out over the same ocean, basking in sunshine, and he remembered the smell of her summer skin. Outside his window, the snow poured like feathers torn from the gray sky. He pictured Nell in her swimsuit on the beach in the summertime and wondered how different his life would have been with her, with Nick as their son. One moment changes everything. He could have gone back to school, made something different of himself. Had a fine house like the Rothmans' place. Had a fine wife, a fine son. But the images were as fleeting as the snowfall. He pictured Holly looking through her office window at the storm, wondering if she should come home.

He stacked the dishes in the sink and made a sea of foam from the soapsuds, and as he scrubbed, he kept an eye on the blizzard outside, half expecting Holly to come through the door at any minute. When he was finished with the bean pot and the cutlery, he went to the phone on the wall and dialed her cell phone, but heard it ring on her desk in the living room. She was so forgetful these days, so preoccupied.

He shook his head and tried her number at the office. After the fifteenth ring, he decided she must be on her way, so he hung up. She was no good in the snow, not having grown up in New England, and besides she had the car without the front-wheel drive and no chains, and he wished she would just show up already. The boys had gone off on one of their games, and he had no one to talk to and a surplus of nervous energy. He dialed her office again, the receiver smelling of soap, but it just rang and rang.

The fidgets threatened to overwhelm him, but fortunately, he remembered the seven lobster pots in the workroom. Earlier in the day when he was mending the slats and mesh, he had noticed how odd and out of place was the new material against the old. The whole stack should be taken outside and given a chance to weather and fade in the cold and damp. Now, he brought them up a pair at a time, and on the third go-around, he decided to save time by taking all three remaining traps. At the threshold, he stumbled into the kitchen, dropping them all and sending one clattering across the floor. Nick and Jip rushed to see what had happened.

"Butterfingers," Tim said. "When you try to save yourself some trouble, you only get more trouble."

"Where are you going with these traps?" Jip asked.

"I fixed them up and thought I could sell them as antiques to the tourists this summer, Lord knows, they're old as sin. But you see where the new wood sticks out against the faded bits. Folks can tell. So I need to get them beat up a bit and exposed to the elements. You boys interested in lending a hand?"

They carried the traps to the mudroom and laid them near the outside door. Tim shoved his hooves into a pair of boots and grabbed a parka from the hook. "Get a coat, Nick, and some boots. You can help me take these round to the back. A good freeze and a couple months of salt air and they'll be good as new. Good as old."

Tim stepped out into the heavy snow, flying thick and steadily, and the boy trailed behind, faithful as a hound, under the bulk of the lobster pot. They trudged to the top of the hill and set them against the railing that ran along the back of the house. The colored lobster buoys hanging there had little caps of snow. At the end of their third trip, they stood to admire their work and watch the storm, white frosting on their hair and shoulders. A good four inches had fallen, creating a smooth and even layer undisturbed by man or beast, except for their own prints along the edge of the foundation and a very fresh and clearly delineated path between the house and the sea. Footprints had been covered over, but the dents in the snow remained. Tracks of someone who had been walking out there at some point in the past few hours. The trail began at the edge of the shore and meandered across the rocks before disappearing around the far side of the house. Tim put his boot into the nearest print and measured its length. Big as a man's foot.

The boy brushed the snow from his head and slicked back his wet hair. Almost immediately a new frosting of snow stuck to him. They did not speak, but by tacit agreement, they set off down to the sea, following the tracks to their source, picking their way around the rocks until the trail petered out at the shoreline. There was no other path to the right or the left. Whatever had made those marks seemed to have come out of the water.

On the tenth ring, Jack Peter answered the telephone. From the vantage of the kitchen window, he could discern the path his father and Nick had made, the heavy flakes covering them like snowmen, white shadows in a world of white. They had nearly disappeared into the page. Because he hated talking on the phone, he almost never picked up a call, but the incessant ringing was worse than his loathing of the instrument. He did not say hello or anything at all, waiting instead for the person on the other end to begin. At first only the sound of breathing filled the void, and then came his mother's disembodied voice.

"Is anybody there?"

"It's me."

"Jack? Hello. Where is your father? It was ringing and ringing."

"He's not here. Nobody's here."

A breath of exasperation escaped her throat. "What do you mean? Where's Nicholas? Where's your father?"

"They are in the water."

"What do you mean?"

"They walked to the ocean."

"In this storm? Are they crazy? What are they doing down by the ocean?"

He dropped the receiver, went to the window to check on the two, and then came back to the phone. "Following the footprints."

"Jack, where did you go? Stay on the phone, do you hear me? What footprints?"

"A monster's."

"How many times do we have to tell you?"

"One hundred times," he said, but she did not laugh. "They went out to take the lobster pots, so Daddy could weather them."

"That man, honestly. Why he felt the need to do it in a blizzard."

"To sell to the tourists."

She laughed, finally. "Listen, Jack, when your father comes in, I need you to tell him to come pick me up. In the Jeep. My car is stuck, do you understand?"

He nodded.

"Are you shaking your head? You know I can't hear that over the phone? Yes, Jack, but listen, I'm not at work. I'm at the church, where Miss Tiramaku lives. Star of the Sea. Can you remember or write that down? Tell him right when he comes back inside."

"Wait." He dropped the receiver again and went to the kitchen where his drawings and pencils had been abandoned. On the back of a picture of the man from the sea, he wrote the name of the church in careful block letters. When he came back to the phone, he could hear her talking to someone else in the room, so he waited until she had finished.

"Jack, are you there? Where did you go? Don't let the phone clunk like that. Did your father come back?"

"You told me to write it, so I had to get a pencil."

"Read it back to me, Jack. So you'll remember."

"Star of the Sea," he said. "Get Mommy in the Jeep."

"You're a good boy," she said.

"You're a good mother," he said.

She laughed again and hung up. For a long time, there was only silence, and then the reassuring dial tone hummed in his ear, but when an angry sound, like an alarm, began to chatter, he dropped the receiver to the floor and stepped away.

Outside, the wind blew the showers across the sky, and the snow had subsumed Nick and his father. Jack Peter pressed his forehead against the windowpane as he peered through the flowing eddies, anxious for sight of them, but they were gone as surely as had they been erased. The trail from the sea to the house was vanishing, too, little more than an impression, and he went from window to window, seeking a sign of where they might have gone. He made a circuit around to the front of the house and there saw a figure approaching, white on white, as though a snowman had come to life and was struggling to find shelter from the storm. As it drew nearer, the figure gained clarity. It was not Jack's father but the drawing man, ghastly thin and naked, his wild hair blowing in the wind, the snow caked in his beard around the horrid mouth. Come for him at last, come to take him away. Take Nick instead, he thought, and realized in the same moment that Nick was outside with his father, leaving him all alone. On bandy legs, the monster crept closer to the house.

His every thought was falling away and let loose into the world. The figure in the window got bigger and bigger, and just as Jack stepped back, the white man reached out both long arms as if to grab at him and pull him through the glass. His long bony fingers stretched and slapped at the windowpane with a report as sharp as gunfire. His face came fully into view, a wretched expression in his black eyes, threatening and imploring, a grimace full of teeth as ruined as tombstones. Jack had seen that face many times before, and now he realized his mistake in drawing it. He screamed, and the creature heard him through the glass. Turning its head as if mounted on a spit, the man glanced over its right shoulder, aware of another presence nearby. The creature quickly retreated, running away from its pursuers. Jack withdrew to the heart of the house, waiting in the kitchen for what was next to come. He was frightened by the uncertainty.

Tim and the boy had stood at the tideline, puzzling over what might have made the footprints that had risen from the sea. These weren't the marks of a coyote or even the paw prints as big as that dead white dog's. They were clearly evidence of a two-legged gait, a man. Tim's mind jumped to the white man. He felt sure that Nick knew it, too, though he dared not ask for fear that he would worry him, for the boy was already anxious in his movements, casting his gaze up and down the shore, anticipating something emerging from the storm.

They slowly climbed the incline toward the house, guiding their steps through the trail they had carved. Curiously, Jip was not spying on them from the window as usual, and Tim wondered what might be occupying his attention. A trough in the snow skirted along the foundation, and below every window was a tramped-down area, as if their quarry had paused beneath each entry point to the house. The windows were all smudged and wet with dirt and melting snow. On the far side, the tracks veered sharply into the pines along the southern border of the property, and Tim and Nick followed them into the trees. Where the evergreen needles had fallen, the snow cover had thinned to a bare coating, and they nearly lost the scent, but the prints picked up again and the length between strides widened, as though the thing was running now and had crossed the road.

Panting, Tim stopped and considered the child at his side, cold and wet and tired. It could be anywhere, miles away, over the rocks or into the woods. As much as he wanted to put an end to the mystery plaguing them, he decided to abandon the chase. "This is no place for a child," he hollered into the wind. "Time to get you safe inside." They retraced the path their own boots had made and circled back to the door by the mudroom. A couple of old towels hanging on pegs allowed them to dry their wet hair into tangled manes. They wrestled free from their coats and boots and their soaking socks, turned up the cuffs on their wet jeans, and marched barefoot into the kitchen. Jip was at the kitchen table, drawing.

"Where were you so long?"

Nick looked like a wild thing, his cheeks bright red and his hair a shock. "We saw footprints out there. It's a blizzard, and we tried to follow them."

"What was it?" Jip asked.

"I don't know. Can't tell," his father said. "Did you see anything from inside?"

Bending down to his paper, Jip resumed his drawing. "Nothing. Just waiting."

They left him at the table and went to change into dry clothes. Tim lit a fire in the fireplace, warm heart to the quiet house, worrying about Holly out in the storm. Nick kept watch at the window, imagining a monster in every shadow. An hour passed before Jip stopped his drawing long enough to report about his mother's phone call and how she said to take the Jeep and find her at the Star of the Sea.

iii.

I'll not have another word about ghosts," Father Bolden said. "You should be ashamed of yourself, filling Holly's head with such tales. A ghost is little more than a trick of the mind at war with itself. A temporary manifestation of psychological conflict." He rubbed his stomach and licked the last of the cherries from the tines of his fork. "No more of your folktales, Miss Tiramaku." He turned to Holly. "Why don't you tell us about what brought you here in the first place? Why don't you tell us about your son?"

At one end of the mahogany table, Father Bolden and Miss Tiramaku sat together as familiar as a long-lost uncle and aunt welcoming her back to the family. The snowy day brought memories of the slant light of other such afternoons, holiday times with her parents and sister, catching up after extended absences, of cups and saucers, dessert plates dotted with crumbs, and feeling that they might never again have the chance to talk this way. She wanted to confess what she had done and what she had failed to do, what she had said and what she had failed to say. She had yearned to tell someone about her dreams and her boy for a long, long time.

"We came to Maine because of Tim. When we were first married, I would have followed him anywhere. It was his dream to come north, find a nice place on the ocean, settle down, and raise a family. His soul, he says, finds its natural rhythm in the tides. He was out of the service and thought he could go back to college here. Study the sea. And I had a postcard view of life, the boats in the harbor, lobster in the summertime, and the light in late September. We were happy here at first, and it seemed that the next part of the dream would come along right away. We'd start making babies, little water nymphs, and set them outside in the sunshine and clean air and salt water and watch them grow big and strong and healthy."

Miss Tiramaku shifted in her chair, and Holly wondered if her story was hitting a sore spot with her.

"We couldn't get pregnant for a long time, and I hope you don't mind, Father, but we tried everything in every conceivable way. . . ." She blushed at her accidental word. "I don't mind saying that I even prayed for a child. Hope had all but run dry, and then a small miracle. Pregnant at last, and those first few months I was expecting, I was deliriously happy. And then I found out what happened between Nell and Tim right before I got pregnant."

"And who is this Nell?" Father Bolden asked.

"She was my best friend. Is. She and Fred invited us over at the end of the summer, and it was nothing really, an indiscretion. We had been drinking, all of us, and they ended up in bed together."

The priest shoved the strudel in his mouth. "Did your husband confess?"

"He never said a word, but she told me, eventually. Months later. Look, if we hadn't both been pregnant . . . I'm over it," Holly said. "Moved on, and our babies coming together made it easier to forgive and forget. Or forget, at least. Though I'm not so sure about Nell. Maybe she brings Nicholas over so much because she still feels guilty."

"Nell is Nicholas's mother?" Miss Tiramaku asked.

Holly nodded and continued her story. "Look, I had a baby growing inside of me, I was so sure it was a girl, and I dreamed of seeing her, holding her, dressing her the way I used to with my baby dolls when I was little.

"Just as my belly was getting big enough to make it seem real, my anxieties took over. Something wrong with the baby. I dreamt it was a fish thrashing around inside, pulled by the tides. So many premonitions and omens. Just hormones and unbridled intuition. But who could I tell those to? Not Tim, surely, because he was just elated, and this baby was the missing piece that would make us happy."

To calm her nerves, Holly took a sip of coffee. "There was Nell, but she had her own pregnancy to think about, so our problems simmered just below the surface. I just spent the last weeks afraid that the baby would not be what I thought it should be. When Jack was born, he was such a beautiful boy, it went out of mind. Until, of course, I saw the infants together over time. Nell's son, Nicholas, was so different. Where Jack was quiet, almost eerily calm, Nicholas was fussy but animated and curious. And even though they say it's best not to compare, what mother can resist to some degree? Especially when it begins to sink in that there's something missing, something odd about your child."

She stopped herself. Her eyes began to water, and she knew she would cry if she went on talking, and she did not want to cry, told herself that she should not. The room went quiet except for the murmur of snow falling against the windows. Father Bolden leaned back in his chair, looking older than his years. "God often gives us burdens as a reminder of the call to sacrifice."

"Please," Holly said. "I would trade that sacrifice to have a normal life for my son. There's no sanctity in the suffering of a child."

"I only meant—"

Miss Tiramaku interrupted him. "He did not mean to diminish what you've been through."

"My apologies," she said. "It's just that people sometimes want to ennoble his condition and struggles, and I would give anything, trade anything, do anything for him to be . . . ordinary."

"I meant no harm," the priest said.

"Tell us how he developed his phobia of the outdoors," Miss Tiramaku said. "What happened that day on the beach?"

"When he was seven, Jack nearly drowned. It was the end of summer, a last day on the beach. Jack and Nick were sitting in the wet sand, just on the edge. The incoming waves were lapping along the shore and wetting their legs and swimming trunks. What could go wrong? It was a bright blue August, a few clouds in the sky. I was reading a novel, an old favorite du Maurier, and looked up from the book and saw that they weren't there anymore. And then I saw Tim racing, kicking up sand, and behind him Nell. Fred was just standing there, dazed in the sunshine, and I knew at once that the boys were under the water. We weren't keeping watch like we should, and I thought the boys were gone. I was paralyzed and couldn't move to save them."

"You were afraid," Father Bolden said.

"No. I wanted to help, that was my first reaction, my instinct, but almost immediately I was, I don't know, relieved that they were gone. Like an act of God was taking them. It was a horrible sensation. It lasted just an instant, but I blame myself for having wished him away."

She stopped suddenly and caught her breath. "I've never confessed before, but I'm sorry, so sorry. I raced across the beach, guilty, guilty, and they had reached them and were pulling them up from the bottom. Jack was alive, sputtering and coughing, but we couldn't find Nick until my husband pulled him from the sea. We all thought Nick was dead, pale and blue and had swallowed the ocean. Jack stared at him, intently, blankly, like he sometimes does, lost in his mind. And then when Tim pressed on Nick's chest, out shot a stream of water. He gasped and came back to us. But they were never the same."

For a second time, she stopped herself on the verge of tears, and she pushed away from the table, turning from the gaze of the priest and the housekeeper. Through the window, she could see the snow shaken from the sky in steady waves. "Look at it coming down. I should have taken the Jeep. I should go before I get stuck."

"I could run you home," the priest said.

"Oh, no, Father. My husband can pick me up, if you don't mind me leaving my car in your parking lot. He can bring me back to retrieve it when the roads are clear." She began rummaging in her purse for her phone.

"Of course not," he said. "But it would be no bother."

"No, no. Just point me to the phone. I seem to have lost my cell again."

On the tenth ring, someone answered the call, and she knew at once that it must be Jack by the resounding silence on the other end. She kept explaining where she was, and he kept dropping the phone to the floor. Each time, she turned to her companions with a look of bemused exasperation. She couldn't imagine why Tim had left him all alone in the house.

"He's done it again," she said. "Everything is so literal with that boy, gone to fetch a pencil I suppose. Jack, Jack, are you there?"

They finished their conversation, and when she was reasonably sure he had taken down the message, she hung up.

"He said the most curious thing. He said I was a good mother."

Miss Tiramaku put her hand on Holly's shoulder and led her back to the table. "He's right, you know. You are a good mother."

"Sometimes I wonder," said Holly.

With a brief smile, Miss Tiramaku forgave the self-deprecation. "Your husband is on the way?"

"He will be as soon as he comes back inside." Holly returned her smile. "According to Jack, he's out chasing monsters again."

iv.

The wipers beat furiously against the glass, and through the nearly impenetrable wall of white, Tim inched along, feeling his way through the storm. He worried about getting to the church a few miles away, and he worried that he would not be able to make it back home to the boys. As usual, Jip balked about going outside, and Tim was in no mood for protracted negotiations, not after he learned how long Holly had been waiting and how his son had completely forgotten to give him the message. Out on Shore Road, he was glad he had decided to leave the boys behind. Even if it meant they would be alone, at least they would be safe.

"Don't leave the house," he had told them. He did not want Nick outdoors tracking the invisible man. "Not for anything, Nick. If there's some problem, call the Quigleys across the road, and they'll help you, and I wrote down the numbers for the police and for Star of the Sea right by the telephone. In this storm, it'll take a while to get there and back, but I don't want you to worry. I've driven through worse."

"Take me with you," Nick pleaded. "Don't leave me alone with him."

Jip locked his fingers around Nick's wrist.

"Listen boys, you'll be all right as long as you stick together." The boy looked heart stricken, and Tim reassured him with a quick hug. "Don't worry, you're safe inside."

"I want to go," Nick said.

"All right, son, that's enough. If for some reason we're not home before dark, make yourselves supper. I'll call in any case before we head on home, just to check in."

The last he saw of them, Jip was lost in yet another drawing. Nick escorted Tim to the front door. "Be a good boy, son. And take care of things. Watch after Jip. I'll be back in a jiff."

Some jiffy, he thought to himself. The snow poured from the heavens. He wouldn't be surprised if a foot had fallen already. There were no other cars on the road, and though the county had plowed once earlier that afternoon, he still found himself searching for tire treads to follow. Round the bend at Mercy Point, he saw it again.

The figure crossed right in front of him. Had he been driving at normal speed, Tim would have run over the man. He could barely make out that there was a man at all, only the outline of his limbs, and the dark mane and beard discernible through the scrim. As Tim drew near, he could see that the man was deliberately standing in the road, a mad look of terror on his face as they locked eyes, provoking a confrontation. Stamping on the brakes, Tim felt the Jeep skid sharply to the right, and forgetting all he had been taught, he tried to steer against the slide but wound up fishtailing and lodging the back wheels between the road and an embankment.

"Shit," he said when the car lurched to a stop. Clutching the steering wheel, he sat in the car for a moment, hoping his heart would quit that awful pounding. He looked through the windshield, but the creature was gone.

Shaken, he stepped out into the storm and hollered at the place the man had been, but there was no reply, and he really hadn't expected one. In the cold and wet, he walked around to the rear and saw that the bumper on the passenger's side had plowed deep, and he could not tell if it was jammed against the earth or simply wedged into a snowbank. If he tried to power his way out of the drift, he ran the risk of sinking deeper without any traction. The Jeep was usually a hog in the dirt and mud, but he'd been stuck before when he'd gone off-roading and couldn't figure the escape angle. Caked in snow, he studied the situation and then got back in, convinced he could rock backward and wiggle his way free. Otherwise he'd have to hope to raise a cell signal in the storm and wait on a plow or the police for help.

"What the hell is that thing?" He sat behind the wheel considering possibilities, some crazed loon escaped from the nuthouse now wandering out to sea. Or worse, a ghost from Holly's ship. Whatever it was, that thing was as big as a man, that much he knew for sure. "White dog, my ass," he muttered and popped the car into reverse as he stepped on the gas. For a brief moment, the Jeep responded as he had hoped, swaying backward, and he could sense the treads dig and catch hold, but he shifted too slowly into drive, and the wheels simply fell back in place and spun a deeper rut. He was stuck. He beat on the steering wheel and mashed the horn, but it only made him feel foolish.

The blare of the car horn sliced through the quiet landscape, and even inside the house, the boys could hear it bleat like a lost sheep. The second sound was just as forlorn, the wailing of a man, and Nick wondered how the car sounded so far away, yet the man sounded so near. He imagined Mr. Keenan crashed on the road, his head striking the steering wheel, and he speculated, if that was so, when help might arrive and how long he would be trapped alone in the house with Jack Peter. The monster boy, the boy monster. He had gone mad these past few days, possessed by some spirit that had him drawing, drawing, drawing all the time. Even now, when they had the run of the place, Jack Peter scribbled at the table, oblivious to everything but his work.

Restless, and anxious about the tracks in the snow, Nick pestered Jack Peter for attention. "Let's do something. Instead of sitting around all day. This is worse than school."

"Let me finish. Leave me alone." He looked up from his work, malice in his eyes. "Do you want them to send me away?"

Nick hated him. He felt nothing but anger and resentment for him. Stupid, why did he have to be so stupid? Why couldn't he be normal, same as everyone else, and just get off his butt and play or fight or talk or throw a ball or break something or go outside? Stuck in the house in a glorious snowstorm with a lunatic. He wanted to smash his face. He wanted to sit on his chest and make him cry. Instead Nick just left him at the kitchen table and went wandering through the house.

He toured the downstairs rooms, picking up knickknacks on the tables and reading the titles of the books in the living room library. Toying with the idea of watching TV, he remembered that only soap operas and cooking shows and programs for little kids were on at this time on a weekday afternoon. He pawed through the mail in the basket by the front door. He thought of his parents out on the ocean in the warm sunshine. Stupid parents. They should come get him from this madhouse. Circling round Jack Peter, still concentrating on the details of his stupid drawing, he made his way up the stairs and headed for Mr. and Mrs. Keenan's room.

The inner sanctum. He had never been in their room without an adult present, and his solitude made him feel like a spy. Behind the door, their robes hung side by side, and he remembered Mrs. Keenan in the nightgown, the spill of her breasts. The bed was neatly made, so he was careful when he got in it, wondering which side was whose, and then he inhaled deeply on the pillows trying to catch their scent. Nothing, so he eased his way off and straightened the covers. In the dresser drawers, all the clothes were folded and sharply stacked, but he hesitated to open the closets, suddenly afraid of what might be lurking behind the door. The shadowy dimness of the space gave him the creeps, and he was about to leave when he noticed a white corner of a piece of paper peeking out from beneath the rug.

Squatting on his haunches, he peeled back the edge and found one of Jack Peter's pictures lying on the floor, but he could not make out the details, so he took the page to the window and held it at an angle to catch the available light. Two boys, half-dressed and floating beneath a wavy line, were locked together, wrestling, surrounded by fish and a ragged-clawed lobster on the sand. One boy pushed down on the other's head while the other boy had his arm round his attacker's shoulder to drag him to the bottom of the sea. The boys were mirrors to each other, a self-portrait fighting with itself.

He did not know what to make of the picture or why Jack Peter had hidden it there, a clue to a crime committed over three years ago. While

Jack Peter clearly remembered the drowning, he had never said a word about it in all this time. Nick set the drawing on the bed and rolled back the rug until it butted against the bedframe. On the floor lay four more sheets of paper, stashed like treasure maps. Four variations on a theme, the underwater wrestlers in different poses, but in each case, twin battled twin. He laid them out upon the bed like pages in a murdered and dismembered book, trying to make sense of the story.

He searched for more. In the linen closet in the hallway, beneath a stack of bedsheets, he discovered two pictures: the naked wild man crouched on a rock overlooking the ocean, and the white dog sprinting after someone who was indicated by part of one leg and a foot, the rest of the person escaping the edge of the page. He left them on the hallway floor by the closet door and then investigated Jack Peter's room.

Drawings had been hidden everywhere.

Another half dozen under his rug, a sheaf of papers tucked beneath the mattress, a batch in the dark cavern under the bed, and still more tucked in the leaves of books. Nick pried open the desk drawer crammed with page after page. It was madness. Hundreds of drawings, page after page after page. All the monsters on sheets torn from the sketch pad, crowding into notebooks, dashed off on scrap paper. Many showed the creature that prowled outside in the woods, by the sea, a wretched haunting thing. He gathered the drawings in a giant pile and spread them out, covering the entire bedspread, thick as snowfall. The pages spilled to the floor. Babies and bodies and bones from the sea. The sight of the pictures quickened his pulse and strained his breathing. His temples throbbed. Glimpsing himself in the mirror, he was shocked by how pale his skin had become and the dark circles under his eyes. Just like an inside boy. Feeling ill, Nick knelt on the floor by the bed and bowed his head to rest in a mountain of drawings. Jack Peter must be stopped.

The wind shifted outside and gathered speed, throwing the snow fine as grit against the windows. The storm made a constant roar, like the ocean in a seashell, but underneath that sound was a human cry, bitter and constant, as if some poor soul was keening. Nick rose from the floor and surveyed the hurricane of papers in the room. Leave it, he thought. When Mr. and Mrs. Keenan come back they will see the mess and realize how far their child has spun out of control. He wanted them to know and in knowing, do something about the problem. At the very least, they could rescue Nick, put him somewhere safe until his parents returned to claim him and take him away from such raw mayhem. He missed his mother and father and wanted to go home. Nearby, the voice outside roared again, pleading and insistent.

He breathed deeply to marshal the courage to go downstairs and face Jack Peter. Perhaps he had gone off his head completely and had been howling from the kitchen, but when Nick arrived, the room was empty. On the table lay his latest masterpiece, another vision of penciled madness, a close-up of the wild man's face, but the boy who drew it was missing. The entire house seemed deserted, though he knew this could not be. Perhaps Jack Peter had intuited what Nick had been up to and what he had discovered, and was in hiding.

"Jack Peter," he said. "I know all about the drawings. I know you are here somewhere. Come out, come out wherever you are."

Not a peep. He tried the mudroom, but it, too, was vacant. Cold air seeped through the slab floor, and Nick could see the steam from his breath when he called Jack Peter's name again. Thoughts of escape leapt into his mind, and he considered how to flee the scene, find shelter, and wait out the storm until the Keenans returned. Hanging on the peg, his coat was damp and stiff, but below it his boots were dry. From the open door, he yelled down to Mr. Keenan's workroom, but it was dark and quiet. He made his way into the living room.

Another log had been added to the fire, for it blazed, popping and crackling behind the hearth. The ornaments on the Christmas tree threw back the light, and the bare furniture absorbed the glow. Had he not thought to look toward the front door, Nick would have missed him. Jack Peter stood with his back to him but ramrod straight, transfixed by a face in the window. The monster was staring back at him, his hands pressed against the glass.

Unable to resist, Nick stepped forward and whispered, "Jack Peter."

The creature's mouth was moving and it appeared to be speaking, though no words penetrated the boundary between the outside and inside. His face was gaunt, marked with smallpox scars and wrinkles, deathly pale with deep circles under hollow eyes and teeth as brown and jagged as a broken fence. Snow covered the crown of his head and clotted in his mangled beard. Below his neck his skin was white as paper and laced with blue veins. His attention had been focused on Jack Peter, but when he saw Nick he thumped his palms onto the window and let out another doleful wail.

Their cups had been refilled and on each dessert plate sat another dainty slice of strudel. Father Bolden was busy sawing through the pastry. "So what happened next, after your son was saved from drowning?"

"I don't know," she said. "I'm not entirely sure. Jack wasn't the same. He became deathly afraid of going outdoors at all, just cried and screamed and threw fits anytime we tried to get him through the door, and it became nearly impossible for us to take him anywhere. The doctors attributed it to the trauma, and at first we thought he would grow out of it, but the paranoia just grew worse over time, not better. We tried everything, but he will not budge. He's just withdrawn into the safety of the house."

With a clatter, Miss Tiramaku dropped her cup onto the saucer. "And he won't go out at all? So it's just been the three of you these past few years? Must be a bit claustrophobic."

"Well, there's Nicholas," she said. "Thank God for Nick."

"I am surprised that you let them play together," Miss Tiramaku said. "After what Nick tried to do that day."

Holly gave her a quizzical look.

"Maybe he didn't mean it," Miss Tiramaku said. "But Jack told me that Nick tried to drown him that day."

A sharp pain lanced through Holly's forehead, followed by ticking, a sound so loud she wondered if the others could hear it, too. The room pulsed along to the beat in her mind, and everything slowed and swayed like the ship in the painting. She felt a swell of seasickness clench at her stomach.

"Don't be absurd," Holly said. She pressed two fingers at the center of her forehead to staunch the pain. The pounding seized her, and she raised her voice, "No, no. He wouldn't pull him under. He wouldn't hurt him. They're like brothers."

"Are you all right, my dear?" Father Bolden asked.

Holly waved him away, steadied herself, and closed her eyes.

Father Bolden interjected himself between the two women. "Perhaps you're mistaken, Miss Tiramaku."

"Yes," she said. "Mistaken. I didn't mean to upset you, Holly. Are you sure you are okay? Perhaps you would care to lie down."

"It's my head, can't you hear? I've been having these terrible head-aches lately."

The priest rose and crossed behind her, and put his hands on the back of her chair to pull it out for her. "We've upset you, my dear, and perhaps you would feel better if we just stopped talking about it. We could go into my study, find you a comfy chair. Miss Tiramaku will find you an aspirin, and you can have a nice rest in the dark while you wait for your husband."

Surrendering to the drumming in her skull, Holly allowed herself to be led into the study. The priest arranged a spot in a soft leather chair and laid a blanket across her lap. Through the leaded windows, she could see the falling snow as it lulled her. In the dark room, the priest sat in a chair across from her, the light from the hallway softening his fea-tures, and he patted her on the forearm. "How long have you been suf-fering these headaches?"

Behind him, the slim silhouette of Miss Tiramaku appeared in the doorway.

"Weeks now," Holly said.

"My own dear mother suffered from migraines all of her life, and she swore she saw angels and heard all kinds of strange things."

The shadow at the door entered the room and perched on the edge of the big black desk that dominated the space. "Is there something that's changed lately? Some trigger where your anxieties might be heightened and causing your hallucinations?"

Holly laughed. "Everything. My son hit me. Claims there were monsters under his bed. Then the wrecked ship and the ghosts come to haunt me. My husband chasing phantoms and coming home covered in blood. Salt water on the walls. Voices in the night."

"Too many ghost stories?" Father Bolden stole a glance at Miss Tiramaku.

"No, it's just Jack."

Miss Tiramaku nodded. "Jack showed me some of the pictures he's been making."

"Jack's monsters? He and Nick go off on these kicks for weeks at a time. Last summer it was baseball cards, and in the fall, they spent every weekend on board games, and then as suddenly as it begins, the craze is over and they're on to some other obsession. I never gave the little monsters a second thought."

Father Bolden said, "Sometimes I think all children are slightly mad. They suffer, finding their way out of childhood."

"The monsters," Holly said. She looked out at the snow. "I wonder what's keeping him."

Tim was sweating in the snow. His hair had frozen into porcupine quills, and he was hot and cold at the same time. On the floor behind the front seat, he found the shovel they kept for such emergencies, and he built a ramp out of hard-packed snow to ride the back tires down, but he was frozen and tired and not sure his plan would work. The lighthouse at Mercy Point glowed soft as a candlestick, a reassurance in the gloom. Nothing came down the road the whole time. No sound at all but the susurrus of snow and his own labored breathing in the miserable wind. From far away, a sudden piercing howl frightened him. He straightened and stood, trying to find the direction and source in the landscape, but he could not determine either. The wailing came from all sides and above and within. Caught between the two poles of his journey, he could only dig more furiously and hope to be soon free.

The engine whined when he turned the key, and Tim cursed his bad luck until the ignition clicked and caught hold. He threw the Jeep into gear and launched down the makeshift ramp and back onto the slippery road, making sure not to stop but to keep moving forward slowly. Following the tree line and the shapes of other landmarks, he found his way and drove carefully to the Star of the Sea parking lot. Beneath a streetlight sat Holly's car, a mound of snow dumped on the hood and roof, and further on, the rectory stood like a gingerbread house decorated for Christmas, with white frosting the roof and ledges, and cheery lights on in the downstairs windows. Gray smoke from the chimney filtered through the ribbons of snow, and he looked forward to a few moments in front of the fire and the chance to feel his toes and fingers again. As he stepped from the car, his left foot landed awkwardly in the slush, and pain shot across his lower back. The spasm seized him when he tried to move. Snow began to sift inside the Jeep and melt against the front seat and floor, for he could not shut the door, could not budge without excruciating stabbing pain. So this is what it is like to freeze to death, he thought. I will just stand here in this church parking lot and turn to snow and ice, and in the springtime, they will only have to thaw me out to bury me. The slightest tic sent fissures of pain along his spine and tightened his muscles into cords of steel. Even a grimace hurt, even a grunt, and when he tried to call for help, he found he could make no more than a choked whisper that even a dog would not be able to hear.

His name arrived on the wind. His wife had come running hurriedly from the rectory, calling for him, the snow whipping around her head and shoulders. Clenching her unbuttoned coat with one bare hand, she first reached out to shut the door of the Jeep. When Holly touched him to see what was the matter, the pressure buckled his knees.

"What's wrong with you?" she shouted over the wind. "What took you so long?"

"Threw my back out," he said, wrenching out each word. "Long story. No message from Jip. Got stuck on the road. Now I can't move."

"Jesus," she said. "We've got to get you inside."

The old priest, dressed more sensibly in a long duster and a hat and gloves, reached them, and Miss Tiramaku was two steps behind.

"What are we going to do?" Holly yelled at them. "His back has locked up."

"Can you try to take a step?" Father Bolden asked.

"No," Tim said with tears in his eyes.

Miss Tiramaku removed her gloves and then took Tim's hand in hers and bared it. "Relax, this won't hurt." Feeling for a pressure point, she located a spot along his wrist and then firmly pressed her thumb in the web of skin and muscle between his index finger and thumb. She held on to him until he began to feel some ease.

"I think I can move," he said. "What are you doing?"

"Tricks up my sleeve," she said.

"I could walk, if someone would hold on to me."

"Take my arm," said the priest, and they all shuffled together through the snow and made their way inside the rectory. While the back pain had subsided to a tolerable degree, he now felt the effects of the cold and the damp, and the others bustled around, finding a heating pad for him to lean against, a cup of hot tea, a warm blanket, and fresh woolen socks for his red feet. The pampering superseded the interrogation, but after he settled in a comfortable chair and had shaken off the chill, he faced the board of inquiry. They surrounded him and fired away, asking for details of his journey, what time he had left and how long it had taken, were the roads passable still. Satisfied with his answers, they all relaxed until the one remaining question popped into Holly's mind.

"But what have you done with the boys?"

v.

The thing beat against the glass, desperate to get inside. Drawn to the creature, Jack Peter stepped forward, and Nick had to catch him by the shoulder to restrain his impulse. Like a caged animal, the white man watched with rapt attention, studying the boys' every movement, and as they started to back away, he bared his teeth in an expression of rage.

Nick pulled hard and spun his friend around. "No, we have to get out of here, understand? You can't let it in." Jack Peter's eyes were dull and vacant. Grabbing him by the hand, Nick dragged him into the kitchen. The monster slid its fingers from the windowpanes and then vanished.

"What is that thing?"

Unresponsive, Jack Peter was already lost in the wilderness of his imagination, staring over Nick's shoulder toward the mudroom. Refusing to let go, Nick forced him to the telephone hanging on the wall. "We have to call. Get the police. Find someone to help."

The outside door to the mudroom broke under the weight of a shoulder, the wood splintering with a loud crack, and the body stumbled through the opening. Tossing aside the coats and boots and skis and empty crates, it made its way toward the kitchen, as Nick hurried to throw the bolt to the inner door before it arrived. Looking for escape and a safe haven, he crossed to the door to the workroom stairs and flicked on the overhead light. There were a dozen nooks and crannies in which to hide, though he did not know how long they could hold out there. Leaving Jack Peter behind, he took the first few steps down the wooden staircase to investigate.

Something scurried below. Nick could sense the movement before he could see it. The floor was covered with them. Those same phantom babies from the other night, mewling and fussing as the sudden light disturbed their shadowy hiding places. Nick screamed and then held his breath, terrified but unable to look away. They swarmed like insects on the floor, tottered on the workbench, sidled by the table saw. Under the glare of the artificial light, they were more defined than they had been on that horrible night when they climbed the walls. Babies with odd bodies, exaggerated eyes misshapen as fried eggs, sketched-in noses, and mouths wide and red as gilled fishes. They were not babies at all but the embodiment of the fevers hatched in the mind of their creator. Drawing made flesh and bone, distortions of reality. Some had jagged marks along their bodies or across their heads, scars that looked taped together. Little demons, fat and squalid and raw. They moved as if lost and blind, hissing like cockroaches, until two and then three took notice of him on the stairs and began to race toward him with unnatural speed. As if waking from a dream, he switched off the light and retreated, banging the door behind him and pushing in the flimsy lock. They cried as though wounded by his disappearance.

The kitchen was empty. Jack Peter was not where he had left him, nowhere to be seen. The inner door from the mudroom was ajar. Cold air slithered in and wet prints of large bare feet dirtied the floor, trailing off to the stairway to the upper level. The smell of fish hung in the air, a pungent odor on the edge of rotten. Making himself small, Nick crouched beneath the table and wrapped his arms around his knees to stop himself from shaking. The table leg vibrated against his body, and he tried to hold his breath and be completely silent, but he could not stop his nervous panting. He could not decide whether to risk running to the phone or to hunt for Jack Peter. Each passing moment heightened his fear. Do something, anything. Willing the Keenans to burst through the open door, he listened but heard no passing car on the road, no turn of the key. The fire crackled in the next room, the fridge hummed mechanically, and the wind whistled through the ruined doorway. Nothing else moved. The creatures in the workroom must be napping in the darkness, and elsewhere in the house not a sound came from Jack Peter or the white man. That silence disturbed every hope for peace, and for the first time, Nick wondered if the monster had stolen the boy and run away and left him all alone in the house.

A half-remembered tune filled his thoughts, providing a balm against the terror. His mother used to sing to him when he was much younger, hovering above him as she gave him a bath. "'Yellow bird, up high in banana tree.'" Her voice was high and pretty, and in the quiet, he could hear it again, the rising and falling melody. He wished his mother were there to save him. "'Yellow bird, you sit all alone like me.'" But she was not there, and her absence intensified his dread. No one but himself to count on.

One of Jack Peter's drawings had fallen to the floor and lay near him under the kitchen table. He scurried sideways and grabbed it, turning the sheet over to reveal the picture. Like a skeletal tree, the white man towered over the two boys, reaching out to them with his branchy arms, and crouching at its feet, the boys were cowering and shielding their faces. He hated Jack Peter and his drawings. Hated all monsters. He tore the paper in two in a swift and merciless execution, separating the creature's head from its body.

From upstairs came an unholy scream, an anguished animal groan that he knew at once came from the monster and not the boy. The drawing, he thought to himself, it's Jack Peter's drawing that has made the monster. He crawled out from beneath the table and found other drawings strewn across the surface. Sifting through the pages till he found another picture of the white man, he quickly ripped the paper from top to bottom. The monster cried out again in pain and anger. He gathered all the sheets together and tried to tear through the stack, but it was too thick. Dividing it in half, he tugged and sheared one set after the other. Below him the babies bawled in chorus, and the upstairs hallway resounded with a high and bitter howling. A door flew open and small feet raced across the ceiling, and in moments, Jack Peter came charging down the stairs, his face red and tearstained. Nick was never happier to see him in his life.

"Where were you?"

"Hid," he said. "Under the bed there were no monsters. When he couldn't find me, he hollered and left to get you."

"Never mind." He held up the torn pages. "It's the pictures. We have to get rid of them."

"No." He was trembling. "Not my drawings."

Like some wild thing, Nick pounced on him, taking his shirt in the talons of his hands. "Listen to me. Do you want the monster to kill us? I found what you hid upstairs. Are there more? Where are the rest of the pictures?"

"Everywhere," Jack Peter said.

The news destroyed him. There were the drawings in the bedrooms upstairs, now lying upon the beds and strewn across the floor, and who knew where the others might be hiding or how many Jack Peter had stashed in secret places. No way to find them all with the creature in pursuit. Above them, the thing clomped from room to room, searching.

"We have to get out of here," Nick said. "Get help. We have to leave the house."

"No." There was no panic in his voice, only certainty.

He grabbed Jack Peter by the throat and shook him hard. "You're coming with me. Get your coat and boots. Now."

A door slammed upstairs and rattled the windows. The monster was on the move, and it was only a matter of time before it came back down the stairs. Nick dragged Jack Peter to the mudroom and tugged him to the slab floor. A pair of new red boots stood in a corner, and he forced them on Jack Peter's unbending feet, like dressing a stubborn toddler. He buttoned him into an overcoat and crammed his fists into a pair of mittens. In the background, the wild man took the stairs one by one, its knees clacking and popping with stiffness. With little time to spare, Nick got himself ready and then pushed his friend down the passage to the ruined open door.

The storm had subsided, but little bursts of snow fell gently in the white world. They stood on the threshold preparing to jump into the abyss. He could feel Jack Peter hesitate at the edge, panic welling up and taking hold. Behind them, the monster had reached the bottom of the stairs, and from the kitchen his ragged breathing sounded like a hunting tiger.

"You'll be just fine," Nick said. "Your father said we should cross the road to the Quigleys if we had any trouble. It's not far, and I'll help you, c'mon."

He grabbed Jack Peter by the arm and pulled him outside.

Tim winced when Holly mentioned the boys, and the pain in his back shot into his legs. Shifting his weight in the chair, he wanted to scream, he wanted the Japanese woman with the fuzzed eyeball to work her magic again on his panicked nerves. The others observed him clinically, their faces mirroring his discomfort with expressions of empathy.

"The boys?" He pinched out each word. "They're fine. Inside. Probably drawing or playing one of their games."

Holly shook her head disapprovingly. "I don't like leaving them alone for so long. If anything happened to Nick while we're away, Fred and Nell would kill us. Do you remember what those boys did when you went off on your wild goose chase a couple days ago? Nearly ate us out of house and home. Pots and pans and dirty dishes all over the place. Lord knows what kind of trouble they might be getting up to."

"Nothing happened," he said.

"Wait here," Father Bolden said. "I've just the thing in the library that will fix you up proper." His boots flapped like clapping seals as he shuffled from the room.

"*Ikiryo*," Miss Tiramaku spat out the word as soon as the priest was out of earshot. "There is one more *yurei* I meant to tell you about: the living ghost. *Ikiryo*. When a person has great anger or resentment, his spirit can separate itself from the body and haunt his tormentors. Sometimes the person has no knowledge that his *ikiryo* even exists, much less is seeking vengeance. I've been trying to remember all day."

Holding a small noggin of whiskey, the priest returned triumphant.

He poured a drop in Tim's teacup and a larger dram in a glass for himself. Lifting it in a toast, he said, "To warm you to the core."

"Any more and my wife will have to do the driving, but thanks just the same, padre."

"Seems like I've interrupted your conspiracy," the priest said. "What goes on here?"

Tim laughed. "No conspiracy here. Miss Tiramaku was regaling us with another one of her stories. The living ghost that leaves the body and seeks revenge."

"*Ikiryo*," Holly said.

"To get rid of the *ikiryo*," Miss Tiramaku said, "the person must give up his fears and resentments."

Father Bolden scolded Miss Tiramaku in stern Japanese, and she looked chastened. Eyes to the floor, she said, "I only want to help their boy. We are so much alike."

Conversation halted, as though she had crossed a line without consent and embarrassed them all into silence. Holly fidgeted in her chair and tapped her fingertips against her lips. The priest stared at his empty glass, and Miss Tiramaku looked past Tim to the little window.

"Snow's letting up," she said at last.

"We'd better get back to the boys," Holly said. "Miles to go before we sleep."

"Ah, Frost. Too bad we don't have a horse and sleigh back of the church," Father Bolden said. "Two roads diverged in a wood, and all that."

As he tried to get up and out of the chair, Tim moaned. "I might need that horse and sled to get me to the car."

Quick as a cat, Miss Tiramaku caught his hand in hers and massaged it, putting pressure on the same points as she had earlier. "Let me help you," she said, and within moments, the muscles in his back had loosened and he was able to walk from the rectory of his own accord.

Holly drove, despite his weak protest, and the Jeep plowed through the deep snow with ease. She kept her gaze fixed on the tire ruts in front of her, but he knew she would feel better if they chatted along the way, counterpoint to her concentration.

"I don't know about that priest," he said. "But she's a miracle worker. I want to know her trick for the future."

"Acupressure," Holly said. "One of the healing arts."

"Wouldn't surprise me if she is a ghost herself, what with that evil eye."

"Tim." She punched his shoulder.

"What does she mean she is a lot like Jack?"

"Same diagnosis. Different name."

Out of habit, Tim braked as she rounded a bend. "Well, she doesn't know him like we do. She hasn't been around, seen what we have seen. Lot of hocus-pocus, if you ask me. Of course he's expressing himself, but maybe he just likes a good scare. Maybe he just likes monsters."

"Or he is acting like a monster," she said. "Out of control."

The tires slid out of the rut, and the car heaved to the left, and she worked hard to correct the course. She kept her eyes on the road. He stared out the passenger's window at the landscape blank and white. They rolled homeward in the late afternoon, lost in their private disputations.

vi.

Jack Peter stepped through the door from the dream house and into the outside world. Snow landed on his face and melted in the warmth of his bare skin. Flakes stuck to his eyelashes, and he had to blink and nod to shake them off. Spangling confetti fell from everywhere, all around, all at once, as the faint light caught the spinning surfaces. Jack in a box of excelsior, in a glitter dome, in a whirl of blown chalk. The air was cold to breathe and left a wet metallic taste on his tongue. Shirred folds in the white landscape ran from the house to the sea, the blanket of snow thick and soft and heavy. He pulled one foot from its hole and noticed the extra weight in his thighs. In the bulky coat, he imagined himself an Eskimo, a musher in the Klondike. When he took a second step, he slipped and stumbled forward, uncertain of how to maintain his balance when his feet no longer worked. Bracing in a spread stance, he looked up.

Outside, outside. He had forgotten the way the air felt, the sensation of the wind pushing against him while it held him upright, the clouds forcing down the sky, and behind them, he imagined, the sun blinked like a great eye. He sucked in a gulp of December that filled his lungs with ice and his lips began to tingle and go numb. The impulse to laugh proved irresistible, and he wiped the wetness from his face and forgot about Nick altogether until he heard his voice calling as though from the moon. Ten feet away, Nick implored him to hurry, to catch up, but Jack could not move. He had forgotten how.

Shuffling through the snow, Nick headed straight toward him, certain as a steam engine. His mouth and cheeks flushed scarlet, and a wet drop hung from the tip of his nose. Snowflakes crossed his face and broke it into a thousand little pieces. From inside the house came the monster's roar.

Nick's hands gripped his arm. "We can't stop here. We have to get somewhere safe. The house across the street."

"I'm outside," Jack Peter said.

Nick wiped his nose with the back of his sleeve. "Yes, right. That's terrific, but it is chasing us. You won't be anywhere for long if we don't escape."

"Outside." He smiled at Nick.

Nearby a dog barked, the sound muffled by the storm. Snow slid off an evergreen branch and landed with a wet thud. Inside the front window, the monster spied them and banged its fists against the glass, and then moved out of sight.

"Yes, let's go." Nick said and tugged on his arm to escape.

In the driveway two parallel indentations marked where the Jeep had pulled away forever ago, and Nick headed for them, thinking it would be quicker to follow the compacted tire tracks rather than wade through the fresh snow. Jack Peter trailed along like a toddler, running stiff legged and trying to pull his arm free. The lights were on at the Quigleys', and a plume of smoke curled from their chimney. He could visualize himself inside that house, tossing a ball to the collie, playing at last with the twins, their surprised but hospitable mother offering him hot chocolate and peanut butter crackers. It was almost as if they were already there, deep in the dream, safe and warm and happy. He could imagine them as clearly as if he had drawn the whole scene.

They heard the dog before they saw it. Barking furiously, it emerged from behind the Quigleys' house, but it was not the little border collie protecting its territory. Churning the snow in great strides, the big white dog from Jack Peter's drawings raced toward them, ears back and teeth bared. "Oh shit," Nick said and grabbed Jack Peter's arm, but the beast braked in a cloud of snow, stopping short at the edge of the property as though an invisible barrier prevented it from stepping onto the road.

"I thought it was dead," Nick said. "I saw it in the back of the car."

With one finger, Jack Peter sketched a fence between them and the dog. "I don't think it can get us," he said. "I don't think it will cross."

Snarling and snapping its teeth, the dog paced on the edge, worrying a path and holding them at bay. They didn't dare move.

Behind them came the monster, picking up their trail from the mudroom. Even from forty feet, they could hear its frantic breathing. The only escape route would be to circle round the other side of the house. If they backtracked, there was a chance they could make it inside again and lock the doors and hope for the best. Failing that, they could simply head for the sea and wait for Jack Peter's parents to return home.

"Run," Jack Peter said.

As she drove the last stretch home, Holly remembered the first time Jack had run away from her. Before the accident, in June of his seventh year, they had driven to a pick-your-own farm and orchard as a Sunday outing. It was the edge of high season, so Tim stayed home to take care of the tourists and summer people, and it was just the two of them. Mother and son gone for strawberries. One moment they were together in the fields, bent low and hunting for red to fill their waxed cartons, and the next moment Jack had vanished. She had been daydreaming, thinking perhaps of strawberry-rhubarb pie or shortcakes for dessert, and when she looked up from the riot of leaves, she could not see any sign of him. He had been scooped up from the earth, plucked from her side. It took a minute to register that he had slipped away without a word. She wound her way through the rows asking the other pickers if they had seen her son, a little boy, a quiet boy, a broken boy who had wandered off. The strawberries had been sown on the bottom flat land next to a small rise, and one party of searchers joined her, while another party struggled up the incline. A blond-haired girl in pigtails and gingham shorts spotted him first. She called out to Holly from the crest of the hill, pointing to a spot far off in the distance. Holly jogged to her and saw the figure in a field, small as a toy. He did not move the whole time she ran toward him, calling out his name, for he had found a quartet of sheep huddled together on the farm, staring back at him and bleating their protests. "See what I made, Mom," he said, and she chalked it up to some random thought buzzing around his brain. When she threw her arms around him, it was like hugging a wooden soldier. The other searchers were bewildered by the sudden appearance of the sheep in the meadow, but she thought nothing of it at the time, just glad to find the little lost boy.

See what I made. Holly recalled his words as she and Tim drove through the virgin snowscape, the yards of the beach houses and summer homes covered white, the pines shagged with ice, everything blank as paper and deathly silent. Was he saying that he made those sheep? The dream house appeared suddenly through the trees, and she saw at once the picture was askew. Zigzag tracks crossed the yard, madcap trails churned through the snow. She lurched the Jeep into the driveway.

From across the street came a series of loud barks. A big white dog paced along a trench it had made in the snow, threatening them from the Quigleys' yard.

"Good God," Tim said. "That's the white shepherd I saw in the back of Pollock's car."

She nearly jumped back in the driver's seat. "I thought you said it was dead."

The dog seemed unable or unwilling to give chase, as though bound by an invisible chain. Keeping the Jeep's hood between it and herself, she sidled around to help Tim manage the snowy driveway. Because of his sore back, he needed to lean on her in order to shuffle through the snow.

"What in the hell is going on here?" Tim asked, pointing to the mudroom's door, open and swinging on its hinges. They stopped to inspect the jamb and the splintered wood at the lock.

"Something's been at it," Holly said. "I've got to check·on the boys." Leaving Tim to fend on his own, she rushed into the house. A lick of water ran down the center of the slab floor, and a pair of cross-country skis lay in an X she had to step over. Coats and hats and boots were jumbled in a heap next to the kitchen step, and the inner door was broken, too. She called to them and entered the room, shocked by the mess. Muddy footprints dotted the linoleum and one of the chairs lay on its back, two legs off the ground. An overturned glass on the counter dripped milk down the face of a cupboard. Papers were strewn everywhere, some torn in half and others ruined with sandy water marks. Moving quickly through the empty space, Holly called for the boys again, glancing at the windows smudged by dirty hands. When no answer came, she stuck her head in the opening to the mudroom and saw her husband straining to pick up a mangled scarf and hang it on a peg. He moved as though he was old and riddled with arthritis.

"They're not here, Tim. What's happened to them?"

The blood drained from his face as he straightened his back. "What do you mean? Have you tried upstairs? Looked all over?"

Frustrated by his lack of trust, she frowned at him and hurried to the stairway, taking the steps in pairs, hollering for Jack and Nick. All of the rooms had been ransacked. The rugs wet beneath her feet. Quilts on the beds, rumpled and bodiless. Closet doors gaped wide and everywhere papers littered the surface of things. She sifted through scores of drawings, bodies and bones, pictures of monsters, the dead dog now prowling in the neighbor's yard. *What has he done?* The pictures stopped her, the awful connections turning in her mind. From the middle of his desk, she picked up one of the drawings lying there: two boys wrestling beneath the sea. She curled it into a scroll and carried it back to Tim.

"How could you have left them alone?"

Trembling with pain, he bent over the kitchen table and steadied himself with two hands. "I've checked the other rooms down here, and the whole house is a wreck, even the workroom. They're not here."

"How could they not be here? Jack is outside?" She hollered and waved the scroll at him. "Where have they gone?"

"I told them if there was any trouble, they should go over to the Quigleys'. Let's not panic. They might be right across the street."

"With that beast waiting for them in the front yard?" She leapt for the phone and dialed the neighbors' number. One of the twins answered with a cheery hello.

"This is Mrs. Keenan," she said. "Is Jack there by any chance? Did he and Nick come over to your house today in the storm?"

The little girl seemed put off by the anxiety in Holly's questions that she hesitated before answering. "No. Jack Peter never leaves the house."

"I know, but are you sure he didn't come over, and you just missed him?"

"No, we've been inside all day. There's no one here."

Holly caught her breath. "Is this Janie?"

The girl grunted a yes.

"Do you know anything about that dog that's out in your yard?"

"Our dog is right here next to me, aren't you, girl?"

The border collie barked in the background.

"No, the big white dog that's out there right now?"

"I don't know what you mean. If there was another dog out there, ours would go crazy. There's nothing out there, and it's been as quiet as church all day."

Holly thanked her and hung up, holding on to the receiver, trying to sort through her fear and anger. "They're not over there, Tim. Someone's got them."

The room looked like a crime scene, signs of struggle and foul play, and it spun in her eyes as if she was drunk. The pounding began in her head, steady as a heartbeat. She hammered on the wall with the paper clenched in her fist till the edges frayed. Papers on the floor, drawings everywhere. *See what I made.*

"They're out there," she said. "Do you remember the sheep, Tim? That day when Jack was lost and we found him with those sheep that just appeared—"

"I'll go look for them."

"Are you listening to me, Tim? I think Jack made them appear somehow."

"Holly, what does this have to do with where the boys are? Let me go."

"You? You can barely take care of yourself. I know where they are. But you need to take care of what's inside. It's the drawings, Tim."

"What on earth are you talking about?"

"The drawings, the drawings he's been doing. Not the ghosts, not the *yurei*. It's been Jack all along. He drew the sheep, and they appeared. He drew the dog, and the dog appeared. Lord knows what else he's made. We need to find all of Jack's drawings, search the house, and burn them in the fireplace. You get rid of them, and I'll find the boys."

He looked at her as if she had lost her mind, but she did not care. She gave him a look as furious as the hammering in her head.

"Don't you see?" she said. "His drawings are coming to life."

The boys ran along the far side of the house and at the rear corner took off for a patch of evergreens, carving a new path through the drifts. The skies had burst, and the snow fell in rippling sheets; and in every shadow, they imagined a new terror. They lost sight of the creature and took the chance to rest for a moment under the pines. With his hands on his knees, Nick leaned over catching his breath, and looking with wonder at his friend, outside again. Red shields appeared on Jack Peter's cheeks, and a rime of frost glistened at the corners of his chapped lips. He rubbed the matt of snow from his hair. Chests heaving, they sucked in deep breaths.

"It's cold out," Jack Peter said. "I'm tired of it."

Nick rubbed Jack Peter's face with the palms of his gloves, trying to help him get warm. "Why did you do this?" he asked.

"They were going to send me away. Too much trouble."

A loud bellow came from behind. The monster spotted them in their hiding place, and they pushed forward, snow flying in their wake, their flapping coats caught in the draft. They left the cover of the trees and climbed the dune. Stretching before them, the canvas flattened into shades of white and gray. Even the waves seemed frozen in place. The smell of salt and fish and seaweed had been drained by the antiseptic cold. Dead quiet, except for their frantic breathing and the whispering snow. The familiar paths to the sea through the maze of granite were obscured, but they had an advantage over the white man. They picked their way around the familiar rocks while it stumbled after them, gaining ground and then faltering, before slipping and landing on all fours, buried face-first in a snowbank. When he saw it fall, Nick ducked behind a large boulder and pulled Jack Peter next to him. They sat and leaned back against the stone.

"Who is that?" Nick asked.

Jack Peter stared at the sea, refusing to answer.

"Did you do this? Did you make the monster?"

"Yes," he said. "I made it all." With the edge of his mitten, he tapped his forehead.

"Well, we're trapped. Between the ocean and that nightmare thing."

Nick peeked around the edge of the rock to see what was keeping the monster. With a howl and a string of filthy curses, the creature rose from the ground. Scorched by the cold, its skin was mottled red and blue and snow sloughed off its limbs in thick clumps. Scouring the beach with its gaze, it found Nick before he could duck back behind cover. The fiend stepped forward, relentless.

There was nowhere to hide, nowhere to escape. Caught in the middle of a great nothing, they had no choice but to move toward the sea. The closer they came to the water, the less snow covered the ground, giving way entirely to sand where the waves lapped the shore, and though they could move faster on this bare surface, so, too, could the monster. They waded into the bubbling wash to the tops of their boots and then turned to face it. The monster lurched toward them and stopped just yards away, tottering on its bare feet and swaying in the storm.

Fire ran along the edges like quicksilver and ignited the drawings in a flash. Tim watched the papers burn and curl upon themselves and the black ash fly up the chimney like a murder of crows. At first he had not understood why Holly had asked him to destroy their son's artwork, but he had obeyed without question or complaint. She rarely ordered him to do anything, and it was not until he actually looked at the images that he began to understand her logic. These were no ordinary childish portraits. Jip had drawn the wild man many times and in many variations, even though he had never seen him, and how could he, with the monster outside and the boy inside at all times? Only he and Nick had seen him, and never in such fine detail and execution, as if Jip had been face-to-face with it, as if Jip had been intimately wired into Nick's mind.

Other disturbing visions populated the pages, none of which Jip could have witnessed. The big white dog appeared in several drawings, even though Tim and Nick were the only ones who had seen it firsthand in the back of the policeman's car. Some drawings were mysteries—an army of monstrous babies, a woman who resembled Nell Weller but vaguely naked and predatory, a pair of bodies with hangers between their bare shoulder blades, bones of a skeleton littering the shore. Tim hobbled from room to room, finding papers scattered everywhere. He searched the entire upstairs floor and brought a bundle down to the fire, pitching them in batches without bothering to inspect the weird subjects, only to stop, stricken, at one drawing that grabbed his attention: the two boys tangled in a violent knot at the bottom of the sea. He guessed at once where Holly had gone, where the boys might be found, and he hurried to the picture window facing the ocean, praying that he was wrong. *Coming to life.*

On feet red and blistered with frostbite, the monster walked closer, and the boys could see the sorrows on his face. Deep-set in bruised circles, his eyes conveyed a world of woe and regret. His mouth twisted and gaped slightly, and he seemed on the verge of telling them something. A plum-colored welt ringed his neck. His tangled hair and beard were curled and twisted as strands of kelp, and he was painfully thin, his bones could be counted through his sallow skin, and he had a look of long hunger. He lifted his arms from his sides and stretched his bony hands toward the boys, in a gesture both beseeching and threatening.

"What do you want?" Nick cried.

As if to answer, the monster opened its mouth, but no words came out, only a sound that began with an infant's urgency and slowly loudened to a long drawn-out wail that resounded and echoed off the rocks and the dream house and sang out to the wide expanse of the sea. A human cry, born out of ancient suffering, turned inside out and full of unspeakable grief and longing.

The boys backed away from the creature, and when the waves struck his legs Nick recoiled from the shock of the frigid water. He heard Jack Peter cry out like a bird. Torn between surrender to the monster to end that tormenting pain and the desire to escape, Nick went deeper. A wave broke over his legs and crashed against his back, soaking him through his heavy coat and pulling him away from shore. As he sank, Nick felt the hands wrap around his waist and force him under.

The water stung like the prick of a thousand needles. The monster cried out in pain, the skin on its shoulders blackening and its hair turning to ash. Flames burst on its limbs, yet it kept marching toward them. Without warning they were going under. Nick had no chance for even a mouthful of air, and he found himself plunged in darkness, trying not to swallow water. The weight of his clothes made him sink quickly, with Jack Peter at his side, dragging and pushing him to the bottom. He fought the pressure on his chest, grappled and pulled at Jack Peter's hands, fighting to be free. The waves, too, gripped and buffeted them, churning the silt and shells, and in the muck he felt as though he was being erased from the page, torn from the outside world.

Holly nearly crumpled to the ground in pain from the cold pressure boring into her skull. The boys had made footprints in the snow, and she followed a pair to the top of the hill. Slipping through the heavy wet snow, she climbed to the crest, the whole ocean spread out before her. Below, one of the boys cried out loudly from the shore. She searched desperately for any sight of them among the rocks or along the sandy shore. Her shouts thinned to a whisper in the blinding whiteness. When she saw a flash of red boots in the water and the navy blue of a child's coat, she ran toward it, the beating in her head finally stilled, her heart exploding with what was in front of her.

They might be dead, she thought, by the time she reached them, but Holly flew to the tideline. She plunged into the water, anesthetized by its iciness, thrashing to the spot where she had last seen her son and diving underwater again and again in desperation. Breathless, she rose from the waves and saw at once Jack in a dead man's float. She cried out his name and seized him by the coat, turned him over on his back, and towed him to the beach. On the edge of the sand, she rested, catching her breath. Black with soot, Tim had arrived and fished out Nick's heavy wet body from the sea, but Holly was barely aware of anything else. They were alone in the quiet of the day, and she cradled her son in her arms, *my boy, my boy*, until the water streamed from his mouth, and his heart stirred.

The little girl with no hair smiled at him across the room, and Jack Peter returned her beatific grin with a smile of his own. When he noticed that his mother was watching, he bowed his head, blushing. Other people wandered in and out of the visitors' lounge—a tired man rubbing the small of his back as he paced; two nurses on a coffee break; an older couple, the husband pushing his wife in her wheelchair and bending to offer some quiet comfort. The Keenans waited for some word, any word at all, now back at the hospital for another long day. Both boys had gone in to the emergency room after they had been pulled from the icy Atlantic. Jack Peter had been treated for mild hypothermia and shock, but Nicholas had not regained consciousness since the drowning. They had seen him once in the ICU, hooked up to a respirator and lying still on his back, a birdlike thing impossible to bear. Father Bolden and Miss Tiramaku had come for a visit and to say a few prayers, but his parents did not pray. They could only stare at the floor as the words were spoken.

Getting Nick's parents off the cruise ship in the Caribbean had proved difficult, and then their flight from Miami to Portland had been postponed because of the blizzard. Texts and phone calls never suffice, and Holly and Tim agreed to keep vigil until the Wellers arrived. A small plastic Christmas tree sat on a table in the corner of the room, and on the walls were cutout decorations: Santa and his sleigh, sprigs of balsam, a blue and white menorah. Holly was grateful that the piped-in music had been changed from Christmas songs to some indecipherable pop mush playing softly in the background. Tim was giving the day's newspaper a third read, and Jack passed the time, thankfully, without drawing. His fingers danced across the screen of her smart phone as he played another mindless game with fanatical desire.

The door swung open and Dr. Ogundipe entered, the same young Nigerian woman who had treated Jack earlier. When she found them, she tugged at the stethoscope around her neck as she approached. "Mr. and Mrs. Keenan . . ."

"You have some news?" Holly asked.

She sat next to Jack and flashed a smile at him. For the second time that day, he acknowledged a stranger's greeting, a good sign. "Nothing about Nicholas, I'm afraid, no real changes, everything's the same. He still hasn't woken up. But his parents arrived at last and have had the chance to see him. They're planning on coming to talk with you shortly."

"How did they seem to you?" Tim asked.

"As you might expect," she said. "Quite a shock, and they are tired from the journey. After you've had a chance to discuss matters with them, let me know what you think about my idea."

Jack squirmed in his chair and put down the game. Earlier in the day the doctor had suggested that he come talk to Nick in the bed, that the sound of a friend's voice might stimulate a response. When he had first heard her proposal, Jack had hidden behind his mother's arm, but now that he had time to consider it, he was willing. He nodded his consent.

"Good boy." The doctor patted him on the leg. "I'll let you all know if we can arrange it." In her crisp white jacket, she projected authority, but her charm had won over Jack. With a nod, she disappeared into the maze of the wards.

They went back to waiting.

"What are we going to tell them?" Tim asked at last. "That a monster showed up and chased them into the ocean? A monster our son made through his drawings. Good Lord, they'll never believe it."

"We'll tell them the story we told them on the phone," Holly said. "That the boys were out playing in the snow and went too close to the water."

He folded the newspaper and tossed it on the coffee table. "They doubted it on the phone, I could tell. They know that Jip never leaves the house."

"Stop calling him that," she said. "'Jip' sounds insulting."

Leaning across the chair, Tim tapped his son on the shoulder. "What do you think, J.P.? Do you feel insulted?"

"Just stop," she said.

"I don't know what's gotten into you."

"Everything, don't you see? There's a little boy lying in a hospital bed. And your own son put him there. And you, you never believe me. Out chasing things." Her face was red with anger.

Fred Weller had slipped into the room and stood directly behind her. With a polite clearing of his throat, he announced his presence. Holly turned to greet him, and saw how his sunburned face had collapsed with worry. Melting in her own grief, she reached for him, and he embraced her as she collapsed into sobs. "I'm sorry," she said. "So, so sorry."

From over his shoulder, she saw Nell enter, flat and emotionless. She did not smile or frown, barely functioning under sedation. Tim rose to meet her, but Nell bowed her head and curved away and would not let him touch her. He seemed so helpless to Holly, abandoned and bereft, that she almost felt sorry for him in that instant.

On the sofa, Jack busily scrolled through the smart phone apps searching for a new game.

"Nell, I am so sorry," Holly said. "It was an accident."

Miles away, Nell stood all alone in the middle of the room. When she began to speak, her voice was strange and low and without affect. "He looks like he is just fading away. Yellow bird, yellow bird."

"I'm sure he'll come out of it," Fred said.

No one moved. Only the hum of the fluorescent lights and Jack's tapping at the screen broke the silence. At last Nell summoned the courage to raise her chin and look at Tim. "I cannot bear to lose him. We thought he was gone three years ago. How could you let this happen?"

"I'm sorry, Nell," he said. "I would do anything to save him. He's like a son to me."

Her face snapped to anger. "Not yours, never yours." She pointed at Jack. "That there's your boy. That's your son."

Tim put his hand to his mouth and slumped into a chair. Holly positioned herself between her husband and her son and rested a hand on Tim's shoulder.

"I'm sorry, Holly," Nell said. "I didn't mean anything by it."

"They're doing everything they can," Holly said. "We all are."

Each adult retreated to a private misery. Jack tapped out another code on the phone and handed it to his mother. A word game in which you used digital letters on faux wooden tiles to spell out words. He had written "wicked."

She laughed bitterly to herself.

When summoned at last by a nurse, they all filed to the restricted area and followed her down the winding corridors. Most of the doors along the way had been left ajar, and they passed strange and sad tableaus of sleeping patients; tired old men staring at overhead TVs; families and friends clustered around a privacy screen, crammed into tiny spaces; and oddest of all, the empty rooms with unmade beds. Nurses came and went, crossing their path without a glance, and they arrived at last at the white room where Nick lay all alone. The curtains had been opened and the last sunset of the last day of the year poured weakly across the foot of his bed. A vase of white roses, sent from the Florida grandparents, perfumed the air. Pale and unconscious, Nick breathed quietly. Oxygen flowed through the thin tube at his nose, and in his arm, a plastic port had been installed, his hand colored with a plum bruise, an ID bracelet curled around his wrist. The thin blanket and sheet over his body were smooth and undisturbed.

Dr. Ogundipe arrived five minutes later, less animated in the presence of the child. After glancing at his chart, she went to Nick's side and held his thin wrist in her hand, counting his pulse, and then she laid his arm against his side and studied the saline drip. "You can talk to him now, Jack."

"I don't know what to say." Jack would not look at the boy in the bed.

"Tell him hello," the doctor said. "Say whatever you are feeling."

Like a wild bird he approached gingerly, two hops forward, one step back, ready to fly away at any threat. At last he found his way a few feet from his friend's head on the pillow but no closer. He cocked his head and looked at Nick slantwise.

"Hello, Nick," he said and waited a few beats for an answer. "Hello, Nick," he repeated in a louder voice. The boy in the bed did not move at all, and Jack frowned at the doctor, confused and uncertain.

"Go head," she said. "He can hear you."

Jack's right hand twitched and his fingers danced. "No more monsters," he said. "All the monsters are gone away."

"Whatever is he talking about?" Fred asked. "What monsters?"

"He won't get up," Jack said.

"Try some more," Tim said. "Tell him you are sorry."

"I don't blame you anymore, Nick. I'm not mad at you. I am just tired of drawing all the time. No more monsters. You can get up now." His shaking hand stilled, and he turned away from the unconscious boy and faced his mother with tears in his eyes and then rushed to her arms.

In the dying light of the day, the others took turns speaking to Nick until there was nothing left to say. The Wellers would be staying the night, but they told the Keenans to go, get some rest.

"Come back tomorrow if you wish," Fred said. "We'll be sure to call you if anything changes."

Blue moonlight reflected off the snow, and the ride home was like driving through a dreamscape, the familiar streets and landmarks transformed by a smooth white cover. Jack studied the windows to catch his reflection when the light was right, so that he could see both himself and the outside world pass by at the same time. As they pulled up in the driveway, their old house same as ever, he imagined his friend Nick waiting there for them to start their next game. But Jack knew he wasn't inside. When her cell phone buzzed, Holly fished it from her purse and lit the tiny screen to read the latest.

"It's the police," she said. "The bone's gone missing. They opened the box and found nothing but ashes."

His father said it would be all right to stay up and watch TV till the ball dropped in New York City, and his mother agreed that it would be okay if he would first change into his pajamas. The empty bed reminded him of Nick in the hospital, but he would soon be just another imaginary now, gone like Red and all the others. On his desk, a quiver of sharp pencils stood in a cup beside the last pages of his sketch pad. It would be easy to sit in his chair and continue as he always had, but he set his mind to resist the temptation. Jack changed out of his clothes and sat cross-legged on the carpet, looking up at the dresser mirror and the moon reflected in the glass, trying to push the last of his friend out of his mind. The lady with the cloud in her eyes would help him. He would talk with her next time. Tell her the whole story.

A soft knock at the door broke his concentration. His mother appeared at the threshold, and when he nodded she came in. "What have you been doing up here all this time? We've been waiting for you to join us. Don't want to miss the countdown."

He rocked gently to and fro, unable to put into words what he was feeling.

"Were you thinking about Nick?" She sat next to him on the floor, and he allowed her to put her arm around his shoulders. After a while, he laid his head against her chest, and she felt a wave of joy rise through her body. They remained together that way for some time.

"Good grief," she said at last, looking toward the space between the desk and his old toy box. "We seem to have caught a mouse."

The forgotten trap had been sprung and the killing bar lay neatly against the mouse's neck. He remembered how Nick had wanted to stick his finger in there. The tiny body was stiff with rigor mortis. His mother got up at once and fetched a plastic bag from the linen closet and wrapped it around her hand and forearm like a long evening glove. Looking away from the body, she picked up the mousetrap and its victim with one hand and tied a knot in the bag.

"Be a lamb," she said. "Take this to your father to dispose of properly."

Jack grabbed the top edge of the bag and held it at arm's length, taking care not to let the dead thing touch him as he walked downstairs. Slumped in an easy chair, his father watched the New Year's Eve festivities on TV, numbed to the presence of his son. His head rested on a wing of the chair, and on his neck, the wounds had healed to pale red stripes, sure to leave faint scars in due course. Jack showed him the bag.

"Mouse," he said. "Mommy wants you to get rid of it."

Tim lifted himself from the chair and accepted the burden. "I will," he said. "And go tell your mother that the show is about to begin."

On the upstairs landing, Jack listened to the soft sounds coming from his room, his mother's exclamations of surprise and wonder. She was seated where he had left her, between the desk and the now open toy box, and she had found his hidden secret. A stack of papers spilled from her lap and smaller piles surrounded her. She looked up when he came into the room, her eyes wide and questioning. She flipped through the drawings and held up a picture of Nick flying a kite.

"These are all of Nick?" she asked.

He bit his bottom lip.

Nick in a classroom bent to his lessons, Nick swinging on a rope over a lake, Nick banging on a toy drum, Nick and his parents sitting on a mountain, Nick dressed for church, Nick catching a baseball, Nick in the winter, spring, summer, and fall. Nick at seven, eight, nine, and ten. Growing older, changing his hair, the style of his clothes, the number of teeth in his smile. A thousand Nicks.

"When did you have time to draw all these?"

He did not know what to say. "Every day."

"What do you mean every day? How long have you been making these pictures of Nick?"

"One drawing every day since he drowned. But I got tired of having to do it. So I drew monsters to chase him away, not me."

Lines of confusion furrowed her brow. "No, honey, that can't be right.

That was only two days ago when you and Nick went in the water, and there must be more than a thousand pictures here."

"Not then," he said. "The first time he drowned. Three years ago."

"But why—"

"Made him up," he said. "Since he died. To keep him alive."

"What do you mean made him up?" She pushed her way to the bottom of the stack and saw the seven-year-old dream boy that Jack had made, and at last she understood. A thousand drawings, a thousand boys, a thousand days. And now Nick was in a hospital bed, fighting to live.

"You can't stop," she said. His mother rose from the floor and grabbed him by the wrist and led him to the desk. Holly shoved him to sit in front of the paper and forced a pencil into his hand. Wrapping her trembling fingers around his, she held him to the page. "Draw," she ordered. "Draw him again."

He faced the blank page and laid down a line.